The Summer Bird

The Seraphimé Saga, Volume One

By

S.M. Carrière

Published 2013 by S.M. Carrière. Copyright © 2013 by S.M. Carrière.

Illustrations and Cover art designed and created by Laura Miller of AnAuthorsArt.com. Cover Copyright © 2013 by S.M. Carrière.

ISBN: 0-9866976-5-6

ISBN-13: 987-0-9866976-5-4

http://smcarriere.com

Other Books in This Series

The Winter Wolf

Other Books by S.M. Carrière

The Dying God & Other Stories

Ethan Cadfael: The Battle Prince

Acknowledgements

I would like to thank everyone who helped me create this book. To my mother, who always encouraged me and never let me wallow. To my father, for his keen eyes and candid opinions. It kept me honest!

To my beta readers, who helped make this story stronger and better.

To Laura, for the beautiful work she has done for me on this book cover and who has been a cheerleader for me from afar.

To all the people I have forgotten to put on this little list who have contributed to my writing, even in the smallest ways, you are so valued and I am so grateful!

With love to my friends. You are my clan, and I could not survive my winters without you.

The Summer Bird

The Serephimé Saga, Volume One

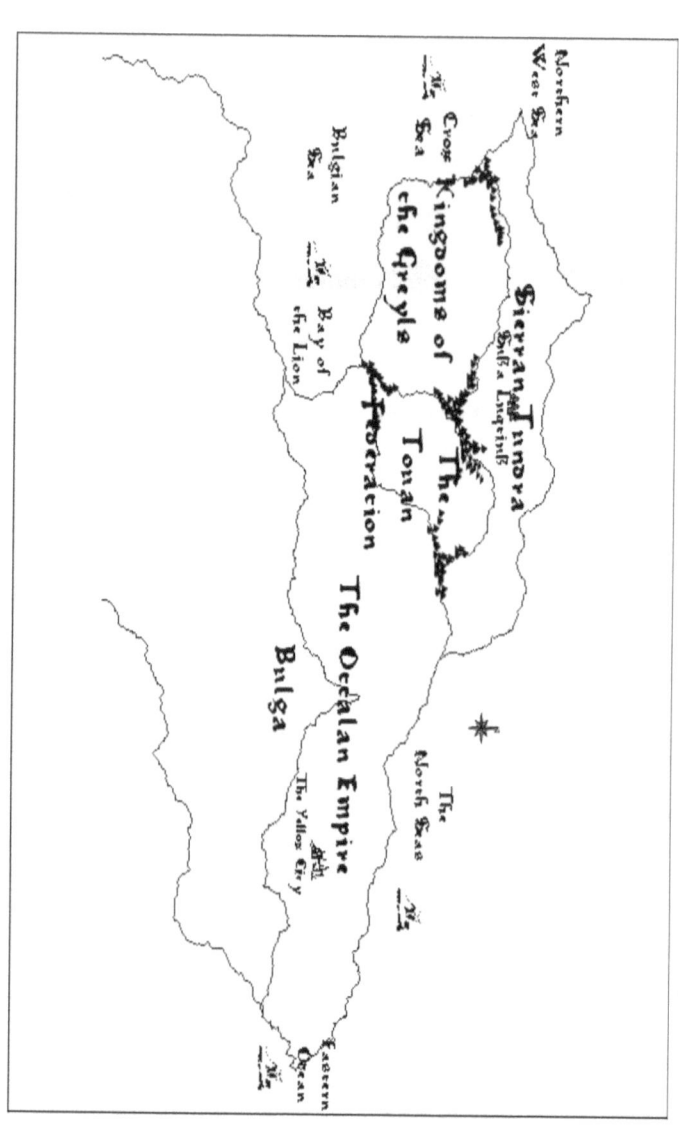

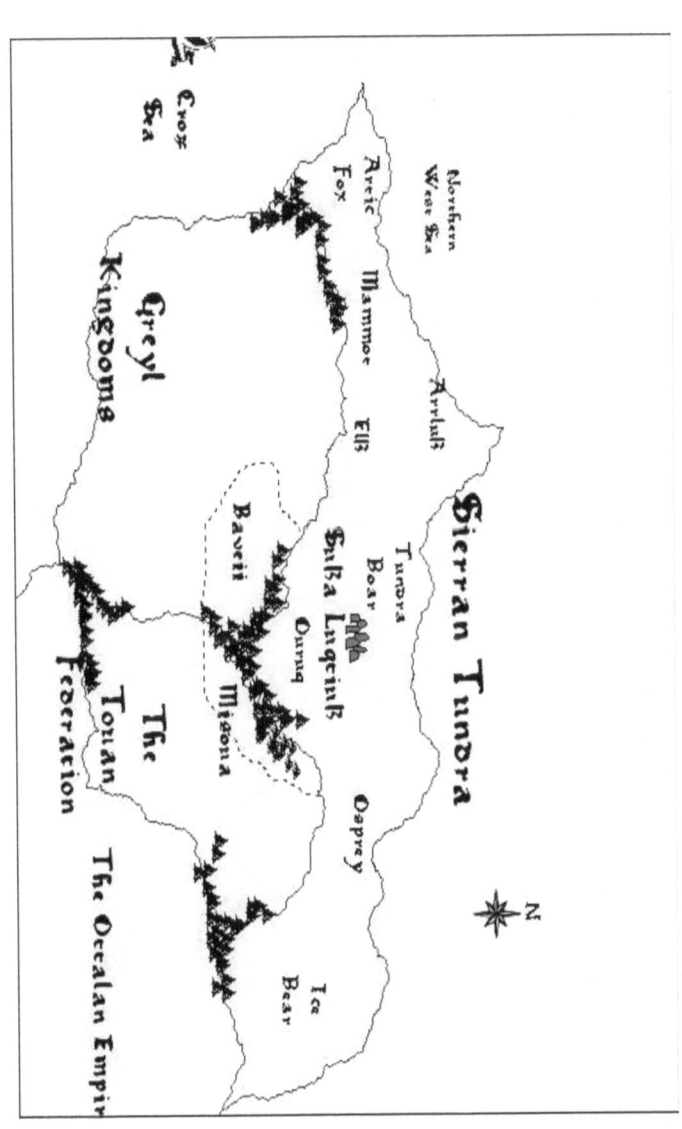

Prologue

The world began a long time before man. Born before life itself, it is, in essence, the first life that ever was. Then came the sun, the heavens, gods, trees, beasts and men. We were born last. Before our race was another kind of Men, of a sort.

They were like us, yet unlike us. We were tall, they were squat. We knew war, they knew not. We lived in warm places, they in cold. None knew how to live on the edge of the walls of ice as they did.

The ancestors first encountered them when the world began to change. The moist grasslands of our home had begun to dry. Slowly at first, then ever more rapidly ponds and lakes shrank and vanished, forcing the beasts to change their movements. They trekked instinctively to where food could still be found. Our ancestors, too, had to move with them, or perish in the drought.

That was how the ancestors first came to know war. As the desert expanded, food and water became scarce. Men fought to the death to claim those necessities of life for themselves and their families. No longer could the ancestors afford kindness to strangers.

War decided land rights, obtained slaves who became mothers, and claimed food and water. Only the largest and the strongest survived. Children grew taller and taller, and stronger and stronger. Many of the ancestors were raised on war. Over generations, war became a part of them until it came to be that they were prepared for battle the moment they left their mother's wombs in a squalling ball of rage.

They were not like that, the ice-dwellers. They had learnt a different lesson from the scarcity of food. They had learnt to aid one another, shelter each other, and share what little they had. They understood, as the ancestors did not, that their survival depended on kindnesses extended beyond the small family unit. Survival depended on kindness given to all the tribes of ice-dwellers.

Once every three years, they would all gather at what was then called Tiq Uellak – Black Rock – the great boulder that had been thrown by Yame, the mountain that spat fire and ice. They gathered there to feast and sing. They exchanged stories, knowledge, reports, and daughters. They traded. That was how they survived.

They were woefully unprepared for the arrival of the ancestors.

Constant war forced some of the ancestors further and further away from their homeland. They fled in all directions to escape, while the victors stole away their land, their water, and their wives. The few that managed to escape settled in adjacent lands. There they eked a living from a reluctant landscape until the next family encroached and another battle was fought. The victor would take and the defeated would flee.

Thus, in ever increasing numbers, our people travelled north in search of unoccupied lands in which to settle. The ancestors were sorely disappointed then, when they came across the ice-dwellers.

The first traces of the ice-dwellers were almost mythic – a shadow in the snow, a mysteriously butchered kill. The first meeting did not go well.

They, long used to helping strangers find food, opened their arms to us, only to be slaughtered for their kindness. In the beginning, they simply fled before us. Later, they began to resist us and, in terrible butchery, were cut down.

Our founding family, the first ancestors to live along the rivers of ice, was small – a father and his two daughters. They fled the fighting in the south and were chased again from their homes in the north. Unable to climb the great wall of ice, they walked along its edge. Westward they walked, cold and hungry until at last their legs gave way and they fell.

They did not die there, that family. A brave wise woman of the ice-dwellers chanced upon them. Her long, wiry hair, once red, was almost the same colour as the ice beneath the three bodies she found. She wore a cloak of greater mammot hide, bones and stones and other strange fetishes tied onto the long, greasy hairs. Her boots were sealskin, with plaited summer grasses on the bottom. On her head she wore a strange, peaked cap of white fox pelt.

Though she had never seen our kind before, she heard the stories. She knew we were born murderers and yet, looking in the pale faces of the children, she felt her heart stir and was moved. She carried all three back to her clan, to fire and warmth, and back to life.

The stories speak of a great argument between the old woman and her kin, for who would willingly house the kind that hunted and killed them? The old woman was adamant, and in the end, none could argue with such a woman as she. Then, as now, Shamanka were both respected and feared.

She nursed the man and his two daughters back to health. She saw in the man's eyes fear when he first looked upon her. The children, however, were different.

They were curious and unafraid. The old woman knew she would be able to teach them; and so she did. She taught them about the northern skies and the fires that danced in them. She taught them about the gods and who they were, how they came to be, and what they did. She showed them how the ice-dwellers buried their dead, and then venerated them every year at Sowyt, the Festival of the Dead.

There were two gods, she taught. One was a man, who was also a stag, who was dead. He had as messengers serpents with the heads of goats. Residing in the spirit world, he seldom came into the world of the living. He cared for the animals of the wild, and all the wild places were his domain. He was King of Aqyn, the Land of the Dead, and ruled over the spirits there. He was the spirit that guided the hunter, or punished him if he hunted foolishly or needlessly. They gave him no name, but a title – The Master of the Wild.

The Shamanka spoke of the Bride of Fire, who held dominion over the hearth and the health of the people. She took special care of mothers and infants. She also inspired songs and dance.

These were the two gods of the ice-dwellers, and each had a host of servants, ancestors of the families who now worshipped them.

Three sisters, Cruenja, Bav, and Mav, served both gods together. In the guise of ravens they came to take the spirits of the departed to Aqyn. In the guise of women, they tended to the family as healers and as warrior defenders of hearth and home.

In time, Ahote, the father, learnt to trust these strange people of the ice as his children had learnt before him. They taught him the paths of the beasts, which ones to hunt and why. They tutored him on which herbs were for eating, which were for healing, and which would kill and mustn't be touched.

The children learnt women's work. They soon wove baskets just as the ice-dwellers did. They knew which of the tough summer grasses that grew in shades of lavender and sage were best for basket making. They learnt how to scrape and cure skins and make clothes from them, and how to assist a woman giving birth. They were taught how to recognise and read the signs left by others, telling them where the herds were, where water could be found, and any other useful piece of news.

For many years they lived with the ice-dwellers. It was their presence that saved their hosts from the invading families of the southeast.

With the help of Ahote and his daughters, other families from the east found a place amongst the ice-dwellers. More and more, families of the ancestors accompanied the ice-dwellers to their gatherings, performed their rites, and walked their treks following the herds of the great beasts of the ice fields.

Those who could not make peace with the ice-dwellers were left to fend for themselves. Unused to life at the edge of the wall of ice, they died slow, miserable deaths of hunger and cold.

Many generations on, the weather began to warm. The ice wall receded inch by blissful inch. Rains returned to the homeland, beckoning some of the ancestors south once more. The retreating ice created the vast Sierran Tundra that now sits in the far north. Yet, for the wet and the increase in food that all reaped, the ice-dwellers began to dwindle, their numbers cut by new diseases and raids by a new, powerful people from the east.

The last of the ice-dwellers was a woman. She had outlived the rest of her tribe and now lived in the far north with a clan of our ancestors known as the Ice Bear Clan. She was very wise, and very, very old. In a feverish dream that would be her last she said aloud, "We are gone now, gone to be with our ancestors. I have been called home at last. I leave this place now to you, Young Ones. Take care of it, and love it as my people have. Do not forget all we have taught you."

Then her soul departed in her final breath, flying upon the winds to the spirits of her kin.

She was mourned greatly as she was buried, and each one of the ancestors, man, woman and child vowed to continue to live as we had been taught for so long. It was not to be.

Some of the ancestors forgot their vows, and began to cut into the flesh of the earth to build. With claims to land on the rise, they made war upon one another. The tundra, however, was not to be tamed and a strange woman in the guise of a tundra wolf came down from the rivers of ice and tore down the follies of the ancestors.

None knew who the tundra wolf was, where she came from or where she went thereafter. Some say it was the spirit of an ancestor, enraged by what she saw. Others claimed it was the tundra itself, claiming back what was rightfully hers. They named her Otsana the She-Wolf.

Some of the survivors of the destruction fled south, beyond the lands of the tundra, and continued to build. Those who remained retook their vows, the vows sworn to the last of the Old Ones. We, their descendants, hold to those vows still, and every three years we gather at the place where the boulder fell, and we feast and exchange stories, and news, and daughters, just as they did.

Yet, it is the way of life that nothing stays the same forever. A change is coming. Dry winds whip in from the east and they bring with them the scent of fear. More and more at the gatherings we hear tales of a strange people who come in and hunt us as if we are no more than animals.

We are now the ice-dwellers. We are now as they once were — hunted, scared, confused. These Easterners are not like us, not willing to learn as we did. We must do now what the Old Ones could not.

We must change, or like them, we shall perish.

Dance 'round the fire
Of the sacred year.
Lay down your weapons.
You are unwelcome here.

Make for the south.
You are lost.
The winter is come.
Pay ye now the cost.

Make for the mountains.
The winter is come.
The wolf and her children
Men's work make undone.

Dance 'round the fire
Of the sacred year.
Thank ye the gods
You are still here.

- Touan Harvest Song

One

"*R*un, Totiuq! Run!"

Totiuq turned and fled, holding his bloodied deer-horn knife tightly as he did so. Behind him the terrible sounds of his clan fighting, and dying, rang loudly in his ears. Tears blinded Totluq as he ran. The memory of his father's brutal murder burned in his mind as his brother's voice echoed over the chaos.

"Run!"

Totiuq flew across the snow, fear moving his legs as swift as any deer. It was not swift enough. An arrow whistled as it flew through the air, landing in his back with a wet thud. Totiuq stumbled and fell to his knees.

"Totiuq!"

Hearing his brother scream his name, Totiuq turned. Another arrow landed, this time in his shoulder. The impact tossed the youth to the ground, pushing the first arrow all the way through his torso. He kept his dark eyes fixed on his brother.

"Inna," he whispered.

The broad young warrior named Inna was struck down, a darkly dressed invader slicing hard into his shoulder. Inna fell to his knees, his eyes hazed with pain. They met the gaze of his younger brother.

"Run, Totiuq," Inna whispered. "Run."

The mighty warrior's eyes rolled. He fell backwards into the snow. The shock of his brother's death knocked the breath from Totiuq's lungs. Something woke in the youth then, strong and swift. It was the spirit of the Ice Bear. Filled with fresh strength, Totiuq pulled himself upright and ran. The other clans must be warned.

"Come back here boy!" a harsh voice called after him.

Totiuq heard the twang of a bowstring. He was certain he would be hit. A strong gust of wind struck suddenly from the north, its frosted breath pushing the arrow far off target. In the howls of that gust, Totiuq perceived his dead father's voice.

Run, Totiuq.

Totiuq grimaced through the pain and pushed on. He ran for half a day before exhaustion and blood loss had their way. Totiuq stumbled once, twice, and fell.

The snow did not feel cold against his skin. It was soft and comforting. Even the winds that blew about him were pleasant. They were the winds of the tundra, of his home. The winds spoke with the voices of the ancestors, and they were happy to meet him. Totiuq smiled.

The world went dark.

* * * *

Totiuq was the fastest of his clan. He had consistently out-stripped his older brother in every race since his ninth birthday. His father had been so proud when, at eleven years old, Totiuq won a race against all the other warriors. He had not even been made a man yet.

"He will be a fine hunter," his father said proudly, clapping Totiuq on the back. "Perhaps even better than Inna. The Chieftain will never want with Totiuq at his side."

Totiuq blushed at that.

Inna grinned at him. "But he still must learn to make a spear," he jested. "And we all know he hasn't the patience for that."

His father laughed.

The laugh changed. It was strange; not his father's laugh at all. Totiuq stirred. He was not at the race's end. He was facedown in the snow, two arrows sticking from his body at odd angles.

"Help," he whispered. Then louder, "Help!"

Someone shouted. In an instant, Totiuq found himself surrounded by hunters he did not recognise. A strong hand turned him on his side. The pain, though dull and distant, still made Totiuq wince.

"He is a child," one hunter said.

"What happened, boy?" another hunter, who knelt by him, asked. He looked kindly down at Totiuq.

"I am Totiuq of the Ice Bear Clan. Forgive me for crossing into your lands without permission." Totiuq's voice was weak, his breathing heavy and strained. "I came... my clan..." Totiuq struggled to find the words.

"Easy now, boy," the hunter said. "It is all right. Can you stand? We will get you inside and warm."

"No!" Totiuq grabbed the furred sleeve of the hunter kneeling by him. "You must go to your chief. Tell him... tell him the Ice Bear Clan is no more. Tell him to prepare... for war.

Totiuq could say no more. He released the man's sleeve and slumped down into the snow. A gentle breeze ruffled the hair on his still head and Totiuq found his voice again, riding the wind with the voices of his ancestors.

"Poor boy," the hunter said, gently closing Totiuq's blank eyes. "Come brothers, let us bury him."

* * * *

"Do you think they will agree, Father?" Seraphimé asked quietly. This night, the youngest princess of the Osprey Clan had chosen to sit with her father in his pavilion. In the birthing pavilion on the outermost edge of the camp, her stepmother screamed and wailed in the pangs of labour.

The Chieftain of the Osprey Clan shrugged his broad shoulders. "I do not know. Perhaps they have not heard of our horses. Once they see them, however, I am sure they shall covet them. They may find the arrangement agreeable. In any case, we must make preparations to send the messengers when the snows clear."

Though Chuchip had more troubles than his wife's present agony to contend with, it was precisely her pain that weighed most heavily on his heart. Earlier that day, his Marshal had come into the village carrying the body of a young boy.

"His name is Totiuq of the Ice Bear Clan," the Marshal had said sadly. "He came to warn us. Chieftain, they have come."

A high-pitched scream pierced the air and the Chieftain winced. "Bride of Fire," he whispered. "Bring her through this."

"Fiacha is strong, Father. She will come through."

Seraphimé had said the same about her own mother many years ago. Her conviction had been shattered when both mother and child died during the birthing. Chuchip marvelled at how Seraphimé could sound so sure now. The Chieftain nodded, but the loss of his first wife during childbirth echoed clear in his memory and he sat in silence, pale and miserable. Seraphimé took his hand.

"Ah, my little Marshal. What would I do without you, child?" he asked gently. He wrapped his thick arm around his daughter's shoulders and pulled her in close. "I should be comforting you this evening, not the other way around."

Seraphimé smiled and quipped, "There are some things that men are ill-equipped to deal with."

The Chieftain laughed. Seraphimé was the second and youngest child by his first wife, and his favourite. He had no sons. Seraphimé, ever since she could walk and talk, had filled that role. She had been taught to ride and fight. She was given all the lessons on leading men that the Chieftain could give or commission.

Now, at ten years old, she had become a beautiful, if solemn, young girl with a strange sort of wisdom and the promise of greater beauty yet to come. Thick waves of auburn hair curled down her back, if ever she was in the mood to let her hair loose. Her eyes sparkled in the most astonishing shade of green. She had a sweet smile, though it was rarely shown, and a very quick mind.

Seraphimé had never been one for dresses, preferring instead to wear the riding clothes of the men. Despite her older sister's disapproval, the Chieftain indulged Seraphimé and had riding and fighting clothes made especially for her. The ensemble included an exquisitely carved wooden training sword.

Wood enough to carve a sword was very rare in the tundra, and very expensive. Seraphimé adored that sword and had since taken to wearing it at all times, tucked into her belt as if it were made of steel.

The fighting men, most especially the Marshal, found it most amusing and included her in all their gatherings. They patiently listened to her ideas and suggestions with gravity and concealed smiles. Often, she would surprise them with a clarity of insight not often afforded to the very young.

Seraphimé's older sister, Gabija, was almost a polar opposite to her younger sister. She was everything a woman ought to be – polite, demure, but not ignorant, generous and kind. She loved dresses and fussing with hair and had often tried to turn her unruly younger sister into a lady. Seraphimé refused point blank, and even offered to settle the matter with a scruff outside. Gabija had given up, hoping against hope that things would change as Seraphimé approached womanhood.

Despite this disparity, Seraphimé and Gabija were close. Both girls were intelligent and lively, and shared a fondness for pranks and jokes. Though they would occasionally squabble, the fight never lasted long and was just as soon forgotten. The Chieftain considered himself blessed indeed to have daughters such as his.

Fiacha screamed once more, drawing both father and daughter from their silent reveries. Then the strangled squall of a newborn sounded bold and clear into the night. The Shamanka entered the Chieftain's pavilion with a smile. The Chieftain stood up abruptly, momentarily forgetting his daughter.

"A girl. You have a daughter," the Shamanka said.

"My wife?"

"Alive."

The Chieftain relaxed visibly, then a slow grin crossed his face. He turned to Seraphimé and picked her up in the air. "A daughter!" he exclaimed as he wheeled Seraphimé around to her delight. "A daughter!" He hugged Seraphimé close. "Let's go meet her! Find your sister and come to the birthing tent!"

"Yes, Father," Seraphimé said as soon as she was set down. She ran out of the pavilion and nearly crashed into her sister.

"Gab!" Seraphimé exclaimed in surprise and joy.

"I came as soon as I heard the baby. What news?"

"Alive, both of them. And it's a girl."

Gabija squealed in delight. She and Seraphimé ran to the birthing pavilion hand in hand. They arrived only moments after their father.

When they entered the pavilion, both girls were immediately struck with the scent of blood and worse. Gabija had been through all of this before with the birth of her sister but this was an entirely new experience for Seraphimé. She had not been permitted in the birthing pavilion after her mother died.

She stared with wide, terrified eyes at the cloths and furs stained with blood as the women began to clean up.

"The first births," Seraphimé heard one say, "are always the most difficult."

Gabija moved forward to her father's side, unafraid, and joined the happy circle. The Chieftain pulled Gabija onto the bed where Fiacha now rested and allowed Gabija to hold the newborn. Seraphimé could go no further. Her stomach rolled and tears streamed down her cheeks. She turned and ran.

Seraphimé could not see to where she was running. It did not matter. She just had to get away from that place, that terrible room filled with blood and pain. She ran until she was well clear of the pavilions.

Sinking to her knees, she emptied her stomach in the snow. She struggled hard to breathe through wracking sobs. Dizzy from the effort, Seraphimé reeled backwards and the world became suddenly dark. No one was there to see her faint.

* * * *

The Marshal found her during his brief patrol of the campground. She lay out in the snow beside the now frozen puddle of her own sick.

"Dear, dear," he said gently, lifting the child in his arms. "That scared you did it?"

Seraphimé did not reply. She shivered silently and unconsciously in his arms.

"I cannot blame you, child," he muttered as he walked quickly back to the camp. "It scares the ghost out of me. Bride of Fire, but that you women survive such a feat is beyond me."

Two days later, Seraphimé awoke from her fever to find her worried father sitting by her bed.

"Papa!" she cried as the man wrapped her tightly in a firm embrace. She burst into tears as he rocked her.

"Oh, my little marshal!" he whispered over and over, pulling Seraphimé ever closer to him.

"Is that how mamma died?" Seraphimé asked after her tears subsided.

The Chieftain sighed and nodded. "Your brother was too big for her. She couldn't push him out."

"I'm never having children," Seraphimé whispered, horrified. Not knowing what to say, the Chieftain held his favourite daughter to him and rocked her until she fell once more into fevered sleep.

* * * *

With the careful attention of the Shamanka and her older sister, Seraphimé recovered from her fever in a little over a week.

"You are strong," the Shamanka said gently when Seraphimé's green eyes fluttered open.

"Sera!" Gabija gasped. She threw herself on her sister in a rough embrace.

"Ow," Seraphimé complained.

"I was so afraid! I thought you were dying."

"Water."

"Here, love," the Shamanka said to Gabija as she handed the girl a water-skin.

"Can you sit up?" Gabija asked her sister.

Seraphimé grunted and pushed herself upright. She felt dizzy from the effort. "Food."

"There is soup coming," Gabija said. "Here, drink."

Seraphimé took the skin and drank down the warm, honeyed water thirstily. "Papa?" she asked.

Gabija took back the water-skin. "With Fiacha. He was so worried. I've never seen him cry like that. Not since Mamma died."

Seraphimé sighed. "I'm sorry." She spoke in little more than a whisper. "I didn't mean to upset anyone. I just... I just couldn't stay in there."

"It's all right child," the Shamanka said. She knelt by Seraphimé's bed and pressed her palm against Seraphimé's forehead. "Seeing the pain a woman must bear to give life to her child is not an easy thing." The Shamanka smiled at Seraphimé. "Your fever has broken. I'll let you out of bed in two more days. For now, though, rest."

Seraphimé nodded and lay back on the bed. Gabija arranged the furs around Seraphimé.

"Stop fussing." Seraphimé fell asleep before her sister could respond.

True to her word, the Shamanka permitted Seraphimé out of bed two days later. Knowing that Fiacha was back safely in her father's pavilion, Seraphimé mustered up the courage to visit her and her new half-sister. Despite her trembling legs, she marched into the pavilion. Her determination was such that anyone could have mistaken her stride as a march to war.

Fiacha greeted Seraphimé's pale face with a bright smile as she held the bundle that was the newborn in her arms. "Hello, Sera," she said gently.

Seraphimé barely managed to nod. She looked ill again.

"Don't worry, tender-heart," Fiacha said encouragingly. "As you can see, the baby and I are quite well."

"Can I see her?" Seraphimé asked, curiosity finally overcoming her fear.

"Of course you can. Come here."

Seraphimé walked forward and climbed up onto the bed. Fiacha sat up and moved the furs that obscured the baby's face. Seraphimé wrinkled her nose.

"Her face is all squished."

Fiacha laughed brightly. "It won't stay like that! Don't you think she looks like your father?"

Seraphimé looked long and hard. Though she found it difficult to distinguish anything about the pink, squashed features that resembled anybody, she nodded.

"Do you want to hold her?"

Seraphimé gasped in surprise. She did want to hold her, but was terrified that she might drop the newborn or hold it the wrong way so that its neck broke. She had heard of such things happening.

"Hold out your arms like this," Fiacha instructed, demonstrating.

Seraphimé did as she was told and Fiacha gently placed the child in her arms. Seraphimé's heart was immediately stolen as the baby yawned and stretched. She opened one pale eye to gaze at Seraphimé and cooed before falling asleep once more.

"She's beautiful," Seraphimé breathed, stroking the little face with her finger.

"Yes," Fiacha said with a smile. "Just like you."

Seraphimé looked up at Fiacha and felt suddenly like crying. Fiacha noticed and opened her arms wide. Seraphimé walked forward on her knees and curled against Fiacha, the baby still in her arms. Fiacha hugged them both close and all three soon fell to sleep.

The Chieftain found them that evening, still in each other's arms.

Two

"Must we treat with these savages, Father?" Algar asked irritably. "Surely they have nothing of value."

"Don't be tiresome, boy," the King of Misoua said, waving at his eldest son dismissively. "They have furs and such to trade, I am sure. Their horses are famous, a breed to be much desired. We could use a cavalry of such beasts against the damned Greyl raids. Besides, it would be a great advantage to us if we were to know precisely the numbers and strengths of the peoples that surround us. That is the true purpose of this mission."

Algar grumbled something under his breath and Alam rolled his eyes. "Father," he said. "I'll go. It might be too dangerous for your eldest son and heir to be so exposed. Besides, I've always been curious about the people of the tundra."

The King grunted and regarded his second son carefully. "Very well, you shall be my designate."

Alam smiled and Algar threw him a look that was both envious and grateful. He did not want to go to the tundra and live amongst the savages. Alam's offer had spared him that, but he resented the way Alam had stolen his father's approval.

"The matter is settled. I shall send them a messenger as soon as spring arrives."

"Good luck finding them," Algar said cheerfully. "They are perpetually on the move, and no one is quite sure where one clan's territory begins and the other's ends."

The King shrugged. That much was true. Though the Touan people had a very rough idea about their northern neighbours, their territories, their lifestyles, and their martial abilities remained something of conjecture. Even the missionaries who returned from the northern climes could offer no greater clarification, save for a few clan names and costume observations.

"I'll be sure to send a man who knows how to live in the wilds."

"The wilds are one thing father," Algar noted casually. "But fields of ice are another entirely."

To this, the King could only grunt his agreement. He decided to send three riders with the offer of trade when the spring finally arrived. It was bound to be a long and difficult journey to the tundra and the King of Misoua could not reasonably expect a response before one year had past, assuming that one of the clans was located swiftly.

The King hoped to meet the Osprey Clan, who had, according to the missionaries' reports, grown quite large, by relative standards, and powerful. The Chieftain of the Osprey Clan was well respected by all the peoples of the Sierran Tundra, his counsel considered weighty and listened to closely. A partnership with him and his family would open a much wider door than if the messengers were to meet another clan.

The first three messengers returned in the dead of winter, having found the tundra empty and seemingly devoid of life. Irritated, the King was forced to wait until the following spring before attempting to reach his northern neighbours again.

This expedition proved even less successful than the last, with only one messenger returning at all. All he carried for his efforts was the hair clipping of another messenger, whom he had found mauled by wolves.

Furious, the King of Misoua, never the most patient of men, abandoned the idea completely until the spring following the next. This time the venture proved to be a success.

"Your Majesty," the messenger greeted with a bow from the door of the King's study. The King had been pouring over copies of the missionaries' maps of the tundra. His sons were disinterestedly playing checkers.

"Come in, my boy! Tell me you have good news for me?"

The messenger's face split into a wide grin. "I do indeed, your Majesty." He walked in and gratefully accepted the vacant seat the King indicated.

"Great Susa! You found someone!"

"Better than just someone, your Majesty. I caught the Osprey Clan as they were heading to their summer lands. Their chieftain, Chuchip, bids you welcome."

"Chuchip?" Algar scoffed. A stern look from his father silenced him.

"You are certain it was the Osprey Clan?" The King asked.

"I am. They had thirty-five mounted warriors, and each man had a family besides. It's a sizeable group."

"Did you take a look at their horses?"

"A good look, your Majesty. They are very fine; sure-footed, brave and fiery when needed. Their riders are skilled warriors in their own right, though in such small numbers will not be a serious threat save to other tundra clans."

"Is there much fighting between them?" Algar enquired.

"No. They are remarkably good-natured. They have very strict rules about trespassing, though they will not withhold aid to anyone in need. A remarkable people."

"You were gone a while," Alam noted.

"Yes. Enough time to learn their language a little. Did you know that they all speak fluent Touan?"

"What?" Algar and Alam asked in unison.

"It took me by surprise too. I tried my best to learn their language in recompense. It seemed only fair."

"What's it like?" Alam forgot the game of checkers and leant in eagerly.

"The single most difficult language in the history of languages everywhere," the messenger replied with a smile. "There are sounds I did not know men could make in it."

Alam grinned.

"What of the offer of trade?" the King interrupted.

"Chuchip was greatly surprised. He had been considering sending a messenger himself with much the same offer. He found the arrangement most agreeable. He said he would send his Marshal with a small host come the autumn, including two hostages of good faith."

The King blinked in surprise. "Do the Sierrans also have the tradition of trading hostages?"

"No, but Chuchip was aware that we Touans do."

"Indeed."

"In any case, the envoy ought to arrive here spring of next year. Prince Alam will return with them, arriving in their homelands near the end of the autumn following."

"Such a long time," Alam mused.

The messenger nodded. "You have been accorded a great honour, your Highness."

"Oh?"

"Your visit coincides with their tri-annual gathering. You are welcomed to it as a guest of honour. I asked if they could recall any other time a foreigner had been permitted at a Great Gathering. They could not."

Alam's eyes grew wide. "I'm invited to a Great Gathering?"

"Yes, your Highness."

"Hah!" Alam shouted, pointing at his older brother.

Algar shrugged. "I shouldn't want to go even if I was invited."

"Liar!" Alam grinned. "You'd love to know what these savages do every three years at their gathering, wouldn't you?"

Algar yawned. "Not in the least. Now, it's your turn. Make your move, little brother. Though, it doesn't matter what you do at this point. I'm still going to win."

Alam could not care less. He moved his piece thoughtlessly. Delight and anxious curiosity set him dancing in his seat while he awaited his brother's next move. He could not wait to see what adventures lay before him in the great white north.

* * * *

Seraphimé turned sixteen the winter the Marshal died. She had been with him in his final moments, sitting patiently by his bed as he shook with fever. He had grown old. Gone was the enormous bear of a man who had rescued Seraphimé from a frozen death after the birth of her first stepsister. In his place lay a thin man, devoured slowly by time and the aching that accompanied it.

"Little Marshal," he rasped, extending his hand out to Seraphimé. Seraphimé took it. He watched her through rheumy eyes. Slightly shorter and quite a bit more broadly built than her elder sister, she had blossomed into an exquisite beauty. The shape of her body was most pleasing, and her green eyes were often likened to fathomless oceans of grass that would drown a man if he gazed in them overlong. She had her father's dark auburn hair and her mother's pale skin and the almond shape of her grandmother's eyes.

"You are so beautiful, Little Marshal," the Marshal rasped. "Long have I wished you were my daughter."

Seraphimé smiled at him and said nothing. Her voice fled her and tears robbed her of sight.

"I have served your father all his life. I watched him grow into a man. I stood by his side when he was married. Twice." He had to pause to catch his breath. It came in short, wheezing gasps. "But I am too old now for those things, and I am dying.

Seraphimé started to protest. The Marshal weakly waved her into silence.

"I have spoken with your father. We both agree. I name you my successor, Little Marshal. Look after your father and his people well."

He touched her hair lightly and then was gone, flying away to join the ancestors.

Sobbing, Seraphimé knelt on the floor by his bed and laid her head atop his chest.

The clan buried him that same day.

* * * *

For three weeks Seraphimé could not be consoled. She went every morning to the late Marshal's cairn and sat at its base, staring at the newly laid rock mound in silence. She sometimes sat there for hours. On occasion, an unusual wind would stir her hair. She knew then that the ancestors were there. They were watching over her.

When the three weeks of her mourning finished, Seraphimé at last donned the leather armour that marked her rank. That evening, an ayal, one of the roving high priests of the God of Death, came to the clan and presented himself to the Chieftain. Welcomed sombrely, he was invited to remain with the clan. No one would dare offend a servant of the Lord of the Hunt by not extending such an invitation.

The ayals were infrequent visitors to any of the clans in the Sierran Tundra. Their presence usually presaged the arrival of grave danger. As such, they were regarded with suspicion.

Seraphimé, however, was not afraid of the Ayal, nor of the stag-god whom he served. Without a single word exchanged, Seraphimé and the Ayal grew fond of one another's company. They would often be seen walking together in the Valley of the Ancestors.

Late that same season, a messenger of the Kingdom of Misoua arrived. Intrigued though she was, Seraphimé remained mistrustful of this new intruder. So too were the men she now led.

Chuchip, however, made certain that the messenger was warmly received. The Osprey Clan surprised the messenger by greeting him and conducting their affairs in the Touan language whenever he was present. In recompense, he set about learning as much of the Sierran tongue as he could manage.

He departed midsummer, having arranged all the details of the offer of trade with Chuchip and his Marshal. Under the lights of the night sky, the Chieftain took the Marshal of the Osprey Clan, his favourite daughter, aside for a long walk.

"You know what I ask of you," he said in his soft voice.

"You want me to go south to collect the Prince-thing."

"Be polite, Sera."

Seraphimé grunted.

The Chieftain laughed. "I want you to stay, as a matter of fact. Send someone else in your stead."

Seraphimé blinked in surprise. "Why?"

"It may be a trap, my daughter."

It was Seraphimé's turn to laugh. "What makes you think so?"

"The Touans are not renowned for their honesty, Sera. I know you mistrusted the messenger. I saw it."

Seraphimé nodded. "I did not trust him, it is true. But I could not detect deceit on his part. He, at least, believed his message to be true. In any case, I am certain the King of the Touans will find it an insult if the Marshal of the Osprey Clan does not arrive as promised."

"Sera-"

"Father, I am your Marshal. I took a vow. I promised an old man on his deathbed. I will not renege on it now. How can I expect my men to trust and obey me if I prove such a dishonourable coward?"

The Chieftain smiled sadly and touched his daughter's face. "You know you make me proud, don't you?" He sounded plaintive, like a child.

Seraphimé took her father's hand and kissed it. "Of course."

Seraphimé and a select number of her warriors spent the next few months preparing to head south, following the geese. She carefully chose her five companions. The remaining thirty warriors were commanded to stay behind and protect the clan as they moved. Alarming reports of more raids from the east had reached Seraphimé's ears. She was determined that her people be protected.

Gabija's eyes filled with tears as they said goodbye. "Be careful," she pleaded.

Seraphimé laughed as she embraced her sister. "Of course I shall."

Three

$\mathscr{I}$t took six months of travel to arrive at the gates of Fredeja, the capital city of the Touan kingdom of Misoua. Seraphimé's tracking had been faultless. She followed the messenger's directions precisely, and found the yellow ribbons that marked their way at the end of every day. She enjoyed this time away, being amongst her favourite men as one of them.

The news of a woman's succession into the position of Marshal did not disturb the men of the Sierran Tundra as it did their southerly neighbours. Women were often found as heads of families, in the ranks of the priestly class and even ruling over entire clans. To the Sierran man, a woman was no less worthy of the rights and positions men enjoyed.

Seraphimé proved a very capable commander and a respected fighter. Many of her own force could not defeat her. What she lacked in strength she more than compensated in speed and accuracy. She was better with a bow and shorter, lighter weapons than she was with heavier weapons. None begrudged her that.

In one match, she out-fought a man thrice her mass. He had chosen a heavy blade and she had only her speed, her wits and two long daggers. That victory had been celebrated for days on end.

For all her prowess, the city of Fredeja made her as uneasy as it did her men. Great towering walls encircled it. A few dilapidated buildings outside clung to the walls like underfed dogs shivering by a fire at which they were not welcome. The countryside had been torn up to make farms and plots of land were fenced in and tamed. The very sight of it made Seraphimé angry. She sat on her horse, well out of range of the archers that dotted the walls like flies over a carcass, and waited patiently.

At length, a guard approached from the gate accompanied by an escort that greatly exceeded Seraphimé's own.

"Who are you?" he demanded.

The men were all dressed in black and red garb with shining steel breastplates. The man who had spoken wore a helmet that was ornate, heavy and utterly useless. Seraphimé highly suspected the haughty man before her had reached his position by birth and was yet to be tested.

She raised her brows at his tone. Her men bristled behind her. "I am Seraphimé, Marshal of the Osprey Clan, come to this kingdom by invitation of your King. Announce our arrival. I will wait here for him."

The guard's mouth twitched in condescending amusement. "You must go to the castle to be announced," he said bluntly, his tone not softening.

Cumus, a burly, squat man whom Seraphimé had chosen as her Lieutenant, rode his black tundra horse to Seraphimé's side.

"We can easily outflank these rats on their little ponies," he growled in her ear. "Let me take the men to the right."

Seraphimé shook her head. "I will not cause a war on account of one rat's ill-mannered address," she replied. She turned her attention back to the guard.

"You have your instructions," she said to him, levelling him with an unnerving stare. Her green eyes flashed dangerously. "Set to them. I will not enter your tomb for the living."

The guard barked a laugh. "You go to the castle, or you wait here forever," he spat. "Not my job to go scampering at some savage's command."

"But it is your job to go scampering after mine," a booming voice said from directly behind the guard's company. The escort immediately parted to find the King, his second son and a large party of palace guards. The guard immediately shrank back.

"Yes, your Majesty," he simpered.

"You will mind your tone when speaking to my guests," the King said in a quieter, but ever darker voice. "Most especially since you are speaking to a Princess. I ought to have you flogged for your insolence!"

"Forgive me, your Majesty," the man stammered. "I did not know who she was."

"Did she not identify herself?"

"Yes, your Majesty, but as a Marshal, not a Princess."

"You spoke so to a *Marshal*?"

The man was rendered speechless.

"Get out of my sight you blithering oaf, or I will have you flogged."

The guard fled, and his escort with him. The King sighed.

"Officers," he murmured, more to himself than anyone. "Think that just because they've money enough to purchase a commission they own the world." He turned to Seraphimé with a bright smile.

Seraphimé could tell that in his youth, this man must have been quite handsome. Tall and broadly built, he must have once been muscular, though years of inactivity had rendered most of the muscle to fat. He ran a thick hand through his receding blond hair and peered at Seraphimé with curiosity. His slate-grey eyes, framed by the strong features of his face, carried the bright spark of humour.

Seraphimé met those eyes with an intelligent gaze. "Good day, your Majesty," she said gently, her tone and seat in her saddle giving her an air of confidence.

Alam observed the boyish young woman on her tall mount. She was wearing leather armour with a sleeveless tunic underneath, though the early spring air was still far too cold for that, to his mind. Her arms were relatively muscular, certainly more muscular than any other woman he had ever seen. Dark auburn hair was pulled back into a braid and remained unadorned.

"Well met," the King replied. "Please accompany me back to my palace. There is a feast currently being prepared in your honour, and rooms made ready for your arrival."

Seraphimé eyed the tall walls of the city crawling with archers and pike-men and the large gates with the portcullis. The scene looked like a monster's sharp-toothed yawn. She shook her head.

"Forgive me, your Majesty, but no."

Taken aback, the King straightened in his saddle. "No?"

"No," Seraphimé repeated firmly.

The King blinked in stunned surprise, his mouth open. He suddenly roared a booming laugh. Seraphimé, unsure what the King found so amusing, watched as he laughed long and hard. His son, for he looked so much like the King that Seraphimé could only presume it was his son, smiled behind him.

"Very well," the King said as he wiped tears of laughter from his eyes. "Very well, in your honour Princess, we shall have the feast brought out here."

Seraphimé smiled. "That is generous of you, your Majesty. We will make the exchange of hostages then."

"Indeed."

With that, both companies parted ways and Seraphimé and her men dismounted. No sooner had the entire greeting party turned around than did Alam look back and note with surprise that the Sierrans had already erected one shelter.

* * * *

"Well I never," the King said as he dismounted in the courtyard. He grinned from ear to ear, having, apparently, greatly enjoyed the exchange that occurred in the field beyond the farms. "Someone fetch the Steward."

One of the many servants scampered across the courtyard. In a matter of minutes, the Steward stood before the King.

He bowed curtly. "You asked for me, your Majesty?"

"Yes. It seems that our Sierran guests mistrust stone buildings. They've requested and been granted that the feast brought to them outside the castle walls."

The Steward raised his brows and looked displeased. "As your Majesty demands."

"Excellent. Make it quick. I do not want to keep them waiting."

"Right away, your Majesty." The Steward bowed again and vanished into the castle.

The King's demands threw the castle staff into a frenzy. They ran this way and that across the courtyard and in and out of the castle, cursing quietly at their superiors. It was such an uproar that Alam barely heard his father speak.

"I rather like that tundra girl."

"She seemed very cool under pressure," Alam noted dryly.

"Indeed," the King said cheerily. "I should very much like to cross wits with her!"

Alam laughed. "Algar will be very sorry he missed this."

Algar had, in anticipation of the Sierran nomads' arrival, taken leave to visit and tour with his cousin in the western provinces.

"It might well change his opinion of them."

"It might," the King agreed. "Unlikely," he added. He grinned at his son. "Well, I suspect you will be expected to stay the night with them, since we exchange hostages after the feast. You had best pack.

"Yes, Father." Alam relinquished the reigns of his horse to a stableman and headed inside to do as his father bid.

* * * *

The feast moved out of the fortified city under heavy guard to avoid a tussle with the poor and desperate. The King and his second son rode at the head of the column, just behind two heavily armed guards. The paraded food made many a mouth water, but none dared try to breach the wall of steel and horseflesh that surrounded it. The parade arrived at the camp of the Sierran nomads just as the sun began its slow descent behind the horizon. The camp made Alam smile. It looked as crude as he had expected it to be.

Two rectangular shelters, each barely waist high and quite long, stood with their entrances facing the walls of the city. The tent hides had not been scraped of their fur and so looked like some bizarre box-shaped animal. A large fire-pit had been dug and a fire blazed cheerily away in its centre.

The small group of men the Marshal of the Osprey Clan had brought with her watched the approaching party warily as they sat around the fire in all manner of positions with no apparent heed to rank. Only the Marshal rose to greet the King and his son. She did not bow.

"Good evening, your Majesties," Seraphimé said.

Her cool confidence both intrigued and irritated Alam. A woman was meant to be soft and demure. She was meant to know all the graces appropriate to her gender. She was not to ride and fight as a man, or walk too freely among them. She was not to be muscular in any way, for such a thing was most unbecoming. Near as Alam could tell, the men did not regard the Marshal as a woman, unless they viewed all women as one of the men.

Still, there seemed to be a gracefulness about the Marshal, of a sort. It was the kind of gracefulness one might admire in the rolling shoulders of a wolf moments before it pounced. It was a dangerous grace, and Alam found that he distrusted the woman before him.

"Well met, Highness," the King replied amiably. "I have brought food enough to feed an army. I hope you and your men are hungry."

"We have travelled a great distance on very little," Seraphimé replied. "We welcome your offering with grateful hearts and very empty stomachs."

The King laughed. "Well then, I shan't keep your stomachs waiting too long."

Seraphimé smiled as the servants were ushered forward and immediately prepared the feast. The boar on offer was considered quite large by the Touans. To the Sierrans however, it appeared small and the pride with which the Touans offered the animal amused the nomads, who nudged each other and grinned. The servants spitted the boar prior to their departure from the castle. They hoisted it on Y-shaped stands so that it hung neatly over the fire.

That achieved, they placed various pots and pans around the flames to keep warm and finish cooking.

"The servants are not very pleased," the King noted as he dismounted, Alam following suit. "They had almost finished preparing the meal when I ordered them to relocate everything."

Seraphimé grinned. "I apologise most profusely for the interruption, but we of the tundra were made for open skies and horizons, not for stone walls and closed ceilings."

The King grunted. "This is my son, Alam, who will accompany you back to the North."

Seraphimé extended her hand in the greeting of men and Alam shook it. She had a firm grip, despite her smaller hands, and they were rough and a little calloused. Alam found it most off-putting.

He forced a friendly smile at this woman that was not quite a woman. "I am excited at this opportunity to travel," Alam said, not lying. "I have been fascinated with the tales of the men in the north."

Seraphimé motioned with her hand and a short, very broad man ambled forward. He wore his suspicion of the southern men openly on his face as he stared at the King and his son. Alam was taken aback by the decided lack of respect for authority the Sierran nomads possessed.

"This is my Lieutenant, Cumus," Seraphimé introduced.

"Pleased to meet you," the King said guardedly. Even his good cheer was not immune to the open suspicion of the Lieutenant. The Lieutenant grunted and waved a hand to the fire.

"Sit," he said in a thick accent. "Eat." Then he ambled back to the fire.

Seraphimé smiled to herself. "Please," she added after the Lieutenant.

The King's easy smile returned. "Thank-you. Uh, where?"

"Wherever you wish."

The King looked perplexed. There were no stools or seats of any kind. The men were sprawled in no particular order, in no particular fashion. Seraphimé waited patiently as the King and his son made their hesitant way to the fire and chose a place to sit on the cool grass. The nomads around them shuffled their positions a bit to make room and Seraphimé joined them.

"I say," the King noted. "I'm not used to such informality."

Seraphimé smiled as she gazed at the fire. "We depend on each other for survival. We do not have the luxury of being overly formal with one another."

The King nodded. "Well, I would very much like to thank you to agreeing to this exchange."

Seraphimé shrugged. "My father thought it would be good for us to extend our trade negotiations south."

"Indeed?"

Seraphimé observed the King in silence for a moment. Her shrewd eyes gave no clue as to what thoughts lay behind that gaze. Alam decided that it was time to break the uneasy silence.

"So tell me, Marshal, what can my men and I expect on this journey?"

"A great deal of walking, Prince Alam," Seraphimé replied.

To this, her small company of men laughed gruffly. Alam wasn't sure if they were making fun of him or not. He decided to smile.

"I am not afraid of walking," Alam replied easily. "It's the stories of giant wolves that terrify me."

Seraphimé laughed. "The tundra wolves tend to stay far to the north where the ice fields meet the tundra grasses. They are rarely sighted."

"Have you ever seen one?"

"Not once since the day I was born."

Alam seemed satisfied by that, but his imagination heaved as the childhood stories of the terrors of the Sierran Tundra came flooding back.

"Is it true that everything on the tundra is bigger? Do you truly have giant boars, and the hairy, tusked monsters?"

"Tundra boars are very large indeed," Seraphimé replied. "But I'm afraid I don't know what you mean by 'hairy, tusked monsters.'"

"Mammot," one of the men said and a light sparked in Seraphimé's eyes.

She laughed. "Oh yes! The mammot! That must be what you mean!"

Alam filled the next few hours with discussions of the various mega fauna of the Sierran Tundra. Alam acted like a schoolboy, asking all sorts of questions, and food did nothing to slow the gush. Seraphimé, the King thought, was very patient to put up with it all.

At length the conversation dwindled and the King rose, a little unsteady from the amount of mead he had drank.

"Though I have enjoyed your company immensely this evening," he said brightly. "I fear I might enjoy the company of my bed more at this late hour."

"In this case," Seraphimé replied with a laugh, "we perhaps should exchange hostages."

"Splendid."

Cumus rose abruptly and left. He knelt by a shelter and something inside stirred. He returned only a few moments later with a young boy and girl. The girl looked terrified.

"My cousins," Seraphimé said. The King bowed low to each of them.

"Do not fret," Seraphimé said to the two children clinging tightly to Cumus' hands. "They won't hurt you."

"And if they do," Cumus growled in Sierran, "I'll hurt them."

Seraphimé's mouth twitched, threatening a smile. She knelt down to her cousins and opened her arms. They ploughed into her in a single rush and she hugged them close.

"Be brave, little ones," she whispered to them. "It will only be for a year."

The little boy pulled away and looked at Seraphimé with large, brown eyes. He nodded, just once, and took his sister's hand. Together they walked to the King, who mounted them both on a spare horse. Seraphimé stood and watched them go with tears in her eyes and an expression of fierce pride.

Cumus reached out and grasped Seraphimé's shoulder. He squeezed gently and Seraphimé sighed. She turned to her men.

"Bed. Show the Prince and his men where they sleep."

Alam quickly learnt that acceptance of authority required nothing more than obeying orders, and that the Sierrans did not ascribe any special treatment to those who were above their station.

He did not like it.

Four

*T*he following morning, moments before the sun rose, the Sierran nomads and their charge left without ceremony. Alam, unused to being woken much before midmorning, did not appreciate the early start, though he did find the swiftness with which the nomads struck camp amazing. The shelters collapsed in an instant and folded neatly so that they might fit on a horse's back without inconveniencing the animal.

Carrying precious little personal effects, the nomads were quickly packed and patiently awaited Alam and his small group to finish their preparations. They watched Alam and his men with small, patronising smiles. One of Alam's men rumbled rather audibly at this and Alam could not help but agree with the unhappy sentiment. Their speed seemed unnatural to him.

Once mounted, Alam suddenly became very aware of the great black horses of the tundra. They were tall and muscular, with thickly feathered hocks and broad hooves. Next to them, his own horse seemed little more than a pony. Alam glanced at Seraphimé.

The Marshal of the Osprey Clan was engaged in a friendly conversation with her lieutenant. Her seat on such a broad mount looked easy and practiced.

She carried about her person a small collection of weapons including two daggers that sheathed neatly into her tall riding boots. At her side she wore a short sword and long dagger. She wore the clothes of men, adjusted slightly to fit the form of a woman.

Alam shook his head. How could the men bear allowing a woman to act as a man? Such unseemly behaviour was severely punished amongst the Touans.

We're not with the Touans now, he reminded himself and so he resolved to be polite to the Marshal of the Osprey Clan, no matter how her appearance and demeanour affronted him.

It took five long months to travel to the borders of the Sierran Tundra. Alam used the time to observe the behaviour of his hosts. They were generally a cheerful people. They did not seem to mind the long days in the saddle, though Alam's own thighs screamed in protest by the third day.

They laughed together freely and, Alam noted with a smile, often played pranks on each other. Seraphimé was quite adept at it and managed to trick Cumus several times before he became immune, much to Seraphimé's disappointment.

Seraphimé once made Cumus believe a ghost was following him. She wove several long grasses together and tickled the back of his neck with them every so often. At first it annoyed Cumus, but when he could not see nor touch the thing that bothered him so, he began to grow fearful.

Over the course of several days, others began to join in the fun, and would complain to each other of a sudden chill. This, Alam learnt, was a sure sign of a ghost. Seraphimé began with her woven grasses again. Alam had never seen a man lift his feet so high in panic. The men laughed so hard that one fellow fell off his horse.

Once adjusted to their habits, Alam noted that though they appeared carefree, they rode in a defensive formation. They also kept a careful eye on their surrounds, even when roaring with laughter.

Alam was wholly unused to loud laughter, his father's booming laugh notwithstanding, for it was very rarely heard. The quiet titters of the members of the court were all Alam truly knew of laughter. Meals amongst the Touan were also quieter, filled with polite conversation spoken in soft tones that rated barely higher than a whisper.

The Sierran nomads were loud and gruff, occasionally raising their voices to shouts in order to be heard over someone else's din. They often told stories around the fire at meal times, ranging from tales about the beginning of time and a strange, wise people known as the Old Ones to more recent endeavours; pranks and hunts and the like.

They would sometimes tell tales of the gods, or the Old Ones, and more often they would recount the exploits of their ancestors. Many, particularly the tales of an ancestor known as Maggog, would garner great guffaws. Evidently, he was an even better prankster than Seraphimé.

Alam and his men remained distant from their hosts at meal times. Though they would sit close to the fire and listen keenly as they struggled to understand the Sierran language, they would rarely interact.

While travelling at least, there would forever be two groups around the fires, divided by region of origin.

When at last the group arrived at the edge of the tundra, the Sierrans gave a small cheer. They didn't particularly like being away from their homeland for so long, and they were keen to get back to their kinsmen.

The Sierran Tundra appeared rather suddenly. For almost a week, Alam noticed the trees thinning. This far north, they did not reach nearly as high as they did in his homeland. Past the mountain ranges, the deciduous trees vanished entirely and for almost a fortnight they travelled through an ever-thinning forest of stunted evergreens. Then, suddenly, there were no more trees, and the terrain stretched northwards in a tumble of tall grass and rocks.

The rocks were covered in hardy lichens, giving them a strange grey-green colour. The grasses were many-coloured, ranging from pale green to lavender and now, as autumn began its rapid descent, pale gold.

"It seems we've gone from spring to autumn, and missed summer entirely," Alam mused.

Seraphimé heard and smiled, but said nothing. She remained at the edge of the rocky ground in stillness for a while, her men waiting patiently behind. Alam was confused by the pause, but the nomads seemed entirely unperturbed.

"What's happening?" Alam asked Cumus, daring to practice what little Sierran he knew.

Cumus turned to Alam with a scowl. "Hush," he replied. He turned again to face the front.

Alam raised his eyebrows and turned his mouth down in disapproving surprise. No sooner had he done so than Seraphimé urged her massive mount forward, and the group was on the move again.

Determined not to be ignored, Alam pushed his horse to Seraphimé's side.

"Why did you pause at the edge?" he asked her.

Seraphimé seemed not to hear at first. Alam asked again, more insistently. At length Seraphimé turned to Alam and smiled a little. There was a secret in that smile, and Alam did not like it.

"To greet her."

"Her?"

"The tundra."

"I see." It was not true, Alam didn't understand at all. Greet the tundra? It seemed foolish.

A loud yelp halted the group and turned Seraphimé's head. She frowned as two more yelps and a whine followed. Turning her horse, Seraphimé went in search of the sound. She shouted back a command, and Alam and his men found themselves encircled by the nomads, each man facing out. Cumus broke the circle and joined Seraphimé as more whines filled the air.

Alam strained to see past the nomads, but the horizon yielded nothing. Beneath him, his dainty horse snorted and shifted, unsettled by whatever made the noise. The southern horses were all discontent. Their northern cousins, however, stood still and steady, their pricked ears the only indication that they were paying attention to the goings on.

Alam ignored his horse and tried to find the direction of the sound, but in the crisp air of the open tundra, it seemed to come from everywhere all at once.

Seraphimé paused and listened before adjusting her horse's direction. The sound came from the east, but not very far away. Each whine cut through her heart as much as it did her ears. It was a sound of pain. Seraphimé needed to search only for a brief moment before she found its source.

Lying in a fairly deep crevice between two stones lay a massive black ball of fur that whimpered and yelped as it struggled feebly, its rear leg caught in a rusted trap.

Seraphimé immediately dismounted.

"Careful," her lieutenant warned.

Seraphimé barely heard. She stopped dead when the animal turned to her. Ruby eyes glittered fiercely beneath a heavy black pelt. The hound looked like a wolf, though it was the size of a small pony.

Seraphimé gasped. Tundra wolves did not roam this far south, yet it was the only dog she knew that could grow to this size. It must be some sort of mutt, as tundra wolves were never the colour of coal. It immediately brought to Seraphimé's mind the tales of the great black hunting hounds of the Lord of the Hunt.

"Hello," she said gently as she took a cautious step forward. The mutt bared its teeth and growled a low warning.

"It's all right." Seraphimé eased forward. "I'm not going to hurt you."

The growl deepened yet more and rose in volume. With Seraphimé's next step, the dog launched itself forward, forgetting its trapped leg. With another yelp, it fell onto its side. At the same moment Seraphimé recoiled and, losing her footing, fell onto her back.

Cumus swiftly dismounted and went to Seraphimé, who promptly refused his aid and struggled to her feet alone.

"There's nothing you can do here," Cumus said. "Leave it be."

"So it can starve to death or die of infection?" Seraphimé retorted indignantly. "No, I think not."

"You'll get yourself killed."

The dog let out a pitiful whine and Seraphimé approached again. The dog twitched, but remained on its side and did not growl. Fear, the only thing keeping its eyes open and fixed on Seraphimé, vibrated through its being, causing it to tremble.

"You poor thing," Seraphimé murmured in a soothing voice. "Poor, poor thing."

The dog was quickly losing consciousness. Its eyes rolled and the eyelids struggled to remain apart. It fought valiantly to stay awake and alive. Seraphimé extended a hand. The dog growled and struggled to rise and attack, but failed miserably. With a sigh, it slumped once more to the ground and did not move.

In an instant, Seraphimé knelt at the mutt's side. She stroked the animal's still head. "Stay with me," she urged. "You're going to be all right."

Moving quickly to the trapped rear leg, Seraphimé barely paused as she worked to open the crudely made steel trap. The wound, Seraphimé noted, must have been quite old.

Several places had started to heal over, only to be torn again by the useless struggles of the wolf-dog that the trap had ensnared. It had festered in places, and grown into new bloody slashes in others. It brought tears to Seraphimé's eyes.

As soon as she pried the trap loose, she tossed it aside, where it promptly snapped shut again. Cumus went over to examine it as Seraphimé ran to her horse to gather medical supplies. In just a few moments, she had cleaned the wound and staunched the fresh flow of blood. Using a scabbard from one of her own daggers, she fashioned a splint for the beast's shattered leg, wrapping a bandage firmly around it. Carefully, she lifted the massive dog and whistled for her horse.

Alam watched from a distance as the horse obediently went to Seraphimé's side and knelt. He found it vaguely amusing to watch Seraphimé struggle with the size and mass of the enormous mongrel dog she laid across the horse's neck. It was less amusing when she mounted and rejoined the group.

"That will get you killed," one of the men noted as Seraphimé resumed the march, the massive mutt slung before her.

"If she survives perhaps," Seraphimé replied, fondly stroking the thick black fur.

"She?"

"Yes, she."

They rode on until dusk and camped in the lee of a valley, where rocks were fewer and soft earth more easily accessible. Seraphimé tended to the dog while the others prepared dinner.

She unwrapped the bandages and boiled them in a pot, while salted water boiled merrily away in another one. She cleaned the wounds again with the boiled brine, taking extra care this time to ensure that all the infected material was removed as well as could be before she applied a thick paste and re-bandaged the leg.

Though the dog twitched on occasion, she did not wake. The twitching as Seraphimé tended the wound was all the indication she had that the dog lived. The Marshal of the Osprey Clan would spend a great deal of time before she retired to bed stroking the animal and speaking to it in gentle tones.

Alam wondered greatly at this, and worried that the dog would suddenly awaken and round on its saviour. Seraphimé seemed less concerned.

"What are you going to do when it awakens?" Cumus asked Seraphimé as she settled inside the rectangular shelter she shared with her men.

Seraphimé shrugged. "Be sad at our parting."

Cumus grunted a laugh and promptly fell asleep.

Seraphimé had, prior to retiring to bed, laid the dog on furs just outside the pavilion entrance, covering the dog with a blanket improvised from Seraphimé's own riding cloak in order to keep her warm and protected from the cold tundra winds.

The first to rise, Seraphimé was greeted by its ruby gaze. She gasped.

"You're awake!"

She disappeared inside the shelter again and emerged with a thick strip of salted meat. The dog growled as she approached, but did not have the strength to move. Seraphimé laid the meat just before the dog's nose and vanished back inside the shelter. She waited quietly by the pavilion entrance and was rewarded with the wet sounds of the dog eating. With a smile, she dressed herself, then kicked Cumus awake. She indicated the dog was awake in perfect silence.

Cumus immediately recognised the impish sparkle in Seraphimé's green eyes and a grin spread over his face. He woke the others, but neglected to tell anyone about the conscious mutt outside.

A loud snarl rewarded the first man to set foot outside the shelter. The man jumped and ran, loosing curses as he did so. Cumus and Seraphimé howled with laughter. For several moments, no one dared exit the shelter, but were encouraged when Seraphimé walked bravely out and, despite a greeting growl, showed no fear as she marched past the injured dog.

It took only a few moments for the hound to identify Seraphimé as the leader and thusly, though it growled at her, the dog would not attack, even when Seraphimé pulled the blanket off and threw it over her own shoulders once more. The enormous black dog remained lying down as Seraphimé struck the pavilion and observed, growling only if Seraphimé came too close.

The mutt shifted its weight to watch as the nomads gathered for breakfast, throwing large chunks of travelling meat into a pot of boiling water. The boiling food filled the air with the scent of meat. She whined with hunger as she watched the people eat.

Seraphimé smiled to herself, but knew animals well. She would not feed the dog until she first had her fill.

The nomads seemed to understand Seraphimé's intentions. Though nothing had been said to them, they left some food for the dog. As the cooking equipment was packed away, Seraphimé approached the mutt with the food. This time, the dog did not growl, but placed her beautiful head on her paws and looked up imploringly.

Seraphimé smiled to herself as she spooned out the steaming mush before the dog and walked away. She turned back to watch with satisfaction as the hound greedily lapped it up while still lying on the ground. She sighed.

They would part ways here for, no matter whether the dog recognised Seraphimé as leader of this new pack or not, she would never let Seraphimé lift her up onto a horse and so must remain behind to fend for herself.

Seraphimé was surprised to hear a plaintive whine as she rode away. She stopped and turned her horse, watching the dog still curled on the ground. The mutt's tail wagged a little when she saw Seraphimé stop. Seraphimé smiled, but did not approach.

"If you want to come with us, you will have to walk," she said quietly.

As if the hound had heard her, she crawled forward and attempted to stand. It took the animal several tries but she managed it and, after a few false starts, hobbled to Seraphimé, who remained unmoving until the dog reached her. The dog kept her head down and her eyes up, with her tail and ears held low in submission as she approached. With a curt nod, Seraphimé turned and moved off again, the dog trailing as best as she could.

The group moved painfully slow that day. Seraphimé deliberately stopped often to allow the wolf-like dog to catch up to them. At each meal break, the dog would sink down and watch from a relatively safe distance as everyone ate. As always, Seraphimé would feed the dog the leftovers, which were deliberately left by the nomads.

Alam heard his men grumble about being served less food each meal, but he was far too absorbed in watching Seraphimé and the foundling mutt bond to bother taking their cause up with the nomads. At the end of each day, Seraphimé ensured she was the last one by the fire. It was less intimidating for the mutt that way.

Each evening, the hound would crawl closer until one evening, she settled cautiously by Seraphimé's feet and curled up, absorbing the heat of the fire.

"I think I'll name you Cabal," Seraphimé said quietly. The dog's ears pricked and she turned her massive black head to Seraphimé. It seemed to Seraphimé that the dog was smiling.

"Cabal it is, then. Goodnight, sweetling." As had become her custom, Seraphimé covered the dog with her cloak before retiring to bed.

Five

$\mathcal{I}$n three short weeks, Cabal's health had greatly improved. So too did her relationship with Seraphimé. She permitted Seraphimé to scratch her ears and ruff. The two would often be found together after the meal, watching the tundra in perfect, mutually enjoyable silence.

Alam had taken to speaking with Seraphimé as often as he could. The distrust Alam held for Seraphimé slowly melted away, replaced by a deep respect for her. She had proven herself to be articulate and intelligent and, now that Alam was more used to the Sierran customs, he could see that her men respected her a great deal.

"When will we get there, do you think?" Alam asked as their horses picked their way through the rocky terrain. It was bitterly cold now, even during the day. Alam found himself shivering violently despite the exertion of horse riding.

Seraphimé shrugged. "It is difficult to judge. We are following the southern trek north. We will meet them eventually."

"The southern trek?"

"Yes. The herds here have different paths when travelling south than when travelling north. Thus, so must we."

Alam rode in silence for a while.

Seraphimé observed him as surreptitiously as she could manage, a remarkably difficult feat for a woman who was more used to direct gazes. She found Alam to be a very handsome man, despite being blond. His eyes were the same grey as his father's and his features sharp and bold. There was something pleasing in the sweep of his cheekbone and set of his jaw.

She turned away again, not allowing herself to think more on it. Think, however, she did, and she could not help but be drawn in by his intelligent banter and pleased by his many looks in her direction.

Perhaps, she thought. *Perhaps.*

Later that evening, Cabal's low growl interrupted Seraphimé's silent reverie. She turned to see who had earned the dog's ire and smiled to see Alam standing awkwardly a few feet away, wrapped in everything he owned.

"Cabal," Seraphimé admonished quietly.

The mutt had grown used to her clansmen, but had yet to take a liking to Alam. With an ill-tempered snarl, Cabal turned and stalked into the night. Relieved not to be facing the dog, Alam came and sat next to Seraphimé.

"Couldn't sleep?" Seraphimé asked.

Alam shook his head. He looked out over the tundra. Save for the sound of the wind whistling between crevices in rocks, eerie silence dominated the landscape.

"Is it always this quiet?" Alam asked.

Seraphimé smiled again. "The ancestors are loud tonight," she replied. "Can you not hear them?"

"I hear the wind," Alam said uncomfortably. Talk of ancestors sent chills through him, most especially since word had spread that the Osprey Clan had been converted by the Holy Yellow Robes several years ago.

"Is it?" Seraphimé replied in a tone that said she knew that it certainly was not.

The wind blew a little harder and suddenly the air filled with humming and other noises that sounded like laughter and speech, though distant and fuzzy. Alam started.

"The ancestors use the winds to speak to us," Seraphimé said, turning her attention back to the tundra.

"And what are they saying?"

"That you have a lot to learn, Alam Misoua."

Alam laughed suddenly. "You almost had me going!"

"Going where?" Seraphimé frowned.

"Wherever you wanted to send me," Alam replied. "Ancestors and all that rubbish."

Seraphimé turned back to Alam and observed him with green eyes deeper than any ocean. Their unreadable depths unnerved Alam.

He turned away. "What makes you so sure there are ancestors around?"

Seraphimé smiled. "I can hear them. When I walk in the Valley of the Ancestors, I can feel them. I dream of them and speak with them. We know they are there because in life, they existed here."

Alam scowled.

"What makes you so sure there are no ancestors?"

"Our religion forbids it," Alam muttered, knowing what reaction it would get. Seraphimé laughed, as he knew she would.

"That is the most foolish thing I've heard," she said.

"Clearly you do not often hear yourself," Alam snapped back.

Seraphimé's laughter died down, but a smile hovered about her lips. There was a dangerous flash that crossed her eyes briefly.

Alam sighed. "I'm sorry," he said. "I'm just tired I suppose. I did not mean to be rude."

Seraphimé shrugged. "Perhaps then you ought to sleep."

Alam nodded, but lingered a while, his gaze never leaving Seraphimé's face. Even when she turned to face him squarely, Alam did not look away.

Seraphimé frowned a little. "What is it?"

Alam could have kissed her then, forgetting for the moment that she was not quite a woman to him. He turned away at the last moment, clearing his throat uncomfortably.

"Well," he said. "Goodnight."

Before Seraphimé could respond, Alam rose to his feet and walked away. Deep in thought, Seraphimé turned once more to the tundra, only to see Cabal streaking across the horizon with surprising speed and agility as she chased a tundra hare.

The morning dawned bitterly cold and Alam shivered violently as he packed away his gear. He noted with annoyance that the nomads were already up and around the fire. Breakfast this morning smelled different. Alam breathed deep and turned to the fire. Five large hares were roasting on a spit. He walked over.

"Rabbit?" he asked. "Where did you get those?"

Cumus grinned as he turned the spit and nodded his head in Seraphimé's direction. He noted Seraphimé standing away from the fire, staring out towards the tundra, Cabal at her feet, tearing into the carcass of a sixth hare.

"The dog?"

Cumus nodded. "A gift for the Alpha," he said.

Alam looked back at Seraphimé and grunted. "Makes a nice change from salt-meat soup," he noted.

Cumus grinned.

Once the hares were ready, Seraphimé was the first to eat, taking her fill before the others were permitted to touch their food. Cabal made sure of it, baring her teeth and growling at anyone who tried to touch a hare before Seraphimé was done. Seraphimé laughed when it happened and, mercifully, ate quickly.

Alam was certain he had never tasted anything so lovely as breakfast that morning, though, he surmised, anything different would be wonderful after endless months on salted meat soup.

As had become his habit, Alam rode with Seraphimé and talked with her as they travelled. Cabal, now fully healed, would run in front, or follow a scent somewhere behind and vanish, only to come running when the group moved too far away. The horses were steadier around the wolf-mutt now, though in truth the tundra horses did not seem so unsettled the first time they encountered her.

Alam, at times, watched Cabal, and other times watched Seraphimé watch Cabal. Sight of the dog relaxed Seraphimé, and painted a perpetual half-smile on her face. That evening at camp, Alam found himself once again alone with Seraphimé.

"You have grown very attached to her," he noted as Seraphimé giggled when Cabal jumped away from swaying grass, having mistaken it for some sort of dangerous animal.

Seraphimé shrugged in response. "Does that seem odd to you?"

"Not especially, except that she was wild."

"And we of the Osprey Clan are so decidedly domesticated."

Alam laughed. "Good point."

"It is not difficult to understand the wild when you live it. A wolf pack is a great deal like a clan. Like the alpha male, the Chieftain protects the pack, but it is the alpha female, like the Head Woman – the Chieftain's wife – who enforces the law."

"Our kings are all men," Alam said with a frown.

Seraphimé nodded. "I know. Though, tell me of a single king who did not listen to the counsel of his wife."

Alam grunted. "I cannot say. I do not know of the pillow talk between a king and his wife."

"Your mother has passed away, am I correct?"

"Yes. How did you know?"

"She did not join us at the welcome feast."

"It could have been that she preferred to eat indoors."

Seraphimé shrugged. "But duty would have overthrown her desire, I am certain."

Alam grunted.

"My mother died when I was young," Seraphimé said. "I no longer remember her."

That explains a lot, Alam thought. He wisely kept it to himself. "You were raised by your father?"

"I was raised by the clan. The Marshal before me, my sister, my stepmother, my warriors, they all had a hand in raising me."

"They taught you to fight?"

"And ride, and hunt, and track."

"Did no one teach you any of the womanly arts?"

Seraphimé smiled. "My sister tried," she replied, amusement thickening her voice like honey. "It seems the gods have something else in mind for me."

Gods. Again. Alam scowled. "Did the Osprey Clan not convert?"

Seraphimé shrugged. "Yes."

"Then why do you continue to make reference to ancestors and gods?"

"Surely you cannot expect us to simply forget thousands of years of tradition, of stories and teachings simply because some fool in a yellow robe tells us we are wrong?"

Alam was taken aback. "If...."

"Peace, Alam Misoua. The clan observes all the traditions your yellow robes taught us."

"As well as the ones they condemned."

Seraphimé smiled serenely and said nothing. Her eyes twinkled however, and an echo of the conversation they had previously floated unbidden through his head. *You have much to learn, Alam Misoua.* Alam sighed and retired for the night.

Travel for another week followed much the same routine. Alam would often find himself alone with Seraphimé. Sometimes he could almost forget that she was not truly a woman, without possession of all the proper womanly graces and arts. He had almost forgotten one evening before Seraphimé's direct question sharply reminded him.

Alam had moved close to Seraphimé; too close for any casual intention. Seraphimé looked him in the eyes and said, "Are you playing with me, Alam Misoua?"

Alam stepped backwards and frowned. "Pardon?"

"For almost a week you have moved as if to kiss me, then turned away at the last moment. Are you simply playing with me, or have you intentions towards me?"

Alam's back immediately stiffened. "Intentions? Forgive me, Seraphimé, I did not mean to lead you astray. I was simply being friendly. I have no intentions towards *you*."

Immediately upon saying it, he knew it was the wrong thing to say. His arrogant tone alone would have earned him a slap across the cheek had he spoken so to a lady of Misoua. He withdrew a little and prepared for Seraphimé's palm to strike his face.

Instead he saw a dark flash across Seraphimé's eyes and her shoulders stiffen.

"And what, I wonder, is so distasteful about having intentions towards me?" she asked bluntly.

Alam was trapped. There was nothing he could say now that would not be a blow to the heart. He decided that truth would be the best course.

"You are very striking, Seraphimé," he said truthfully. "And you should know that I respect you a great deal, but you are not what I am used to. You are not like the women of Misoua and though I find it refreshing, in truth I could not cause myself to..." He groped. "...To have intentions towards you."

Seraphimé remained silent for a long moment, her eyes clouded. She looked at Alam. "I greatly pity the women of Misoua, who must pretend to be weak to protect the fragile egos of their men."

A simple statement, but Seraphimé's tone was cold, her words coated in ice to protect them from the heated inflection of hurt and embarrassment. She said no more, turning on her heels and walking away, her head held high. Alam watched her leave, pained. With an angry sigh, he retired for the night without eating, proclaiming a headache.

Cumus watched with curiosity as Seraphimé sat at each meal in sullen silence and Alam vanished into the shelter provided for him and his men. He very shrewdly guessed what was behind both Seraphimé's silence and Alam's early retirement, and could barely believe it. Seraphimé had never shown any man preference, and any man for whom she did so would have to be a fool to shun such a rare gift.

Six

*T*ravelling together now awkward, Alam remained with his men for the most part, sometimes riding forward to speak with Cumus or other nomads. Seraphimé refused to speak with him. Should he ever attempt to speak with her, her flat stare sent him back to his men in irritated silence. After several days, Alam refused to be cowed and rode beside Seraphimé regardless.

They rode in silence for three days.

Alam, tired of Seraphimé's silence, had turned back to join his men. He was in a foul mood, wondering when Seraphimé's frost would melt, even if only a little. He could understand it, of course.

Rejection was never easy to take. Still, he expected a more feminine response, in spite of everything. There should have been a temper tantrum, tears, anything but this cold indifference. He shifted in his saddle, glowering ahead at Seraphimé's form.

Seraphimé herself rode mostly beside her lieutenant, finding comfort in his wide, brown face. She sat easily in her saddle and appeared perfectly at ease. Beside her loped the foundling mutt she had rescued on the way. The dopey animal's pink tongue lolled happily from its mouth as it trotted beside Seraphimé's horse.

The dog seemed happy enough at this distance, but Alam knew that as soon as he approached she would turn as vicious as any wolf. Seraphimé was the only one Cabal responded well to.

Two she-wolves, Alam thought bitterly to himself.

As if the mongrel could read his thoughts, she paused and turned to Alam, her red eyes narrowing.

Alam shook himself. It was not possible. It was nothing more than pure coincidence, aided by the fact that the half-wild mutt hated Alam. He pulled his gaze away from the dog and the Marshal of the Osprey Clan and instead looked about him. Everywhere he looked, the view remained the same.

The windswept tundra stretched out into eternity, an uninteresting wasteland covered in patches of hardy grasses that grew in between the green-grey rocks. Every so often, sparsely covered shrubs or the occasional tall monolith broke the flat, colourless terrain. Alam often mused on the monoliths, wondering what they were for and how old they were.

Possibilities muddled his mind, making it difficult to think clearly. They could be territorial markers, or simply landmarks designed to aid navigation in an otherwise featureless terrain. They might be gravestones or some strange, featureless effigy for an equally strange, featureless god. Alam had no clue, and his guides were most reluctant to answer him when he asked.

His simple question, 'What are they?' was simply answered, 'Standing stones.' It irritated the Touan Prince.

They had passed several standing stones on their journey into the heartland of the Osprey Clan. Each one looked so weathered as to be ancient, though it might well be that the continual winds had made them appear so and they were actually quite new.

He understood from Cumus that the stones were in fact ancient, having been erected by the ancestors many thousands of years ago. Though why the ancestors bothered was something Cumus either did not know or refused to tell.

The gait of Alam's horse suddenly changed, surprising the Prince and rousing him from his meandering thoughts. The horse moved from the uneasy steps the dainty-hoofed animal had to adopt amidst the rocks into a smooth, easy walk.

Blinking in surprise, Alam looked down and found that the group now followed what looked like a paved road. Although shrubs and grasses had sprouted in the cracks between cobbles, there could be no mistaking that they were now walking along a road. It looked sophisticated and provided a startling juxtaposition against the wilderness that enveloped the party.

"This is a road!" Alam exclaimed aloud.

The entire party halted to look at him.

"Sorry," he mumbled. "I'm surprised that a nomadic clan would have need of a road, that's all."

Seraphimé smiled slightly. "This road was built by the ancestors," she said. "Cut from the white stone of the Quiranese Mountains. In a few moments we will pass where the rough cuts were honed down for paving stones."

"Really?" Alam was intrigued.

His city had existed as a city for thousands of years. Whatever history it contained was likely buried deep under more modern buildings. He did not have such unrestricted access to his own history as these people did.

True to her word, Seraphimé stopped a few hours later at the site where the rough stones were refined. It was painfully clear, even in the fading light that Alam now sat in front of a well-organised honing quarry.

Unshaped stones lay in a heap on the left. On the right and slightly closer to the road itself sat a small pile of shaped stones stacked in a tumbled-down pyramid. The site could have been abandoned yesterday, for all Alam could tell.

"It has remained untouched this way for tens of thousands of years," Seraphimé said, her voice barely a whisper. "Do you see on the flat rock? There are the groove marks of the cutting implements. Smoothed now by ice and wind, but still they are there. The tools have been taken away by the ice long ago."

"I did not know that the Osprey Clan had the tools necessary for cutting cobblestones," Alam said. He had not meant to sound patronising.

Seraphimé's mouth quirked. "We do not. The ancestors abandoned the craft and so it was lost."

Alam grunted. He wanted to ask why the ancestors abandoned their building efforts, but knew that all he would get was a grunt and a shrug, if that.

"We will make camp behind the next ridge," Seraphimé said, turning her horse.

It took another half hour to arrive at the campsite. This site was another great mystery. A large, round space paved in stones of different colours marked out a swirling pattern surrounding a close huddle of standing stones. The plaza showed no signs of having a roof – no postholes, no broken stone columns. It had been intended as an outdoor space, Alam felt certain.

He noted with surprise that the plaza had a set of stairs, marked by two waist-high, carved pillars that led down onto another road. The road beyond, however, had all but disappeared, destroyed by the ravages of time. Only the occasional square paving stone hinted at its presence.

Alam rubbed his hands together in an effort to create warmth as the sun began to set. He took out his bedding and unrolled it, noting that he was the last to have done so. With a sigh, he watched the flames of the evening's fire roar to life.

Alam gratefully sat down next to its orange warmth. His men followed suit wordlessly, but he knew well what they were thinking. He thought it also.

It was too damned cold, and winter had not even arrived yet. He had no idea how the people of the tundra managed to live with it. Yet they seemed completely unbothered by the now subfreezing temperature.

A clansman poured cold water into a pot and set it on the fire. It had amazed Alam when he first saw the water being gathered. Upturned stones revealed sheets of crystalline ice that were chipped away and melted.

His awe at the Sierran Nomads survival strategies did not stop Alam from grimacing at the sight of the strips of dried, salted meat that were cut and thrown in the pot.

Salty meat soup, a favourite up here. Alam hated it. Still, it was food and it was warm. He wouldn't turn it away. He sat patiently as the water began to bubble and the smell of salt and leather filled his nostrils.

"Travelling food," one of the Osprey horsemen grunted almost apologetically. "Good to keep you warm."

"Like eating boiled leather," Alam noted dryly.

The horseman grinned and nodded, evidently not understanding Alam's tone. Alam sighed and pulled his furs closer around him.

The horsemen of the Osprey Clan were typically loud, talking quickly in their strange language and laughing. In contrast, their Touan guests were quiet, too cold to expend the extra energy to speak. Alam noticed, more sharply this time, Seraphimé talking with her men. Though treated with the respect one might expect for a Marshal, she was evidently as much one of the horsemen as the rest.

Alam grunted. He wondered if there were any gender distinctions between the men and women of the Osprey Clan, besides the obvious physical ones. Then he wondered that if there were none, how on earth could a man be a man without appearing womanly? It hurt his head, so he gave up on the thought.

The meat, having been so thoroughly dried, broke down into something akin to stringy mush in the water. Served with a spoon and a large, unappealing chunk of dry bread, Alam nonetheless gratefully accepted the bowl of salty meat mush. Lacking in flavour though it might be, it promised a full belly and some warmth.

The meal granted both. Warmed and full, Alam and his men turned in for the night to find rest. They found it quickly, fading into gentle sleep.

The same could not be said for Seraphimé.

She remained awake, even after her own clansmen retired to bed. She poked at the slowly dying fire before giving up and leaving it to perish on its own. She walked to the top of the short stairway and stood at its edge, staring out into the moon-soaked tundra. Away from the eyes of her men for the moment, she could finally let flow the anger and disappointment she kept hidden.

Hot tears streaked down her cheeks and instantly turned cold. It had not been easy to hide her emotions, and the only way she managed it was to become like the tundra – cold and indifferent. Seraphimé idly wondered what trauma had turned the plains to ice.

Had the maiden that was the plains been shunned by a lover, thus turning her to a land of bitter frost? Surely that was the only fate that awaited a spurned woman. She sighed in her melancholy and turned her attention to the stars.

A quiet, high-pitched whine drew Seraphimé's attention to her feet. There stood Cabal, her foundling hound. The dog looked at Seraphimé as if to enquire after her.

Seraphimé smiled down at the mutt and the latter wagged her shaggy, curled tail. Seraphimé reached out and stroked the dog's head and ears. Reassured, the dog settled happily at Seraphimé's feet and Seraphimé turned her thoughts once more to the tundra and then onto the ancestors. Had they broken the heart of the plains?

Alam, still unused to sleeping on hard ground, shifted in his sleep. His constant turning and tossing ended with his head sliding off his makeshift pillow. It hit cold stone. He woke with a grunt, his open eyes falling to the figure of Seraphimé.

A halo of light surrounded her as the rays of the moon reflected from the frost on her cloak. She stood quietly on the edge of the camp staring blankly out into the vast tundra, her mongrel dog lying beside her. The hunter's green cloak flapped dully in the frigid night breeze. Alam watched her a moment in curiosity before he approached. The dog growled at him as he did so.

"Hush, Cabal," he heard her murmur in her velvety voice.

"It's a cold night," he noted as he came to a stop beside her.

"It's always cold on the tundra."

"Indeed," he remarked dryly. "It has chilled your tone."

She did not reply for a while. "You should be asleep," she said finally.

"So should you. This is the third night you haven't slept."

She made to reply, then shut her mouth, pressing her lips together tightly.

"Say it, Seraphimé."

"Go away, Alam."

"Say what it is you want to."

"Go. Away."

The tightness in her voice warned Alam not to press the issue further, but some strange pressure in his chest drove him on.

"Seraphimé," he said gently.

She closed her eyes and drew a deep breath before turning to look at him.

Not for the first time Alam noticed how truly beautiful she was. The gentle light of the moon made her even more stunning. For all of the promise of her features, her expression was hard.

"You already know," she grated. She turned sharply on her heel and stormed away.

Alam sighed. "Seraphimé," he called quietly. For all her anger and hurt, the gentle tone in his voice gave her pause. "You are a hunter and a tracker, a horseman and a master of war."

Seraphimé turned to face Alam once more. "I am, and I have worked all my life to become so. Yet for all of that, I am still a woman." She said no more, turning again from Alam and disappearing into the murky night.

Cabal remained where she was, her teeth bared at Alam.

"Come, Cabal," Seraphimé called softly from the darkness.

The dark, wolf-like mutt rose to her feet and trotted towards the sound of Seraphimé's voice, but not before giving an ill-tempered snap in Alam's direction. Alam shook his head and took Seraphimé's place, staring blankly out over the silver-touched tundra. He wondered if the tundra had once been a beautiful paradise full of promise.

Seven

The next morning dawned just as cold as the night had been. Alam grumbled quietly to himself as he packed his bedding. He could not understand why anyone would travel through, let alone opt to live on, the sparse, frost-covered plains of the north. He had been so excited to go to the tundra. Now all he wanted was to go home. Somewhere, a pack of wolves howled in defiance of the cold. Alam's horse shivered as he dressed the beast.

"I'm sorry," Alam said to the mount as he forced the cold metal bit into its mouth. It snorted in protest. "I warmed it up as best I could."

Alam took some time to look around. The tundra-dwellers were already packed and waiting atop their massive, thick-limbed horses. Seraphimé sat amongst them quietly, deep in thought. Her dark auburn curls were buried beneath the traditional peaked, fur caps of the Sierran people. The frost crystals which still adored her long travelling cloak lent the green a greyish hue. Had she simply been amongst the rocks instead of on her horse, Alam would never have seen her.

Her lieutenant leaned over and spoke in her ear. Seraphimé nodded and nudged her mount. She reined him in to a stop just before Alam.

"The wind speaks of snow," she said blankly. There was no hint of the wounded woman who had hissed at him the night before. "Will your men be much longer?"

Alam could not help but smile. The question was not asked to seek an answer, but to prompt a little more haste. "I'll have them ready to ride very soon."

"Good." She turned her horse and trotted back to the Sierran tribesmen that made up her personal guard.

Alam turned back to his men, who were moving as if already frozen solid. "Snow is on the way," he barked. "Mount up now or get left behind."

That was enough. No one wanted to be left behind in this forsaken land of frost. The men finished packing and were up in record speed. Alam had never seen them move so fast. With a grin, he led his men forward to join Seraphimé and her guard. The two columns of unlikely travellers pushed forward at an urgent trot.

"How much further?" Alam asked Seraphimé.

"No more than a day, if your horses can keep their pace." It was not Seraphimé, but her lieutenant who provided the answer.

Alam scoffed. "Ours can if yours can," he muttered to himself.

The Lieutenant heard him and grinned wildly. He declined to respond. Instead, he mentioned it to his neighbour, who roared with laughter. When Seraphimé looked back with an enquiring gaze, the Lieutenant repeated the story.

Though Alam did not speak the language of the Sierran horsemen, he could tell what they were talking about. Seraphimé smirked at Alam when the brief story was told, but did no more. Alam was glad.

The first few flakes of snow began to fall during the midmorning break. Alam could hear his men groaning. He was not far from it himself.

"This is intolerable!" he muttered darkly to himself. He looked over again at his hosts. Not a single one of the nomads seemed at all bothered by it.

They sat amongst the rocks so at home that, were it not for their laughter and movement, Alam might have mistaken them for stones. They shared bread and jerked meat between them while Alam's own men huddled close together, cold, hungry, and miserable.

"You should eat," Seraphimé's lieutenant called over. "Or you'll feel even more cold."

"I can't bloody eat," a man named Bully grumbled. "My jaw is frozen!"

"It's warm enough to flap in complaint," Alam noted, earning grins from the other men. Bully simply growled.

"Cumus is right," Seraphimé noted. She had walked over largely unnoticed. Without any further words, she handed Alam a large loaf of bread and hunk of meat for him to share amongst his men.

"Thank-you," Alam said as he collected the food, but Seraphimé had already walked away.

"Cold bitch," Bully noted.

"It's all this living in the ice and snow's that done it," Bully's brother, Gremmet, said. Alam sighed. That wasn't the reason, but only he and Seraphimé knew it. Alam looked over his shoulder and noted the Lieutenant's dark eyes fixed on him.

The Lieutenant too, Alam revised. He turned back to the circle of warmth that was his men and shared out the food.

Later that day, Alam found himself in conversation with the Lieutenant. The snow now swirled through the air in thick plumes.

"Why the hell would you live out here?" Alam grumbled to the squat man.

The man shrugged. "No one bothers us up here," he replied.

Alam laughed. "I can imagine. No one is crazy enough to be out here except you lot."

The Lieutenant grinned. "That is why it is safe."

Alam grunted. He glanced at Seraphimé, who scanned the horizon alertly, another warrior beside her, at the head of the column.

"You look at her a lot," the Lieutenant observed.

Alam shrugged. "She's not so difficult to look at."

"But too difficult to bed?"

Alam looked sharply at the man. "That is none of your business."

The Lieutenant shrugged and squinted up at the sky. He murmured something in his native tongue.

"Cumus!" Seraphimé barked from the head of the column.

The Lieutenant immediately pushed his horse to the front. Alam watched with interest as Seraphimé handed him a length of coiled rope, keeping a hold of the end herself. The Lieutenant then stopped his horse and handed the rope to each person who walked past.

"Here," the Lieutenant said, shoving some rope into Alam's hand. "Hold this. It will connect you to everyone else and you won't get lost."

"What's going on?"

"Wall of snow." Cumus pushed Alam on.

Alam frowned and took the rope. He nudged his horse forward. Despite the chill, Alam found himself sweating. He clung so tightly to the rope that his hand went numb. He was very glad he did.

When the wall of snow hit, he could not even see his hand in front of his own face. Everything was white. Still, connected by the rope, they trudged resolutely forward.

"How do they know where the hell they are going?" Bully called from just behind Alam.

In the howling wind, Alam could barely hear what the man said, but he understood it nonetheless. The same question plagued him. Knowing there was no way to answer and be heard, he simply chose to ignore Bully and plod on, despite his reservations.

The storm lasted for several bitterly long hours. When it finally cleared, everything was covered in a glistening blanket of white. Alam had to admit, cold though it felt, it looked stunning.

He looked around at the sparkling landscape with wide eyes. The sun came out and shone so strongly that the glare bouncing off the snow hurt his eyes. He looked back. Everyone was still there, brushing the snow from their persons. Cumus came trotting up the line, coiling the rope as he went. He threw Alam a broad wink as he passed.

"Didn't lose anyone," he said.

Alam nodded.

As soon as Seraphimé had the rope in her possession once more, the party moved forward. The southern-bred horses had some trouble over the snow-covered rocks of the tundra, their smaller hooves more likely to slide into unpleasant cracks and crevices. The broader-hoofed northern horses strode easily over the terrain, and so several times the nomads had to stop and wait for their southern guests to catch up.

The Lieutenant leant over to one of his comrades and said something in his unintelligible native tongue and the whole company of Sierran horsemen laughed. Alam did not understand the language, but he could guess at its meaning: *if yours can, ours can.*

Alam scowled, prompting more laughter.

Seraphimé cut the comedy short though she, too, smiled. "We're almost home," she said. "But behind schedule. We will ride until we arrive. No stops."

"Except to have your horses catch up," the Lieutenant added to Alam, before turning his horse and leading the column for a while. Seraphimé seemed content to let him do so, and fell easily in line in the space he left.

Alam muttered darkly as he pushed his horse forward.

The great northern horses were gifted with feathered hocks, keeping in their body heat and protecting their otherwise fragile legs from the cold. The southern horses did not have these and Alam feared that they would suffer some serious injury, or fall ill from trudging through snow.

There wasn't much to do but think or talk on the way to Seraphimé's village and Alam had found himself doing plenty of both. For now, however, he eyed the setting sun with some trepidation. Though the sky was cast in stunning colours of flame reflecting those colours with shadows of purple across the snow, he found himself removed from the beauty of it.

All this cold made him appreciate home all the more. He longed for a hot bath, fresh meat and the comfort of his own bed, perhaps with a willing woman in it. This thought plummeted Alam into deep contemplation. Not for the first time, he considered the nomadic Princess, Seraphimé.

He could admit to her beauty, but seemed incapable of seeing her the way men see women. She was not a woman. She was a warrior. She was a horseman. She was a commander. And she was damned good at it. Alam respected her a great deal, but he could not imagine her in his bed. He sighed as the last vestiges of light faded from the sky.

"Four hours of light," Gremmet grumbled.

Alam shrugged.

"How can anything live on just four hours of light?"

"They can't, that's why you don't see any trees out here," Bully answered.

Gremmet grunted.

"Do you see that?" Bully asked.

"See what?" Alam asked in return.

"That light."

Alam frowned and narrowed his eyes. High in the sky and far to the north, a light traced lines through the night sky like multi-coloured flames. The flames in the night sky captivated Alam and it took him a moment to realise that the party had stopped. He reined his horse in as Seraphimé dismounted. He watched as she reverently sunk to her knees and the mounted horsemen bowed their heads, each chanting quietly in perfect unison.

After only a moment Seraphimé mounted once more and the group moved again. Alam nudged his tired horse forward to Cumus.

"What was that all about?" he asked the Lieutenant.

Cumus seemed almost in a trance and it took him a moment to recover. He grunted as he roused himself. "The lights in the sky," he said simply.

Alam waited for more information to come, but none did. "Yes," he said at last. "I saw them too."

Cumus shrugged. "That's what it was about."

Alam rolled his eyes. He obviously had to ask more direct questions. "What are the lights in the sky?"

Cumus shrugged again. "Ancestors."

For all of Seraphimé's actions to the contrary, Alam still held to the happy news that the Osprey Clan had converted. Cumus' answer surprised him.

He had heard that some of the lesser Sierran nomads still retained their antiquated beliefs, but according to the missionaries sent out of the holy citadel of Wetoua, none of the Sierran nobility now followed the heathen path. It had been a great victory for the Wetouan Council. After all, where the leaders went, the rest would follow. Alam scowled.

"You are surprised?"

Alam's frown deepened. "We had been told that Sierran nobility had converted," he replied.

"Most have," Cumus said. "But Seraphimé is one of the few who did not."

"Why not?"

Cumus shrugged. "Who knows? Why do women do anything?"

Alam grunted. Not content with this answer, he approached Seraphimé.

"I was speaking with your lieutenant," he said casually. "He noted the ceremony we just witnessed was for the ancestors?"

"Yes," Seraphimé answered in her distant, cold manner.

"I thought the nobility had converted."

"Most."

"You didn't."

"No."

"Why not?"

Seraphimé looked at Alam briefly. "Because."

Alam waited for more information. It did not come. "Because what?"

Seraphimé smiled. "Because I didn't want to."

"There must be a better reason than that."

"Must there?"

Alam sighed. "Fine," he muttered. "Keep your secrets."

Seraphimé smiled. "There will come a day, Alam of Misoua, when you will learn that each soul must walk its own path. One cannot force a tree to grow."

"A soul is not a tree."

"You do not know that."

"And you do?"

"In my fashion."

Alam grunted and pulled his horse back, now troubled. If Seraphimé had not converted, then it is likely that her father also had not. Could he be walking blindly into trouble? Somehow he doubted it.

The people of the Sierra Tundra were famous for their honesty. Still, the Council of Wetoua, following the example of their superiors in the Holy Yellow City, declared war on the enemies of their faith. Perhaps the Sierran nomads were preparing for some sort of pre-emptive strike?

Anxiety plagued Alam as he crested the hill overlooking the valley that currently contained the mobile village of the Osprey Clan. His brow sparkled with sweat, though the temperature remained below freezing. His shoulders were square and tense. Even after travelling with them for months, he had no idea what to expect of the nomadic horsemen. He was astonished at the level of sophistication displayed by the barbarians of the Sierran Tundra.

Large pavilions dotted the valley on either side of a narrow, shallow stream. The pavilions themselves were made of thick hide, probably belonging to the giant bison the Sierrans called ouruq. The hides were decorated with lines and dots and depictions of animals in seemingly haphazard patterns of white ochre. Against the black hides the effect was quite striking.

The pavilions were a strange design, round like a ball, but with very long tubular central spires out of which rose smoke from the hearths inside. They looked something like painted onions sitting on the ground. Alam grinned at the thought.

He turned as he heard shouting and watched as several girls ran towards them, squealing in delight. He remained mounted as Seraphimé, grinning, dismounted and ran to the girls. The youngest, who could not be more than seven or eight, Seraphimé caught and swung up into the air.

The girl screamed and giggled as Seraphimé pulled her close, blowing a raspberry on her cheek. The girl hugged Seraphimé moments before two other young girls almost bowled over the Marshal. Laughing, Seraphimé hugged them all close.

Alam noticed one young woman holding back, smiling maternally at the scene.

Her features were rounder than Seraphimé's own, making her appear kinder somehow. Her mouth was parted in a smile, which displayed pretty dimples on either side of her full lips.

He watched as the three girls detached themselves and Seraphimé and the pretty one embraced. He could hear them talk. Seraphimé's rich voice of velvet juxtaposed the other girl's higher, sweeter voice. They were clearly glad to see each other.

Seraphimé turned and walked back to her horse. "Cumus," she said. "You and your men are dismissed for the evening. Thank-you for your aid."

Cumus inclined his head. He turned his horse and vanished without a word, his men trailing behind.

Seraphimé turned to Alam. "A pavilion has been prepared for you and your entourage. There is a hot bath ready. We will send for you in an hour for the welcome feast."

"Thank-you," Alam said, his eyes flickering to the woman standing behind Seraphimé.

Seraphimé noted the look, but made no issue of it. Men preferred her sister. It had always been that way.

"Follow me," a clear voice said to Alam's right.

Alam turned and noted a young boy dressed in blue. The boy smiled and Alam nodded. He turned his horse and followed the boy, his men in tow.

Eight

"Our guest is very handsome," Gabija noted to her sister as the latter sat on her bed and unlaced her boots.

Seraphimé shrugged. "He's blond."

Gabija laughed. "So?"

Seraphimé shrugged again and Gabija's mirth died down. "Why do you not want to speak of him?" she asked.

Seraphimé pressed her lips together and Gabija sighed. "So you aren't immune to handsome men after all, even if they are blond."

"I don't want to talk about it."

"Perhaps if you did something about it this time?"

Seraphimé almost growled. "He won't have me," she said bluntly.

"Oh." Gabija sat down beside her sister and gently brushed a loose strand of hair from Seraphimé's face. "You have such beautiful hair," she said. "You should wear it down for the feast."

Seraphimé scoffed.

"You should! And wear a dress."

"No."

"Seraphimé, how do you expect to attract a man if you refuse to make the effort?"

"Any man who dares call himself such should be able to see who I am regardless of what I wear."

Gabija sighed. "Men aren't as bright as that. You have to trap them first. You need the right bait."

"Then I'll live without. I don't want to bed an idiot."

Gabija giggled.

"I'm serious," Seraphimé said with a smile. "What if stupidity is contagious or worse yet, hereditary? You know I couldn't cope with stupid children."

Gabija laughed brightly. She helped her sister with her bath and washed her hair. Despite Gabija's best efforts, Seraphimé refused to wear a dress and opted for a slightly fancier version of her armour and riding clothes.

* * * *

The eating pavilion was loud as the clan and their guests gathered for the evening meal. Alam noted with some surprise that there appeared very little distinction between the Chieftain and the other members of his clan.

For all Alam could tell, the difference was merely in the style of dress. Even at that, the only notable difference was that the Chieftain wore jewellery of amber and carried a ceremonial soapstone axe.

Alam found it difficult to concentrate on his conversation with the Chieftain. There were far too many distractions.

The Chieftain's three youngest daughters were squealing with delight as they played chase with some scruffy-looking boys. Many of the clan members looked on and laughed occasionally as they talked to one another. The two eldest princesses were yet to arrive.

It was a raucous gathering, and very different from the quiet, polite functions of Alam's own people.

"So you have five daughters?" Alam enquired.

The Chieftain grinned. "And one more on the way," he said proudly motioning to someone.

Alam smiled when a young, heavily pregnant woman approached. Her dark hair was braided back except for one strand that was beaded with amber at the end of which an osprey's feather was affixed. Her high, broad cheekbones and angular eyes were completely foreign to Alam, but he found her beautiful nonetheless.

"My wife," the Chieftain announced proudly. "Fiacha. She thinks it's a boy, but I'm hoping for a girl."

The woman smiled, revealing white teeth, as Alam bowed. "My Lady," he said. "I am honoured."

Fiacha giggled and said something in her native tongue.

The Chieftain grinned. "She said that you are all limbs. You look like a bone-eater. She's never had a bone-eater bow to her before."

"A bone-eater?"

The Chieftain grinned again. "A white-skinned spirit that walks the winter and eats people who stray too far from their clan."

"Ah."

"It is a compliment," the Chieftain said laughing. "Bone-eaters are said to be very handsome."

"I see," Alam said with a smile, though he wasn't sure if he did.

The Chieftain wrapped one thick arm around his wife's shoulders and kissed her on the top of the head. Fiacha leant on her husband and smiled to herself.

The pavilion fell silent suddenly as everyone's attention diverted to the entrance where stood the two eldest princesses.

Alam noticed Gabija first. She wore a dress of red wool and a blue cloak. Her light brown hair was loose and it framed her face in gentle waves. She too wore beads of amber in her hair.

Seraphimé stood behind her sister. She looked much the same as when Alam had first met her. Her thick waves of dark auburn hair were tied back in a braid and she wore a mail shirt over a brown tunic. A sleeveless green smock fitted tightly over the mail shirt. She carried weapons at her side. Tall riding boots and britches completed her boyish attire.

Still, her face was as striking as ever, and her green eyes sparkled with wit. When her gaze met Alam's own, they issued a silent challenge, as if she dared him to question her femininity.

"My girls!" the Chieftain greeted warmly, extending his arms as he strode towards his two eldest. They both embraced their father, but there was extra warmth with Seraphimé.

"I've missed you so," the Chieftain whispered in Seraphimé's ear.

Seraphimé smiled, but said nothing. Kissing both his daughters on the cheek, Chuchip took Gabija's hand and led her to where Alam and his men were standing, Seraphimé walking behind.

"Your Highness," the Chieftain said. "May I present my eldest daughter, Gabija."

Alam bowed low and kissed the young woman's hand in the fashion of his own people. Gabija looked surprised for a moment then smiled graciously.

"It is lovely to meet you, your Highness," she said in her sweet voice, her Touan touched lightly by an accent.

"Please, call me Alam," Alam replied as charmingly as he could manage.

Behind Gabija, Seraphimé rolled her eyes.

Catching the movement, Bully could not help but laugh. The fact that he tried to suppress it turned the laugh into something like an explosive grunt.

Alam turned on his heel and glared at him in irritation. Bully returned Alam's expression with an innocent one of his own. He threw a quick grin at Seraphimé when Alam turned back to Gabija. She returned it and immediately reversed Bully's opinion of the nomadic Princess.

"Come, come," Chuchip said. "Sit, sit."

Alam escorted Gabija to her seat beside the Chieftain's wife and sat down beside her. His men arranged themselves beside him. The Chieftain sat with his wife on one side and Seraphimé on the other. Next to Seraphimé the three youngest princesses sat in order of age. The rest of the clan arranged themselves haphazardly around the low, semi-circular table.

They sat not on chairs, but on an array of cushions and furs and reclined in any manner they felt comfortable. Again Alam was struck by the difference between the relaxed atmosphere here and the strict formal setting of his own country.

The lull in conversation soon forgotten, the volume of the gathering rose once more as they awaited their meals.

"How does this work?" Alam asked Gabija. "Are we expected to get our own food?"

"Yes," Gabija said with a straight face. "But first you much catch it, skin it, brine it…" She trailed off as Alam's eyes grew wide, then burst into laughter. "Will you believe anything I say?" she asked with mirth.

Alam grinned. "Perhaps. I'm always confounded by a beautiful woman."

Gabija cleared her throat. "Thank-you."

Eager to change the subject from Alam's overt admiration, Gabija hurried to answer his question. "Today is the Day of the Hare. So we will be served by the youngest daughters of each family."

"Are you still playing with me?"

Gabija laughed brightly. "No indeed! I am very serious."

Alam was sceptical, but quickly found that Gabija had been telling the truth. Four young girls entered the tent carrying large jugs of warmed, spiced wine. They served each person, the noble family and their guests first, without a word before vanishing from the pavilion. Alam thought it odd, but said nothing since his hosts did not think anything by it. He did notice, however, that no one took a single sip before the Chieftain raised his cup to his lips. After his first sip, the drink flowed freely.

"Your mother seems very young," Alam noted by way of conversation.

Gabija smiled. "She is not my mother."

"Oh?"

"Seraphimé and I were born to Queen Sinopa. She died in childbirth along with our brother."

"I'm sorry," Alam murmured.

Gabija shrugged. "It was many years ago now. The other three girls are Fiacha's daughters."

"I wondered at the age difference. Your father mentioned that he was hoping for another daughter."

Gabija laughed. "That sounds just like him."

"Even though he has no son?"

"He doesn't need a son," Gabija said, her voice tinged with some sadness. "He has Seraphimé."

Alam's gazed shifted to Seraphimé, who was engaged in two separate conversations – one with her father, and the other with her half-sisters. It took Alam a moment to realise that his gaze had lingered too long and he smiled at Gabija in an effort to hide it.

"That certainly explains a lot," he said lightly.

Gabija smiled sadly. "She must surely be something of a shock. I understand that Touan women are very different."

"To Seraphimé?" Alam replied. "Most certainly. It is inconceivable that they would ride and fight as a man, let alone dress like one."

"It must be very constrictive," Gabija said.

Alam shrugged. "They know their place."

Gabija politely did not comment.

Alam continued to make light conversation with Gabija, who very graciously answered any and all of his questions. The serving of the first course marked the arrival of a man dressed in a deer-hide hooded cloak. The hood was somehow attached to a deer's skull, which served as a helm. The antlers of the deer skull poked through holes in the hood. The hood and helm combined to prevent anyone from seeing his face. The stranger walked tall, but carried no staff, as Alam had been told religious figures of the nomads did.

The hall fell into respectful silence as the antler adorned man walked to the Chieftain, bowed low, then made his way around the table to sit cross-legged behind the noble family in silence. Once he was seated, the chatter began again as if the nomads were not concerned by his presence at all.

Alam was. "Who is he?" he asked Gabija in hushed tones.

"He is an ayal, a priest of the Lord of the Hunt, Master of the Wild and the King of the Dead." Gabija's voice was hushed as she spoke, indicating either great respect or fear.

Alam grunted in disapproval.

"He lives apart from us in a small tent near the Realm of the Dead," Gabija continued.

"The Realm of the Dead?"

"Yes, where the ancestors now live."

Alam looked at Gabija, not comprehending.

"The entrance is where their ashes were interred," Gabija prompted.

Understanding flooded Alam's eyes. "A graveyard," he said.

Gabija, not familiar with the term, had no choice but to simply assume that it was so. She grimaced.

"You don't like this subject?"

"The very thought frightens me," she admitted. "The dead scare me."

Alam looked back at the ayal and noticed the hooded man place a gloved hand on Seraphimé's shoulder.

"But not your sister," Alam noted.

Gabija smiled and shook her head. "She was always the brave one. She once told me that the living do much worse than the dead ever will."

"In this," Alam said, "I can only agree."

"You both have had the advantage of seeing battle, I suppose."

"I'm not sure I would call than an advantage."

Gabija smiled at Alam.

Alam smiled in return. "Who is the ayal?"

"I don't understand."

"Who is he? What is his name?"

Gabija looked down at her plate. "He does not have a name. His is simply the Ayal of the Osprey Clan."

"He is just a man. Surely he has a name, an identity?"

Gabija sighed. "He was once called Harom, and he was a proud warrior of twenty summers when he..."

"When he what?"

Gabija looked at Alam. "When he died."

"He died?" Alam blinked and raised his brows.

Gabija nodded. "He was slain in battle. Then he woke, just moments before the funerary flames were to set into his flesh."

Alam frowned. "I'm not following."

"In order to become an ayal, you must first die. Something happens in the realm of the dead. I assume a pact is made with the King of the Dead. Then you return to the realm of the living."

"So his name is Harom?"

"No."

"But you just said…."

"The part of him that was Harom was left in the Land of the Dead. You see, an ayal is one who had died a man and returned as something else. Harom is dead. The Ayal is not that warrior, though he might wear his face." Gabija shuddered.

"I'm sorry, my Lady. I'll not press the issue further."

"Thank-you."

As if sensing Alam's gaze, the Ayal turned his head. The gaze trapped Alam instantly. Though he could not see the Ayal's eyes, they caught the Prince and would not let go. It was as a serpent might charm its prey. Though Alam struggled in silence, he could not break free until the Ayal released him, turning his head and resuming his cross-legged pose in silence.

Alam turned back to the table, bathed in sweat. His eyes burned and his limbs hung heavy and weak from his body. Whatever it was, the Ayal possessed incredible power. He could understand Gabija's fear. He could not understand Seraphimé's absence of it.

He glanced quickly over at Seraphimé. She cradled her youngest sister, who had fallen asleep in her arms, as she spoke quietly with the Chieftain.

"Your father and sister are close," Alam noted.

Gabija nodded. "She has everything a king could want in a child."

"In a son, you mean."

"And in a daughter."

Alam scoffed.

"Think on it Alam of Misoua. Would you not want to know that your daughter would be able to protect herself should something happen to you?"

The thought gave Alam pause. "I suppose," he grudgingly admitted. "Though I would ensure that she was married so that her husband could look after her."

"And if something happened to her husband? Or what if no man would take her?"

Alam fell silent. Having a sister of his own, he knew that women talked, sometimes about the strangest, most obscure or vulgar things imaginable. There was no doubt in his mind that Gabija knew that Alam had spurned Seraphimé.

"Or she would take no man," Alam countered, deciding that it was best not to start discussing the events of four nights ago with the woman he hoped to bed before long.

"Then the man she does choose should consider himself very lucky indeed," Gabija replied smoothly. "For favours rarely bestowed are all the more precious for it."

"Unless he prefers the favours of another."

Gabija smiled. "Is there someone back home who has your heart, Alam of Misoua?"

Alam laughed. "No. Not back home."

Gabija did not meet Alam's eyes as he gazed intently at her.

The young serving girls carried in a large tundra boar on a spit and broke the moment. The boar filled the pavilion with the most intoxicating aroma of cooked pork and spices. Alam's stomach rumbled. He cheered with the rest of the feasters as the servers brought the food forward.

Dinner was delicious. The discomfort of the loaded exchange between Alam and Gabija evaporated as delectable food passed hungry lips.

The summer berry wine flowed freely and no cup was ever empty thanks to the vigilance of the day's serving girls. Alam felt quite cheerful by the time the evening drew to a close. He had forgotten his earlier suspicions and the cold and misery of their long journey.

Unlike the events in Misoua, there was no formal end to the evening as Alam was accustomed to. People simply began to filter out of the pavilion, bowing to the Chieftain and his family as they did so. Early in the parade of clansmen excusing themselves, Seraphimé stood. She turned to her father.

"May I be excused, Father?" Her youngest half-sister snored gently in her arms. "I have not had much sleep on my journey and am very tired. I'll take the little one to her cot first."

The Chieftain nodded. "Of course, of course, you may go. Sleep well, Sera."

"You too, Papa," she said. She bent over and kissed her father on the cheek, threw a smile at her stepmother and left, taking her sister to her bed.

Alam watched her go before turning his attention back to her older sister.

Nine

*S*eraphimé's departure marked a precedent. The pavilion soon emptied of all the riders who had arrived that night. Not quite sure how he managed it, Alam found himself walking with Princess Gabija, escorting her to her pavilion.

"What happens when the Chieftain is gone?" Alam asked. "Will there not be an issue of succession?"

"Why would there be?"

"There is no son."

"So?"

"Won't that cause an issue?"

"Not at all. Unless I am deemed unfit to rule, I shall become Chieftain of the clan."

"Won't your sister have an issue with it?"

"Why would she? I am older than she and will make a competent Chieftain. We have discussed it at length and she wants nothing to do with the Chieftainship. She has promised to remain as my marshal."

Alam smirked. "A female chieftain and a female marshal."

"What of it?"

Alam smiled. "It is unheard of where I am from."

Gabija laughed. "Our men aren't so selfish."

Alam grunted. "That might be true." He looked up at the sky. It was clear and the stars shone brightly in various colours. Struck by the display, Alam forgot to take the next step and remained in place, one foot off the ground, his step unfinished. A little way to the north, the fire in the sky danced.

"Are you all right?" Gabija inquired.

"I can't remember the last time I've seen the stars like this."

"Do they not appear in the southern sky?"

Alam shook his head. "They do, but the lights of the city are so bright it blots them out."

"That is a sad fate indeed."

Alam grunted and they continued their walk. They did not walk for long before the pair arrived at the entrance of Gabija's pavilion.

"May I ask a favour, my Lady?" Alam asked as Gabija opened her mouth to bid him goodnight.

"But my favours are so rarely granted," Gabija teased.

"Then it is all the more precious to me."

Gabija's smile faded. She wanted to protest, thinking of her sister. It was pointless, Alam stepped in and stole the kiss regardless. He was skilled, and Gabija found herself responding without a thought.

A small sound roused Gabija from the kiss and she turned, sighting her sister. Seraphimé had just rounded the pavilion. She froze in place and the two sisters gazed at each other for what felt like an eternity to Gabija.

"Forgive me," Seraphimé managed to say at last. "I'll return later."

"Sera," Gabija called. She ran after Seraphimé, who walked away at a phenomenal pace. Left behind and forgotten, Alam felt strangely guilty. He sighed and wandered back to his tent.

"Sera," Gabija said. She caught up with her sister, who stood on the hill overlooking the Valley of the Ancestors. She watched the lights in the sky, her face impassive.

"Sera, I'm sorry. I know that you –"

"It's nothing, Gab," Seraphimé said.

"If it was so, you wouldn't have run away."

Seraphimé sighed, but did not reply.

"It won't happen again, Sera."

Seraphimé shook the tension from her shoulders. "Don't allow me to dictate your happiness, Gab. He didn't want me, who am I to deny him to you?"

"You are my sister."

"And no man will change that." There was a long pause before Seraphimé spoke again. "I envy you Gab."

"Why?"

"Because you are a woman; everyone sees it and no one doubts it. Go to him. He had been long without a woman for company."

"Sera…"

"I want to be alone now."

Gabija shut her mouth and nodded. Without another word, she turned and made her way down the hill and back to her pavilion. With marked relief she noted Alam had not waited for her.

* * * *

Seraphimé waited until the sounds of her sister's steps were well and truly swallowed by the blanket of night before descending the hill into the Valley of the Ancestors. Here, countless mounds and barrows lay arranged in a pattern dictated by the stars, the sun, and the moon. They were bathed in starlight and moonlight. The flickering lights in the sky to the north sent light and shadow dancing across the valley.

Seraphimé knew exactly where she was going. She had been there many times before. She threaded her way through the mounds and barrows until she came to a medium-sized mound. She sank slowly to her knees, then curled herself up against the side of the mound.

"Grandma," she whispered, pressing her palm against the snow that still covered the mound. "I could use some of your wisdom now. I miss you."

The tears Seraphimé had been fighting for days finally came to the fore. They slid down her cheeks in warm, briny rivulets. Silently she prayed for a reprieve from her loneliness and while praying, fell to sleep.

* * * *

He had seen much in his journeys between worlds. He knew much. Tonight, he walked alone in the crisp autumn air. The snows had come early. There was a warning in that. Yesterday he had found an osprey dead, killed by an eagle. The omen had chilled him to the core. He had sought counsel with the Lord of the Hunt.

The Great Stag had been cryptic and though the Ayal was a part of the god, his connection to the mortal world shrouded his sight. Tonight he stalked across the snow, summoned to the Valley of the Ancestors. The spirits had called for him and their voices were sad. He followed the whispers and the soft white lights until he came to a stop before the royal mound. Curled in the snow at its base slept Princess Seraphimé, her cheeks wet with tears. The Ayal sighed.

* * * *

She felt familiar people around her; people she knew were long dead. Yet they were there. She could feel them, smell them and, in her sleep, was comforted by them. A warm hand brushed the tears from her cheeks. She felt herself being wrapped in a thick blanket.

"Grandma," she whispered. "I miss you so."

* * * *

The Ayal sighed as he knelt beside her in the snow and kissed Seraphimé gently on the cheek. "Sleep now, little one," he whispered. "Sleep. You are safe in the arms of your forebearers. Sleep in their warmth and under the protection of the Lord of the Hunt."

The Ayal watched with a strange, detached melancholy as a small smile stretched Seraphimé's lips. Sighing, the Ayal rose to his feet and left.

Cabal loped in from the darkness and, after taking a few moments to find a suitable angle, curled up beside Seraphimé, tucking her thick body into Seraphimé's stomach.

From the gloom a stag, the likes of which had long since vanished from the mortal plane, walked in on tall, slender legs. The great stag sank onto his side beside Seraphimé, the length of his body pressed against her back. He rested his noble head on Seraphimé's shoulder.

Unseen by anyone of the Osprey Clan, the fire in the sky flickered and danced in the shapes of the great beasts of the tundra.

Ten

"May I enquire as to your purpose here?" Gabija asked Alam as they walked.

Not five days after the Touan Prince and his party arrived, the entire village had been struck and the clan moved on. They followed a large herd of elk south, but would go no further than the boundaries of their territory. When they reached that invisible line, they would set camp and stay there the rest of the winter.

Alam found it odd and wondered greatly why they didn't make a permanent camp at the southern edge of their territory. He did not bother to ask. Honest as they were, the tribesmen of the Sierran Tundra, he had quickly learnt, were masters at shirking direct answers.

"I believe that a treaty is being drawn up between our peoples," Alam responded. "My father thought it wise for at least one of his children to learn your language and customs so that we might communicate with each other more effectively."

Gabija smiled. "Indeed," she murmured.

"You doubt our intentions?"

"Keep your friends close, and your enemies closer. This is a saying of your people, is it not?"

Alam nodded. "Yes. Though I doubt very much my father has anything untoward planned. We don't know how to survive in such a frozen wasteland as this. This land is useless."

Gabija smiled serenely.

"Perhaps in time, Alam, you will learn that one people's desert is another's oasis." It was not Gabija that spoke, but Seraphimé. She wore her usual unreadable expression and kept her tone neutral, though Alam was certain she kept it so to politely mask her contempt. It made him tense. He gritted his teeth.

"It seems you still feel I have a lot to learn," he noted, doing well to keep the irritation from his voice.

Seraphimé turned to him and her lips twitched as if she was trying hard not to show patronising amusement.

Gabija said something to her sister in her native tongue. Seraphimé grunted and walked on, guiding her horse up to where the Ayal walked in silence.

Alam watched them for a while. They did not speak to each other, yet they seemed to share an understanding and an enjoyment for each other's company.

"Both know what it is to pretend to be something they are not," Gabija said cryptically. "Were he still a man, it would have been a good match."

Alam scowled at the thought of the Ayal touching Seraphimé in that way. He had no explanation for the hot flush of anger that rushed through him at the thought.

A black shape darted past Alam, drawing him from his brooding with a sharp jolt. Gabija giggled when Alam jerked in surprise. He smiled sheepishly at her when he realised that the shape was nothing more than Cabal, returning from the wilds to Seraphimé's side. The dog licked Seraphimé's gloved hand before commencing her loping trot by the Princess' side.

Almost instinctively, Seraphimé scratched Cabal's head. The Ayal turned. His mouth twitched into something resembling a smile, even if only briefly. Alam raised his brows.

"There may be some humanity in him yet," he grunted to himself as he continued to trudge through the snow, leading his exhausted, cold horse.

"It's no wonder there is so little fat on you people," he noted to Gabija, who did not appear phased by the journey.

Gabija looked at him enquiringly.

"You walk so damned much."

Gabija laughed. "You get used to it."

Alam grunted his suspicion at the assertion and Gabija laughed again. It was a light, pleasant sound. Alam loved to hear it.

He looked up at the blue sky. It was clear of clouds. Days like this, he discovered, despite being bright and full of sun, were colder than days it snowed. Long ago realising that even if he put on every single garment he owned all at once, the southern dress was much too cool for these northern climes. He instead very gratefully accepted the Chieftain's own clothes of leathers and furs to keep him warm. He even wore the pointed hats he had previously found so ridiculous.

Initially the sleeves and legs of the clothing had been much too short. Fiacha kindly remedied that by sewing on thick strips of fur to the ends of each. The Sierrans had laughed when they saw, but they understood better than anyone that practicality far outweighed fashion, so their laughter was not ill intended.

Alam looked around him. His own men were huddled together, presumably in an ineffectual effort to conserve heat. They did not speak to one another, but trudged on in abject misery.

The Sierran nomads, by comparison, were spread out and laughing gaily. Not for the first time, Alam marvelled at how hardy these people were. Not a single one of them groaned about the cold, or about the daily long walks to the next campsite. Not a single one, down to the last child, stopped their relentless marching until the Chieftain did so.

He looked across at his own men, blue-lipped and miserable and suddenly felt as if he was somehow less of a man for being so unhappy. Even Gabija, girlish as she was, did not complain or stop. Again Alam's gaze shifted to Seraphimé.

No sooner had Alam's eyes moved than the Princess and the Ayal suddenly stopped, turning their heads west and scanning the white horizon. Cabal's hackles rose, making her appear even more wolf-like, and she issued a deep growl. The whole caravan of people ground to a halt and fell silent.

"Sera?" the Chieftain called from the head of the caravan.

Seraphimé did not respond. Cabal's growl grew louder and Seraphimé placed a comforting hand on the mutt's head.

"What is it?" Alam asked Gabija in a low voice.

Gabija frowned and shook her head. She did not know.

Seraphimé gave a signal with her hand. Immediately the warriors of the clan unveiled their lances and launched themselves into their saddles. The caravan moved again, this time under the profoundly imposing guard of the Osprey Clan warriors. Seraphimé rode point with Lieutenant Cumus at her side. The riders were alert, but even they were not prepared for what happened next.

A hail of arrows rained in from the sky. Screams and panic followed as many of those arrows found their mark in clansmen and horses. In an instant the mounted fighters gathered on the western flank of the caravan. Almost before the arrows had landed, a large band of mounted men charged in. They were terrifying to behold.

Yellow and black war paint covered their faces. They wore dark clothes that billowed out behind them. As they bore down on the startled Sierrans, their painted lips split into wild grins. Their teeth were stained orange, and some had even filed them into sharp points.

The clash was brutal. The Osprey Clan were sorely outnumbered. A single charge left Seraphimé with half her fighting force. Nevertheless, the warriors of the Osprey Clan rallied fiercely, forcing the invaders back to regroup.

"South!" Seraphimé screamed at Alam. "Take them south!"

Alam immediately understood. There was no way for the Osprey Clan to win this fight. They would seek asylum with Alam's family. Alam suspected that Seraphimé hoped for a fighting retreat. This way they could protect the clansmen until they reached Misoua.

Seraphimé and Cumus were especially proficient with the bow, and together with the first volley of hurled lances, they managed to hold back the attackers long enough to create a safe distance between the refugees and the strange horsemen who thundered in from nowhere.

With the strangers in pursuit, those that could put their loved ones on horseback and fled. The Chieftain was their beacon. Alam and his men rode behind the group, shouting encouragement and turning back often in case the attackers broke through Seraphimé's line of defence.

Night fell swiftly. The clan ran well into it until at last Alam and his men stopped them. The Touan horses could not travel well over this terrain during the day, let alone in the treacherous night. They camped that night without a fire, lest the defenders had all been slaughtered.

A few minutes before dawn the Chieftain noted, with profound relief, his daughter and twelve men galloping towards them. Seraphimé dismounted on the fly and immediately went to Cumus' aid. He had been badly wounded and barely made it off his horse without keeling over. Cabal was nowhere to be seen.

"Ayal," Seraphimé called.

From somewhere in the close throng of people, the Ayal appeared. He knelt in the snow beside Cumus. The man struggled to breathe. A close examination of the Lieutenant's wounds immediately told the Ayal that there was no hope. He looked up at Seraphimé and silently shook his head.

Cumus stopped breathing.

Seraphimé sank to her knees and stared blankly at the squat, broad-faced man. Her father went to her side, wrapping his thick arms around her shoulders.

"I am sorry," he whispered to her. "I know he was a good friend."

Seraphimé closed her eyes briefly.

"Who were those men?" Alam demanded.

Seraphimé opened her eyes and looked at Alam in irritation. "I do not know," she replied.

"Why would they have attacked?" Gabija asked.

Seraphimé shook her head. "They were not from here. I did not recognise their garb, or even their weapons. It could be a raiding party on the hunt for slaves. I did not think the Ottals had come this far west."

Alam frowned. He knew precisely who the Ottals were. A savage people of the desert; people of an empire that made its living in the slave trade, raiding nearby peoples in order to acquire their goods. The holiest of places stood in Ottalan territory. The Ottalan faith was also the faith of the Touan Federation. It made Alam's blood boil.

"What do we do?" Gabija asked her sister.

"Will your father take care of my clansmen?" Seraphimé asked Alam.

Alam nodded. "If he doesn't, I shall."

"In that case, everyone will rest here for a moment. Then continue south. The men and I will try to buy you some time. If we prove successful, you should have a day or two between them and you."

Gabija gasped.

"That should be enough time to get you safely into Touan territory."

"That's suicide!" Gabija cried, horrified. "Is there no other way?"

Seraphimé shook her head. "No. Not if the clan is to survive at all."

"You can have some of my men," Alam said, numb with shock at the matter-of-fact way Seraphimé willingly spoke of her imminent death. His heart cramped painfully.

Seraphimé nodded her head in appreciation. "Thank-you. I will take no more than five," she said. "Should they slip past us, you will need fighters with you."

Alam nodded. He turned to his men and immediately five, including Bully and Gremmet, stepped forward. Their respect and open admiration for Seraphimé compelled them forward. Alam nodded in approval.

The manner in which Seraphimé commanded her men, her ability to ride and fight as well as any man, and her unflinching devotion to her clan had earned her a place of legend amongst those men.

"Good," Seraphimé said. "Now everyone get some sleep. I'll start watch."

Sleep did not come for the Osprey Clan. In a savage attack at first light, the Ottal raiders struck again. They came from the east this time. It was too late for many of the clan before a defence could be mustered.

Seraphimé led the charge. Grim-faced and determined, even the fierce Ottals shrank before her. At the cost of two warriors, Seraphimé once again put some distance between the Ottal raiders and her clansmen. The latter mounted and fled south at a dead run.

Seraphimé and her men fought just long enough to ensure that their clansmen were safely away. They turned and retreated a distance to reform. Out of range of the Ottalan short bows, they stopped again and faced the Ottals.

Their enemy grinned with orange, roib-stained teeth and charged. Seraphimé's defenders pushed back, nevertheless finding themselves almost at their clansmen's heels.

As the clan fled, the heavily pregnant Fiacha felt the first nauseating spasm in her womb.

"No," she whispered. She stumbled and fell.

The Chieftain turned and went to the aid of his wife. Alam realised too late. He turned his horse and called his remaining fighters to the Chieftain's aid.

Seraphimé noticed and immediately drew her men in a line to shield the Chieftain and his wife. The Ottal raiders loosed their arrows. Nothing could prevent the arrow that pierced Fiacha's skull. She tumbled forward into the snow, spraying it red with blood and brains.

In shock, the Chieftain drew an axe from his belt. He turned and bellowed an ancient war cry. Vision blurred by rage, he raced towards the Ottal raiders. He burst through the line of his own horsemen, taking them by surprise. His quest for retribution earned him an arrow through his shoulder and another through his gut. The broad man fell over backwards in the snow.

Gabija screamed. She tried to run to her father. Alam grabbed her, preventing her from also breaching the line of horsemen that protected them. They struggled against one another. Alam almost lost. Gabija was surprisingly strong.

Seraphimé, however, Alam could not save. She turned to her warriors.

"Protect the clan."

She pushed her horse forward, escaping her own men to charge headlong at the remaining Ottal raiders. Her warriors could do nothing. They obediently herded their clansmen back.

Seraphimé breached the Ottal formation.

"No!" Gabija screamed. "Sera!"

"There's nothing you can do," Alam grated, forcing Gabija back.

The hysterical woman would not listen. She fought Alam every step backwards. Alam forced Gabija onto his mount. He spared one look at Seraphimé as she battled the remaining Ottal horsemen. His breath was kicked from him when a cruel knife slipped under Seraphimé's armour. Blood sprayed from her mouth as she was dragged off her horse.

"No," Gabija whispered.

To Alam's left, the Ayal growled. The sound was so guttural, so animal, it turned Alam's head. He watched on, numbed to the point he did not notice his own weeping.

The Ayal leapt into the air, changing form into a large, black, wolf-like mongrel. The dog raced into battle. It leapt onto the Ottal raider who stood over Seraphimé, axe raised.

Arrows rained on him as the dog tore into the man's throat. He turned and leapt again, taking down two more men. Still the arrows flew and hit until he was so full of arrows he resembled more a porcupine than a dog.

The Ayal, in the form of a hound, snarled his last breath. He collapsed in a twitching mass at Seraphimé's side. Of Cabal, there was no sign.

Unable to believe what he had just witnessed, Alam turned his horse. He rounded up his men and the remaining members of the Osprey Clan, and set out at a hard gallop for Touan territory.

Eleven

The Ottal raiders now numbered only five. They would not give chase. This raid had cost them too much. They stood in a circle around Seraphimé. She was still breathing.

"It's a woman," one noted.

Another grunted. "We take her then. There has to be something to show for all this blood."

"Damned Sierrans," another said. He spat in disgust, his black and yellow war paint smeared. "Tougher than they look."

The first one to speak nudged Seraphimé with his toe. "I know she'll fetch a higher price if unbroken," he said. "But this bitch killed Uma."

* * * *

Gabija did not stop her weeping for an entire day. Eventually, the grief took its toll. Unable to fight the exhaustion it caused, Gabija fell to sleep in Alam's arms, rocked into a dull ache by the awkward gait of Alam's horse.

The remaining members of the Osprey Clan did not cease their desperate flight until dusk. Even then they stopped only because the horses were too tired to continue. The risk of doing them some serious injury was too great.

In numbed silence, the Osprey Clan set up camp, forgoing their onion-like dwellings and opting to carve out banks in the snow to shelter them from the winds. With their help, Alam gently lowered Gabija into one such shelter. Elderly women tended to the their newly made Chieftain and Alam sought the comfort of his own people.

"Did I see what I thought I saw?" Bully whispered to Alam. He, too, was in shock. Gremmet had been slain before his eyes. "Did that man really just turn into a giant dog?"

Alam blinked. He had almost forgotten about the remarkable transformation the Ayal performed, though how he could have forgotten was beyond him.

"I... don't... know," he managed to say at length. By all accounts it ought to be impossible. No one could simply change form at will.

"Some sort of devilish trick then?" Bully asked.

Alam shook his head. "I don't know, Bully," he replied. "I really don't."

A man named Frid cleared his throat. "Uh," he said. "I have heard that they believe their gods can change shape like that."

"How would you know that?" Bully asked.

"Alam's not the only one capable of learning another language, you know," Frid sniffed.

Alam frowned. "Go on."

"Well, the Sierrans believe that the ancestors look after the people, while the gods look after the land or cosmic balance or something. The gods can do anything they want – change the weather, cull or grow herds, command the animals, shape-shift... anything."

"So why do they pray to the ancestors?"

"Because the people do not know how to deal with the gods, but the ancestors do. The ancestors and the gods have a good relationship. The ancestors act as intermediaries between their descendants and the gods. If the gods' wrath is not easily justifiable, it's the ancestors who petition the gods on the people's behalf."

"And if it is justifiable?"

"The ancestors will do nothing, knowing that the people ought to be punished."

Alam grunted. In some perverse way, it made sense. "So you think this ayal was a god?"

"Unlikely. The gods don't come to this world anymore, or so it is said."

"So what was he then?"

"An ayal," Frid replied.

Alam fought an overwhelming urge to slap him on the side of the head. He glared at Frid.

"A living ancestor," Frid said, shrugging his shoulders at Alam's ire.

"But you said it was the gods that shape-shifted," Bully objected.

"An ayal is attached to a god," Alam said, thinking back to what Gabija had told him at the welcome feast a week ago. "In this case, the God of Death."

"God of Death?"

Alam grunted again. "I don't get how he could just change like that though, if he wasn't a god."

Bully suddenly burst out laughing. "Listen to us," he managed to croak. "Just half a year out in the blistering cold with one tribe of barbarians, and already we're talking like heretics."

That ended the conversation. Denial was the easiest option. None of Alam's men would ever speak of the impossible again. Alam turned back to the Sierrans. They remained in shocked silence, barely even moving. Alam could not blame them.

In one, confusing, rapid swoop, they had been stripped of their kinsmen, their lands and their beloved Chieftain and his brave daughter.

Alam's eyes fell to Gabija in the snow. He could not fathom what nightmares she would have, after having witnessed the brutal murders of those she loved best. Sighing, Alam rolled into his bed and closed his eyes. It would be a long journey back to Misoua.

* * * *

The great stag approached the slaughter on long, elegant legs. His noble head crowned with a very fine pair of many-tined antlers. Large soft eyes turned hard as the scent of blood reached his flared nostrils. The great stag nevertheless walked forward until he stood beside the body of the Ayal of the Osprey Clan. He breathed a short sigh as he observed the handsome warrior, his body so bristled with arrows he could have been mistaken for a rush of reeds. The warrior had died twice.

"Harom," the stag said quietly.

The Ayal's eyes opened and, as if he had never been struck, he rose to his feet. "My Lord," he said, speaking for the first time in almost thirty years.

"Where is she?"

The Ayal looked about him. "They have taken her," he intoned, an edge of anger colouring his otherwise impassive words. He began to remove the arrows from himself. "Eagles. From the east."

The great stag's eyes narrowed. He reared angrily. Suddenly, in place of the stag, stood a man, dressed as the Ayal had been. Unlike the Ayal, the Lord of the Hunt carried weapons.

A full quiver of stone-tipped arrows graced his hip and a spare one was tied to his back. He carried a short but powerful bow as well as an array of perpetually sharp stone knives made of a peculiar rock that looked like black glass. On his other hip hung a carved hunting-horn made of the proud horn of the now extinct ice-beast. He whistled.

From somewhere in the wilds galloped a broad-hoofed black tundra horse. A smaller, wilder, more archaic version of the horses the Sierrans now bred and rode, it carried neither saddle nor bridle. Without a word, the Lord of the Hunt mounted. He turned to the Ayal.

"Guide the spirits of the dead to Aqyl."

"Yes, my Lord. And you?"

"I'm going hunting." The Lord of the Hunt's grin was vicious as he raised his hunting horn to his lips. He blew three long blasts and smiled with satisfaction as his three hounds, Guira, Valla and Cabal came loping over the nearest ridge. Each the size of a pony and black as pitch, their sparkling ruby eyes were hungry for the coming hunt.

The Lord of the Hunt blew one more baleful note. With his snarling hounds at his side, he galloped from the slaughter.

* * * *

The Shamanka of the Osprey Clan raised her ancient head and gasped. She was not the only one who heard and paled as the long blast of a hunting horn travelled the winds. She trembled.

"What is it, High One?" one of the surviving horse-warriors asked in a low voice.

"He's here!" the woman whispered, her eyes wide with fear. "He's here, and he's on the hunt."

"Who is here?"

"*The Hunter*," she hissed. "And he is angry."

Alam overheard. He frowned out into the night.

* * * *

The man laughed cruelly. His filed teeth flashed orange as Seraphimé struggled desperately beneath his weight. Her clothes had been harshly ripped away from her by five pairs of rough hands.

She remained unbound, the nature of her injuries rendering her as good as chained. It did not stop her from fighting, however. She kicked and bit, scratched and punched, all to little effect.

Every movement sent terrible pain ripping through her. Her right side where she had been stabbed gushed blood with every movement. The blood lost made her efforts weak.

The man overpowered her easily. He found his way between her legs and forced himself inside. Seraphimé bit her lip to stifle her scream of pain and rage.

The man finished pleasing himself quickly.

Seraphimé found herself accosted by a different man. She could not fight this time. Consciousness slid from her grasp as the four remaining Ottal raiders took turns slaking their lust.

Perhaps it was because they were so frenzied in their quest for vengeance against Seraphimé that they did not notice the tall, hooded, stag-helmed man astride a black, steaming mount. He deliberately kept his approach quiet. Equally as deliberately, he sat in plain sight and very leisurely knocked his arrow. He casually took aim and let the first one fly.

The arrow pierced the head of the man currently on top of Seraphimé, striking with such force that the man tumbled sideways and slid a fair distance. The arrow broke cleanly through his head on both sides. The four remaining raiders dived for their weapons, their trousers still down around their ankles.

The Lord of the Hunt fired three more arrows, each in rapid succession. He did not aim to kill. Three of the four screamed with pain as the arrows struck shoulders and thighs. The forth, having recovered his weapon, kicked off his trousers that stubbornly refused to tie back up and rushed for the intruder.

The Lord of the Hunt sat unmoving on his horse. He smiled grimly. The smile told the attacking raider he was about to die.

A large, wolfish dog leapt from somewhere out of sight. The creature snarled viciously as it clamped its fanged mouth around the man's weapon arm and yanked. The arm tore clean away from its socket.

The man screamed in agony. More snarls filled his ears, soon followed by the screams of his friends. The sickening sounds of snapping bones and tearing muscle joined the screams of the men in a nauseating cacophony.

The black hounds took perverse pleasure in tearing apart their quarry, dismembering them slowly. It took the men a while to die. The last to die found himself staring up into the liquid brown eyes of an enormous stag, the likes of which he had never before seen. The stag emanated anger.

"A fair trade," the stag said without moving its mouth. "For all you have done."

"A fair trade," the Ottal raider rasped.

His eyes fell blank, his life gone.

The great stag turned around and, changing form again, strode to Seraphimé's side. He touched her temples, sending her mind far away from the dull pain that plagued it even in its current state.

"You are safe now," he said in a voice of liquid silk. He smiled sadly as her body relaxed. Removing his cloak, he covered her over before becoming a stag once more. He lay down beside her, as did his hunting dogs.

Under a mass of living pelt, Seraphimé slept, protected from the cold.

Twelve

$\mathcal{S}$he awoke in an unfamiliar place. A small clearing surrounded by dense temperate forests greeted her hazed eyes. Snow fell gently in enormous flakes. They were large and fluffy, like the moult of a gosling. Seraphimé sat up and stared around in wonder.

Though she had heard of them, she had never seen trees this size. The trees in the forest around Misoua were nowhere near as grand. She could never have imagined they could be so large, so tall, so *beautiful*.

"Where am I?" she wondered aloud to herself. She struggled to her feet, unaware of the other presence in the clearing.

"You are on hallowed ground," a soft, masculine voice said from behind her.

Seraphimé spun around and came face to face with a hooded figure in deerskin hides. On his head rested a large stag's skull. The tall many-tined antlers stuck out from holes cut into the hide. Shrouded by a large hood, only the man's lips and chin were visible.

"Ayal," she said. As soon as she uttered the greeting, she knew that the man she faced was not the Ayal of the Osprey Clan.

"In a manner of speaking, Seraphimé Princess," the man replied with a smile.

Seraphimé's eyes widened in shock as she realised that she stood now before the Lord of the Hunt, King of the Dead.

"Am I dead?" she whispered.

The Lord of the Hunt shook his head. "You stand now where the First stood in his first fever dream."

"The First?"

"When the boy had taken a bite of poisonous fungus and collapsed. For a brief moment, which to him seemed an age of the earth, his spirit left his body and came here, to me. It is here we talked and here he learnt all he knew."

"What did he learn?"

"That the stars have eyes, the beasts have thoughts, the wind a voice and the trees have memories."

"Oongus," Seraphimé breathed. "The First Shaman."

The Lord of the Hunt nodded. "His first vision. He was but ten years old."

"And you, you are our ancestor too. The First Hunter."

A smile crossed what little of the Lord of the Hunt's face Seraphimé could see. "Not quite," he said.

Seraphimé frowned. "I don't understand. We were taught-"

"I know what you were taught," he said softly. "And there is some truth to it."

"But you are not our ancestor?"

The Lord of the Hunt shook his head. "No. I am older than even the first beginnings of your people. I belong to the people who came before; the people who vanished, leaving you as wardens of this land. None of their blood survives now in yours."

Seraphimé stood in silence as the Lord of the Hunt unveiled his story.

"I was not yet born when the drought struck our homeland deep in the south. With drought came famine and plague. The scarcity of food caused discord, something that was new to us. My family broke from their clan and went north, knowing that certain death awaited them if they stayed. They arrived on the central plains. What is now tundra was then a vast, grassy plain bordered by broad forests. It was colder here, but water still flowed freely on the surface and there were many fruits to eat.

"I was the first born in these strange lands. In a sense, I belonged not to my clan, but to the earth itself. I grew up amidst these immense trees, and running with the herds on the vast plains. My youth was a time of great joy. Yet great hardships awaited us.

"Even as the drought in the south grew worse, it grew colder and colder here. The winters lasted longer. The summers barely came. Still, snow was simply cold water and we managed to live well until the fruit trees began to dwindle.

"It was then we first turned to flesh for food. I was but sixteen when we stumbled across a freshly killed mammot. The wolves had been done with the carcass only moments before. Starving from eight months of winter, we dragged the beast back and ate it.

"And so it was we became scavengers, following the wolves and long-toothed cats and taking their kills when they were done with them.

"The meat was tough and our wooden tools did not aid us. It was my father who first discovered the blade of stone.

"Scavenging grew dangerous as the disappearing land meant fewer animals. We were in constant competition with more competent killers than ourselves. I lost my brother to a long-toothed cat. Fuelled by a desire to ensure that it never happened again, I turned our stone tools into stone weapons. We would never be hunted again. We would become the hunters.

"I studied the movements of the great cats and the wolves. I watched bears in their pursuit. I became them. In so doing, I came across a large litter of ice-dog pups that had been abandoned. Of the eleven pups, only three survived. I took them, and they became my pack. I had truly become a hunter.

"I made my first kill here," the Lord of the Hunt said, sadness creeping into his voice.

Seraphimé opened her mouth to question him, but the Lord of the Hunt simply nodded past Seraphimé's shoulder, indicating something now approached. Seraphimé turned.

To her great surprise, a young man of no more than twenty summers, carrying a short, heavy-looking, stone-tipped spear and an array of stone knives approached. He was dressed in the dark hide of an ouruq that had been covered in white ochre paint to match the snow. His features were strikingly handsome.

Long black hair was pulled back from a broad, high-cheeked face. His eyes were angular and the colour of dark silt. His skin was the colour of light honey. In his hair he wore various sized beads of blue. It was clear from his crouched walk that he was hunting.

A soft snort to Seraphimé's right made her jump sideways. She turned to see a large stag with antlers of many branches. Its legs were striped and its hind was speckled in tan and brown. The pelt was otherwise red. Large liquid eyes of brown gazed out in the wrong direction. This beautiful creature knew nothing of its impending demise.

Seraphimé stepped back, guided by the Lord of the Hunt's gentle touch. She watched as the young man, the Lord of the Hunt as a youth, spied his prey and approached. It was over in a matter of moments. The stag sensed the danger, but all too late. The Lord of the Hunt burst from the snow-laden bracken and with a well-timed thrust, pierced the stag through. The triumph of the hunt was not what it should have been.

Seraphimé watched as shock took hold of the young Lord of the Hunt. She watched, surprised and touched, his dark eyes fill with tears as they gazed at the emptiness of the dead stag's eyes.

"Killing changes you," the Lord of the Hunt said quietly, his voice filled with sorrow. When Seraphimé looked, his eyes glistened with tears.

The scene became hazy and faded. It changed to a scene near a cave. A thick hide covered the mouth of a cave, protecting those within from the fierce, snowy winds. It was clearly shortly after the hunt, for Seraphimé spied the young Lord of the Hunt near the outside fire as the stag was being roasted. His expression was one of intense melancholy.

"Though I took the stag home, I grieved for three weeks at his passing. I did not partake of the feast of his flesh and I buried his bones afterwards. Here, in the clearing where he was killed. It was all I could do for him.

"Shortly after his funeral, I felt myself overcome with gratitude, both his and mine. He had returned on the wind to thank me for my respect. I, in turn, thanked him for his life for it saved the lives of my clansmen.

"That night I dreamt of him. He came to me at the place of his death. It was a dream I shall never forget. I unearthed his skull and still I wear it to this day in his honour – the great stag. He is a part of me now.

"The following weeks were harsh and bitterly cold. The meat lasted us only a few weeks before we had to hunt again. The clan turned to me, but I could not bring myself to kill again. Instead, I taught them to hunt.

"Every time the hunters returned with a kill, before it was butchered, I went to it. I connected with its spirit and I expressed my grief for its passing, and my gratitude that in doing so, it kept my loved ones alive. Perhaps they too heard the animals' voices in the wind, for before long we all bowed our head in grief and thanks before the kills were butchered.

"Every year the winters grew worse, harsher, colder, longer until at last all the world was covered in ice and the summer never again came. The seasons became only two – the season of light and the season of dark. It took only a few years for this to happen.

"Even still, other clans drifted north, trying to find respite from the drought – a drought that was caused by the vast plains of ice in the north. They trapped all the water.

"Wherever the clan came from, we could recognise them, and they us. Gladly we shared our knowledge, for we knew that without it our kith would not survive long.

"For all of our kind who passed through our new homeland, I never found amongst them a wife. I died unmarried and with no children."

The scene changed again. Seraphimé and the Lord of the Hunt were back in their clearing, but there were no trees. It was now so blanketed by snow that Seraphimé could hardly recognise it. Dusk painted the scene in soft purple.

Seraphimé watched a slow funerary procession approach. The Lord of the Hunt's clan, four of whom bore a stretcher weighed down with his lifeless body, wrapped in deer hide and wearing his stag skull helmet, walked in mournful silence through the snow.

At Seraphimé's feet, a deep grave had been dug, possible only because the sharp prongs of a great deer carved easily through the ice that lay only inches from the surface.

"It was our custom to bury the dead beneath the floors of our dwellings," the Lord of the Hunt intoned behind her. "I was different. The winds had told our elders that my spirit belonged to the wilds. So they buried me in the clearing in a grave beside the one I had dug for the stag."

Seraphimé watched in wide-eyed awe as a tall stag walked purposefully into the clearing, bearing witness to the funeral. The funerary party seemed unsurprised. Once the Lord of the Hunt's body was covered in soil and snow, and his grave marked by the first ever, albeit small, cairn and standing stone, the elders bowed low to the stag and left.

"Every year thereafter, the hunters would bring their kills here and lay the body across my grave in order to thank the beast, and thank me for teaching them to hunt, the singular skill which enabled them to find food and live here in the land of snow and ice.

"In this way, my memory was kept alive and with each blessing my spirit grew stronger.

"It was only one generation later when they began to ask for my assistance during their hunt. They also prayed that I help the herds stay strong. They understood that without the herds of ice-beasts, ouruq, elk and deer they would starve. I became the Master of the Wilds as well as the Lord of the Hunt.

"So it went for years beyond count. Then one day, things began to change. It started to get warmer. Slowly, year by year, the snow began to melt away and the ice retreated ever further north. For the first time in hundreds of years, there was a summer. It brought with it grass and, later, trees, and something yet more sinister."

Seraphimé looked at the Lord of the Hunt. "My ancestors," she whispered.

The Lord of the Hunt nodded. "At first my kind thought you kith, for we knew of no others who walked on two legs and hunted with spears of stone. You were not. Your people came from the southeast, a place untouched by ice, a place of such plenty that you were unaware and unwise. Your hunting of the great herds of ice-beasts decimated their numbers.

"In just a few hundred years, they had all been killed; the herds of great deer, greater mammot and horned rhiba, all taken under by the continual encroachment of the southeastern tribes. For all my effort, I could not save them. I wept bitterly for such foolishness."

Seraphimé's eyes filled with tears as she saw her ancestors, wearing battle fetishes, tracking and killing the mightiest of the ice-beasts, destroying the vast herds from the inside out. Then she watched horrified as they began to hunt the gentle people of ice. The images flashed before her eyes, just as the Lord of the Hunt had witnessed it.

"It was not long before the spears of your ancestors turned upon the flesh of my descendants. They called my name, but I could do nothing. Even spirits have limits. All I could do for them was to collect them and have their souls brought safely to a place of rest.

"All too late, some of them sought to make peace amongst my kith and learn from them. For though summer had returned, it was still cold and harsh here. That is when your kith learned of me, learned of what it was that I had been called upon by the voices of the living to do.

"The day the last of us died, a boy was born. When that boy turned ten, he chanced across an unfamiliar fungus. One small bite threw him so near death, he called my name as my kith's elders had taught him. I came to him, expecting to collect the soul of a kinsman.

"Yet this boy was not one of my kind and he was not willing to die. There was wisdom deep in his eyes. I had not seen it in your kin before then. He was as an old man, yet with the curiosity of a child.

"Whatever questions he asked, I answered, for the trees seemed to know him and the winds whispered his name. His name was Oongus, and he became the First."

Seraphimé frowned. "The First Ayal, the great Shaman Oongus. Why are you telling me this?"

"To let you know Seraphimé that your kin have become mine. To tell you, Seraphimé Princess, that you are not alone. Trust in me. Let the winds and the animals and the trees guide your path, for their voices are mine."

"Many have turned their backs on you," she said.

"But you have not."

"They call you a god now," she said.

"Then I will be your patron god."

Seraphimé smiled. "Have you not always been?"

The Lord of the Hunt smiled in return. "You have felt it too, then."

"You sent Cabal to me."

The Lord blinked in surprise. "How did you...?"

"She has knowing in her eyes," Seraphimé said. "She was wild, yet tame. More interesting still was that, for all the animals she would hunt, she never once touched a deer, nor its flesh."

"When did you know?"

"When I saw you weep for the stag you killed as a youth."

The Lord of the Hunt reached out and clasped Seraphimé's shoulder with his gloved hand. "Memory of me dims with each passing year," he said sadly. "Soon I shall be forgotten."

"What happens then?"

"I will join my kin in the realm of the dead. I will die."

Seraphimé turned sharply around. "No!"

The Lord of the Hunt smiled. "Even gods die."

"Who then will tend to the wilds?"

"That task will fall to those who live."

Seraphimé shuddered. "To those who have forgotten all the lessons of their past."

"They may yet remember."

"You are more hopeful than I."

The Lord of the Hunt stroked Seraphimé's face. "You are beautiful," he murmured. His gloved hand moved lower until he pressed his palm against her chest. Unused to a man's touch, Seraphimé's heart raced.

"Too beautiful to be so angry."

Seraphimé's eyes stung with tears, which she tried to blink back. "I have been hurt," she whispered.

The Lord of the Hunt nodded. "I know," he whispered to her in return. The gentleness in his voice overwhelmed Seraphimé and though she continued to struggle against them, tears fell from her eyes.

Taking her face between his large hands, the Lord of the Hunt gently kissed the tears away. Seraphimé felt that she might fly apart with all the conflicting emotions that raged through her.

Grief and anger fought with the simple yearning to be held and loved, and the strong animal desire that surrounded the Master of the Wild pulled at her. She could not resist as he drew her close into a strong embrace.

Some of the wild moved through her and she let herself grieve, howling her pain and rage into the air until both were spent. She relaxed against the Lord of the Hunt's strong frame.

He held her tightly as her sobbing died down and her breathing returned to normal. When at last her trembling took on a different tone, he pulled away from her.

Not altogether in control of the wild desire that swirled through her she reached up and, very carefully, pulled off the Lord of the Hunt's stag skull crown. He appeared to her just as the twenty-year-old vision of him she had seen, though his dark temples were touched with grey.

"Ancient and young," she murmured. Her expression hardened slightly. "I was raped."

"I know."

"Make it go away."

The Princess of the Osprey Clan did not miss the lustful flash in his dark eyes. It fanned the flame of her own desire. The Lord of the Hunt remained motionless, his unfathomable eyes boring deep into her as she unclasped his cloak. He did not move as she removed her own tunic and breeches. She stood naked before him.

With no clothes to hide her form, she was unmistakably a woman, totally and utterly feminine; made even more so as she unbound her thick auburn curls. They fell about her shoulders in a shimmering cascade.

Bestial by nature, the Lord of the Hunt could no longer keep his hands from her. He pulled her close, kissing her hard. Seraphimé's mind went blank. She clawed desperately at his leather armour until it fell away and she could run her hands over smooth, honey-coloured flesh pulled taut over a muscular frame.

Together they fell to the soft fern-strewn floor of the clearing and there, the talented Master of the Wild reduced Seraphimé to a pool of sensation.

Their lust adequately slaked, Seraphimé curled into the Lord of the Hunt's embrace and wept until peaceful sleep took her. All through her sleep, she felt his warm, strong arms surround her.

She smiled.

Thirteen

For close to a day, he had been on the trail of perhaps the largest deer he had ever thought imaginable. The tracks, unsurprisingly for this time of year, headed south. What did surprise Inna was the fact that the deer was on its own. There were no other tracks that might hint at a herd.

Inna had lived by the northern ocean with his clan his entire life. Now numbering only three, his clan stood on the brink of extinction. Countless Ottal raids had devastated his clan. It had once been the greatest clan in the Sierran Tundra; the mighty Ice Bear Clan, now faded into obscurity.

Inna forced his thoughts away from the past. Nothing could be done about it. The day dawned bright and warm, surprisingly mild for this time of year. Inna felt a little too warm as he followed the tracks in the snow. He shrugged away the discomfort and clutched his heavy, stone-tipped spear tighter.

The third day of his hunt Inna received a shock that made him question his sanity. An hour before dawn, the cool, soft snout of his quarry awakened the hunter. Startled, Inna shouted and leapt backwards out of his bedding.

"You hunt very slowly," the great stag said to Inna.

Inna could not discern any movement that would denote the physical act of speaking. "You can talk," he said stupidly.

"You can think," the stag replied wryly.

Inna blinked, then laughed a little.

"There isn't time," the great stag said, urgency in his deep, soft voice. "She will not last without care."

"Who?"

"The She-Wolf."

"I don't understand."

"Follow the pack, and you will find the She-Wolf. Hurry." The great stag said no more. It turned and bounded gracefully away.

Inna watched it until his eyes fell upon a small pack of three large, black wild dogs that looked like some kind of wolf mix. They loped towards him, ignoring the stag that crossed their path, their heads low and ruby eyes fixed intently on Inna.

Inna swallowed hard and reached for his weapons as the three dogs fanned out. Their trot slowed to a walk and then they stopped. The three dogs sat in a semi-circle around Inna. One took a cautious step forward, then sat down again. Its pink tongue lolled out of its mouth as the mutt looked expectantly him.

"Do you know where she is, this She-Wolf?"

The dog cocked its head, its gaze never wavering.

"You don't speak," Inna said, a little disappointed. The dog whined.

"All right," he said, turning and collecting his things. It only took him a moment. "Lead the way."

All three dogs turned and loped away, heading south. Inna had to run to keep up with them.

The journey took most of the day. The dogs came to a skidding halt just before what appeared to be little more than a rock. It was surrounded by pieces of people. Five torsos, mangled and chewed, lay scattered about. Inna recognised the yellow war paint and filed, orange stained teeth on the disembodied heads. Ottal Raiders.

Around them were horse and deer tracks as well as prints that could only belong to the three hounds that were sniffing the rock and whining. Inna approached the scene cautiously.

He then noticed that the rock was in fact something wrapped up in a dark mottled cloak. He didn't particularly want to know what lay wrapped in the cloak. It might be a mound of severed limbs, or a heap of bloody bowels, or worse. Gathering his courage, Inna approached. He gasped at what he saw.

A woman lay wrapped in the cloak. Thick curls of dark auburn hair fanned out around her pale face where they had escaped her braid. Her large, wide-set eyes were closed, framed by a high brow and pronounced cheekbones. She definitely resembled a member of one of the plains tribes; southern by the pale skin and distinctive lack of tattoos. That meant she knew how to ride. He wondered briefly if the horse tracks belonged to her horse. Where the mount might be now, Inna could only guess. It had probably been stolen and taken back to the Ottalan Desert.

Inna looked around him again. She had been raped, from the look of things. What had become of her clan, Inna could not discern. Perhaps, like his own clan, they had been destroyed by the seasonal raids of the slave-traders of the east.

Whatever the case, these raiders met a most unpleasant end. It looked to Inna as though they had been torn to shreds by the dogs. He glanced up at them. All but one happily ignored him. They chewed at the remains littering the snow. The other one kept a disturbingly intelligent eye on Inna.

Sighing, Inna wrapped the cloak tighter around the girl. He hauled her unconscious weight onto one shoulder and began the laborious trek back to the remnants of his clan.

* * * *

Seraphimé stirred as the Lord of the Hunt shifted his weight. They were still in the forest clearing. As far as Seraphimé could tell, they had only been asleep for a few hours. She felt the large, calloused hand of the Master of the Wild run through her hair and she smiled.

"I have to go," he said at length.

Seraphimé's eyes flew open. "But-"

"You are safe now," he said, his voice still gentle and loving.

"I don't want you to go."

"I know."

"Please." Seraphimé began to cry again. The thought of leaving his warm embrace distressed her.

"Hush now," he said. "Sleep."

As if on command, Seraphimé's breathing eased and she fell once again into sleep. She did not feel him gently lower her onto the bracken floor and vanish.

* * * *

"What happened?" the elderly Shamanka said as Inna lowered the fever-stricken girl onto the floor of the pavilion.

"It is a long story."

"Is there no food for your ten days away?"

Inna grunted. "No."

"Then go out again. We're hungry. I'll tend to her. You can tell me the story when you come back."

Inna nodded and vanished into the cold again. The Shamanka looked down at the girl and sighed.

"You must be the She-Wolf," she whispered to her.

Inna did not get far before he stumbled across a freshly killed seal. He blinked, then looked up. His eyes spotted one of the wild dogs, now alone, sitting a fair distance from the pavilion and watching on with interest.

Shrugging, Inna butchered the animal where it lay and dragged it back. He entered the pavilion to gather the wood for the fire.

"That was quick," the Shamanka noted.

"I had help," Inna replied before vanishing again.

The seal meat sizzled on a hot stone that sat on the fire outside the one and only remaining pavilion. The rest of the meat was sitting in a bucket of seawater. It would remain there for three days, then be dried in the smokehouse. With so few mouths to feed that single seal ought to last the clan a few weeks. Inna returned before long, the scent of cooking meat filling the air.

"I had a dream when you were gone," the Shamanka said.

"Oh?"

"I dreamt that an osprey had been killed by an eagle and from the body of the osprey rose a wolf, and the wolf and the eagle fought."

She-Wolf. Inna felt uneasy. "Who won?" he asked.

"I don't know," the Shamanka said. Her voice cracked with age. "I woke up."

Inna grunted. He looked around. Ur was fast asleep in the Shamanka's bed, curled so tightly into himself that he looked half his size; a difficult task as Ur was already small for his age.

"How is he?" Inna asked.

"The same. He cries out still, sometimes."

Inna grunted. Ur had lost his sight during the last of the Ottal raids. One of the raiders had removed his eyes with hot pokers. The raider intended to teach Ur's mother a lesson. She had bloodied him some as he raped her.

Ur had been left for dead, as had Inna himself. Were it not for the Shamanka's careful attention, both Ur and Inna would have died. His blood began to rise. Inna forced his mind back to the girl on the floor in an attempt to curb an explosion of temper.

"I found her amongst bodies of Ottal raiders. I counted five. They had been torn apart. It looked like wild dogs."

"I see." The Shaman seemed unsurprised.

"The deer I hunted woke me up," Inna continued. "It spoke to me."

"What did he say?"

"How do you know it was a him?"

"I have only ever heard of one talking deer," the Shamanka said with a smile. "And it is a him."

"Who?"

"The talking deer."

"No, I mean who is he?"

"Who is who, dear?"

"The deer."

"Who?"

"The talking deer! Who is he?"

"He is the King of Aqyn, and his three hounds guard its gate. He is the Master of the Wilds, and his three hounds stalk the land. He is the Lord of the Hunt, and his three hounds accompany him. The Hooded One. The Horned One. He has many names."

"Three hounds?"

"Yes, three. Ancestors to the wolves – big and black and vicious. Pity the fool who angers the three hounds of Aqyn. Pity more the fool who angers their master."

"There were three wild dogs," Inna whispered.

"So it was him."

Inna paled. He'd had a conversation with the God of Death, and he did not even blink. It could have gone very badly for him. He looked down at the girl.

"She is important to him," he said blankly.

"She is important to the tundra," the Shamanka replied.

Inna scowled, not understanding. That was why, he supposed, the Shamanka was the Shamanka. Such intricacies were beyond his limited grasp.

Ur stirred a little and sobbed.

Inna immediately went to him. "Hello, little man," he said, resting a hand on the blind boy's shoulder.

"Inna," the boy murmured.

Inna smiled. "It's me."

"When did you get back?"

"Less than an hour ago."

"Oh."

"Ur, we have a new guest."

Ur frowned. "Who?"

"We don't know her name," Inna said. "I found her while out hunting. She's not conscious."

"She was attacked," the Shamanka said. Inna shot her an irritated look. Evidently the Shaman did not care, for she continued. "By Ottal raiders."

The boy went rigid and the colour drained from his face. "Are they back?" he whispered.

Inna sighed. "Not any more."

The boy frowned.

"The Hunter has taken them."

The boy blinked. "But gods do not walk on this earth."

"For this girl, it seems, this one does," the Shamanka mused, almost to herself.

"What does it mean?" the boy asked.

The Shamanka shook her head, sending her turquoise beads tinkling. "I do not know."

"Do you think this is about your dream, old mother?" Ur asked. "Is she the wolf who will fight the eagle?"

Inna blinked. It never ceased to amaze him how the simplest minds could grasp the most difficult things.

"I do not know," the Shamanka replied. "But it seems likely."

The boy crawled forward, feeling his way with his hands until they connected with the limp hand of their unconscious guest. He pulled himself closer, clasping her hand in both of his.

"Can you hear me, Otsana?" he asked her quietly.

She showed no signs of doing so.

"If you can hear me, we need you, Otsana. We need your help." Ur curled up beside the girl and fell to sleep, never letting go of her hand.

With a sigh, the Shamanka pulled a fur over them both and left to finish cooking dinner.

* * * *

Mtsusa, a Tigil of the Fortu Guild sat on his dainty, hot-blooded horse on the edge of the ice plain and growled. His raiding party had been gone too long. They had been out almost a month and should have returned days ago. How was it possible for them to fail? They had over sixty men, the same size as one large Sierran clan, and all of them fighters.

He rubbed his bald head with a hand that glittered with rings as he stared into the white horizon. He growled again. Where were they?

"Tigil," the Braddard called. The Tigil ignored him.

"Tigil, it is time to go."

"My men have not returned."

"Then the snows claimed them," the Braddard said. "We must go. Now. The Suma is expecting his goods."

"He'll get less than he expects if we leave without my men."

The Braddard shrugged. "He knew the risks of attacking the tundra."

"The simple tribesmen. We came for the tribesmen, not the land," the Tigil growled.

"They say that they are one and the same. Now we must leave. We have a deadline to meet, and we are already behind."

The Tigil growled again, sounding much like a wounded dog. He did not move his horse.

"Or you could stay and wait until you freeze to death," the Braddard said with a shrug. The fat man turned on his sleek mount and trotted to where the caravan of chained slaves awaited the order to move out. He signalled. The camels and horses, wagons and newly made slaves began to inch forward over the frozen ground.

The Tigil noted the sounds, but refused to move. He sat belligerently on his horse and scanned the horizon for any trace of his sixty-five strong raiders. It took a second look for the Tigil to understand that a lone figure approached.

He squinted, trying to make out the figure. It walked slowly through the distant snowfall. Mtsusa was forced to wait for a clearer line of sight.

He frowned when at last the details came into view. The stranger was dressed in black robes that covered archaic leather armour. On his head, beneath the hood, the stranger wore the skull of a great stag, the antlers of which were sticking up through the hood.

The horse the figure rode was clearly one of the broad-hoofed tundra horses, though it looked a little smaller. As with the larger mounts of the Sierran Tundra, it was black with a muscular build and feathered hocks. It wore no tack.

Flanking the horse were three beastly-looking hounds the size of ponies with shaggy fur. They looked more like wolves than dogs. They loped this way and that, weaving in and out of their formation in order to keep at the horse's pace and not get too far ahead. Their heads were low to the ground as they trotted through the snow. The Tigil could see their muscular shoulders roll as they padded quietly beside the mysterious rider.

The rider held something in his left hand. It was, the Tigil realised as the stranger came closer, a head on a spear. Mtsusa tensed. He reached for the hilt of his blade, a movement that the hounds evidently saw, for they began to growl. The sound put the Tigil's hairs on end.

As the rider approached, the Tigil recognised the head, or at least, to whom the head belonged.

"Uma," he breathed.

The rider stopped at the line where the snow disappeared and the frozen grass began. He raised the spear and drove the sharpened butt into the ground. He then straightened and looked directly at the Tigil, clearly unafraid.

Mtsusa shrank from his gaze. An awesome power surrounded this robed man and his animals, and it curdled the Tigil's stomach.

"Uma," he said again, loudly enough for the stranger to hear.

The stranger turned his head and looked impassively at the head. At least, the Tigil imagined that the man's expression was impassive. Beneath the hooded skull, only the stranger's mouth could be seen.

The hooded figure turned his head back towards the Tigil. "You are not welcome here, eagle of the desert," the man said in a soft, though deadly, voice.

The Tigil started. The man had not moved his lips. "What?" the Ottalan raider demanded, noting with chagrin that his voice squeaked a little.

The stranger cocked his head in an animal-like fashion. "This is the tundra, man of the desert. You are not welcome here."

"The Ottals go where we please!" the Tigil hissed. He turned his uneasy horse and rode after the caravan at a gallop. Behind him, one of the wolf-mutts howled. The Tigil looked behind and saw that in place of the man on the horse stood a great stag, his large, liquid eyes staring after the Tigil. The mongrel dogs milled around it. Sick with fear and confusion, Mtsusa turned away and urged his horse to go faster.

Fourteen

*T*he Braddard, master of four Tigils and their companies, turned at the sound of thundering hooves coming near. He spied the Tigil Mtsusa and smiled. The smile faded as the Braddard noted the former's pasty face.

"Tigil," he said. "You look like a snow covered stone. What happened? Did you see one of the famous ghosts of the tundra?"

There were stories the old women told their children at night. They talked of the strange spirits of the tundra that protected that land. Any Ottal who ventured too close risked being devoured by these ghosts; these ugly, white wisps that rode the winds. Such stories were frightening when told to a child, but increasingly ridiculous as the child grew into adulthood.

The Tigil shook his head mutely as he reined his horse in and started to walk beside the Braddard. Slowly gaining control of his irrational fear, the Tigil explained all he saw to the Braddard, who promptly laughed at him.

"The cold has gotten to your head, Tigil," he said. "Stags and dogs are not friends."

"If you doubt me, turn back and tell me you do not see Uma's head on a spike!" the Tigil snapped.

"All right," the Braddard said, full of bravado. He signalled the caravan to a halt. "You come with me."

The Tigil nodded and, with a selection of other guildsmen, they set off for the line of snow that marked the beginning of the tundra.

What they saw chilled them all.

Sixty-five heads on spikes lined the border of the Sierran Tundra. Each one the Braddard and the Tigil recognised. The Braddard pulled his horse up short while one brave soldier rode forward to investigate. He frowned as he observed the tracks in the snow.

"Very large deer and wolf prints," he called back, riding the line up and down. "But there are none leading to or away from the border."

"Impossible!" the Braddard snapped.

"Come see for yourself, Braddard," the soldier said.

The fat man on his slender horse did so and noted with disbelief that the soldier spoke truly. Wolf and deer prints were dotted all over where the spikes were set into the ground, but there were no tracks leading to or from the site.

The Braddard turned back to the Tigil. "What is the meaning of this?" he demanded.

Mtsusa shrugged. "I do not know, Braddard," he growled back.

"How is it possible that these simpletons cut down our entire party?" the Braddard asked. Accusation coloured the Braddard's tone.

The Tigil narrowed his eyes. "I. Don't. Know."

"Clearly the wind blew the tracks away," the Braddard said dismissively. "Soldiers," he commanded. "Remove those spikes. We'll be taking the heads with us to the Guild Master. He'll want to know."

The soldiers obediently dismounted and went to the spikes. Grasping them firmly, they pulled with all their strength, but the frozen ground would not yield its prize. Each soldier tried in earnest while the Braddard and the Tigil looked on. They even abandoned their first spikes and tried again on different ones. Nothing yielded.

They then tried to remove the heads. It was as if the heads had been born on those spears. Though the soldiers pulled with all their might, the frozen heads would not come off the spikes.

"They won't come out or off, Braddard," one soldier finally said as he tried to catch his breath. The Braddard rolled his eyes, not noticing that the constant breeze of the tundra had stilled into dead air.

The Tigil did notice, however. He looked around nervously.

"Then cut the damned spears, you idiot," the Braddard roared, his voice loud in the silent, frozen air.

Shrugging, the soldier drew his blade and swung it full force at a spear. The sword shattered on impact. The wooden shaft of the spear bore no mark at all. The soldier yelped and leapt backwards in surprise.

At that moment, the tundra winds rose to a deafening gale. Through the howling winds whispered the words, *you are not welcome here.*

The Tigil struggled to keep his watering eyes open against the wind. Beyond the row of spiked heads, he thought he could see white wisps.

They were indistinct at first, then, at times, they formed the approximation of a person. They were approaching. The Tigil was not the only one to have seen them, or hear the words whispered on the winds.

"Ghosts!" a soldier shouted as a wisp appeared and vanished just as suddenly immediately behind the spear that carried Uma's head.

In a flurry, the soldiers were on their horses and galloping away. The Tigil barely managed to hold his horse in check as the Braddard roared his commands and curses.

"Get back here you yellow-bellied lizards! It's a damned snow drift!"

The Tigil heard the blast of a hunting horn and before the Braddard could utter his next curse, he was flat on his back, an arrow through his throat. Tigil Mtsusa stared down in numb shock. The Braddard stared up at him with an expression that mirrored his own.

Mtsusa's attention turned to the arrow. It was not tipped with steel as it ought to have been, but chipped stone – a stone that was black as night and gleamed as if made of glass. It was an ancient arrow.

The Braddard's mouth opened and closed as he tried to find words to speak. Thick streams of blood escaped his wound and stained the frozen ground until at last his life was gone, his open eyes blank. The Tigil looked up and saw the silhouette of a great stag, obscured a little by the thick drifts of snow the howling winds had torn from the ground.

Screaming like a child, the Tigil turned his horse and bolted for the safety of the caravan and desert.

The laughter of a thousand voices mocked his retreat.

* * * *

Gabija looked terrible when she woke. They had been travelling for close to a month and were nearing the Touan boarder. She felt and looked as exhausted and ragged as everyone else. Eyes, made red and puffy from the tears that would not stop coming, stared listlessly out at nothing. Clothes that once fit hung loosely on a frame Gabija could not bring herself to feed.

Alam was concerned. Lovely though she was, Gabija lacked the steel nerve of her sister, the sister that now lay somewhere on the tundra, probably being gnawed on by one or more of the tundra's various carnivores. Gabija's eyes watered again and Alam turned his attention to the front.

He could not bear to see her cry.

The rear guard reported that no one followed the party, but Alam pushed hard, just in case. After all, the yellow-faced devils had appeared out of nowhere the last time.

From what little he knew of the Ottals, they were the kind to attack without provocation, seeking only to acquire slaves, whom they then sold for a considerable profit. The slave trade was a booming economy in the desert.

The Ottals originally came from the east, at the edge of the eastern desert near the sea. Now they controlled the entire desert. It was they who had founded the holy Yellow City, and it was ultimately to the Yellow City that the Touan Federation, including the kingdom of Misoua, owed their allegiance.

The Sierran tribesmen themselves knew nothing of the men who had attacked them a week ago but for stories they had heard from other tribes. It gnawed at Alam.

He knew well that his loyalties would ultimately have to lie with the holy Yellow City, yet he had come to care a great deal about his host Sierran Clan.

In the past, tribal movements had often adversely affected the safety of the Touan people. Tribal movements still caused some measure of trouble. Yet this was different. It was not a tribe encroaching on another's territory. This was a declaration of war, tantamount to genocide. The relatively peaceful Sierran peoples were poorly equipped for what had befallen them.

Alam knew that Gabija had made the same realisation. The thought must have weighed heavily. He turned to look again. One of her mounted warriors had pulled his horse up beside her and was speaking to her.

It was evident in his expression and tone that he was frightened that the girl might collapse or shatter. It was a concern that none of the warriors would have spared for Seraphimé. That woman had been forged of hard, impenetrable ice. Alam worried that without Seraphimé, Gabija would not be able to rule effectively.

His fears proved largely unfounded. Made of sterner stuff than her delicate appearance might have suggested, Gabija proved a capable leader in the months it took to reach Fredeja, Alam's home and the capital of the kingdom of Misoua. Alam sighed in relief. On this early spring day, only a thin layer of snow covered the ground. It did nothing to hide the rolling grasslands before the fortified city.

The Osprey Clan had noted the change in landscape with some suspicion. They did not like the warmer temperature, and they hated travelling through the temperate forests even more. They did not like being unable to see the horizon. They felt closed-in and vulnerable.

The palace guard met Alam on the road. They saluted smartly as they spied Alam and his entourage crest the hill. Alam was surprised and relieved to see them.

"Your Highness," the Captain said. "We received your message yesterday and were riding out to find you."

"No need, but my warmest thanks. Is there space for my guests?"

The soldier nodded. "Your father has cleared a wing for them."

"Good."

Gabija rode forward. The soldiers looked at her strange appearance with interest.

"We would prefer to camp outside," Gabija told Alam.

Alam blinked and then smiled. "It's much safer in the city."

Gabija shuddered. "We cannot be so closed in. Did you not see what the forest did to my people's nerves?"

"Gabija," Alam said as if speaking to a child.

Gabija's eyes flashed dangerously. "I insist," she said coolly. "We will camp near the walls if you are concerned about our protection, but not within them."

"Considering what you had just been through," Alam replied. "I thought you might feel safer within the walls."

Gabija smiled slightly. "Thank-you, but we would not."

Alam sighed. "We'll try and find you a suitable space behind the city near the merchant houses," he said. "But for now, please humour us with your presence."

Gabija frowned a little in thought, then nodded slowly.

"Thank-you," Alam said. He really could not understand these people of the tundra. Surely they had realised by now that fortifications helped keep the threat out? He shook his head and with the guard in the lead, he escorted the train of refugees through the city and into the courtyard of the imposing fort.

He noted with relief that his older brother, and younger brother and sister waited for him in the courtyard. Although pleased to see Alam, they were equally saddened to hear of the misfortune which befell his host clan. Waiting with them were the two Osprey Clan hostages. To Alam, they looked as if they had aged at a rate disproportionate to the length of their stay.

He dismounted and his sister rushed into his arms. He embraced her closely. Gabija observed from a safe distance, still mounted on her broad-hoofed horse. None of the Sierrans had dismounted. As was their custom, they would wait for their chieftain, though the two Sierran hostages were practically dancing with anticipation.

Gabija took careful note of the royal family of Misoua.

Alam's siblings were much like he was. They were tall and mostly limbs. Though exempt from the lanky height of her older brothers, Alam's sister was nevertheless as wiry. Gabija thought her much too slender, for bones showed through where there ought to be flesh. She immediately disapproved, not of the girl, but of the girl's caretakers who surely must not be feeding her.

She looked down at her own hand and sighed. She appeared no different from the Misouan Princess now. She had been unable to eat much during the journey south, and must appear as skeletal as Alam's sister. Gabija returned her attention to Alam's family.

Like Alam, they were all blonde, the eldest son having some red in his hair. The sister was so blonde her hair was almost white. All of them had blue eyes, though in different hues. The two eldest had iron-grey eyes, the younger brother and his sister had sky blue eyes.

"We were so worried," the girl gushed in a high voice. Her blue eyes were as large as platters. She had all the airs and graces of a perfectly vapid girl; sweet, but vapid.

Alam smiled affectionately. "I told you that I was unharmed in my note."

"I know, but we were worried all the same."

"Alam," the eldest said taking his brother's hand and shaking it firmly. "Welcome home."

"Thank-you," Alam replied. "It's good to be home, Algar."

Algar rumbled a laugh. "The tundra was not to your liking, little brother?"

Alam smiled again. "It is a cold, harsh place. I do not know how anyone survives there." Alam turned and noted that the Sierrans were still mounted, and they huddled close to one another in tense suspicion. Many of them were eyeing the high stone walls and the pikemen atop them with open ill-ease. Gabija was still on her horse awaiting…. something.

Alam went to her. "You are most welcome to my home," he said with a small smile, extending a hand to her.

Gabija, appreciating the gesture, took it and dismounted. As the rest of the Osprey clan followed suit, the two Sierran hostages tumbled over one another to race into Gabija's waiting arms.

"Gabija!" the girl exclaimed. "I've missed you so."

"What happened?" her brother asked. "Where is uncle? Where is father?"

"Hush," Gabija said gently. "I will tell you everything once we're inside and rested."

Fighting tears, the siblings pulled away from their cousin and were soon taken away by their clan.

The Misouan royal family looked on. Alam's siblings all wore uncharacteristic expressions of surprise. It made him grin.

"Would you like a bath?"

Gabija smiled graciously. "Yes, please."

"Come, I'll introduce you."

Gabija followed Alam to where his sinewy siblings stood.

"Gabija, these are my siblings. Crown Prince Algar, Prince Brandt and Princess Anthia."

Each person bowed low as their names were uttered and Gabija bowed in return. Her movement made it painfully evident that she was completely unaccustomed to the ritual of bowing.

"This is Gabija, Chieftain of the Osprey Clan," Alam said. He had to catch himself before he introduced her as the Princess of the Osprey Clan.

"Welcome to Misoua. We have readied the west wing in anticipation of you and your clan," Algar said with all the princely charm he could muster. Alam tensed slightly and Gabija smiled.

"Thank-you, your Highness," Gabija said gently. "But we have already arranged to set our pavilions outside of the walls of the city."

Algar raised an elegant eyebrow in surprise.

"It seems the stone walls make the Sierrans uneasy," Alam explained.

Algar recovered graciously. "Indeed? In that case, we will spare some soldiers to guard your camp."

Thinking it unnecessary, but not wanting to upset the royal family's favour any further, Gabija bowed awkwardly again. "Thank-you."

"Until then, I have offered the Chieftain a bath," Alam said.

"Of course. Come inside and we will have baths and food prepared for you and your clan."

"Thank-you," Gabija said again. She was suddenly overcome with fatigue and desperately wanted a warm tub to sink into. She turned to her waiting clansmen. Understanding the unspoken signal, the newly elected Lieutenant walked forward.

Alam's siblings noted in silence that the man did not bow. In fact, other than obeying his chieftain, there appeared to be no sign of deference from the man at all. Algar did not approve, Brandt found it fascinating, and Anthia thought nothing of it at all.

The two conferred together in their native tongue. After a moment, a consensus had been reached. Gabija turned back to her hosts.

"My lieutenant and I have agreed, it would be easier if the camp was set up as soon as possible. He will take a few of my clansmen to prepare it and join us immediately the task is complete."

Algar nodded. He looked at Alam. "Do you know of a suitable location for them?"

"There's the meadow beyond the wall at the merchant's quarter."

Algar nodded. "By the old oak tree." He turned to Gabija. "I will have an escort for those who are setting up your lodgings. They will remain so they can escort your men to the bathing room. The city is something of a maze, and it is very easy to get lost if you do not know where you are going."

"That is kind, thank-you."

Algar nodded. He soundlessly indicated to two guards. They approached the Crown Prince and bowed. They bowed again once Algar had finished relaying his instructions.

The Lieutenant and Gabija exchanged glances with a look that spoke volumes. The Lieutenant made it clear that he would not bow and Gabija made it clear that she did not want him to.

Alam almost laughed.

All the necessary preparations were made quickly. Alam personally led Gabija's twenty-strong group to the west wing, where five tubs of steaming water had been prepared. With a smile, Alam delivered the group and let the servants take over.

Unused to such intimate assistance from strangers, Gabija felt odd as the servants helped her with her own clothing and, once she was in the water, washed her hair. They even made to towel her down, but Gabija thought that went much too far.

"Thank-you," Gabija said gently. "But that will be all." Bowing, the servants scurried away. Never once did they look Gabija in the eye. She found it disturbing, but tried not to think on it as she dressed herself.

Now that she was finished and dressed, the bathing room flooded with people. They each took turns to bathe, not caring for their nakedness in front of their clansmen. In the bathroom's antechamber, Gabija sat and combed through her brown hair. She dressed in what the servants had left behind, finding the style strange, though not uncomfortable. Her own clothes were much too heavy and warm for this climate.

With the baths all taken, the members of the decimated Osprey Clan each sought a place in the west wing. Comfortable as much on the ground as on any of the many pieces of furniture, the Sierrans sprawled in every posture imaginable. Some sat, some slept. Very few talked.

Gabija found it difficult to keep her eyes open, but forced herself to remain awake. When she was simply a princess, she could have gotten away with falling asleep. She was the Chieftain now, and chieftains must put their needs behind the needs of their clan. She sighed and waited patiently.

It was an hour later when the Lieutenant and a few others arrived. With a curt nod in greeting to their clansmen, they vanished into the bathroom and emerged shortly thereafter, clean and grateful to sink onto the floor to join the muted conversations of their clansmen.

The servants could not help peering curiously in on the twenty or so strange people who sprawled anywhere and everywhere in the large bedchamber of the west wing. They stopped as they scurried by, and then giggled to each other at the complete lack of refinement displayed by these savages.

Overhearing the muted chatter and giggling of the servants, some of the ladies of the court decided to do the same. They peeked in on their guests and mocked them in hushed voices. There they remained until interrupted by Prince Alam.

Fifteen

*A*lam cleared his throat behind the growing number of female spies gathered around the entrance to the wing in which the Sierran clan rested. Surprised, the group immediately disbanded without so much as a word and Alam entered the room.

Gabija stood, swaying slightly on her feet.

Alam frowned. "You are exhausted," he noted.

Gabija shrugged. "No more than you."

Alam grunted. That much was true. "I've been instructed to escort yourself and your lieutenant to the dining hall."

"What about the rest of my clan?"

Alam smiled. "The kitchens have prepared a grand feast for them as well, but I'm sure they would be more comfortable dining in their own camp."

Gabija thought briefly. Though she was well aware that this display of apparent kindness was simply employed to make the dismissal of her kinsmen more palatable, it was, nevertheless, the truth. She nodded in agreement, much to Alam's relief.

"That is well."

"They shall be escorted immediately."

The Sierran tribesmen got to their feet, groaning with the effort. With the exception of Gabija and her lieutenant, they followed the two pike-men who were selected to guide them to their pavilions.

Once the last of the Osprey Clan trudged from the room, Alam turned to Gabija and smiled. He held out his hand. Not knowing what else to do and eager to not insult her host, Gabija took it. With the glowering Lieutenant behind them, Gabija and Alam walked to the dining hall.

Gabija gasped when she walked into the massive room. The ceiling seemed as high as the sky itself, but made of ornately carved stone. Triangular panels in the ceiling were painted in detailed frescoes and illuminated by several crystal and gold chandeliers.

Long tables and benches running the length of the very long room were laid out in straight rows and were crowded with people. The head table ran across the top of the hall on a raised platform. Covered in a white cloth and decorated with bowls of fruits and candles set into gold and silver holders, it appeared ornate and crowded. The wealth on display was stunning, but looked somewhat uncomfortable.

"I apologise," Alam said quietly. "But our father is touring the kingdom now, and will not be joining us for this feast."

Gabija nodded, gazing intently at a servant who approached them.

"Do as I do," Alam whispered. Gabija nodded silently.

The servant arrived and he bowed to them. They bowed in return. The servant then turned and escorted Gabija and Alam to the high table where he left them, but not before bowing and being bowed to.

They were approached again, this time by a servant dressed in a different set of colours. He bowed to them, and they bowed in return. The servant then led them to their respective seats. He bowed to each of them and they bowed back. A servant who was stationed behind each seat pulled out their seats for them. As they sat, the seats were pushed in again. Gabija seemed to be in shock as she tried to make herself comfortable.

Alam smiled reassuringly at her. "You did very well," he said.

The Lieutenant did not do as well. He did not appreciate being separated from his chieftain, and liked the bowing even less. He disliked it so much, he glared icily at anyone who bowed before him, and bluntly refused to bow in return, choosing instead to cross his thickly muscled arms before his chest.

Alam smiled a little as he watched, noting the shock and outrage that the Sierran caused. At length, with a grunt, the Lieutenant sat down beside his Chieftain.

"I do not like these people," he growled at Gabija in his native tongue.

"Their customs are strange," Gabija agreed in kind.

Alam laughed to himself. He wondered if they realised just how strange they themselves were.

"What's this for?" the Lieutenant asked Alam roughly as he grabbed a fork at random and held it up.

"That particular one is for the fried rock hen livers."

"You have so many," Gabija noted in dismay as she looked down at her place setting.

"They're all the same," the Lieutenant growled.

"You'll note that some are larger and some are smaller," Alam explained. "They are each for particular courses."

"Why do you have so many?" the Lieutenant asked gruffly.

"So you don't have to use the same one twice," Alam explained with crumbling patience.

"What a waste," the Lieutenant grumbled, more to himself than anyone else, but he made sure that Alam heard it.

Gabija giggled. She agreed with her lieutenant. What's more, she felt very ill at ease in this setting. The chairs were high-backed and, despite their plush cushions, not at all comfortable. They forced one into a rigid, upright position – wholly unnatural.

Everyone spoke with subdued voices. Their laughter sounded closer to snickers – cold and disingenuous. They were nothing like the laughs of her own people, who only laughed when truly amused.

Nothing about this supposed celebration felt sincere. It was stilted and cold, a ritual without warmth or meaning.

"It's not like the feasts of your home," Alam said to her, rousing her from her home-sick musings.

Gabija nodded. "I am out of my depth here," she said.

"As I was in your home," Alam said.

Gabija laughed. "Perhaps," she said. "But for one difference."

"And what is that?"

"In order to be comfortable with the Osprey Clan, we ask that you only be yourself. Here, it seems, we must all pretend to be someone else."

"How do you mean?"

"Listen to the laughter."

Alam listened. Certainly the tittering here and there was more subdued than with the Sierran tribesmen, but he could discern nothing from it. He looked at Gabija quizzically.

"They are not truly amused," she said. "They laugh to keep up appearances, but not one of them laughs for mirth."

"Politics is a game," Alam said, a little sadly. Gabija's observation had, he realised upon reflection, been correct. "You stay on the good side of the people who can help you."

Gabija shuddered. "It's a wonder your kith have survived at all, if you are all secretly at each other's backs with daggers and poisons."

Alam's mouth quirked. "A wonder? It's a damned miracle."

"Though easily explained," Algar said. He had been quietly listening in to the conversation since the pair had been seated.

Alam and Gabija both turned to him in surprise.

"The lands in the south are a good deal more yielding than those of the tundra. We rely less on each other for survival."

"That cannot be true," Gabija said with a frown.

"Oh?"

"Do not tell me that the lords and ladies seated here in this hall know anything of the proper times to till the soils, to plant and harvest the crops as the peasantry know. You rely on their expertise to feed you, and they rely on your martial prowess to protect them."

Algar smiled. "Indeed," he agreed. "But lords have little need for other lords."

"That is also untrue."

Algar blinked. "Indeed?"

"As the peasants require protection from their lords, the lords require protection from their king, who in turn requires the aid of the lords."

"For what, pray tell?"

"Clearly for the running of the kingdom."

Algar regarded Gabija in silence and Alam did the same in astonishment.

"A kingdom is too broad a land to be run effectively by only one man," Gabija explained, unsure if these men had been taught anything about their own system of governance. "So a king divides his land amongst others who have sworn allegiance to their king. They are entrusted with the governing of that land and in turn, when asked, the king will lend his power, money and other resources to protect the lords. They in turn, will do the same. It is a mutually beneficial arrangement."

Algar blinked, then roared laughter. It was a loud, unexpected sound, but much to Gabija's enjoyment, it sounded genuine. "By the yellow robes of the Holy Order!" Algar muttered between laughs. "My girl, I had quite underestimated you!"

Gabija smiled gently.

"Where did you learn all this?"

"My grandmother was most insistent that we, as children, learn all we can of the peoples that surround us. In that way, we are ever prepared to deal with them."

"Deal with them?"

"Yes. For the most part, we are concerned only with trade, and little enough of that."

"For the most part? And what is the other part?"

"Protection, your Highness."

Algar continued to grin. "I see. Was it your grandmother who taught you our language? Father noted that when Alam was collected, his guide spoke it fluently, as do you."

Gabija's mood turned unhappy. "Seraphimé was a fast learner. She was speaking it before the rest of us were. It was my father who insisted that we learn. 'A people prefer to trade in their own tongue,' he told us. It had been our intention to reach out to you first, but your messenger arrived before ours was even dispatched."

"For trade?"

"Yes, for trade."

"What would you have traded?" Algar asked, not unkindly.

"Horses," Gabija said, her voice barely a whisper.

Algar noted that Gabija was now drawing on painful memories of the past in order to answer his questions, but his burning curiosity could not be ignored.

"Permit me one more query, my Lady," he asked, fully prepared to silence himself if she did not acquiesce. Gabija nodded.

"If we truly wanted your horses, surely we could simply invade and take them."

Gabija did well to quell her shock. "That was father's fear also," Gabija said quietly as she looked at her lap. She lifted her eyes and looked squarely into Algar's own. "But we are not a warring people, and he felt that trade would shield us from harm."

Algar grunted.

"I don't think we could have," Alam said to his brother.

"Hmm?"

"I don't think we could have invaded," Alam repeated.

"How so?"

"Algar, it snows in the summer. It was early fall when, during our travels, we were hit by a snowstorm so thick I couldn't see my own nose. The Sierran people know how to deal with that weather. We would all freeze to death. More still, those black Sierran horses are better over that terrain. Our own horses could not keep their step. And," Alam hesitated, wondering if he should mention it at all. "And a small fighting force of no more than thirty Sierran riders destroyed all but five of a party of eighty or more Ottal raiders."

"There weren't that many," Gabija said quietly. "More like forty."

"Sixty-five," the Lieutenant interjected. "There were sixty-five." He grunted. "Bastards," he snarled.

Gabija closed her eyes as the memory of her father and sister's murder flashed before them.

"Forgive me," Alam said gently.

Gabija shook herself out of her melancholy. "There is nothing to forgive, your Highness."

"I am impressed," Algar murmured. "Who led them?"

"Who? The Ottals or the Sierrans?" Alam asked.

"Seraphimé," Gabija answered, unaware that her quiet voice was being listened to by almost everyone in the room, which had fallen silent since Algar's barking laughter. "My younger sister by two years. She was our Marshal, our General, if you will."

"Was? She is not among the survivors?" Algar asked.

Gabija shook her head and drew a long, shaky breath. "No, your Highness. She was slain in battle, avenging the lives of my stepmother, who had fallen into labour as we fled, and my father, who turned back to help her."

Algar made a strange sound in the back of his throat that sounded a bit like a sympathetic grunt. The first course, a light, broth soup was served and Algar turned to matters that were a little lighter.

"Tell me about your horses."

Sixteen

"Hello, Otsana!"

The sound of a young boy's voice hit Seraphimé's ears before sight of him reached her bleary eyes. When light did finally pierce the darkness, her vision was far too blurry to make anything out. Seraphimé struggled with the focus until she gave up in exhaustion and closed her eyes once more.

"It's all right," the boy's voice soothed.

She felt a small pair of hands stroke her forehead awkwardly.

"Old mother will be back soon, and so will Inna. She's gone to find lichen for your fever, and he's gone to find food for us all. He says there is a black dog lurking around the outside of the camp, scaring away the prey."

"Cabal," Seraphimé murmured.

"Cabal," the boy repeated.

She found his voice soothing, something solid to cling to, something to pull her out of the fathomless murk that clouded her senses and her memory.

"One of the three Hounds of Aqyn. You have a strange guardian, Otsana. They normally rip people apart."

Seraphimé groaned in fevered agony.

"Shhhh," the boy soothed again. "It's all right. You are safe. Would you like me to sing to you? I will sing."

The boy sang. He sang a quiet dirge, an old lament that spoke of a wise, kind people murdered by the hands of ignorance. He sang of how they taught the Ice Bear Clan all they knew, and how the clan would have died were it not for them. He sang of the loss of the last of them, taken by age at last to join her kinsmen in the Aqyn. He sang of how grateful the Ice Bear Clan was and how they would never forget Aguna, the last of the Old Ones.

As the boy sang, in a voice so clear and true it would have drawn tears from ghosts, Seraphimé dreamt. She dreamt of Aguna, who sat on a stone by a fire. She wore the furs of the now extinct greater mammot, the long, oily hairs knitted with bones and stones and other strange fetishes.

Aguna lifted her head as Seraphimé padded close, her four clawed paws silent on the dense snow. The Old One's deep-set brown eyes sparkled with wisdom and love and her heavy brows rose in greeting. She smiled.

"Hello, She-Wolf," she greeted. "I am honoured at last to meet you."

* * * *

"Old mother! Old mother!" Ur called from the pavilion entrance, clearly excited.

"What is it, Ur?" the old Shamanka croaked as she pushed the blind boy back into the warmth of the tent.

"Otsana woke today!"

This surprised the Shamanka. The strange woman's condition had remained the same for almost an entire season. Every day that passed it seemed more unlikely that the girl would survive much longer.

"Did she?"

"Yes," the boy breathed. "And she told me the name of the hound that haunts us."

"Indeed?"

"She said her name was Cabal."

The Shamanka barely contained her gasp. She immediately recognised the name of the Black Hound of Aqyn. Truly it must have been as the migrating elk were saying, the Lord of the Hunt walks the earth again. She shuddered. Things must be grave indeed, for the Lord of the Hunt rarely walked the earth, not since the last of the Old Ones perished, thousands of years ago.

"Ancestors," she breathed as she knelt by the dark head of the suffering girl. "I need to speak with you."

A bitter wind rocked the pavilion. The ancestors heard her, but could offer no solace. The wind rose to a howl. In that howl was a warning; war was coming, a war that would change everything.

The nomads of the Sierran Tundra stood on the brink of obliteration.

The Shamanka shook her head to clear her eyes of tears. She could not imagine the tundra at war. The people who lived here were, for the most part, as peaceful as the Old Ones had been. Their gentle influence had seeped into the bones of the Sierran people. The Sierrans knew nothing of war. War was unnatural to them, yet it was coming nonetheless.

"Old mother," Ur asked, placing his small hand on her forearm. "Why do you weep?"

"Goodness, child," the Shamanka said, hastily wiping the tears from her eyes. "How did you know I was weeping?"

Ur smiled sadly. "I could feel it."

It was more than the Shamanka could bear. She broke down and pulled the boy close. She wept as she held him. If he could have, the boy would have wept with her.

It was a scene that Inna did not expect to see as he parted the entrance flap to the pavilion. His first thought flew to the strange girl lying unconscious, wrapped in fur near a warming stone. The stone had been heated with embers from the fire outside and would remain warm the entire night.

"Old Mother," Inna whispered.

"Oh Inna!" the woman said. She stretched out an arm in his direction. Immediately Inna went to her and fell into her embrace. The three remaining members of the Ice Bear Clan hugged close as the Shamanka struggled to control her tears.

"Is it the girl?" Inna asked quietly when at last the Shamanka could breathe again. The Shamanka laughed and shook her head.

"No, my boy," she said, wiping the tears away from her face. "She is growing stronger. Ur said she woke today."

Inna looked at Ur. "Is this so, little man?"

Ur smiled and nodded. "She spoke. The hound's name, she said it was Cabal."

"Cabal?" Inna asked. "As in the Black Hound? The Hunter's favourite?"

The Shamanka nodded. "His favourite."

Inna breathed out a long, slow breath.

"Mmm," the Shamanka said in reply.

Inna left the circle and went over to where Seraphimé lay. He removed his mitt and placed his large hand on her forehead.

"She is still with fever."

"Yes."

"It has been almost five months now."

"Yes."

"What will that do to her?"

"I do not know. Some fevers take the mind. Others take the heart. We shall not know until she wakes properly, and she has slept much longer than most."

Inna sighed. "Either is a fell blow."

"I do not think that she shall suffer from the after-effects of fever," the Shamanka said quietly.

"Oh?"

"Just a hunch."

Inna grunted.

"What did you bring us to eat?"

"What would you like? The hound went south and brought us back an elk. I have fish myself."

The Shamanka laughed. "That dog is a better hunter than you," she teased.

Inna shrugged. "But less reliable I'd wager."

"Hmph."

"Smoke the fish. And make some soup of the elk. I'll try and wake her once it's done."

"Soup?" Inna enquired.

"It is easier for an ill stomach to digest."

"Oh."

"It is a good thing I am here, Inna, or she'd have died long ago."

Inna grinned. It was true enough. He left the tent to do as he was asked.

The elk was large, and it could feed them for almost two months. Not much was needed for the soup, and with only three other's to feed, there would be little else used. The rest Inna threw into the small icehouse – an underground structure carved entirely from the ice that lay only a few centimetres from the surface where meat was usually stored in the summer.

Inna even cut a large piece for the hound, though the mongrel was nowhere to be seen. He walked a small distance from the camp and lobbed the meat into the air. He watched it fly.

Cabal startled him when she emerged from somewhere beyond knowledge and launched herself into the air, taking down the large slab of meat. She growled and barked at it even as she tore it to shreds and ate it.

She looked up once during her feeding at Inna, her gaze neither hostile nor particularly grateful. Inna shuddered and turned back to prepare the meals.

The soup was the first to be prepared and the last to be finished. Inna squatted outside by the fire and stirred and stirred and stirred until he felt he might fall asleep for the monotony.

Ur broke that monotony by venturing outside the pavilion for the first time in over three years. He wordlessly squatted down beside Inna, finding his way without difficulty. He breathed deep.

"That smells good!" he said.

"What does?" Inna asked. "The soup, the cooking elk steak or the smoking fish?"

"All of it. It reminds me of the Great Gathering. Do you remember it?"

Inna smiled at the memory. Every three summers, all the clans of the Sierran Tundra gathered for a feast like no other. The festival lasted an entire month.

There were games – spear throwing, archery, both mounted and on foot, horseracing, contests of strength. There was dancing; all the women would dance to the sacred drums as the congregations raised their voices in song. Necessities and luxuries were traded and betrothals made. At the end of the celebrations, there was a mass wedding and each new family went with their maternal clans back to their tribal lands.

The Great Gathering was held in the centre of the tundra. All the clans gathered around a small circle of stones there called, Suka Luqtiuk, The Lady's Navel, in the centre of which stood the black boulder. In the circle blazed a fire that was never quenched. One virgin daughter from each clan always tended to the fire, ensuring it never died. In all, there were eight clans, so there were always eight virgins who tended the eternal flames.

Inna grew melancholy. The Ice Bear Clan had not attended the last gathering. The virgin of the Ice Bear Clan must be concerned.

Next Gathering, Inna promised himself. *Even if I go alone.*

"Why did you not take a wife at the last one?" Ur asked.

Inna blinked.

"Even the Chieftain of the Tundra Boar Clan took a wife, and he had been without for nearly eight years."

"How would you know? You were barely walking!"

"Old mother mutters about it sometimes."

Inna sighed. "I didn't see anyone I wanted except...." Inna almost dropped his stir stick. He stared wide-eyed into nothing.

"What is it?" Ur asked.

"Her name. She is Seraphimé! Princess of the Osprey Clan! I knew I've seen her before!" He grabbed Ur's elbow and hauled the boy into the pavilion.

"She is a Princess of the Osprey Clan!" Inna almost shouted.

The Shamanka looked up from her sewing at Inna. "Yes," she said. "I know."

Inna frowned. "You do?"

"Yes."

"How?"

"She had a dream," Ur answered. "An osprey killed in the snow by an eagle."

"Oh." Inna looked crestfallen. "Why didn't you tell me that was her?"

"I thought you knew, or at least would figure it out before now. Ur did."

Ur giggled and Inna scowled.

"Stop scowling," the Shamanka said without looking up. "Is the soup ready yet?"

Grumbling, Inna trudged back outside and resumed his position by the fire, stirring and stirring and stirring. Behind him, he could hear the Shamanka rumble a quiet laugh. It was the first time he heard her laugh since the Ottalan raiders first came. Despite himself, he smiled.

It took another half hour before the soup was ready. Inna took the beaten copper pot from the fire and walked into the pavilion. He set the pot down onto the warming stone and went to fetch the steaks for everyone else. He returned quickly and gave out the meals. The meat was thrown onto plates that had been fashioned from ice-smoothed stones.

The Shamanka ate quickly, then took up the pot of soup. She walked over to Seraphimé and knelt. Eating slowly, Inna watched on in interest. Ur sipped his soup noisily, his head turned in Seraphimé's direction.

"Otsana," the Shamanka said, shaking the girl by the shoulder. "Otsana time to wake up. You must be fed."

Inna sighed when Seraphimé did not stir. She had become gaunt in the months that she had remained unconscious in the pavilion. Fed only broth, there could be no expectation that she would retain any of her strength. Surely it was too much for her and she would slowly fade.

Ur finished eating. He wiped his hands and walked to Seraphimé's other side. "Otsana," he said gently, laying one small hand on her brow. "Otsana, awaken."

It was as if the boy's simple command could have moved stone. Seraphimé stirred.

"Awake, Otsana. It's time to eat."

Seraphimé groaned and her eyes fluttered open. Ur smiled in his sightless knowledge.

"Hello, Otsana," he whispered.

"I can't see," Seraphimé said quietly.

Ur smiled again. "Neither can I." He took up Seraphimé's hand and placed her fingers where his eyes used to be. Seraphimé gasped as soon as she realised.

"Ottal raiders took my eyes before taking my mother," he explained, his voice choking though his eyes could shed no tears. He need not have shed them, Seraphimé did for him.

"I'm sorry," she whispered, quickly weakening again.

"That's enough now," the Shamanka said kindly. "Your sight will heal. I have food for you, Otsana."

Seraphimé nodded weakly.

The Shamanka fed Seraphimé in silence. The Princess was surprisingly hungry. She managed to finish her bowl of broth and chewed weakly at the small chunks of meat that were left over. She ate everything in her little bowl before she collapsed back into sleep. It pleased the Shamanka.

"I believe she'll recover well," she said to the others. Inna barely heard her, he was too busy staring at Ur with an open-mouthed expression of astonishment.

"Close your mouth, Inna," Ur said, turning his sightless head towards him. "You'll catch flies."

The Shamanka laughed brightly.

Seventeen

*I*t had been close to a month since the Osprey Clan set up camp in the field by the fortified city of Fredeja. This far south, there was barely any snow and the people of the tundra felt anxious. Though the migrating birds were not yet due to fly for another few months, the Sierrans were restless. It was time to journey back home.

They had a longer trek than usual this coming spring, and they were concerned that they would miss the herds. They must move soon.

"That's absurd!" Alam exclaimed when Gabija explained everything to him. "You clearly are no longer safe on the tundra!"

Gabija sighed. "I thank you for your concern, your Highness, and for your protection until now. But our people were not made to be sedentary. Already we have stayed too long. Everyone can feel it. I fear the rising tension will bring with it violent discord." Gabija smiled graciously, though her tone told her hosts she would not be dissuaded. "We must take your leave, but do not feel we are ungrateful for all you have done for us."

Algar brooded in his seat as Gabija spoke. "You truly would rather risk another Ottal raid than remain where it is safe?" he asked quietly.

Gabija smiled. "My Lord, there is nothing like the open sky and the plains and the winds. There is nothing like watching the ice yield to grass and all manner of life. We have freedom on the tundra, not self-imposed prisons of stone. I would take a short life of freedom over a long life of imprisonment any day."

Algar smiled. "You make it sound romantic, this nomadic life of yours."

"Only because it is," Gabija replied.

"You truly love the frozen plains?"

"Yes, my Lord. With all my being."

Algar sighed. "We shall be sorry to see you go, Gabija, Chieftain of the Osprey Clan. You were a breath of fresh air."

Alam felt himself flush and his blood heat up. Gabija and his elder brother got along well. It irked him.

Ever since the welcome feast the previously aloof Algar would visit the Chieftain in her camp. He had once told Alam that he was envious of Alam's expedition into the northern plains of the Sierran Tundra, now that he had gotten to know the tribesmen.

The sudden switch was something to behold. Algar had always disdained the nomads of the north, claiming them to be unwashed, uneducated vagrants. It was always Alam that had defended them, and now Algar reaped all the rewards. Alam sulked.

"If it pleases you," Algar said. "I wish to escort you to our northernmost border."

Gabija bowed. "That would please me."

"I'm sure it would," Alam growled under his breath.

"We shall be ready to depart in the morning."

"Alam, I trust that you will be able to manage affairs until I return?" Algar asked.

"Of course, your Highness," Alam said, barely keeping the sour notes from his voice. Algar could hear them all the same and annoyance flickered across his face. Sensing tension between the two brothers, Gabija bowed and made a hasty retreat, eager to tell her people the good news.

They cheered when she did. Her clansmen hugged her so often and so strongly that she could scarce draw breath. It was not difficult for the clansmen to pack up four months of their lives. They did so with much haste, leaving only their blankets and pavilions for the night. Even at that, no sooner did the cock sound his morning call than the pavilions were struck and the camp of a little over twenty was ready to ride for home.

Algar was a little behind, not used to waking up quite so early. He was still stretching the sleep from his limbs when his horse was brought to him. In typical style, his personal guard sat ready and waiting in the cold pre-dawn air before they even spied a light in his window.

"Lazy git," growled one soldier.

"It's his prerogative," their commander snapped and the restless guardsmen fell silent.

The Commander was a grizzled veteran of two wars and any number of smaller skirmishes. He had served the royal family since he was a child and knew nothing else but loyalty to that family. He did not begrudge them their luxuries. In his opinion, it was not their fault that they were born to them. The family never squandered their wealth in excessive fashion. As far as rulers go, the Misouan family could be much, much worse.

The group moved out as soon as Algar was on his horse. He met with Gabija shortly thereafter. In a long column guarded by palace soldiers and mounted Osprey Clan warriors alike, they journeyed to the north in the thinning snows.

* * * *

Seraphimé laughed brightly as Ur struck Inna with a snowball the size of Inna's fist. That the boy seemed to instinctively know where people were and what they were doing had long ago lost its novelty and the three Sierrans played snow wars together in the hazy afternoon sun.

The worst of the winter was behind them, and they played during the little daylight they had. The darkness remained largely unbroken in the winter, though spring saw the duration and strength of daylight increase daily.

The Shamanka laughed also, reminded both of her youth and of the days before the Ottal raids began, when children freely played in the snow and did not care for the noise they made.

Cabal, the Hunter's favoured hound, joyfully danced around Seraphimé, emitting an occasional bark. It was a jubilant sound. That she and Seraphimé were firm friends was no wonder to the Ice Bear Clan. Seraphimé had shared the tale of the hound's rescue with them on one of the many long, dark nights. Ur was especially enthralled.

"All right! All right!" Seraphimé said laughing and out of breath. "Enough. I surrender." She collapsed in the snow, grinning. Inna immediately dropped his snowballs and went to Seraphimé's side laughing.

"Need help, Princess?" he asked moments before a snowball hit him in the side of the head.

Ur squealed with delighted laughter as Inna turned and, imitating the sounds of a bear, chased him. The boy almost flew over the snow he was so swift. Inna himself was not so fast, and found himself falling nearly waist deep into unexpected drifts.

Seraphimé laughed as she watched. She picked herself up and went to the Shamanka, who sat by the fire outside the pavilion entrance stitching a hood of snow hare pelt.

"Phew!" she said as she flopped down onto the snow.

The Shamanka laughed. "You should be careful, Otsana," she said. "You are still recovering."

Seraphimé grinned. "I am almost there. In all honesty, I believe the fresh air and the sight of the sky is helping."

"I saw you last night," the Shamanka said quietly. "On your knees beneath the fire in the sky."

Seraphimé nodded. "I am not ungrateful for my recovery."

"The ancestors must be pleased they have at least one supporter left amongst the Osprey Clan. It was a great shock to us all when news of your family's conversion reached our ears."

Seraphimé grunted. "It wasn't meant. Father just said as much to get those damned preachers out of our territory without declaring war."

"That's the way it usually starts."

Seraphimé frowned.

"Time has a way of making these things more permanent than they were intended," the Shamanka said.

Seraphimé sighed. "I would not let that happen."

Ur suddenly let out a shriek and it drew the attention of the two women. Seraphimé laughed again as she spied Inna lift the boy onto one shoulder and trudge back to the fire. The snow deceived him again and he tripped and fell. Seraphimé laughed as Ur quickly covered Inna's head in snow.

Cabal came to Seraphimé and flopped down at her feet, exhausted. Without thinking, Seraphimé scratched Cabal's ears.

"You surely must have the Hunter's favour, to have his favourite hound for a guard," the Shamanka noted.

Seraphimé smiled. "I dreamt of him often when I wandered from the land of the living," she replied.

The Shamanka grunted. "What is dream and what is real?" she asked, not expecting an answer.

"All is dream, all is real," Seraphimé answered.

The Shamanka smiled. "You speak as an ayal."

"They do not speak."

"They do, but only when absolutely necessary."

Seraphimé nodded.

"Was he handsome?" the Shamanka asked.

Seraphimé looked at the old woman quizzically. "Who, Old Mother?"

"The Hunter. Was he handsome?"

Seraphimé smiled a little wistfully. "Beyond words."

The Shamanka chuckled.

"Otsana," Ur asked, having finally reached the fire and winded from his play.

"Yes, little man?"

"Will you travel to your tribal lands when you are well?"

At this reminder, Inna and the Shamanka grew sad. It was an unspoken law, but nevertheless binding, that no clansmen may cross the bounds of another clan without an invitation from that clan's Chieftain. It was considered rude to ask to do so. They would not be able to go with her.

Seraphimé smiled. "I will wait until the next Gathering and we can all journey together."

"If you wish to go sooner," Inna said, "I can accompany you as far south as the border."

Seraphimé smiled. "I do not know if any of my clan escaped the attack. I hope that they did, and the Prince of Misoua also, but I do not know. The next gathering is in two summers. I can wait until then."

"If they have survived, will they not miss your company?" Ur asked.

"Yes, as surely as I would miss yours," Seraphimé replied. Ur smiled and curled up on the snow, resting his head on her lap. "I will wait," she said.

"That is well," the Shamanka said quietly. "I fear the shadow of the eagle still haunts the tundra."

"They will not stop until every clan is destroyed," Inna growled bitterly.

"Then we must stop them," Seraphimé said.

"How?"

Seraphimé shrugged. "We were not so different from them once. The Old Ones taught us a different path. Perhaps we can teach them."

"I do not think it will be so easy," the Shamanka replied, looking strangely at Seraphimé.

"Do you think that the Old Ones found it easy?" Seraphimé answered. "We had almost killed them all before we realised our error."

"With one small difference, child," the Shamanka said. "We were looking to live in the tundra. The eagle is not. It comes only to feed and cares little for the land. It will return home when the food is gone. I fear it will come to war."

With that, Seraphimé was silenced and a chill settled into the bones of all four as they sat around the fire.

The sun slipped once again from sight.

Eighteen

"*D*id you hear that?" Gabija asked Algar, turning her head east.

"Hear what, Chieftain?"

"A howl."

"A wolf?"

"No, the howl was different."

"How can you tell? One howl sounds much the same as another."

Gabija smiled. "When your life depends on you knowing the difference, Crown-Prince, you can tell."

"I didn't hear anything."

"I did."

Algar could not fathom how. The only sounds he had heard for the past four and a half months were the talk and laughter of the people he accompanied, the occasional whinny and snorts of the horses and, on the rare occasion, the whispering of the wind.

Gabija shrugged and fell silent, wishing that her sister were here to make her feel better. She could tell the difference very easily, and even tell the purpose of the howl. Some were calls to a hunt. Others were simply calls to find one another and, in the rare instance, some were howls of pain and rage.

Sighing, Gabija looked up at the blue sky. She had never felt so happy to see it, she was certain. They had cleared the mountain forest after three months of travel and all of her clansmen were happier for it. Daylight hours had begun to lengthen as they did when the winter yielded slowly to spring. Here in the south they were much longer than the Osprey Clan was used to for this time of year.

They chased the winter north and thus far, they were still ahead of the birds. That was well. The birds came first, then the herds. Normally the clan would leave their southernmost camp and begin to travel to their first hunting post when the birds came. That way they could intercept the herds as they passed through to the newly grown feeding grounds. The herds usually arrived a day or two after the clan.

It was uncertain whether the clan could now arrive on time for the first hunt of the season. They had been too far south and, despite their early start, many were afraid that the balance would be upset. Life was not easy on the tundra. Everything depended on that balance.

Gabija turned her mind to happier matters, such that could be found. It was sunny. There were no more closed-in trees and closed-in walls and all of the foolish games and intrigues that went on behind them. At last they were free of the heavy air of the city into the clean, fresh air of the free plains. In another month they would be in the tundra, hopefully before the birds, so they might get at least a day's rest before the first march of spring.

"A searling for your thoughts," Algar said to Gabija.

Money, Gabija thought. *Yet another foolishness of the south.* She did not understand money and probably never would.

"I was thinking how good it felt to be free of all the closeness and to see the horizon once more."

"Do you not feel exposed and vulnerable out here?" Algar asked.

Gabija smiled. "I was more exposed and vulnerable in your great castle," she said. "I have never been so scrutinised in my life."

Algar grunted. That was true, especially by the ladies of the court, who were eager to judge ill of anyone and everyone. Gabija had been unused to such intrigues and games of deception and had fallen prey to their petty plots more than once. It seemed that her gods were smiling upon her, however. She usually saved herself at the last minute by a personal choice.

Algar smiled as he recalled hearing how the ladies tried to dress Gabija in the traditional garb and make-up of a whore before an important feast. After thanking the ladies of the House of Rent, she decided to remain true to her nomadic roots and arrived instead in her traditional garb. Algar was perplexed when the two sisters of the House of Rent looked utterly crestfallen. He had severely chastised them for their actions against Gabija as soon as he had found out. Whatever games the ladies of the court played, it all backfired. The memory of it made Algar grin.

"And what are you thinking, your Highness?"

Algar's grin widened. "Oh, only how you showed the ladies of the court what it is to be a true lady."

Gabija smiled, embarrassed.

"Don't be embarrassed," Algar said. "It was remarkable!"

"How on earth can any woman trust another, if they all behave like that?" Gabija mused, more to herself.

"They don't, I imagine," Algar answered anyway.

Gabija shook her head. "That is a terrible fate indeed," she said. "There are some things that only women understand. It is a great comfort to have women who are close that one can divulge these things to."

Algar shrugged. "I don't presume to know the workings of the female mind," he said.

"Well, as a female," Gabija replied. "I can tell you that it is not much different from that of a man's mind."

"Oh, indeed?" Algar enquired, not convinced.

"Well, yes," Gabija said. "Only we have more to concern ourselves with than public displays of grandeur."

Algar blinked and, noting Gabija's cheeky smile, roared with laughter.

"It is only natural," Gabija continued.

"How so?"

"All males in the animal world display their physical strength, and sometimes beauty, to attract a mate. Those animals who walk on two legs are no different."

"I'm not an animal," Algar protested.

"Of course you are. You live on this earth and eat her fruits just as any other animal."

"We build castles."

"So too do ants."

Algar blinked. He had seen the tall anthills in the semi-arid grasslands of Bulga. Sometimes they were taller than a man, and riddled with labyrinthine tunnels in which ants scurried to and fro. Inside, it was said, lived the Queen. She directed the actions of all other ants. The ants even had an army – large-headed soldier ants whose sole responsibility was the defence of their 'castle.' In that light, ants were very much like men.

Algar fell silent and Gabija laughed quietly.

* * * *

"Hello, Otsana," a pleasant masculine voice greeted Seraphimé as she stepped through the trunks of the massive, broad-leafed trees. Seraphimé smiled before she saw the man. She knew him by the sound of his voice.

"Hello," she replied when at last she faced him.

They were in the sacred clearing again. The line of tall trees broke here and gentle sunshine found its way through. It was summer, early morning, by the tilt of the sun, though snow still lay on the ground.

The Lord of the Hunt had forgone his armour and cloak and stood before Seraphimé in nothing but his riding trousers. Seraphimé was pleased. He was as she remembered him, golden-skinned and in fine form. About his neck he wore a torque of twisted copper and gold.

The God of Death did not miss Seraphimé's searching gaze. A smile threatening to cross his lips, he held out his hand. Seraphimé took it and he pulled her into him, wrapping his free arm around her waist. Seraphimé closed her eyes and rested her head on his chest.

"You are longer of limb than the Old Ones," she noted.

The Lord of the Hunt smiled. "I am as you are, more or less. Many do not remember what the Old Ones look like, and so my image resembles more your people."

"Strange," Seraphimé murmured. She kissed him on his clavicle, and smiled to herself as she felt his body grow taut. "I know this is only a dream," she said sadly. "I do not want to wake."

The Lord of the Hunt laughed quietly. He pulled away and cupped her face in his hands. "So delicate," he said, stroking her cheeks with his long thumbs. "Yet so strong."

"The tundra does not allow for weakness," Seraphimé replied.

"That's not wholly true," the Lord of the Hunt replied with a small smile.

Seraphimé raised her brows in surprise and opened her mouth to argue. She was never given the chance as the Lord of the Hunt pulled her into a hard kiss.

Seraphimé understood his meaning immediately. Through the kiss she smiled and surrendered herself to it, allowing her weight to press against him. His hands slid from her face to her shoulders, over her breasts and lower still, seeking the laces that kept her clothing around her, shielding her body from him. Seraphimé did not resist. She craved this as much as he did.

They submitted to their weaknesses with passionate haste and the Lord of the Hunt was soon inside her as they rolled together naked on the soft, snow-covered bracken floor.

Many delightful hours later, Seraphimé lay with her head on the Lord of the Hunt's broad chest, her thick auburn curls unbound. The sun shone brightly through the snow-laden leaves and though snow covered all, Seraphimé did not feel cold. The Lord of the Hunt ran his fingers through her hair as they lay in silence.

"Do you know of the kingdoms of the Greyls?" the Lord of the Hunt asked in his soft voice.

Seraphimé stirred a little. "They are the warriors of the south west," she replied. "Mercenaries and raiders, no better than the Ottals."

"Yet they know me there, and they honour me."

Seraphimé frowned and pulled herself up to look at the Lord of the Hunt's face.

The Lord of the Hunt smiled up at her, his dark eyes turned to liquid honey by the sunlight. "You must seek them out."

"I don't understand."

The Lord of the Hunt sighed. "The Ottals have been warned. The ancestors and gods of the tundra both have warned them away from the land and those who live here."

"You fear they will not heed the warning."

The Lord of the Hunt nodded. "The tundra does not know war as the Ottals or the Greyls do. Should the Ottals attack..."

"Can you do nothing?"

The Lord of the Hunt sighed. "It is beyond my power," he said. "I care for the wilds, for the animals and, in the south, the great woods and dark forests. Who rules the lands I care for is not for me to decide."

"And who decides that?"

"The land does. She decides who will rule over her."

Seraphimé frowned. "Is the land a god, like you?"

"The land is a power far older than myself, and truly beyond my understanding. The animals know, and they understand. It is the land that directs all life. Her concern is that of balance. When the balance of life is threatened, only then will the land be roused into action."

"And you believe that balance is being threatened now?"

"Yes."

"By the Ottals?"

"The Ottals are animals of the desert. They have no place in the tundra."

Seraphimé remained in silence, contemplating, and the Lord of the Hunt continued to speak.

"In my living time, the land dreamt. In her dream, she stalked upon her own slumbering form in the guise of a tundra wolf. Long limbed and white, the She-Wolf came only to us in winter, when the land could slumber and dream a mortal dream. I saw her once, the She-Wolf.

"Her eyes looked right into mine, right into my very soul and any pretence of grandeur was cut from me. In that instant, I realised how insignificant I was, how weak we all are. The moment she chooses, the land can destroy everything with less effort than we take to blink. I was humbled."

"And do you think this wolf has returned?"

"Yes, though now she walks in the form of a beautiful woman."

"Then she will intercede?"

"Only if the woman awakens to the power that is within her."

"Surely the land knows herself?"

The Lord of the Hunt laughed then. "The woman is the power of the land made manifest, a dream of mortality, not the land itself."

Thoroughly confused, Seraphimé closed her eyes and tried to puzzle through what the Lord of the Hunt had said. "Are you always so cryptic?" she asked him.

"Think of it this way, in my life I was one of what you have called the Old Ones. I was not a god until I died, and thus awakened to my true strength."

"You had told me your godhood was bestowed upon you by your people."

"Yes, that is true. Their memory of me kept my spirit alive."

"Then is it so different for the land?"

"Yes, for she is not mortal and does not live in the form of a woman. That form is a dream and for the dream to be made powerful, she must remember, she must learn to draw from her physical self to strengthen her dream self."

"And men, they only see the dream self?"

"They see the dream self, and walk upon the physical self of the land."

"Then are we all but dreams?"

"Perhaps. And if that is so, then I am simply a dream within a dream."

"This is making my head hurt."

The Lord of the Hunt laughed again. It was a pleasant rumbling sound that started deep in his chest. He tightened his arms around Seraphimé.

"My precious Otsana," he whispered. "The tundra needs you. Unite the clans. Go south, go to the Greyls and learn war from them. Make allies of them and bring their warriors north to meet the Ottals. Promise me."

"I promise."

"You have precious little time, Otsana. The Ottals will come soon, and they will come hard."

Seraphimé felt herself drift into sleep as the deep, seductive voice of the Lord of the Hunt washed over her, filling her with the message he carried. She felt him pull her yet closer to him and smiled as the last of consciousness drifted from her.

* * * *

Seraphimé woke gently as Inna quietly made preparations to go hunt. She opened her green eyes, taking a moment to realise that she was not in the clearing with her god, but wrapped warmly in blankets in the one remaining pavilion of the Ice Bear Clan.

"Inna," she murmured.

"You shouldn't be awake," Inna said gently. For the first time, Seraphimé saw how similar Inna was to her precious god. Though he did not have his height or the long limbs of the Lord of the Hunt, he did have the same thick, dark hair, dark almond-shaped eyes and skin of dark honey. Seraphimé frowned.

"Is something the matter, Otsana?" he asked.

"Otsana," she replied. His voice was not the voice of her god. "Why do you call me that?"

Inna shrugged. "It was Ur who began it."

Seraphimé turned her gaze to Ur, who was curled against the belly of the Shamanka, smiling. He turned to face Seraphimé, his smile full of knowing. Though the boy had no eyes, it was clear he was looking at Seraphimé, *into* Seraphimé.

"That is what *he* calls her," Ur said quietly.

Seraphimé's pulse quickened and Inna looked at Ur and then back at Seraphimé. Inna grunted, guessing correctly at Ur's meaning. The Shamanka herself noted that Seraphimé belonged to the Lord of the Hunt, and that she dreamt of him often.

"The birds will be returning soon," Ur said as he curled back up and fell slowly to sleep. Inna grunted. It seemed irrelevant.

"I must leave," Seraphimé whispered. "I must go to the Greyls."

Inna blinked.

"When the first bird arrives," Seraphimé finished, taking her cue from Ur and falling quickly into a dreamless sleep.

Inna grunted again and left. He had plans to return with a particularly fat seal he had seen earlier.

Nineteen

$\mathcal{G}$abija heard the loud, disjointed honking of the first of the tundra geese as they flew in a split *V* overhead. She turned her eyes skyward with some dismay. They were a day away from their usual winter camp. Algar and his entourage had been left behind just under a week ago.

Algar had been very difficult to be rid of, though he stopped short of insisting he accompany Gabija and her people the rest of the way. They had moved much faster without his men and were much relieved to be rid of their grumbling about the cold.

Gabija's lieutenant turned to look at her as he too heard the geese overhead. Gabija nodded at him. He knew. There would be little rest at their winter dwelling. One night was all they could spare. Any longer and they would miss the herds and go hungry for the spring. He sighed in irritation and picked up the pace.

* * * *

"Tell me calmly what happened you gibbering idiot, or I'll have your tongue," the Suma growled. A powerful slave merchant, he had acquired less than anticipated on his investment with the Fortu Guild and was in a foul mood.

The Tigil Mtsusa had driven the caravan so hard that most of the slaves needed to be tended to before they were sellable. He wasn't likely to run much of a profit from this lot. He was, at least, grateful for the rich pelts the guildsmen had thought to bring back. White fox and hare were precious indeed, and trimmed the coats of the wealthiest Ottalans. They, at least, were unharmed.

One of the Fortu Guildsmen, the hired soldiers used to protect caravans, knelt before the Suma blubbering something about a deer that was an archer and tundra ghosts.

"I'm sorry about this," the Fortu Guild Master said, still gripping the soldier's elbow tightly. The Guild Master had brought the soldier before the Suma at the latter's request some months after their arrival back from the tundra. He had previously gone to great lengths to conduct his own investigation.

The Suma, however, was not impressed with the Guild Master's report. In the interest of re-establishing their working rapport, the Guild Master had capitulated to the Suma's demands to conduct an investigation of his own. The Guild Master shook the soldier gruffly.

"I'll have you thrown from the guild," he growled.

"I'm n-n-n-n-not sure," the soldier replied. His teeth chattered as if he was still in the tundra. "The Tigil, his men hadn't returned when they were supposed to. He was waiting, and waiting. The Braddard left without him. We were all on the march when the Tigil came roaring back, as white as the field of ice we left behind. He said Uma's head was on a spike."

The Guild Master raised one eyebrow. He had heard this story countless times, but still couldn't believe it. Uma was one of his best, a professional in every respect and a brilliant fighter. The soldier swallowed and tried to steady his breath before continuing.

"We all went back to find sixty-five heads on spikes right at the line of frost."

"You just said that the Tigil said there was only one head on a spike," the Suma said irritably. The story changed more times than he cared to count. The soldier nodded vigorously. "That's what he said at first, but when we went back, all the heads were there."

"Where are they now?"

"I don't know. Still there, I think. The Braddard ordered us to remove them, and we tried. Suma, I swear we tried. They wouldn't budge, neither head nor spear. Then the Braddard told us the cut the spikes, and I tried."

"You tried?"

The soldier nodded. "My sword... it shattered... as if it was made of glass. It shattered as I tried to chop the wood." The soldier fell silent.

The Guild Master shook him again. "And then?"

"And then the wind started." The burly man kneeling before the Suma looked as if he might start to cry. "Terrible wind that howled... and it spoke to us."

The Suma raised his eyebrows. "The wind spoke to you," he repeated, his tone expressing his disbelief.

"Y... Y... Yes."

"You're starting to sound like one of those damned tundra crones."

"Please Suma, we all heard it. It said, 'You are not welcome here.'"

The Suma regarded the soldier the way he would an imbecile. The soldier trembled.

"Then we saw them."

"The ghosts."

The soldier nodded, coming close to a breakdown. "Like wisps of fog in the wind, but shaped like people. And their eyes... their terrible empty eyes." The soldier shuddered. "We ran, but the Braddard and the Tigil stayed behind. The Braddard was shouting and then he stopped, halfway through. I didn't turn around to find out what happened, but it was only the Tigil who caught up to us. He told us the Braddard was dead – an arrow through his throat. Please Suma, that is what happened, I swear it."

The Guild Master let the soldier's arm go in disgust. He looked at the Suma, who sat silent and deep in thought. He turned to the Guild Master.

"Bring me the Tigil."

The Guild Master bowed and, kicking the soldier heavily with his boot, removed himself and the hired sword from the Suma's attendance chamber. The Suma sighed and pressed his fingers to his lips.

The Guild Master returned before long, the Tigil in tow. The Tigil looked much more together than the soldier had. He had eaten, bathed and shaved, and it was clear that he had slept. The months between the strange events and the current investigation had been good to him, it seemed.

"You are looking remarkably well," the Suma said wryly. "Considering."

Mtsusa grunted. "I'm no common sword," he growled.

"Indeed." The Suma knew the Tigil Mtsusa's story well.

The bastard son of a warlord, the Tigil had been well trained before he came to the Fortu, the Guild of Hired Swords. A bastard in a hard man's court, he had to make a living somehow. His father certainly wouldn't recognise him and any inheritance was out of the question.

"Tell me the whole of it."

The Tigil did in a steady, reasoned voice. Much of it was as the blubbering sword had mentioned before. There was one detail the Suma found most interesting.

"The arrow," the Tigil said. "The design was archaic - ancient, even. The tip was made of knapped stone and held fast with fire glued vine."

"Indeed? What kind of stone?"

"It looked like glass, to be honest. Black at its thickest point, virtually clear at its thinnest. Sharper than any metal could ever be."

"And do you have proof of this?" the Suma asked.

The Tigil shook his head. "No. I fled before I thought to retrieve the arrow. I can draw it for you if you like."

"No doubt you can," the Suma murmured. "Would you say you are an ambitious man, Tigil?"

The Tigil's sharp eyes narrowed. "What are you insinuating?" he asked. "That I created an elaborate ambush for the Braddard and killed him myself in the hopes of being promoted?"

"We do know that there are only a select number of Braddards in the Guild," the Suma replied, examining his perfectly manicured nails.

Mtsusa barely held his temper. "I did not murder the Braddard. That fat ass could've kept the damned job."

"Indeed? Your father would be disappointed. Content with being just a Tigil. Surely you ought to have grander ambitions?"

"That is for my half-brothers," the Tigil replied stiffly.

The Suma smiled benignly and leant forward. "So you don't want to prove yourself to daddy-dearest? You don't want to show that a whore's son can make it in the world?"

The Tigil growled and the Guild Master restrained him lest he attack the Suma. After only a moment of brief struggle, the Tigil straightened, calm enough to speak evenly.

"You asked me what happened," the Tigil growled darkly. "And I've told you. I now take my leave."

"Stay," the Suma barked as the Tigil turned on his heel. "You are under arrest, Tigil, until I can uncover the truth of the matter."

"I've told you the truth!"

"I'm sure you have," the Suma sneered. "Only I don't believe in ghosts and in deer that can shoot arrows. They have no opposable thumbs for heaven's sake!"

"I would strongly suggest," the Tigil replied, oddly calm. "That you question the slaves from the tundra about a man who is also a great stag."

Behind the Suma one of his slave girls, a child of the tundra, gasped.

Twenty

"Are you sure?" the Shamanka said, wrapping dried fish and meat in a mat of seaweed.

"I must," Seraphimé said quietly. "The birds are on their way. I cannot wait any longer."

"It will still snow. You know the tundra."

Seraphimé nodded. "Of course, but the spring snows are not so hard to endure. I will not be in any danger."

"But the bears and the wolves and the...."

"Hush Old Mother," Ur said impatiently. "She will be safe. *He* is looking after her."

"I doubt even the First Hunter is a match for an ice bear."

"Then we must trust that the ice bears understand Otsana's need."

Inna and the Shamanka both looked at Ur, then exchanged a silent questioning look between them. The boy simply smiled placidly. He turned to Seraphimé.

"I'll miss you, Otsana," he said.

Seraphimé smiled and embraced him. He had grown strong over the winter, the illness of the mind he suffered due to the last Ottal raid all but a dim memory.

"I'll miss you too, little man," she said. She stood and turned to Inna. "And you Inna." She kissed him gently on the cheek. "Make sure you look after them."

Inna nodded. "I promise."

"Well, child," the Shamanka said. "Take care on your journey. And do not trust the Greyls. They are an uncouth breed."

Seraphimé smiled and she embraced the old woman. "Thank-you for all you have given me, Old Mother," she said.

"Well, well," the Shamanka replied with a dismissive wave, though her eyes filled with tears. She waved Seraphimé away again. "You'd better go, or it'll be summer soon."

Seraphimé laughed. "Look for me at the Great Gathering." She pulled up her furred hood and began to walk south.

Ur took the Shamanka's hand and sighed as he leant into her. Had he eyes, he would have wept.

* * * *

Seraphimé had been walking for several days when Cabal bounded happily in the snow towards her. At first mistaking the massive mutt for a foe, Seraphimé tensed. Cabal's dopey joy gave her away as the mongrel dog approached Seraphimé, bounding in the thick snow like a bizarre rabbit. Seraphimé immediately started to laugh. She dropped her heavy bag of supplies and ran towards Cabal with arms outstretched.

They met bodily, Cabal's happy leap knocking Seraphimé onto her back. Cabal licked Seraphimé's face frantically in greeting.

It took a moment or two before Seraphimé could stop giggling and a few more moments to wrestle Cabal's considerable weight off her. She sat up in the snow and affectionately scratched Cabal's ears and ruff.

"Hello, my sweet," she said. "Where have you been?"

Cabal panted in return, her bright pink tongue lolling out of her mouth. It seemed to Seraphimé that Cabal was smiling and that, in turn, made Seraphimé smile. With a sigh, Seraphimé struggled to her feet.

"Come on then, you dope," she said. She retrieved her pack and commenced walking again, now with Cabal for company.

* * * *

Gabija sighed as they reached the familiar site of their winter dwelling. She was happy to see it yet, all the same, it brought fresh pain to her as she recalled the last time she had rested here. It had been a happy time. Her clansmen were experiencing the same flood of emotions. Many wept openly as they set about their tasks.

The pavilions were not raised. They would stay but a night before moving on to the herd paths. Despite her heavy heart, Gabija was happy to at last reach this place and she felt invigorated by the achievement. She dismounted from her horse and paused, breathing in the crisp late spring air in the fading light.

"Home," she whispered to herself.

Her clansmen must have felt it too, for, despite the grief, the mood lightened. The weeping gave way to songs as the fire flared to life. Laughter accompanied the preparation of the meals. Shelters were dug into the snow and, shortly after the evening meal, the clansmen disappeared into their snow hollows.

To the outside eye, it looked like a hastily abandoned site. Horses herded together, a few piles of folded pavilions and possessions littered the snow haphazardly and small pits of glowing embers lit little mounds in the snow.

Morning came quietly. Though the sun was late to rise, as it did in the spring, the Osprey Clan was not. Cooled embers were brought back to life and a hot breakfast soon warmed each clansman's stomach. They worked quickly despite the low light and were soon on the march – hours before the first rays of the sun broke through the night.

Gabija closed her eyes a moment, enjoying the warmth of the sun's rays. Winter meant very little sun this far north, and no sun at all just a little further north of the Osprey Clan's lands. The return of the sun signalled the return of life and Gabija loved it. Spring was her favourite season.

Eager to get more than an evening's rest, the clan travelled as quickly as the snow would allow, trying to get to the herd paths ahead of the great migration. It would be close this year.

Though the birds were only ahead of them by a day, the clan nevertheless felt a profound sense of urgency. It drove them forward at a good pace. Gabija thought of her sister then, and how Seraphimé would whistle back to the earliest birds as they sang to one another, looking for a good nesting site for the rest of their flocks. Gabija's heart hurt with the joy of the memory and pain of knowing there would be no more moments like it.

For a week the clan marched determinedly to their regular site. They arrived feeling elated. The speed with which they marched ensured that they were well ahead of the herds. They could spend at least three days in blissful rest.

The herd paths were a day away from this site. Only the hunters would approach the paths. The scent of too many people would cause a change in the migration pattern of the herds. For now, the clan simply set up their pavilions and, under the bright sun, they engaged in their first spring snow-fight.

* * * *

The Tigil Mtsusa was decidedly unimpressed. He sat on the long, thin bench that served as his bed in the sweltering hot cell and stared angrily at the floor. His mind raced. He should not have told the truth. He should have lied and said that his men had been ambushed by some savages of the tundra. Now, in the heat of the day, he began to wonder if he really had seen what he believed he saw.

A giant deer? *Ghosts*? Surely it had all been some trick of the eye. Ghosts did not exist. It probably was nothing more than drifts of snow kicked up by the wind. As for the hounds, those large, snarling mongrels…. The Tigil had no idea what to make of them. He shook his head.

Whatever he saw, he knew one thing, he did not kill his own men and then line the border with their spiked heads. What would that have gotten him? Nothing. Nothing but a short stay in a sweltering gaol and the loss of his own head. The Tigil growled, wondering what was happening with the investigation and whether or not he might live out the week.

* * * *

"It makes no sense," the Guild Master told the Suma. He paced the Suma's attendance chamber, fretting for his Tigil. "I've known him a long time. He and Uma were good friends. He would never have killed him, and certainly not for social advancement."

"There are no limits to ambition, Guild Master. You of all people should know that."

"Every man has limits. The Tigil would not have murdered his own men and then fabricated some wild story about deer, hounds and ghosts. He knows we do not hold to the superstitions of the tundra. He knows such a tale wouldn't be believed. Call him a bastard, but that man is no fool."

"Then why did he tell us that wild story?"

"Perhaps it's what he saw."

The Suma gave the Guild Master a flat look.

"I didn't say that is what actually happened. The cold is a difficult thing to bear, Suma. Perhaps it toyed with his head and he genuinely saw those things."

"And the other soldiers too I suppose."

"A mass hallucination, perhaps."

"I see." The Suma pretended to ponder. "Or perhaps he and the men conspired together to kill the Braddard. It is well known that he was disliked."

"All Braddards are disliked," the Guild Master answered. "It's their job to get results, not to be liked."

The Suma grunted.

"Did you speak to the girl about the giant stag?" the Guild Master enquired.

"I did."

"And?"

"She refused to tell me his name, claiming that it provoked some terrible wrath to call on him directly without cause."

The Guild Master waited in expectant silence.

The Suma sighed. "She said he was the Lord of the Hunt, the Master of the Wilds and the God of Death and that gods never walk this earth unless there is dire need."

"A god."

"Yes."

"She cannot be serious. A *god*?"

"That is what she believes."

"You are certain she was genuine?"

"Absolutely. She did not talk until I pressed a hot iron into her side."

The Guild Master grimaced. "Mtsusa could not have known this."

"He is the one who suggested it."

"Perhaps he spoke to one of the slaves on the way back and acquired the information that way?"

"Perhaps. In either case, it still leaves one of your Braddards dead, and my profits severely damaged."

"But with no proof to condemn anyone."

"Let the Tigil go and there'll be more deaths," the Suma warned.

"That is also unproven."

"Damn the Guild!" the Suma roared unexpectedly. "I want his head!"

"I'm sorry, Suma. Without adequate proof, the Guild will not hand him over to you."

"We have the whole story before us!"

"And all of it nothing but speculation. I'm sorry. I know you're upset about the slaves, but the extra pelts should more than make up for it. You cannot have the Tigil."

The Suma sat down, sulking. "Fine," he snapped. "Take him back then, and watch as every Braddard in your pathetic organisation is killed. I'll be laughing."

The Guild Master smiled slightly. "That is the Guild's concern." He bowed abruptly and left.

The Suma grumbled to himself as he watched the broad-backed man exit. In a temper, he knocked over his silver wine decanter and goblet and stormed from the hall.

* * * *

The Tigil looked up at the jangle of keys. The gaoler was unlocking his door and behind him stood the Guild Master. Without a word, the gaoler opened the cell door and stood aside. The Tigil walked out and stood in front of the Guild Master. They acknowledged each other in silence. The Guild Master turned and marched from the Suma's residence, the Tigil in tow.

The Guild Master remained silent as they walked back to the Fortu Guild House through the dusty streets of whitewashed, single story houses. The Tigil knew that meant the man was furious. Having no other choice, the Tigil walked a step behind in sullen silence. Once safely inside the Guild House the Guild Master rounded on the Tigil, throwing him hard against the wall with surprising strength for his age.

"Now tell me what really happened," the Guild Master growled.

"I told you," the Tigil spat back. "I've already said it!"

"You know damned well what we think about ghosts and gods," the Guild Master growled back.

"Gods?" Mtsusa asked. "I didn't say anything about gods."

The Guild Master let the Tigil go. "A tundra slave did."

The Tigil snorted. "About the stag?"

"Yes."

"Camel shit!" the Tigil snapped. He turned and stormed up the stairs to his room, the Guild Master in pursuit. The Guild Master found the Tigil frantically packing his furs and his weapons.

"What are you doing?"

"I'm going to find that shape-shifting bastard and bring his head back," the Tigil growled. "God my arse."

"The hell you are!" the Guild Master growled back.

"That son of a bitch killed Uma!" the Tigil yelled.

He reached his hand into his satchel and withdrew it quickly with a startled oath. An object fell out of the bag as the Tigil pulled his hand back. His hand had a deep gash and dripped thick blood, but the Tigil's attention was on the object on the floor. He bent down to pick it up. Turning around, he held the object out for the Guild Master to see.

It was an arrow, a shaft of white wood with a fletch of raven feathers. The head was not iron, but stone. Glasslike, the arrowhead was black at its thickest point, and clear at the edges; edges now stained with fresh blood and still razor sharp. The Guild Master snatched it from the Tigil's hands. He looked up at the Tigil, who now looked as white as chalk.

"A warning, perhaps?"

Twenty-One

Bran was considered a very handsome man, though he himself remained blissfully oblivious to that fact. Almost six feet tall, with thick black hair and deep blue eyes, the young ladies of the Baveii court would swoon whenever he walked past them. They admired most the breadth of his shoulders. His skin was, in the winter at least, milky white.

In the summer, his constant training out of doors turned his skin a light shade of brown, much to his mother's consternation. Something of a dreamer, Bran often preferred training weapons by himself than courting ladies. That also vexed his mother.

"Lord knows he'd be married by now if he didn't ignore every girl he's ever met," she complained to her sister one evening over a quiet dinner. With her son out in the yard exercising his horses, his father busy with his first wife, Amwyl, third wife of the King of the Baveii had to content herself with her sister's company for now. She did not mind. Her sister was a great comfort and wise beyond her years.

"Perhaps he is not intended for an ordinary life," Catrin replied, accepting another offered sweet bread. "Or ordinary women. Who have you tried to match him up with?"

"There was Alis, and Delwen, the youngest of the Habetti family."

Catrin snorted. "She's a troll!" she exclaimed. "No wonder he wasn't interested."

"Don't encourage it!" Amwyl complained. "He's already turned down all the pretty ones. There isn't much left over but trolls!"

"He doesn't prefer men, does he?"

"Oh no. He's bedded plenty of willing women - none of them marriageable, of course. Can you imagine him marrying the stable boy's sister? That would be a travesty!"

Catrin laughed. "He might enjoy it though. I hear she's as feisty as a filly in her first oestrus."

"You're no help."

Catrin laughed. "Don't you worry, sister dear. One day he'll meet that one woman he just can't get out of his mind. Then you'll see. You are fussing for no reason."

"Hmph."

Bran, oblivious to the gossip of his mother and his aunt, trained his favourite horse out in the free air in the very first week of summer. The warm sun drew beads of sweat from his skin as he put his horse through its paces. He paused a moment and closed his eyes, enjoying the warmth of the sun and the gentle breeze.

"You know, Rusha," he told his horse. "This is just perfect. What a beautiful day!"

The horse snorted and tossed its head impatiently.

"All right, all right," Bran said with a laugh. He pressed his heels into Rusha's flanks and continued his exercises.

Bran loved being outside. The round wattle and mud houses of the city were too closed in for him. He often dreamed of the wilds, of living just as his forefathers had. Even still, he was mindful of his duties as a prince of the Baveii. He knew he would have to marry soon. The thought weighed on him heavily.

He had yet to meet a woman he fancied he could live with all his life. Worse still, he knew that once he was married he'd be expected to have children. Once that happened, all his dreams of freedom would have to be abandoned. It was a depressing thought. So, to keep from getting overly disheartened, Bran kept himself as busy as possible with his training and horses.

To keep his dreams alive, he spent his time with people who knew the value of the freedom he desired. Of course, that meant that he spent little time amongst the nobles, preferring the wild men and women of the lower classes. He knew that his father disapproved and his mother constantly worried, but Bran would not be dissuaded.

"Bran!" his mother shouted from the door of their spacious home. "Come inside for some sweet bread, and say hello to your aunt!"

Bran gritted his teeth in irritation. "Yes, Mother," he called back.

Grumbling, Bran dismounted and led his horse back to the royal stable beside the massive feasting hall. He took his time, grooming for half an hour before he made his way back to his mother's private house. He sat at the table with a grunt.

"You look glum, Bran," his aunt noted, stealing another sweet bread.

Bran shrugged. "I'm inside and it's beautiful and sunny outside."

"You'll get brown if you stay out in the sun too long," his mother chided. "Look at you, you're brown already. It's most unattractive."

Bran rolled his eyes so only his aunt could see. She grinned at him.

"Yes, Mother," Bran intoned dully.

"Don't be cheeky."

"Yes, Mother."

"Honestly Bran, you are such a handsome boy. Why you take no pride in your appearance is beyond me."

Bran wanted to groan.

"It is the fate of every mother to believe her son is the handsomest boy to have walked the earth," Catrin said with a smile. "But in your case, Bran, your mother might just be right. You are very handsome."

Bran gave his aunt a flat stare.

"And you should take better care of your appearance."

"Don't you start," Bran grumbled.

Catrin smiled again. "You are a prince, Bran."

"One of eight. The last one of eight."

"Nevertheless...."

"Let my brothers worry about marriage contracts," Bran snapped. "I want no part of it."

"Bran," Amwyl tried to reason. "Marriage contracts are the responsibility of all princes and princesses."

Bran stood with a sigh. "When I marry, mother, it will be because I am in love, and no other reason. My marriage won't be like yours and Father's."

With that, Bran left, taking his short bow and quiver as he did so. He needed to train more. Amwyl sighed.

"He has a point, Am."

"Oh shut up, Cat."

* * * *

Bran had been at it for hours. His fingers were red and raw from pulling the bowstring. He did not care. He was angry. His mother was more concerned with propriety than Bran's happiness.

"It was unseemly," she had once told him, "for a young man to remain unmarried over long."

Her nagging had wriggled its way under Bran's skin. The fact that she was right grated at his nerves. Bran gritted his teeth in pain and irritation as he knocked another arrow and pulled back the string. He never loosed his arrow.

He drew back the string and aimed, but a small noise in the brush pulled Bran's attention away from his target, a wooden carving of a boar. His eyes widened when a small, half-dressed figure emerged from the forest.

The figure, he realised after a moment, was a young woman. She was dressed strangely and staggering from the effort of walking. She carried an empty satchel and dragged a heavy-looking fur cloak behind her.

Long auburn waves tumbled down her neck and shoulders in a glistening cascade. Her skin was pale, though flushed with heat at the moment. Full, pink lips and beautiful almond-shaped eyes pulled Bran's gaze from her frame.

She looked profoundly lost and a little dazed. When at last she lifted her head to mark her surrounds their eyes met. Bran gave a start, and his heart fluttered sharply in his chest. The woman's eyes were a stunning shade of green, at once bright and deep, and they were glazed over.

No sooner did she see Bran then she collapsed, falling to the ground in a heap. Bran gave a startled shout, dropped his bow and arrow and raced to the girl. He skidded to a stop and dropped to his knees by the woman's head. Though his breath caught once again at the sight of her face, he worked quickly, taking her up in his arms and setting off at a sprint to his mother's abode. He startled the guards as he hurtled passed them.

"Mother!" he called as he raced through the dirt paths that served as roads in the royal compound. He had run the entire length of the town, the woman in his arms, setting the hamlet abuzz. Though his body ached with the effort, he did not slow.

"Mother!"

With some relief, he saw his mother poke her head out of the door. As soon as she spied Bran and his burden, her eyes went wide. She immediately opened her door wide and ushered her son inside.

"What happened?" Amwyl asked as Bran laid the girl on his mother's bed. Catrin soon joined them. She gasped on seeing the frail-looking woman unconscious on the bed.

"I don't know," Bran admitted. "I was at target practice and she just walked out of the woods and collapsed."

"She's horribly flushed," Catrin said. "It must be heat fainting. And no wonder! Look at what she's wearing! I'll fetch a cold bath."

"Thank-you, Cat," Amwyl murmured. She hastily began to undress the girl. "You may go now," she said to her son.

"But..."

"Out. Now."

Bran sighed. "Yes, Mother."

"Make yourself useful and fetch some cold sweet water and some bread and cheese would you? She'll be hungry when she wakes, I am sure."

Bran grunted and went to do as he was bid.

The territory of the Baveii was fortunately placed. The royal grounds rose on the tallest of the hills on the fertile plains. The plains were bordered on the southern side by tall mountains that were perpetually peppered with snow.

Every day, the water bearers travelled up into the mountains to the line of snow, and filled buckets with the frozen water. The ice melted by the time they brought it to the royal grounds, but it remained refreshingly cold. They used honey to make the water sweeter.

In the heat of the summer, there was nothing better to quench the thirst. Bran returned quickly, eager to learn the fate of the beautiful stranger. Amwyl uncharitably forced him to wait outside the door.

Behind the bathing room door, Amwyl dabbed the girl's feverishly hot forehead. It worried Amwyl. She had to bring the girl's temperature down a little before plunging her into the cold water. It would be too much of a shock to her body. Some hearts were not strong enough to withstand that sort of shock.

Even simply dabbing the girl down with cool water and allowing the gentle early summer breeze to breathe over her had a profound effect. The girl's skin prickled in goose flesh and she began to shiver.

"My poor girl," Amwyl said gently.

"It's no wonder she was heat struck," Catrin said. "She was wearing furs and leathers. What was she thinking, wearing furs and leathers at this time of the year?"

"Clearly she isn't from here."

"Where then?"

"You can be terribly dense sometimes, Cat. It still winter up in the north. In fact, if you go far enough north, it is always winter. They would have to wear leathers and furs all year. Perhaps she is from there."

Cat shot her sister a terribly unimpressed look. Amwyl didn't much care.

"You don't know that."

"No, I don't, but it seems most logical, does it not?"

Cat grunted. "She ought to be cool enough now."

Amwyl nodded. Together the sisters lifted the stranger's limp body and lowered it gently in the tub of cool water. The reaction was instantaneous.

The stranger sucked her breath in quickly and arched her back. Her green eyes fluttered open. She gave a start as she saw the two strange women and simultaneously realised that she was naked. She drew her knees up to her chest and sat in the water, shivering.

"Hello, love" Amwyl said gently.

The girl glared at her warily. Amwyl smiled. "It's all right, sweetheart. I'm not going to hurt you."

Amwyl put up both her hands with her fingers splayed in a universal sign of peace. The girl seemed to understand. She rested her chin on her knees, still warily observing the two women.

Seraphimé's head swam sickeningly. She felt faint and uncomfortable. Where her frame was submerged, she felt as cold as ice, but where her skin was exposed, it burned like fire. She watched the two women before her, unsure what to expect.

Amwyl smiled kindly at the girl. "You're suffering from the heat," she explained. She took a small jug and dipped it in the tub. She slowly poured it over the girl's exposed back, letting the water wash away the heat. The girl shuddered, but started to relax.

"There you are now. Let's get you cooled down. Cat?"

"Yes, love?"

"She's about Eilwen's size. Will you fetch one of her summer gowns from the chest?"

Catrin gave a start. Amwyl had never spoken of Eilwen since the red fever took her over five years ago. Bran had been fourteen when he lost his younger sister and the only full-blood sibling he had. He had taken it very hard, though he remained outwardly strong to care for his mother. Amwyl had taken Eilwen's death harder still. She barely ate for almost a year.

"Stop gaping Cat and fetch Eilwen's gown please."

Cat silently did as she was told, leaving Amwyl, who poured a new jug of water over the stranger's head. The stranger bowed her head and accepted the cool water gratefully.

"You are a pretty little thing," Amwyl murmured. She smiled at the girl, who smiled back. It was a shy smile, unsure and barely visible. Amwyl began to sing as she bathed the stranger and watched with satisfaction as the red flush began to recede and the shivering died down.

Cat returned with Eilwen's favourite summer gown; a simple deep blue linen, sleeveless gown, fastened at the shoulders by two finely wrought golden brooches, each set with a single glistening sapphire. Atop the neatly folded gown sat a girdle of finely spun golden thread, the centre of which held another sapphire. Cat held a pair of gold thread sandals in her left hand.

The stranger did not notice. She sat in the tub with her eyes closed, enjoying the cold water as Amwyl sang and washed her down. Catrin watched with a small smile for a moment before excusing herself. She found Bran anxiously pacing the main room. He spun on his heel when he heard Catrin enter.

"What's going on?" he demanded.

Catrin smiled a little. "She's awake now," she replied. "You're mother is bathing her. She'll soon be all right again."

Bran grunted and resumed his pacing. Catrin had to use all of her considerable willpower not to burst out laughing. "Do sit down, nephew mine. There are sweet breads that need finishing."

Bran waved them away impatiently. "Not hungry," he managed to grunt.

"Sit," Catrin commanded.

Bran sighed and collapsed onto a chair. He stretched out his long legs and crossed them at the ankle. Catrin sat down next to him and smiled to herself.

"Why are you grinning like that," Bran asked suspiciously with a sidelong look.

"No reason."

Bran grunted again. He didn't believe her. After a moment he broke the silence.

"Did she speak?"

Catrin contained her smile well and simply shook her head. "I don't think she speaks our language. Your mother thinks she is from the Sierran Tundra in the north."

Bran nodded absently. He knew precious little about the nomads of the north. They kept largely to themselves and bothered no one. The little he did know of them was from the legends his tutor had taught him.

'We were all the same once,' he recalled his aged tutor explain. 'All of us, right up until the line of the desert. But time has a way of sundering what once was whole and now we are all different, turned down different paths by nature – ours and the one out there.'

The historian had waved his hand vaguely around which Bran took to mean the air and the trees and the earth. 'Those to the east of us have gone over to the religion of the desert-dwellers now. They have become very different. But the northerners, they have changed least of all from the early days. They still know the true gods and they still worship their ancestors as we used to. We would do well to learn from them, learn from them and understand who we are.'

The old historian had died last year, desperately unhappy that he did not get to travel north and witness the fabled Summer Solstice celebration the Northerners called the Great Gathering. It was supposed to be something to behold.

Bran sorely missed that old man. He had instilled in his student a fascination with worlds before his own time. Bran missed most the vague mumblings and sharp tongue of a man who believed that the past was more important than the future. He sighed and rolled his ankles back and forth whilst awaiting news of the stranger.

Twenty-Two

Seraphimé was certain that her hosts did not mean her any harm. The woman who bathed her was gentle and motherly and the cold water felt good on Seraphimé's burning skin. The fatigue all but melted away. Though she was tired and her muscles ached, her head was clear again and it felt less like she was drowning when she breathed.

Her body temperature now normal, she relaxed as the woman began to bathe her in earnest with sweet-smelling soaps. Once clean, the woman motioned to Seraphimé to stand. Still in a haze, she obeyed and clean, cold water poured over her. She rinsed the soap from herself. Gratefully accepting the offered towel, Seraphimé stepped out of the tub onto the paved stone floor.

The floor felt cool and pleasant on her feet. She dried her skin while the woman, singing quietly, took a towel to Seraphimé's thick locks.

Those tasks completed, the woman guided her to the bed and sat her down. She began to comb out Seraphimé's jumble of curls, applying a small amount of rose-scented oil to help with the tangles.

Seraphimé had been walking for months and had neither the time nor the inclination to comb out her hair during her march south. It took the woman a long while to sort through the multitude of knots that had developed. Then the woman turned to Seraphimé's skin.

Using a thicker oil, the woman began to rub it into Seraphimé's arms, back and legs. She gave Seraphimé the vial so that she could anoint her breasts and stomach herself.

Amwyl then fetched the clothes. She lowered the gown over Seraphimé's head and adjusted the laces in the back, cinching the gown in at the waist. She placed the girdle around Seraphimé's waist, adjusting the girth a little to allow for Seraphimé's slightly broader frame.

Sitting Seraphimé down again, the woman slipped on the sandals. They were a little too large, though not so much that a slight adjustment of the laces could not fix it. The woman laced them up deliberately slowly to ensure that Seraphimé could see and learn. Seraphimé watched carefully.

Finished, the woman stepped backwards and observed Seraphimé, who stood up, feeling self-conscious. She smoothed the front of her dress and played with her fingers.

"Well now," Amwyl said, tears stinging her eyes. "You look well enough for royalty." She exhaled in a long, low sigh. Seeing her daughter's dress on another person was painful and yet gratifying. She smiled at the stranger who smiled shyly back.

"Come on then," Amwyl said. "Let's get you some water and some food." She beckoned and the stranger followed.

The door to the third queen of the Baveii's bedchamber opened up into the spacious living space and Amwyl stepped through. She stood aside to allow the stranger in the room.

Bran leapt to his feet when she walked in. She was a vision in her dark blue gown. Bran, struck dumb as his heart skipped several beats, opened his mouth to speak. His mind fell blank and no words would come.

Catrin eyed her nephew and, concealing her laughter but not her smile, she stepped forward and took the girl's hands in her own. She squeezed them gently and led the girl to the table where the silver decanter of cold sweet water awaited.

Bran stood beside the table, staring. His expression gave him the appearance of a man just shy of a half-wit. The girl paused and looked at him a moment. He smiled or, at least, Catrin was certain that was what he tried to do.

"Come," Catrin said, guiding the girl the rest of the way. She poured the water into a glass and handed it too her. The girl sniffed it, then took a tentative sip. Having decided it was pleasing to taste, she quickly drank down the entire glass. Catrin smiled and indicated for her to sit and she did so, joined by Catrin and Amwyl.

Bran was the last to sit. He did so slowly and blindly, never taking his eyes away from the stranger.

Amwyl poured the girl another glass of sweet water and cut her some bread and cheese. With everyone served, Amwyl started to eat and the others followed suit; everyone except Bran.

He remained uncharacteristically unaware of the food in front of him. All he could see was the girl. His mother noticed and she elbowed him hard, bringing him back to reality with a jolt.

"Stop gawking and eat!" she hissed at him.

Abashed, Bran looked down at his plate and began to eat. Catrin could no longer hold in her laughter and she giggled. Bran shot her a dark look from under his bowed head. Amwyl did nothing but smile and the girl, confused, ate in silence.

They ate until they could eat no more and Amwyl noted that the girl was almost falling asleep where she sat. Amwyl stood and offered her hand.

"Come," she said.

The girl seemed to understand that word readily enough. She stood and followed Amwyl into the bedroom. There, Amwyl tucked the stranger into her bed. The girl was asleep before Amwyl finished adjusting the sheets. Amwyl smiled and quietly made her exit.

Bran and Catrin waited expectantly.

"She's asleep," Amwyl said.

"She must be presented to the King," Catrin said.

"Yes, but it can wait until she's well enough to entertain the lords of the house. Bran, would you be so kind as to go to your father and explain."

"Of course," Bran replied. He left quickly.

It was a peculiar custom of the Greyls to treat all visitors as if they were friends. Perfect strangers were housed, fed and given whatever else they might desire before any questions were asked. Warlike though they were, none could ever find fault with the hospitality of the Greyls.

King Gofron sat in his study, playing Hamma with his eldest son. His Marshal and the court Wise One sat in silence behind him. Both had been, prior to Bran's arrival, watching the game closely.

From the expression the King wore as Bran relayed the news, it was clear that he already knew of the girl's arrival and that she was currently housed in his third wife's home in the royal compound. Still the King listened intently to Bran's report.

"And where is she now?" he asked in his deep voice.

"Asleep in Mother's bed," Bran said. "Recovering from her ordeal."

"What on earth could have driven a northerner from their beloved ice plains?" Merven, the King's Marshal, mused.

The King grunted. "It cannot be good news," he said. "The northerners never leave the frozen plains." Gofron turned his attention back to his youngest son. "Thank-you Bran," he said. "Tell your mother I will receive our guest as soon as she is well enough."

Bran nodded and bowed, excusing himself quickly.

"And you *will* appear in court this time, Bran," the King said after him. "It will not do to remain a wilding all your life."

Bran sighed. "Yes, Father," he said and the King smiled. Bran exited with another bow and the Marshal turned to his king.

"I've seen that boy training," he said. "I could use a man like him."

"My son will not be a common soldier, Merven."

"Then permit me to make him an uncommon one."

"No."

Merven sighed. "What would you make of him instead?"

The King smiled a little sadly. "A happier youth than I was."

"You spoil him, Father," Cumal noted.

Cumal, the King's eldest son, looked most like the High Queen of the Baveii. Fair hair curled wildly around his heart-shaped face. Pale, steel blue eyes sparkled with wit and good humour. He was considered handsome by any measure.

Already with one wife, Cumal was currently considering another. Though Cumal was brave, intelligent and would make a fine ruler after him, the King had a soft spot for his wilder youngest son.

Cumal suspected that it was because all the King's sons looked like their mothers; all except Bran. The youngest prince looked almost exactly like his father save for the deep blue eyes. The King himself had the same shade of steel blue as his eldest son.

Bran's head of dark hair, his height and the ever-increasing breadth of his shoulders reminded the King of himself in his youth. Bran's impetuous nature reminded the King of all the dreams he was forced to abandon the moment they set the crown upon his head.

King Gofron resented that crown. He resented having to give up his solitary rides into the wilds. He resented having to marry women he had no affection for in order to procure beneficial alliances. He even despised the manner in which people fawned before him, as if they had all lost their self-respect and memory of themselves as soon as the King was crowned. His friends were now formal and distant, and his enemies were falsely pleasant. It was enough to make a man mad.

Bran would never have to wrestle with these problems. He would always be free of the responsibilities of ruling, the responsibilities the King despised so much. Gofron admired it; the wildness that had been scourged from his own person. He wanted Bran to keep that, to remain wild, so at least one of his bloodline would know what it meant to be free.

The King sighed. "You are right," he admitted to his eldest son. "I do."

"And you don't intend to change that," Cumal noted with a smile. Personally, he did not envy his youngest brother one bit. Bran would never be of much consequence amongst the Baveii. Only slightly better than a bastard was the youngest son of a king by his third wife, even if he was handsome and broadly built.

"He will never learn to be a prince unless he is made to."

The King sighed. "He does not need to. He is the son of my third wife, one of eight."

Cumal furrowed his brow and the corners of his lips turned down in an expression of disapproval.

Gofron laughed. "You had the misfortune of being born first, and to my first wife. The responsibility of learning to rule, I am afraid, falls to you."

"I do not begrudge Bran his freedom, Father," Cumal replied honestly. "But I do fear for an unruly younger brother. He is a man, well old enough to be married, not a boy. I cannot count on him if he remains a wilding."

"Some spirits," the Wise One in his plain brown smock said quietly from his corner. "Cannot be tamed. The little crow is one, as is his rescue. She is wilder still."

The King turned to him. "What do you know?"

"Only that the north winds speak her name. Otsana — the She-Wolf. She comes with war on her heels. She comes with the promise of life in one hand and the God of Death in the other."

"Speak plain," Merven snapped.

"I just did," the Wise One shot back. "It is not my fault you have lost the ability to listen."

"That's enough," the King said wearily. "Tell me, Wise One, with whom do the northerners war?"

"They struggle against an eagle."

Merven grunted. "Superstitious bollocks."

The King smiled grimly. "Does this eagle have a name?"

"If it does, it has not been revealed to me."

King Gofron grunted and turned back to the game of Hamma he was playing with his son and the study returned to its normal state, all minds occupied with the impending war the Wise One warned of.

It was his fourth warning in as many weeks, and it worried those who still believed in the ancient powers of the Wise Ones. The study fell into brooding silence.

"Father," Cumal said.

"Hmm?"

"It's your turn."

"Oh."

* * * *

Bran practiced archery again. It could not be helped. He was vexed, and there was little else of a savoury nature he could do to keep himself from going mad.

He could spend the rest of the day pacing in the main room of his mother's house waiting for the girl to awaken, but that would be a waste of a perfectly sunny day.

The horses had already been exercised and he even mucked out his favourite's stall. No doubt it would surprise the stable-hand when he came to do his chores.

Bran's aim was impeccable. Even as distracted as he was with thoughts of the stranger, where she came from and why she came at all, he still managed to hit the targets with deadly accuracy.

"I really could use you, my Lord," Merven noted from his place against the wall.

Bran jumped at the sound of the unexpected voice and silently cursed himself for allowing anyone so near him unawares. He should have been more alert. He should not have let his mind wander.

"You'll have to ask my father," Bran said with a half-smile.

"I did." Merven's tone was sour.

Bran laughed. "Oh dear."

"Exactly."

Bran laughed again. "Perhaps it's for the best. I'm not sure that I want to be a soldier."

"And what would you be instead, my Lord?"

Bran shrugged. "I don't know. Not a soldier."

Merven sighed. "You cannot be a professional dreamer, my Lord."

Bran grinned. "Watch me!"

Merven laughed. "Your brother is right, your father has spoilt you. You shall become a good-for-nothing lay-about with stars in your eyes and nothing in your head."

"If that ever happens, you have my permission to run your sword through my gut."

Merven sighed. "Your mother is trying desperately to get you married, you know," he noted nonchalantly.

Bran made a face. "I know."

"You don't want to be married?"

"I don't want to be married to a woman I feel nothing for. Both of us miserable, wishing we were with someone else. I would seek other wives to fill the hole and father all manner of bastards on other, ambitious women. She would be left to deal with her jealousy and abandonment."

"You are not your father, you know."

Bran scowled and shook his head. "I will not marry unless it is to the woman I can see myself with all my life, the woman whom I will never cease to desire."

"Yep," Merven said with a smile. "A true dreamer."

Bran smiled sadly.

"If ever you change your mind, my Lord, and fancy some excitement – travel, battle and a willing woman in every town, let me know."

"You make it sound glorious," Bran said with a smile. "But I am not such a dreamer that I do not know the other side of battle – the maiming, the dying, the screams and terror. And for what? A few coins in the purse?"

Merven grunted. He bowed and wandered back into the royal compound. Bran drew another arrow.

Twenty-Three

All the princes were bid to dine with their father. It gave the King of the Baveii particular pleasure to be surrounded by his sons. Eight healthy boys was an achievement worth celebrating. They dined together in the grand hall.

The hall itself was typical of the halls of the tribes of the Greyl kingdoms. Pillars of carved and painted wood lined the hall in two columns. In the centre sat an enormous hearth that roared brightly, casting dancing light and gentle heat throughout. Tapestries of all kinds lined the plain wooden walls, most depicting battle scenes.

Quite normally, the royal family would sit at the long, rectangular table that sat permanently on the raised platform at the back of the hall. It was the King's wish, however, to see and speak with all his sons on evenings such as this, so they all sat at a large, round table just below the platform. It was a loud and joyful gathering.

Throughout the dinner, Bran remained uncharacteristically silent. He sat in his chair with a slight slouch, devoid of his normally phenomenal appetite and barely touching his mead. The King noted it once the remains of the main course were cleared away.

"You are quiet tonight, Little Crow," he said, snapping Bran back into reality.

Bran looked up. He blinked as if not quite remembering where he was. "Sorry, Father. I was thinking."

"First time for everything," Bullis, the scrawny first son of the King's second wife sneered.

"Says the weed who cannot spell," Bran shot back.

Bullis was about to retort when the King raised his hand.

"Enough," he said gently, silencing Bullis with a stern look. The King turned to his youngest son. "What's on your mind, Bran?"

"Merven wants me to join his mercenaries."

The King stiffened. "Is that so?"

Bran smiled a little. "You know it's so. He told me he already asked you."

The King grunted and waited for Bran to continue. Bran looked down into his mead cup and swirled the contents around for a moment before sighing and putting it down. "I was thinking of taking him up on the offer."

The King raised his greying brows. "Why?"

Bran shrugged and looked his father directly in the eye. "I'm not good for much else, am I?"

Cumal stood abruptly. "Come brothers," he said. "Father and Bran need some time. We'll take our mead to the women and entertain them this evening."

In curious silence, the seven older princes of the Baveii filed out of the room, occasionally looking back at Bran. He sat with his head resolutely bowed as if the old wooden table held something fearfully fascinating in its crumbling knots.

Gofron regarded his son in silence for a short while before he sighed and rose from his seat. He went to his son's side and sat down beside Bran sideways so that he faced his son squarely.

"Why do you think that, Little Crow?" The King had called him Little Crow the moment he was born. He was the only son to have been born with a full head of dark hair. Though Bran would never admit it, he had grown quite fond of the pet name.

"Because it's true. Isn't it?" Bran looked at his father, who did not answer. "Isn't it?" he demanded.

"Bran...."

"I know my place, Father," Bran said, all the force gone from his voice now. He spoke softly and sadly. "I will inherit nothing. You have seven older sons than I, all demanding some inheritance. For the last three, you would have to take lands away from one of your loyal clans to give them the lands that their inheritance deserves. Two of them are fortunate. They can serve in their older brother's houses."

"You could serve in one of your half-brother's houses, Bran."

"Not without taking a title away from someone else, Father. You know that. I am... unimportant."

The King was shocked and saddened all at once. He had believed he treated his sons equally. He believed that he made sure they were loved and knew it. How long had Bran been feeling like this?

"I am so lost," Bran admitted. "I have no direction - nothing to work towards. Perhaps becoming a mercenary would give me something; some sense of purpose."

The King put down his cup of mead and put his strong arms around his son's shoulders. Bran allowed the embrace, feeling like nothing more than a small child rather than a man of twenty.

"You are important to me," Gofron said quietly. "I will not have you parted from me this way. You are destined for greater things than mercenary life, I can feel it."

Bran laughed softly and bitterly. "Like a life of indolence?"

"No, my son. You will see."

"I wish I could."

The King released his son and, taking him by the shoulders with meaty, scarred hands, looked him directly in the eye. "You are a prince of the Baveii, not some common soldier. You are my son. There is not one of our bloodline who was ever unimportant. That includes you."

Bran tried to smile, but it turned out more like a sloppy grimace.

Gofron laughed. "You are young yet, Bran. Enjoy it while you can, childhood ends soon enough."

"Mother is trying to marry me off."

The King laughed loudly. "Indeed? Of all people, she ought to know better."

That cut Bran more than he would let others know, but the King could see it. He sighed.

"I don't like being King, you know," he said. "None of my marriages were truly my choice, but were necessary. They were my duty to perform and nothing more. That is a King's curse."

"Were you ever in love?"

Gofron shook his head sadly. "There were many pretty girls I fancied, but the great love that some people seem to have was ever denied to me. I never met her and now, it seems, I never will."

It was the King's turn to be unhappy. He slumped a little in his chair and turned his mug around on the spot. Bran watched in silence. The King roused himself.

"Your mother," he said. "Is she unhappy?"

Bran smiled a little. "No. Resigned, perhaps, but not unhappy."

Gofron sighed. "Would that I could've loved them all as fiercely as I love their children."

"It's not too late to try," Bran replied.

The King looked over at his son and smiled. "Perhaps not. Will you make me a promise Bran?"

"What promise?" Bran asked suspiciously, and the King laughed. That Bran was ever himself around him was something the King was truly grateful for.

"Promise me that you will be true to yourself, no matter what. Answer the call of your heart. Don't do what I did."

Bran smiled and nodded. "I promise."

"Good." The King clapped Bran on his shoulder, downed the rest of his mead and stood. "Now, I think it is time to sleep. Goodnight, Bran."

"Goodnight." Bran watched his father leave before he too left the dining hall and made his way back to his bed in his mother's home. He hugged his mother closely before crawling onto his bed. For the first time in many nights, Bran slept deeply.

* * * *

Amwyl checked in on the girl. She was still soundly asleep on Amwyl's bed. Amwyl thought her stunningly beautiful, if a little dark-skinned. With a quiet smile, Amwyl checked in on her son, who was also soundly asleep. Quite normally, he would wake when he heard his bedroom door creak, but now he barely even stirred. Amwyl entered the room and covered her son with blankets to guard against the night. Spring had barely departed and there was still a chill in the air when the sun left the sky.

She exited again to find a royal messenger in her home. She stopped short in surprise. The messenger bowed stiffly.

"Forgive the intrusion, my Lady," he said. "The King has requested your presence."

A slight frown on her face, Amwyl bowed and the messenger took his leave. Her heart a-flurry, Amwyl searched her room for something decent to wear. She changed her dress as quietly as possible. Her mind was scattered.

It had been a long time since the King had requested Amwyl's presence, and she could not imagine that it was now for the same reason as it once had been. Perhaps Bran was in terrible trouble. Perhaps the King had finally decided to remove her. That would be grievous indeed, most especially for Bran.

She brushed her hair and anointed her wrists and neck with rose oil. For the first time in many years, she donned the thick gold torque that marked her as a princess. Nervously chewing her bottom lip, she exited her house and went to the palace proper.

Amwyl was directed to the King's study, where he was pouring over meticulously drawn maps. He looked up as she entered. Even now, with grey in his hair and lines around his eyes, he was strikingly handsome. She bowed.

"Amwyl," he said in his deep, quiet voice. He looked her over appraisingly. "You dressed up."

Amwyl nervously rubbed her arm. "I couldn't present myself to my king in rags," she said with a small smile.

Gofron smiled. "I am flattered by the effort. Come here, Amwyl." Caught by his gentle tone, Amwyl took the hand the King extended.

"Is something the matter, my Lord?" she asked. "Has Bran...." She did not get to finish her question. The King put his forefinger on her lips to stop them moving. She stood in confused silence as he studied her face, tracing the lines of her cheek and jaw with the back of one hand.

"You truly are a beautiful woman," he murmured. Then he did the unexpected. He kissed her. Amwyl was breathless when the kiss ended.

"My Lord," she managed at last. "I'm not sure I'm prepared for this. It has been a very long time."

"For you and me both," the King said and he kissed her again.

Amwyl capitulated to her re-awakened need, and the rest of the night was spent in forgotten pleasures. The following morning, for the first time in almost five years, Amwyl attended court.

Twenty-Four

Bran entered the courtroom dressed as a prince ought. His formal armour had been polished so much that he could see his own reflection amidst the swirling patterns of the worked leather. He wore a dark sable cloak fastened across the shoulders with a gold brooch. About his neck he wore a thick torque of twisted gold and bronze and across his brow he wore the thin circlet of red gold as befitted a prince of the Baveii.

The ladies of the court whispered and swooned as Bran walked passed, the last in a procession of the King's very large family.

Before him walked the King's second wife, her eldest son at her side and her two daughters behind her. Behind them walked her youngest son, who managed to inherit his father's strong frame if not his height. Ahead of them walked the King, with his first wife by his side and their children behind them.

Bran glanced over at Amwyl, who walked beside him in a beautiful summer gown of red. She seemed radiant today. Though she looked the same, it was almost as if she was glowing. Bran decided that it must be some trick of the light.

Once the royal family had arranged themselves, the King and his first wife on the two thrones atop the dais and their children arranged on ornate seats below the platform, the court session began.

On the King's left stood his lesser wives and their children and on the Queen's right stood the rest of the noblemen who attended court.

"It seems that we have a guest to greet," the King said. "Will someone summon the Lady Catrin and her charge?"

A messenger left. The regular daily business of the court began. Wolves were a problem this spring. They were taking too many lambs and the flocks were in terrible danger. The King promised the shepherds of the Kilgurret Clan that he would send twenty men out to them to deal with the wolf problem.

That was as far as Bran's attention lasted. His mind wandered as he observed the courtroom of the great wooden keep. Bran marvelled at the simple beauty of the room. The walls were lined with tapestries of the finest needlework that anyone had seen. Scenes of hunts and wars and peacetime played across the face of one. On another was a strange procession of giants and beneath it a similarly strange procession of animals. Bran had been taught that the giants were the gods, and the animals beneath them were the gods in mortal form.

The tiny, yet bizarrely slender people that surrounded the tapestry in a strange, corporeal border, were said to be spirits, some of them good, some of them bad. The spirits talked to the gods and did the work of the gods in the mortal realm. That was an unnerving thought so Bran forced his mind away from it. He turned his head to the view beyond the window instead.

The sun shone brightly outside making the weather pleasantly warm. It was not yet so far into summer that the day would be uncomfortably hot.

Birds sang in the sunshine and both sun and song poured into the courtroom in fantastical displays of joy. It made Bran happy. He was certain it made everyone happy, for even the King looked more relaxed than usual.

"...Lady Catrin and her guest!" the Herald announced.

That brought Bran's attention sharply back into the courtroom. The crowd fell silent as the heavy doors swung open and Lady Catrin walked into the room with the foundling girl in tow.

Today, Catrin had dressed the girl in a summer gown of deep green. On her head, she wore a golden-threaded and moonstone-studded hairnet that captured half her dark locks while the other half poured down her back in silken waves. Bran's breath caught and his mouth fell open slightly.

The girl observed the mead hall with wide, green eyes, taking particular note of the exquisitely carved pillars. She was so distracted by the hall that she failed to realise that Catrin had walked forward. When she did, she had to run to catch up. There was a small titter of laughter from the crowd as all eyes followed the strange young woman.

She walked always half a step behind Lady Catrin and moved a half beat behind her in her actions. It was clear that the girl had no idea of the manner in which she was to behave and took her cue from Lady Catrin. Catrin bowed low before the raised platform and so too did the stranger.

Most eyes would have missed the signal that Catrin gave to the girl, but Bran did not. He was certain that it was the only reason the girl remained where she stood and did not follow his aunt, who went to Amwyl's side.

The girl fidgeted uncomfortably as the entire hall regarded her in silence. At length the King spoke.

"With all my heart I welcome you. We are the Baveii."

The girl remained silent, a slight frown on her face.

"I am the King, this is my Queen. My name is Gofron."

The girl bit her lip as the King fell into expectant silence. She looked helplessly at Catrin and Amwyl.

"Forgive me, my Lord," Amwyl said. "She does not speak our language."

The King grunted.

"Father," Bran said, rather unexpectedly. "May I?"

The King observed his youngest son for a moment, then gave a curt nod. Bran smiled gratefully and stepped forward.

"Oh, this will be interesting," Bran heard Bullis sneer quietly to his mother, who hushed him, but not before laughing an oily giggle. Bran ignored them.

The girl watched his approach rather warily. Though she appeared relaxed, there was something in the shift of her weight and the placement of her feet that instantly told Bran that she was preparing to fight should it be necessary. He smiled to himself. *She knows how to fight.*

Bran stopped in front of the stranger with his hands up at his shoulders, and palms facing her, indicating he was unarmed and meant no harm. He bowed low. When he stood upright again, he noted that her green eyes were no less suspicious. He smiled at her and then pressed one hand against his chest.

"Bran," he said simply.

The girl's frown deepened slightly. Bran pointed at her and raised his eyebrows to indicate a question. When the girl remained silent, he indicated himself again and said, "Bran." Then he pointed at his father.

"Gofron." He pointed at his mother. "Amwyl." Then at his aunt. "Catrin." He pointed at her again and now she was smiling.

She touched the smooth skin above her chest. "Otsana," she said.

Bran's face split into a wide smile. "Otsana," he repeated, pointing at her.

She nodded, then she reached out and unexpectedly touched Bran's chest. Bran felt his pulse race and hoped that his face did not give him away with a blush.

"Bran," she said.

"Yes," Bran replied, nodding. For a moment, the sparkling emeralds that were her eyes caught him and it took a considerable amount of effort for him to turn away and face his father. He bowed low to the King, then returned to his place by his mother.

"Well done," Amwyl whispered to her son, squeezing his hand briefly. Bran felt himself flush.

The King stood and descended the platform to stand in front of the beautiful young woman.

If Seraphimé thought Bran was broadly built, his father was the breadth of a house, and almost as tall. His blue eyes were very blue, though nowhere near as dark as his youngest son's. His peppery grey hair had once been jet black. It was as if Seraphimé looked at Bran who had aged suddenly.

"We are very pleased to welcome you Otsana," he said in a deep, gentle voice. He bowed before her, as it was a king's duty to humble himself before his guests. "I would like to invite you to stay a while until you can tell us of your ordeal and why you travelled from the north."

Seraphimé understood naught but the name she had given them, however the tone was kindly and she could detect no deceit in him. She glanced over at Catrin who smiled at her and nodded her head. So, not really having any other option, Seraphimé nodded.

The King smiled. "Bran?"

"My Lord?"

"Since you and our guest have established a rapport, I am placing you in charge of learning all you can of her and her purpose."

It took everything Bran had not to give a joyful yelp. Instead he smiled benignly. "Yes, my Lord."

The King returned to his throne with a secretive smile. With the exception of Amwyl, there was no one who could read the Little Crow better.

After Gofron took his seat, he spoke. "Very good then. I suggest we welcome the guest with a feast for to break our fast."

The gathered nobles cheered and the morning's court session was complete. Bran and Catrin went to the stranger called Otsana and escorted her from the hall as it immediately began to be rearranged for the breakfast feast. They went to Amwyl's residence where a kettle of water boiled cheerfully.

In silence they sat at the table as Catrin poured the hot water into a pot filled with spice leaves and flower petals. The room immediately filled with a heady aroma that set Bran's stomach rumbling. They sat in silence until Amwyl arrived.

Catrin rose to pour the spicy brew, keeping an eye on her nephew. Bran could not take his eyes off the girl, and the girl clearly noticed. She shifted her weight uncomfortably and barely glanced at him, trying to avoid his intense gaze. Catrin could not help but smile. If she knew her nephew even a little, the girl's coyness would only make him try harder. Failure had never been an option with Bran.

Amwyl kissed her son on the back of his head when she entered. She moved to her chair and sat down, gratefully accepting a cup of steaming tea from her sister.

"Thank-you, Cat," she said. "Bran, you did very well today. I'm proud of you."

Bran grunted and looked down. "Anyone could've done it. Making someone understand you isn't that difficult."

"Your half-brothers likely would have simply raised their voices and frightened the poor girl."

"Hefa's sons maybe, but Hafwen's boys wouldn't. They have brains enough."

"Yes, and are exceedingly polite and what have you," Amwyl said with a little distaste.

Bran smiled slightly. It had been a long time since his mother had been jealous. He wondered what had effected the change.

"They are good boys," Catrin agreed. "And Hafwen is a good woman, steady and not like to anger quickly. She was a good choice for High Queen."

Amwyl snorted but said nothing further. Bran turned back to observing the girl. She listened intently to the conversation. He was certain she understood nothing, but she tried. Bran found it endearing.

"Otsana knows how to fight," Bran said in order to change the subject.

"How would you know?" Catrin asked, handing him his steaming cup.

Bran thanked her. "A fighter can tell another fighter. In the courtroom when I approached she behaved in exactly the same fashion as a fighter would behave. She did not attack because she did not know if I was a threat, but her body shifted ever so slightly so that she could respond if she needed to."

"I have heard that sometimes women lead men into battle in the north," Amwyl said thoughtfully. "Perhaps she is one such woman."

"She wouldn't well be on her own if that was the case, now would she?" Catrin said.

"Unless her clan was somehow destroyed," Bran said with a frown. He looked at the one called Otsana, and she met him with an even gaze.

"Well, you're in charge of finding out."

"In order to find out, I'm going to have to teach her how to speak our language."

"Or learn hers."

"Both," Bran said. "I'm going to do both."

That was precisely what Bran did. Every morning Bran spent exercising his horse, he took Otsana with him. He showed her how to saddle them. She needed no help in grooming the horses.

Early into the daily excursions, she gave him a shock when she mounted one horse without a saddle. He tried to pry her off, but she would not have it, and she galloped the horse out to the stable yard. Bran chased her and, laughing, she directed her horse to dodge his every attempt to get a hold of her.

It turned into a game and it was not long before both Bran and she were laughing as he chased and she fled. Cleverer than he, Otsana could not be caught. In the end, Bran did not have the strength to chase anymore. He collapsed in the dirt with a grunt.

He also took her to weapons training in the afternoons, showing her what he knew. It seemed that they were equally matched in this. She knew things he did not, and they learnt from one another.

So it went through the hot, easy days of summer. Otsana learned quickly. By the end of the summer, she had a good grasp of the Greyl language. Bran had more difficulty.

Otsana's language was filled with complex sounds that did not exist in Greyl. He had trouble forming the sounds and often ended up saying something nonsensical.

Amwyl was certain that he sometimes did it on purpose to make Otsana giggle. It was clear the both herself and her sister, Catrin, that Bran had fallen hopelessly in love with the girl. Amwyl often caught him looking at her.

Though Otsana appeared to like Bran a great deal, there seemed nothing more in her regard for him than friendly intent. Amwyl fretted that her son would suffer a broken heart before long, but, as Catrin had mentioned more times than Amwyl cared to count, there was nothing for it.

"Love is something young men have to navigate on their own, Amwyl," Catrin said as she and her sister observed Bran and Seraphimé departing for a walk together.

Bran took his time extracting the information his father required. He did not want to pry too much into her privacy and there were some things that Otsana seemed too hurt over to speak about. When at last Bran worked up the courage to ask, Otsana told him everything.

She told him that she was the second daughter of the Chieftain of the Osprey Clan in the north, and his Marshal. Her clan had been attacked and decimated by the Ottals of the East. The attack had been unprovoked. Otsana suspected that it was for nothing more than their slave trade. Her warriors managed to kill all the attackers, save five. Of her fighters that had not been ordered to go with and protect her people, only she survived.

She was raped.

A hunter by the name of Inna, who was one of three remaining members of the now annihilated Ice Bear Clan in the very far north, found and rescued her. Ottal raids, she said, had also destroyed his clan. The Shamanka of the Ice Bear Clan nursed her back to health, and as soon as she was well enough, she struck south in the hope of forging an alliance with the famous Greyl warriors, who counted her gods amongst their own.

She was willing to pay handsomely in good horses. Bran was excited about that.

The sure-footed, even-tempered, strong horses of the north were legendary. Of course, there was the promise of preferential treatment in trade also. Furs and beautiful stones and other status items were all on offer. To the northerners, it was a king's ransom. To the Greyls, however, it was a meagre, though honorific, offering.

Horrified and angry, and not caring to disguise it, Bran relayed the information to his father and eldest half-brother. He paced furiously on the rug in the study, looking very much like a caged bear as he told everything to his father. The King listened in silence until both Bran's information and anger were spent.

"That is a fell tale indeed," he mused.

"We have to help," Bran said, still pacing.

Gofron raised his brows. "Do we?"

"How can we not? The northerners know nothing about war. How could the attack have been provoked? Such injustice should not be permitted!"

"Yet the injustice is beyond our borders, Bran. To willingly engage in rash action might well likely bring the Ottals down upon our own heads, and from what I hear of the Ottals, you don't want them crashing on you."

Bran's mouth hung agape for a moment, before he straightened. "That can't be your decision," he said.

The King sighed. "I share your outrage, Bran," he said in an even tone. Bran looked like he was about to argue, but the King raised his hand.

"We must think of what is best for our people, Bran," Cumal said, imitating his father's tone so perfectly it set Bran's teeth on edge. "Though it might grieve us, we can't just go rushing off to war at every outrage."

"It is a King's curse," the King agreed heavily. "War is costly, in coin and lives. The people to suffer the most will be the peasants. We cannot enter this war carelessly."

"We can't stand aside and allow genocide either!" Bran fumed. "Did both of you miss the lesson that taught that the Greyls and the Sierrans are from the same stock?"

"Yes, and the Touans too," Cumal replied wearily. "We know the stories."

Bran opened his mouth.

"Enough now, Little Crow," the King said.

Bran shut his mouth, making a thin line of his lips so that his father might see his displeasure. It did not have the effect Bran hoped it would.

Gofron simply smiled. "Cumal," he said.

"My Lord?"

"Will you excuse us? Bran and I must talk."

Cumal smiled also. He rose and left without complaint.

"Sit, Bran," the King commanded.

Bran sighed and sat in Cumal's seat.

"Tell me about this Otsana. What is she like?"

"Thinking of taking a fourth wife, Father?"

The King grunted a laugh. "I should never have taken a second. One woman is trouble enough."

Bran grunted, but remained silent.

"I'm not blind Bran, and neither is your mother. We've seen the way you look at her."

Bran blushed a little.

"It's nothing to be ashamed of, Little Crow," the King said, his smile crinkling the corners of his eyes. "While your mother is worried, I am rather pleased. What is her regard for you?"

Bran shrugged. "I don't know. She seems friendly enough, but I can't tell if it she feels as I do."

The King grunted. "Would you marry her?"

Bran didn't need to think. "Yes," he said instantly.

"Think on it carefully, Bran."

"I don't need to. I love her. I have never felt like this about anyone. Ever. I cannot see myself apart from her."

Gofron nodded. "Very good. You may go."

"Father...."

"That will be all, Bran."

Bran sighed and bowed, leaving his father to his thoughts.

Twenty-Five

"*Y*ou cannot be serious?" Amwyl blurted as the King relayed his plans later that night.

"You do not approve? I thought you would be happy to see your son married."

Amwyl was caught. She did want to see her son married, but the maternal feelings for the northerner called Otsana were also profound. Amwyl knew that she did not love her son. Forcing a marriage upon her was, to Amwyl's mind, unthinkable.

"My Lord, she does not love him."

"When has that ever been a consideration in marriage?"

"Bran himself said that —"

"That he would only marry for love, and he loves her, Amwyl."

"It will not do!" Amwyl fretted. "You condemn them both to a loveless marriage. I cannot bear to see either suffer that pain."

"She will grow to love him."

"Oh, my Lord, I wish it were so! But she is a strong-minded woman, determined and incredibly stubborn. She will not take well to the offer of marriage."

"I'll make it worth her while."

"How?"

"She will gain the aid she needs, if she accepts the contract. We will be sworn to protect her people as our kin."

Amwyl's eyes filled with tears. "A terrible choice for a free spirit; chain yourself to misery in order to save your people. Are her horses not enough?"

The King pulled Amwyl close to him. "You are upset. This is not the reaction I had imagined."

"I am a woman, my Lord, who married young and for duty. I know the pain she will suffer."

Gofron sighed. "I know I am not a good husband," he murmured.

"No, my Lord. I didn't mean...."

The King pressed a finger to her lips to silence her. "Bran loves her. He *wants* to marry her," he said quietly. "She will have a better husband than you do."

Amwyl gently pried the King's finger from her lips. She kissed the top of his hand. "But he will have an unhappy wife. She will be miserable and because of it, so will he."

"Then warn him if you must, but I fear Bran has marriage on his mind. However stubborn the northerner is, Bran is ever more so."

Amwyl sighed. "Will you not offer her aid if she does not marry Bran?"

"No. I cannot. She would not be kin. There is no way I could move the council into action for anyone less than kin, let alone a complete stranger."

Amwyl nodded. "They will be no less reluctant when she is married."

"A little lie will move them into action."

"And what lie would that be, my Lord?"

The King smiled. "Watch, and you will see."

"I never had a taste for politics."

"It is fun, on occasion."

Amwyl shook her head. "The poor girl."

The King released Amwyl from his long embrace and looked his third wife in the eye. "Don't fret, my wife. It will turn out for the best."

"I hope so," she murmured, and they kissed.

* * * *

Amwyl found her son the next morning sitting on the wooden catwalk that ran the length of the palisades.

"Are you not training this morning?" she asked her son.

Bran shook his head. "I can't concentrate."

"Otsana," Amwyl said sadly as she sat down.

Bran nodded. He looked like he was in pain. "Mother," he said. "I'm in love. I can't stop thinking about her. I dream about her, if I manage to sleep at all. I can't eat."

"I know."

Bran looked at her.

"You aren't especially subtle, Little Crow."

Bran sighed and swung his legs over the sides. "I'd do anything to have her."

Amwyl sighed. "That is why I've come to you this morning. Your father told me of his plans to marry you two."

Bran nodded. "I am apprehensive about it," he admitted. "I do not know how she feels for me."

"I do."

Bran looked at her hopefully. His wide-eyed gaze was so innocent and child-like that Amwyl wanted to lie in order to protect his precious hope. She could not, for both Bran and Otsana's sake. She could not lie to him about this.

"She likes you Bran, but she does not love you. There is nothing more in her regard for you than an offer of friendship."

Bran slumped, looking utterly crushed and Amwyl's heart broke for him.

"Did... I mean... did she tell you this herself?"

"No, but I know."

"Then you might be mistaken." That thought seemed to fortify Bran and he smiled at his mother, still hopeful.

"Oh, Bran," she said. "Were I mistaken, that would make me the happiest mother alive! My son married to a woman who loves him!" Amwyl drew a breath. "I urge you to reconsider your father's plans to have her marry you."

"You think she will turn me down?"

"I think she will marry you. Not because she wants to, but because she has to. For the sake of her beleaguered people, she would marry you. That you might bring the full force of your warriors to her people's aid, she would marry you. But Bran, it will be an act of duty, and nothing more. And I am come to warn you, that wild things trapped and made captive turn bitter and vicious. You will not be happy in your union."

Bran remained silent a moment. "She will grow to love me."

"You are too much like your father!" Amwyl snapped in exasperation. "You know nothing of a woman's heart! I beg of you Bran, if you truly love her, you will let this summer bird fly free."

Bran's brow furrowed in thought. "I want her," he said finally. "I will marry her."

"Then you do not love her." Amwyl had nothing more to say. She rose and left the palisade, knowing full well she had, for the first time in her life, earned the ire of her son. If she was lucky, he would consider her words carefully.

Knowing Bran, however, he would brace his back and charge forward heedless, if just to try and prove her wrong. She prayed as she returned to her home in the royal grounds that she was wrong. She desperately wanted to be wrong.

* * * *

That evening, all the royal family were invited to dine with the King. It was a private family dinner, the likes of which had never occurred. It was generally considered foolish to have all of one's wives under the same roof. The bickering would be unbearable.

This evening, however, fighting had been decidedly absent. Curiosity overrode all and even the King's second wife refrained from lashing her sharp words at Amwyl. That in itself was a miracle.

"Send for Otsana," the King said before the meal commenced. "I have something to discuss with her."

It was not long before Otsana stood before the King and his family. Today she was resplendent in a summer gown of deep red and sandals of gold and garnet. She bowed deeply before the royal family.

"Good evening, Otsana," the King said gently. "Please, sit." He snapped his fingers and immediately a cushioned seat was brought for Seraphimé.

Frowning a little, she sat. "Thank-you, my Lord," she murmured in near-perfect Greyl.

The King smiled. "I have a matter to discuss with you."

Seraphimé remained silent.

"I have been informed by my youngest son of your situation."

Seraphimé's eyes flickered to Bran. "Then you know what I might ask of you, my Lord," she replied.

The King nodded. "I know," he said softly. "I am truly grieved for all you have suffered, chieftain's daughter," he said. "But I do not think I could move the council to act on your behalf."

Seraphimé's beautiful face fell.

"There is a way," the King continued.

Seraphimé looked at him in hopeful silence.

"If you were to become kin, if you were to marry into my family, I might be able to convince the council to move north and help you defend your people."

Seraphimé's already pale face paled even more as the King spoke. *Marry*. The word hung in the air like a birding net.

"Marry Bran," Gofron continued, oblivious to the tears that had struck Seraphimé's eyes. Amwyl did not miss them, and her heart cracked.

"My Lord," Seraphimé whispered, not sure if she could hold back the tears if she spoke any louder. "I am promised to another."

Gofron raised an eyebrow and he set his jaw in a fashion that told all present there would be no compromise. Though he kept his voice soft, there was some steel in it when he said, "Then you must break that promise for unless you are kin I am afraid I cannot help you."

Seraphimé seemed stricken. "Please, my Lord," she said. "I love him."

This time, Bran paled. Though he did well to remain upright, he seemed somehow smaller than he ought. His shoulders slumped a little and his blue eyes hazed. Amwyl was not sure whom to feel sorry for the most.

The King sighed. "That is a luxury you can ill afford," he said quietly. "I am sorry, Otsana. Though I am honoured by your promised gifts, the council will not be easily moved. If you were to wed Bran, and we were to pretend a recent attack, I could move them. But not if you are not kin."

Seraphimé was torn, as Amwyl well knew she would be. The poor girl looked ready to dissolve, and only her damnable pride and stubborn refusal to break in front of an audience held her together. Slowly, she stood and bowed.

"Will you grant me some time to think, my Lord?"

The King nodded. "Do not take too long, child," he said gently, his steel finally beginning to crack in the face of Seraphimé's beautiful misery. Seraphimé nodded and bowed, leaving the hall quickly but gracefully.

The King looked over at Amwyl, who, with nothing more than her expression, conveyed one simple message: *I told you so.*

A moment of shocked silence from the King's children filled the hall. To Bran, that silence was deafening.

The young ladies of the court had been viciously clawing their way through each other in an effort to have Bran notice them. Everyone that had tried to ensnare him into marriage had failed miserably. There was not a woman Bran could not have amongst the Baveii and yet this girl, this insolent stranger, had all but refused him.

Bran's half-siblings stared at him. Though he kept his head resolutely bent over his plate, he could tell. He had lost his appetite and did not eat. The pressure of his temper too great to contain, Bran abruptly stood and left the hall.

The King sighed, but could not abandon his other children this night. With nothing more than a glance, he told Amwyl to go and see that his son was all right. Amwyl nodded and quickly followed her son.

She found Bran in the stables, destroying everything he could get his hands on. Amwyl waited patiently for Bran's temper to cool. He spied her before it had run its course.

"She loves another," he spat bitterly.

Amwyl nodded once.

Bran grunted and turned away. "I am a fool," he said, the bitterness not gone from his voice. "How could someone not have claimed her heart before me? Why would I have thought she would want me?"

"Bran," Amwyl said gently stepping forward and touching his arm.

Bran shook her off and stepped away. "I love her!" he almost shouted it.

The confession broke him, and he fell to his knees, angry tears stinging his eyes and dogging his breath. "I love her." The words were barely more than a whisper.

Amwyl ran to her son and put her arms around him.

He allowed the embrace and even fell into it. "Mother," he sniffed.

"I'm so sorry, Little Crow," she said. She felt him stiffen and he pulled away from her. The expression on his face reminded her of his father when he dug his heels in. Her heart sank. Otsana would not escape.

"She needs our numbers," Bran declared. "I will have her."

He said no more, and stormed from the stables, leaving Amwyl desolate behind him.

"My poor children," she whispered, feeling equally sorry for her son and Otsana. She thought on Bran, whose foolishness would condemn him to a miserable marriage. There was nothing for it now, though, and Amwyl retired to her home, where she hoped to find and comfort Otsana.

Twenty-Six

Seraphimé could not be found in the house, or even in the royal compound. She had fled to the graveyard beyond the walls. There, she went to the oldest mounds, which looked very similar to the ones her people still made for their dead. At one that felt friendly, she sank to her knees and prayed.

"I know that you are not my ancestors," she whispered to the silent stone mound as tears spilled down her cheeks. "But I'm asking for your help regardless. Please. I cannot marry him. Please, please, please find away to give my people the aid they need without this marriage. Please."

Seraphimé begged and pleaded late into the night, until Bran found her.

"Otsana," he said in surprise. "What are you doing here?"

Seraphimé stood, but did not turn to him. "I came here to find some peace and clear my mind." Her voice was calm, but now devoid of the warmth she had formerly used when speaking to him.

The chill in her tone hurt Bran. He walked to her and placed a hand on her shoulder. He had meant the gesture to be comforting, but he felt her tense beneath his touch. He dropped his hand. "I will not make a bad husband, Otsana," he promised. "I will love you and honour you...."

"I love another," Seraphimé replied sharply. She knew the words would cut and took some satisfaction in seeing that they did.

Bran responded the way only a hurt man could. "You have little choice," he replied, anger in his voice. "You need our help. It will not be given otherwise."

Seraphimé grated her teeth. It was true. With no rebuttal, She turned on her heel and marched back to Amwyl's house. She fell into the bed that had been made for her and curled into a tight ball. Too soon she fell to sleep, and in her dreams, she sought out her god.

* * * *

"Hello, Otsana," the Lord of the Hunt said quietly as Seraphimé stepped into his clearing. It was late summer now and the snows had all melted away. The moon shone brightly into the clearing, casting everything in a silver light. The Lord of the Hunt sat on his own grave, scratching Cabal's ear.

"Cabal!" Seraphimé said.

The dog barked happily and bounded down to meet Seraphimé with a lolling tongue and wagging tail.

The Lord of the Hunt observed impassively. "It is unusual for her to take to anyone so well," he noted.

Seraphimé smiled a little. "Do you know why I have come?"

The Lord of the Hunt nodded, his face betraying no emotion.

"I need your help."

"You have it."

"I need you to tell them, tell them that I cannot marry, tell them to help my people without the union."

The Lord of the Hunt smiled sadly. "I cannot," he said.

This surprised Seraphimé and she did not care to conceal it.

"Otsana," the Lord of the Hunt said gently. "My domain is the hunt, the wilds and death. The politics of men is beyond my authority."

"But you are a *god*."

"Yes, of the wild, the hunt and death. Nothing more."

"You are lying. You could. You could go to them and tell them." Rising hysteria caught in Seraphimé's throat.

"It is not for me to do. I will not intercede."

Seraphimé sank to her knees.

"Otsana," the Lord of the Hunt said, rushing to her side and hauling her to her feet. He kissed her tears away. "Otsana, even gods have rules. There are boundaries I do not dare cross."

"I cannot marry him. I can't."

"You must, or there will be no alliance and the clans of the tundra will fall one by one."

Seraphimé could barely breathe. "I do not love him."

The Lord of the Hunt smiled a little and brushed Seraphimé's hair away from her face. "But you love your people. Marry him."

"And what of you?"

The Lord of the Hunt tensed a moment. "I will always be at your side, Otsana, but I can no longer be your lover. You will be his."

The words dug barbs into Seraphimé's chest and tore her breath away. She tensed and pulled away.

"Otsana," he said gently when he saw the angry steel that flashed through Seraphimé's eyes.

"I was just a diversion for you," she hissed. "It is you I love. And you hand me to another. I love *you*." Broken-hearted, she turned from the Lord of the Hunt and fled his clearing, tears blurring her vision and choking the air from her throat.

"Otsana!" the Lord of the Hunt called after her, a strange, unfamiliar feeling rising in his chest. He did not chase her, however. He stared after her with a frown until the trees swallowed her.

He turned around to see an elder woman dressed with the fetishes of the Osprey Clan. She looked at him with a knowing sparkle in her deep green eyes. Her tone was impish when she spoke to him.

"You are an idiot."

* * * *

The sun did not wake Seraphimé. Her own wracking sobs did. It was still dark outside as she wept her storm of tears. She could not breathe for the grief that pressed on her chest and burned bitterly in her throat. She hacked and coughed as she tried to draw breath to little avail. Nor could she control her keening, though she tried hard to keep it quiet. Amwyl's sudden presence confirmed that she had not succeeded.

"Child," Seraphimé heard Amwyl say as the concerned woman climbed onto the bed. "Goodness child, come here."

Gladly, Seraphimé let Amwyl lift her into a tight embrace. With Amwyl here to mother her, Seraphimé's tears fell with less restraint. She cried with such force that Amwyl's shoulder was soon soaked with brine. Every wracking sob that shook Seraphimé rattled Amwyl as well.

For hours Seraphimé mourned as Amwyl rocked her, trying what she could to soothe her. To Amwyl's distress, nothing but exhaustion seemed to have any effect on the grieving girl.

"There, there," Amwyl said as Seraphimé sank back down onto the bed, too exhausted to weep any longer. "My son is a stubborn boy, but his heart is good. You will see. He will make a fine husband. You shall want for nothing."

"I love him," Seraphimé whispered before she drifted off to sleep. Amwyl was certain she was not speaking of Bran.

"A parting of lovers is a death," Amwyl whispered, stroking Seraphimé's hot forehead. "I am glad I have never known that pain."

Amwyl settled herself beside Seraphimé and fell to sleep there, lest the distressed girl wake in tears again.

Seraphimé did not wake again in the night, nor did she wake the following morning, or afternoon. At length Amwyl had to leave her to tend to her chores. When she returned, Seraphimé was nowhere to be found. Panicked that the girl may have run away, Amwyl called upon her sister, Catrin, and they searched hard for her.

Bran found her. He knew where she would be. She stood still amidst the stone mounds of the graveyard, dressed in white, the colour of mourning.

He approached cautiously, not knowing what welcome he could expect. Seraphimé did not move though he was certain to make his approach known. When he stood beside her at last, she turned to him.

"I will marry you," she said simply.

The words should have lifted Bran's heart. Yet for Bran, Seraphimé's tear-streaked cheeks and swollen, red eyes and with the deadness in her voice, it was no victory. He watched sadly as she walked away from him, defeated. His mother's words echoed in his head. *Let this summer bird fly free.*

"I'll be a good husband," he promised Seraphimé in a fierce, unheard whisper. "None will love you as I do."

A cold northern wind drifted south.

Twenty-Seven

$\mathcal{T}$he wedding was, if nothing else, beautiful. Bramble arches laced with strings of summer flowers in purple and yellow were erected, creating an open pergola in the centre of which Seraphimé and Bran stood.

Seraphimé wore a gown of red, trimmed in gold, with a hairnet of fine gold thread set with garnets. Her smooth neck was unadorned, though she wore a red gold bracelet set with a polished red river stone. She wore a long cape of red velvet, also trimmed in gold. It flowed down around her like a river of blood.

Upon her head, she wore a crown of flowers, woven together on a thick string. For all her beauty and splendour, Seraphimé was a joyless bride.

Bran wore blue. His wedding cloak was a sleeveless, floor length piece of wool, with a high collar that fastened at the neck. It was richly embroidered with floral patterns in silver thread. Around the neck, he wore a torque of twisted silver. A sapphire adorned each side of the open necklet. A thin silver circlet crowned his brow and he wore a ring his father had ordered to be made for him especially for this day.

He was painfully handsome, with his dark hair and blue eyes, yet he seemed tired and drawn.

In the centre of the circle of bramble and flower arches, Bran and Seraphimé held hands and the Wise One wrapped a thick ribbon around their clasped hands.

"In this binding," he intoned sombrely, "do I bind your hearts. In this joining, do I join your lives. In this rite, who all have witnessed, are two made one, one heart, one mind, one life. My Lord Bran, you may kiss your bride."

Bran stepped close. Throughout the entire ceremony, Seraphimé's eyes had been cast down. Bran gently stroked her cheek and hooking one finger under her chin, lifted her face so that now she was forced to look him in the eye.

The depths of Bran's blue eyes were kind and gentle, and even a little sad. He smiled a little for her, and she tried to smile in return. Bran's kiss was gentle and shy.

The crowd roared their approval nonetheless, and immediately joined hands and danced in a ring around the couple, singing as the musicians played their stringed instruments.

It should have been the perfect wedding. The sun shone brightly and birds sang gaily in the morning air. Sunlight sparkled off freshly fallen dewdrops, turning the grass and trees into glittering jewels.

A magnificent feast had been prepared and awaited the guests just to the right of the wedding circle. The festivities would carry on well into the night. Yet for all of that, Amwyl was unhappy. It was painfully clear to her, if not the singing crowd of dancers, that the northerner called Otsana was miserable.

Though she did not shed a tear and, at times, smiled bravely for the sake of the revellers, melancholy tainted everything she did. Otsana looked pale. The light in her eyes fell away into unfathomable depths of grief.

Bran, too, looked strained. His smiles were tight and he seemed exhausted. Amwyl knew well the cause of his exhaustion. A great internal battle had been fought the night before the wedding. Valiantly did Bran's love for Otsana struggle with his want of her. His desire won over the moment his father reminded him that the help Bran so desperately wanted to provide for Otsana's people would not happen without this union.

Amwyl sighed as she sat third on the left of the King's chair. The King himself looked very pleased, but he was a man, Amwyl reasoned, and so did not understand the situation as fully as she did. Neither did the crowd. They were just happy at the prospect of feasting.

Many of the young ladies were desperately in love with Bran, and would never understand why his bride would be so reticent. Amwyl knew.

A bird had its wings clipped today, and would never fly again.

Briefly, her eyes met Seraphimé's and a quiet understanding passed between them; a woman's understanding.

Otsana would be a dutiful wife in every regard, but she could not be anything more than dutiful. Her heart belonged to another. That was the full of it. Bran would be denied the love she felt for this other man, of whom she would not speak. That broke Amwyl's heart, for she could see that her son was very much enamoured with this girl. He was such a good man. He deserved to be loved.

At length, the singing and the dancing were done and Bran led Seraphimé to the table of honour for the early afternoon feast, their hands still bound. Once seated, their hands were unwrapped and the wine flowed.

The feast was loud and full of laughter and song. Bran was much engaged with his father's conversation and he smiled and laughed as he ate and drank, though Amwyl could well see that each smile was laced with a strange kind of pain.

He knows, she thought. *He knows what the future holds for him now.*

Amwyl shifted her gaze to Seraphimé. She sat with her hands folded neatly in her lap, her food untouched. More often than not, she had her eyes averted from the scene before her, staring down at the table. Amwyl filled her glass with wine and went to her.

Sitting in the seat recently vacated by Seraphimé's side, Amwyl thrust the wine beneath the bride's nose.

"Here, Otsana," she said. "The wine helps."

Seraphimé blinked and looked up at her new mother-in-law. She tried to smile, but all she managed was a wan grimace.

Amwyl smiled kindly in return. "It helped me."

"Did you... did you love him?" Seraphimé asked, glancing at the King.

Amwyl sighed and shook her head, noting that Seraphimé had not taken the glass from her. "No," she said. "I did not love him. Not even a little. And no woman in their right mind would want to be a man's second wife, let alone third."

"Why did you, then?"

Amwyl shrugged. "I am one of many daughters to a minor lord with little lands. My father's wealth came through trade. I thought the best marriage I could have hoped for was to a wealthy horse-breeder or some such rubbish." Amwyl sighed. "When the King began to make negotiations with my father, I was very surprised. He was then as he is now. Embittered by his life of duty, his 'King's Curse,' as he calls it. Still, he was kindly and gentle and in the end, it wasn't so bad."

Seraphimé looked sad again.

"I am well kept," Amwyl said cheerily, trying to encourage Seraphimé. "I have my own home that is well kept by servants. Nothing I desire is denied me. It is a very comfortable life, Otsana."

"I do not need this finery," Seraphimé whispered. "I need the horizon, and the snow. I need the fire in the sky. I want to go home."

Bran, who had been listening in, turned away from his father and took Seraphimé's hand, startling her. He smiled a little as Seraphimé jumped.

"I will take you home, Otsana," he told her in a low voice. "I will take you back to your sky and plains of ice, and your family. I promise."

Seraphimé smiled, but her eyes welled with tears all the same.

Your kindness is killing her, Bran. Amwyl thought. *A hard man is easier to hate.*

"Thank-you," Seraphimé whispered.

Bran smiled and Amwyl again noted the pain that strained at his mouth. Everywhere around them swirled laughter and song, a strange juxtaposition to the pocket of sadness enveloping Bran and Seraphimé both.

Amwyl quietly excused herself, taking the wine back with her. Bran continued to gaze intently at Seraphimé, who had turned her eyes back to the table.

The wedding took place in high summer. The sun would not set until quite late. Already it was late evening, and the sun still shone as if it was early afternoon. Bran stood. He had to get Seraphimé away before she lost her composure. He was certain she would be happier away from the loud crowds. He took her hand and stood. She rose silently at his side.

"My friends," he said with a bright smile. "Though the sun might try and fool us, it is quite late, and long past the hour my bride and I are to be away. Enjoy the feasting and dancing, we beg your indulgence and retire."

The crowd gave an almighty cheer. With a comical bow, Bran turned away and led Seraphimé to their new home; a home apart from his mother's and his father's in the royal compound.

It was as most of the royal houses were, large and spacious. Built from square-cut grey stone, the house had two levels. The downstairs was open and airy, with rugs and rich tapestries. Comfortable chairs and lounges filled the otherwise cavernous space. A big fireplace, currently empty, stood to the far left of the room.

Stairs that lead to the second landing lined one wall. They led up to the bedrooms. There were three in total, as well as a private study for Bran and Seraphimé each, a sewing room, a music room and several other spare rooms besides.

"Welcome home," Bran said kindly, before leading her upstairs.

As she walked behind her husband, she thought, *This isn't my home.*

Bran led her to the enormous main bedroom, which had been completely furnished under Amwyl's careful command. Seraphimé could see Amwyl's touch in everything and she smiled gratefully when she saw a black tapestry decorated with white embroidery in all the images of the beasts of the tundra. Though the style was not exactly Sierran, Seraphimé nevertheless appreciated the effort. She immediately went to the tapestry and touched the rough-spun black wool.

"My father thought it was hideous," Bran said as he watched her. "But mother insisted. I'm certain it's not accurate, but they did the best they could."

Seraphimé smiled at Bran, the first genuine smile since the marriage proposal was set forth. It sent Bran's heart fluttering.

"Here," he said, walking to her. "Let me take that." He carefully unclasped Seraphimé's long cape. Its weight surprised Bran.

Though he tried to behave himself, he deliberately brushed the exposed skin on Seraphimé's shoulders as he did so, then silently reprimanded himself for doing it. He turned and slung the cape over the back of one of the chairs that faced the fireplace. He removed his wedding vest and hung it over Seraphimé's cape. He turned to her. She was still studying the tapestry.

"When did you want your warriors?" he asked her.

Seraphimé looked at him for a moment, her solemn green eyes boring into him. It made him uncomfortable.

"I do not know," she answered at length. "I don't know what it's like up there. Who, if any, have survived. I promised Inna that I would return at the next Great Gathering."

Bran nodded. This was a relatively simple conversation to have and it filled the awkward silence. He turned and sat down on the chair that held their robes and unlaced his boots, kicking them off with satisfaction. It was much too hot for boots and he found formal wear uncomfortable. He sighed happily when a breeze floated over his bare feet.

"Well," he said. "I can accompany you with a small fighting force to the Great Gathering that we might take better stock of the situation and determine what needs to be done to remedy it. When is the Gathering?"

"Next summer."

Bran nodded and smiled at Seraphimé. "That's plenty of time."

"Thank-you," Seraphimé murmured, lowering her eyes again.

Bran held out a hand to her. "Come here," he said.

Seraphimé could do naught else. She took Bran's hand and allowed him to gently guide her to his lap, where he folded his strong arms around her. He held her a moment in silence before his desire got the better of him. He stood, still cradling Seraphimé in his arms, and walked over to the bed.

He laid her on the bed, feeling her tense as he did so. Denied her lips with a simple turn of her head, Bran ignored the hurt and kissed her neck. Bran was as slow and gentle and kindly as his desire would allow and when he was finished, he kissed Seraphimé deeply. The sun set and darkness fell over the house.

Bran, however, could not sleep. He lay on his side and let the loneliness and uncertainty wash over him. He had what he desired; yet it did not fulfil him.

Seraphimé had been obliging, but it was not desire that made her lie with him. She had lain with him out of duty; cold, unfeeling duty. Now Bran lay on his bed, feeling alone and guilty. He curled into himself and willed himself to sleep.

* * * *

Bran awoke in the late morning. He did not remember falling asleep. With a grunt, he rolled himself out of bed. He looked back. Seraphimé was still on the bed asleep. Even now, she took his breath away. Being as quiet as possible, Bran dressed himself. Before he left the room, he leant over Seraphimé's sleeping form and kissed her gently on the cheek. She barely stirred. Bran left.

As soon as the door closed behind Bran, Seraphimé opened her eyes. She had not wanted to face Bran that morning. She was miserable and couldn't bear to see his wide, hopeful eyes. It angered her. She hated it.

Most of all, she felt guilty — guilty for not being able to love this man who was so kind to her, guilty for hating him for his kindnesses. She was so torn between the pieces of herself that it drove her to tears, and for the remainder of the morning, she allowed herself the luxury of a crumpled composure.

Later that afternoon, Amwyl arrived to rouse Seraphimé and teach her all she needed to know about a wife's duties. The marriage had been so hastily arranged that she had not had time to do so before the celebration.

Seraphimé learnt quickly, and was glad for Amwyl's company. Amwyl was sympathetic and kind and did not meddle too much in Seraphimé's private affairs. She also often brought along sweet cakes and hot flower brew and they talked.

Amwyl was most concerned that Bran treated her well, and Seraphimé kindly assured her that she had no cause for complaint. That much was true. Bran was a kind and considerate man. He always treated her gently. Still, Seraphimé found that she had little love to spare for him, though she was accommodating and dutiful in every respect.

Bran often visited his mother and aunt, asking them questions about what pleased women. He strived with great effort to please Seraphimé, but his gifts would often go unused or unwanted. Even still, he swore to honour his wedding vows, to remain true to her.

He took on no other wives, despite his father's counsel, and worked every day for one of Seraphimé's precious, rare smiles. Just one would light his heart for an entire week.

The effort began to show on Bran's young features. His fretting over her affections wore a line of worry into his brow and permanent wrinkles about his eyes. Amwyl watched sadly. She could do nothing but lend her ear and counsel.

Seraphimé and Bran both were terribly lonely.

Twenty-Eight

"*H*ear that, deer-man?" the crone said as another desperate howl filled the private world of the Lord of the Hunt.

"Go away, hag," he said.

The old Osprey clanswoman cackled. "Or else what? You gonna kill me? I'm already dead, m' Lord. Can you kill me twice?"

The Lord of the Hunt growled at the crone and she smiled impishly in return, all the while her green eyes sparkling merrily.

"That's my granddaughter," she said, pointing in the direction of the sound of the howls. "And she's crying."

The wolf had been howling nightly since the Lord of the Hunt had sent Seraphimé away to wed the Greyl Prince. The howling was filled with a heart-wrenching note of desperate longing.

"It cannot be helped."

The woman grunted. "You're the one who sent her away," she said. "It could've been helped."

"She is another man's now."

"Also your doing."

The Lord of the Hunt threw his hands in the air and shook his head.

The old woman sighed. "You love her," she said. It was not a question.

"In my fashion," the Lord of the Hunt replied haughtily. His tone was insincere, sounding as if he said it only to silence the woman.

The old woman laughed again. "Then tell me, why, if you do not care for her, do you think of her? Why do you miss her? Why is it snowing here when it ought to be summer?"

The Lord of the Hunt scowled.

"You love her."

"Enough!" he barked. The woman fell silent. "Without that union the tundra does not stand a chance!"

The old woman sighed and scrambled down from the rock. She placed her papery hand on the Lord of the Hunt's shoulder. "I know you did not mean to love her," she said. "But you do now, and you wound yourself as much as you wound her."

The Lord of the Hunt shook his head and set his jaw. "It cannot be helped."

"She is the Tundra Wolf, my Lord. You know it as well as I."

The Lord of the Hunt nodded. "Yes," he said at last. "She is."

The crone sighed. "What will you do?"

"I will wait."

"For how long?"

"As long as I have to. Forever if I must. She is...." The Lord of the Hunt could not find the words to describe how he felt. He did not need to.

"I know, my Lord. I know."

* * * *

Seraphimé entered the study quietly. So quietly, in fact, that Bran barely heard her. Only an accidental glance from his scrolls informed Bran of her presence. He smiled warmly.

"Otsana," he said.

"You called for me?"

"I did. It occurred to me the other day that you have been speaking my language every day since you first learnt it. I, on the other hand, haven't been speaking yours."

"You haven't learnt it properly."

Bran smiled. "I mean to remedy that. In this house, at least until I'm comfortable with the Sierran language, you will speak exclusively your own tongue. That way I'll be forced to learn."

Seraphimé blinked in surprise.

"I also mean to document it."

"Document what?"

"Your language. That way I can teach it to others."

"To what end, my Lord?"

"Please, Otsana, call me by name."

"Very well, Bran. To what end?"

"So that the men I take with me to the Great Gathering will be able to speak it comfortably."

"If they speak Touan, the Osprey clan knows it."

"That's not the point, Otsana," Bran said. *The point is to make you happy.*

"The point is, a husband should be able to communicate well with his wife's family and it would help expedite things if I didn't have to continually say the same thing twice over."

Seraphimé almost smiled. "I could teach them, my... Bran."

"I am your Bran," Bran quipped with a quick smile. "And that is not a bad idea. The snows will start soon, and the men will have nothing to do."

"Have you selected your men?"

"Uh, no. Not yet. I was thinking I might hold a contest in your honour, and those who win would be selected to accompany us to the Great Gathering."

"In my honour?"

"When is your birthday?"

"The Day of the Dead."

Bran blinked. "Really?"

"Truly."

He grinned. "Perhaps not the best day to have a contest of arms."

Seraphimé did smile at that. "I would think not."

"Then we'll hold it before. The middle of next moon, perhaps."

Seraphimé smiled again. The Touans and the Greyls both had taken to counting time in terms of the light, but the Sierran tribesmen still counted time by the nights. For them, the day began when the sun set, and ended at sundown the following day. Without realising it, Bran found himself speaking in Sierran terms when it came to time.

"That will do. It should not be too cold for your men then."

Bran laughed softly. "In the tundra?"

Seraphimé nodded. "Though, the ice will have already come."

"Very well. It is settled. A contest to decide who is to come with us."

"Have you told them?"

"Told them what?" Bran asked innocently. He knew perfectly well what.

"The contents of our marriage contract."

"Um... no."

Seraphimé's mouth turned down in disapproval.

"Politics is a strange game, Otsana." Bran explained hurriedly. "If they know you married me just for the warriors, they will not be willing to help. But if they think we married and then your people just happened to find themselves in trouble, they will rally to your cause without a single thought."

"That is lying."

"No, it's just not telling the truth. It'll get us your warriors without any opposition, Otsana."

Seraphimé sighed. "Then I cannot object."

Bran smiled, allowing himself the small pleasure of examining Seraphimé's face once more. He could do so a thousand times over and he would never tire of it.

Seraphimé was immediately uncomfortable. "Will that be all?"

"Yes."

Seraphimé turned to leave.

"Otsana?"

"Yes?"

"I love you." Bran had said it hundreds of times since the day they were wed. He never expected her to respond in kind, though every time she did not, it cut him deeply.

She looked helplessly at Bran, and seemed to be struggling to find voice enough to say the same.

"It's all right, Otsana," Bran said softly. "I don't want you to say it unless you truly mean it."

Seraphimé closed her mouth and bowed before wordlessly exiting the study. Bran closed his eyes a moment to guard from the tears that threatened.

I love you, he thought fiercely. *One day you will love me too.*

* * * *

"Did you hear?" Alam asked his brother Algar over dinner one evening.

"Hear what?" Algar replied.

"One of the princes of the Baveii has married a woman from the northern tribes. They said she had walked all the way south from the ice coast and collapsed at the prince's feet."

Algar grunted.

"Poor girl," Alam continued. "I imagine the Ottals have destroyed her clan."

Algar looked at his brother. Alam shrugged. "Why else would a northern woman be wandering the southern wilds alone?" he replied to his brother's unasked question.

"What's her name?"

"Who?"

"The northerner. What's her name?"

"Ossa, or something to that effect."

Algar grunted again. Despite their shared heritage, the Greyls and the Touans were often at odds with one another. The Baveii tribe was one of the friendlier of the warrior-pastoralists, but that did not stop the occasional raid. It was useful for the Touans to keep a careful eye on the Greyl tribes, most notably because they had stubbornly refused to convert.

They were proud and belligerent, prone to anger quickly and seemed to have no fear of death. Why fear death if you believed you would live again?

"They are holding a tournament in her honour."

"Are they?"

"Yes. The prize is interesting."

"Is it?"

"Honestly, Algar, you could at least pretend to be interested in what I'm saying."

"I am interested, little brother."

Alam narrowed his eyes in suspicion.

"You should know by now that our eldest brother does not speak much when others are talking, Alam," Brandt noted with a smile.

Alam ignored him. "The prize for winning is the journey with the young Baveii prince to the Great Gathering in the north."

"Why would the Baveii bother with a Great Gathering?"

"Curiosity, I suppose," Alam answered. "It's his wife's family after all. In truth, I would love to see one."

"As would I!" Brandt added. "I can't imagine what it would look like – a gathering of all the northern savages together. It must be quite a sight!"

"They're not savages," Alam and Algar reprimanded Brandt in unison. The two eldest brothers exchanged an irritated look as their youngest sister giggled.

"Mayhap they're looking for an alliance," Algar noted. "If the Sierran fighters were as brave and skilled as you said, the Greyls are likely to want a few."

Alam grunted.

"Perhaps we ought to go to a Gathering."

Alam immediately perked up. "Might we?" He was excited at the prospect. He'd get to see what was promised to him, and Gabija would be there.

"No," their father said flatly, not bothering to look up from his meal. "Can you imagine what the Yellow Robes would say if my sons were out at some heathen festival?"

Algar sighed.

"We could make the excuse for trade," Alam said hopefully.

The King grunted. "Time's past. They'd never buy it, and though you vex me greatly, I rather like seeing your heads on your shoulders. There will be no more excursions to the tundra!"

"We wouldn't lose our heads if we severed our connection with the holy Yellow City," Algar growled to himself.

"Father's just bitter the last expedition didn't go so well," Alam murmured to his older brother.

"I heard that," the King snapped. Algar and Alam grinned at each other before returning to their reading.

Anthia's giggles turned to hiccups.

Twenty-Nine

*N*ews of the contest spread throughout the Baveii's expansive territory quickly. Clan leaders prepared their sons immediately on hearing it. A contest of arms was always fun. There were feasts after the fights, and most of the matches were friendly enough, if people could hold their tempers.

Several years ago, the three Crows of War touched one man and he lost his mind, beheading his own clansmen who had sought to calm him. They had to put three arrows through his chest before he stopped fighting, though he was still thrashing his sword around as he died.

Seraphimé watched with interest as the various warriors arrived. The Kildurrow Clan sent one fighter from each of their families. There were eight in total. Their entourage was enormous, numbering several hundred with armourers included. Octagonal pavilions sprouted like geometric mushrooms outside the Baveii royal city of Hambt where the contests were to be held.

Since the contest was in Seraphimé's honour and arranged by Bran, both were required at the King's side to welcome each of the clans and their contingents.

Seraphimé felt she had never smiled so much in her life and by the end of the second day, her cheeks ached from the effort. Not one of her smiles reached her eyes.

She smiled falsely, something that was uncomfortably close to lying for her. Yet she did so for Bran, who had been nothing but kind to her and had arranged all this so that she might have the warriors she needed to defend her people.

Every noble that arrived cast curious looks at Seraphimé. No doubt they came to see the woman who had so enchanted and ensnared the famously wild Prince Bran. Such a woman must be extraordinary. After all, he had turned down a large number of very beautiful ladies before his marriage.

Not for the first time, Seraphimé looked across the King to Bran and studied his handsome features. Handsome and kind, and yet Seraphimé could not love him. She wondered why that was so, and at the injustice of it.

As if he could sense her gaze, Bran turned to her. Green eyes met blue. He smiled at her and Seraphimé smiled wanly back. When the last greetings for the day were done Bran walked around his father's throne and held out his arm for his wife, who gladly took it, leaning a great deal of her weight on it.

"You look tired, my love," he said, kissing her lightly on the top of her auburn head.

Seraphimé nodded. "My cheeks hurt from false smiles," she said wearily.

"Are you not glad to see them? They come for you."

"Come to stare at me, more like."

Bran grunted. He had noticed the curiosity. "They will not dishonour you," he said. He wasn't as certain of it as he sounded. Many of the men were brothers and fathers of potential brides Bran had slighted.

"Mmm," Seraphimé murmured.

Bran laughed. "You must wear that smile of yours a little while longer. The contest will be over in a fortnight, I promise you."

Seraphimé rolled her eyes and forced her groan into silence.

* * * *

The contest, once it began, was loud and very busy. Men, and a very few women, fought one another on horseback and off. There were contests of archery and javelin from chariots and on horseback and on foot. There were single-combat sword fights, knife fights and fist fights. There were contests of horsemanship without weapons. Chariot races, steeplechases and military manoeuvres performed as if they were a dance.

Seraphimé greatly admired the Baveii cavalry. She watched with keen interest as they performed in unison at the opening of the contests. The horses were very well trained, and the riders more so.

"You like that?" Bran asked during the show.

"It's remarkable," Seraphimé answered breathlessly. She could not take her eyes off the performing cavalry.

The greatest contest of all was the melee that occurred at the end of the fortnight long contest. The objective was to capture the opponent's flag across the field. Bran formed two mock armies, of equal strength, and ensured that the rules were clear.

For the most part, both armies played well together. Men who were struck lightly understood the blow would put them out of action and so quietly made their exit.

One man had the misfortune of falling from his horse during the initial rush and was trampled to death. It horrified Seraphimé and she quite lost her taste for the whole thing after that. It was one thing to watch men in battle. A man dying in play, however, was completely different.

Yet she stayed by Bran's side and clapped when she ought. Bran often lent over to her and explained the names of the ploys each side was using during the fighting. Seraphimé's sharp eyes missed nothing, and sharper mind easily grasped what each trick strove to achieve. Whether or not each ploy worked depended on the skill and tactics of the opposition.

A great roaring cheer erupted as Mace Kildurrow stole the flag from its hold and galloped with great speed back to the beginning position of his army, grinning ear to ear.

Defeated, the opposing side laid down their arms, only to be roughly embraced by their celebrating foes.

Bran, having stood, declared the winner to the adoring crowds. The warriors then retired to bathe and have their wounds tended to before the grand feast that evening.

It was a grand feast indeed. Goose and duck and hens of all kinds were brought forward stuffed with blackcurrants and apricots and summer savoury and glazed in honey and butter. Pork pies and mutton stew and fruits Seraphimé had never seen before sat on the tables. Wine and ale and mead flowed freely. The hall filled with laughter and song.

Seraphimé remained silent, half of her listening to the stringed instruments the Greyls loved so much. She could understand why.

The music they created was thoroughly enchanting. The other half of her listened carefully to whatever snatches of conversation could be heard above the roar and din of the feast.

"... I think he's lost his mind, she's not...."

"... I certainly hope I get selected. I would love to see a Great...."

"... They say she is a witch...."

"...I heard the same...."

".... Well of course he is, how else...."

So many voices from different places, Seraphimé could not imagine who spoke them or their full meaning. She did manage to pick up an undercurrent of resentment towards her, even though her wedding to Bran was legitimate and its true purpose largely unknown. Seraphimé listened more closely.

"... Beautiful...."

".... Yes, I'd...."

"... Fights well. He's his father's...."

Seraphimé gave up and turned instead to her meal. She was hungry, she realised, and the duck with plum sauce was too good to pass over.

"You have a beautiful wife, my Lord Bran," Seraphimé heard the old man at Bran's side tell her husband. "I've never seen anyone so fair."

"Neither have I, Gerard. She is the brightest star in my sky."

Seraphimé felt a pang of guilt, and her appetite left her. She put down her fork and tried her hardest not to listen.

"I am surprised she is not heavy with child yet," the old man continued. She felt Bran tense beside her.

"If she has trouble conceiving, I have a crone who knows how."

"There is no trouble there," Bran said a little tersely. The truth of the matter was that Bran did not often lie with Seraphimé. He still, perhaps foolishly, hoped for the day Seraphimé would desire him enough to take him for more than duty. Until then, he would submit to their passionless lovemaking only as his desires became too great to withstand.

Yet he still refused to lie with any other woman. He had made a vow to be faithful, and he intended to keep it. It was not an easy thing to do. More than one pretty girl was attempting to lure Bran away from his cold prize.

Seraphimé's distress must have been evident, for the woman sitting beside her touched her arm.

"Are you all right, my dear?" she asked with genuine concern.

Seraphimé tried to smile at her and failed.

"You look awfully pale," the woman said again. "And your skin is cold. You might be getting ill."

At that Bran turned around. "Otsana?" he inquired with a furrowed brow. "Are you all right?"

"I'm fine," Seraphimé managed to say.

"You do look pale," Bran noted touching her forehead.

"Please don't fuss," Seraphimé urged. Her annoyance gave her voice an edge.

Bran seemed not to hear her. "Perhaps we should retire. It has been a long fortnight."

"No, Bran," Seraphimé said firmly, despite the fact that she was feeling a little light-headed now. She did not want to admit weakness to anyone, especially not her husband.

Bran glanced at her plate. "You haven't eaten," he noted calmly.

"I'm not hungry."

Bran sighed. "Come then, we'll retire."

"No!" Though it was just a whisper hissed at Bran, it was fierce.

Bran recoiled a little and Seraphimé felt that now familiar pang of guilt again. *When did I become like this? When did I turn into such a bitter old woman?* Seraphimé forced her expression to soften.

"I do not want to insult any of our guests," she said gently. It was a lie. Seraphimé did not give a damn about what the others thought of her, other than being seen as weak.

"If you are unwell, they will understand."

"Bran, I used to command warriors of my own. They would never have followed me anywhere if I even once proved weaker than they. It is the same with your chosen."

"They understand that you are only a woman...."

Seraphimé silenced him with a look that could have frozen the deepest bowels of hottest Hell. Her beautiful lips pressed together to form a thin line. She turned away from Bran and said nothing.

Bran had never angered her like this before. This new development made him nervous. He began to babble. Every word made Seraphimé more and more angry.

"I only mean that, well, women aren't like men. They're not as strong... or...." Bran babbled until the woman beside Seraphimé cut him short.

"My Lord," she said.

Bran continued to babble.

"My Lord!" she said, sharply this time.

Bran shut his mouth. The woman shook her head at him and Bran sank back into his chair flustered and upset. He kicked himself for upsetting his wife on one hand and appearing completely at her mercy on the other. He resented the last a great deal. He clenched his jaw and turned away from his wife.

When the feast was over and most of the revellers drunk and asleep where they sat, Bran and Seraphimé retired to their residence in stony silence.

"Why are you so angry with me?" Bran snapped as they entered their residence. He barely shut the door before the question shot from his mouth.

Seraphimé did not answer. She pretended she did not hear and went to move past him and up the stairs. Bran would have none of it. He grabbed her roughly at the elbow and pulled her back. Seraphimé gasped in surprise and pain as she was forcibly spun around to face him.

"Let me go!" she commanded.

"Answer my question," Bran spat back. He was angry and frustrated. His jaw clenched and unclenched in rapid succession and a vein pulsed in his forehead. His eyes burned with fury when he looked at Seraphimé.

"You're drunk," Seraphimé muttered. "Go to bed and leave me be."

"Not until you answer my question," Bran spat.

Seraphimé's pulse quickened. She forced herself to be calm. An icy bitterness swept through her and she pressed her lips together in spiteful silence.

Bran shook her hard. "Why are you so angry with me?" he demanded again. His gentle blue eyes were now as hard as ice.

Seraphimé was afraid. Gentle as he usually was, Bran was a good deal larger than her, just as skilled and extremely strong. His grip was crushing.

"Let me go," she demanded again, straining to keep the fear from her voice.

With a snarl Bran threw her hard against a wall. Seraphimé fell to the ground. It would have been better for her if she knew how to be weak, if she had stayed on the ground and wept. The tundra wolf, however, was not easily cowed and though afraid she stood and faced her opponent, anger turning her green eyes to fire.

"We were friends before this," Bran growled.

"We were," Seraphimé answered. It was clear from the hostile tone of her voice that she no longer considered him a friend.

Bran snapped. "Curse you!" he snarled. He grabbed her arms and threw her against the wall again, pressing his full weight against her. "All my kindnesses, my gifts, my hopes!"

"I asked for none of it," Seraphimé hissed.

Bran threw her again. This time, Seraphimé struck back. Fast as any snake and with all the cunning of a wolf, she was still no match for the angry bear of a man she railed against.

All it took was one heavy backhand to breach her defences, and she was sent sprawling to the ground, her lip broken and bleeding. The shock of the pain rendered her useless for too long.

Bran was on top of her immediately, wresting her onto her back, his weight pressed against her.

Suddenly, she was back in the tundra, cold and wounded after the brief battle.

Five Ottals laughed cruelly at her vain struggles as they used her. The man atop her grunted like a hog with each violent thrust. Searing pain tore through her loins, and she tried to kick.

The man laughed. "More," he whispered hoarsely. "Do that again."

His tongue travelled from her ear to her mouth and her cries were drowned in a hard, wet kiss. She struck him twice in the side of the head. He laughed again and grabbed her wrist. He forced it back down in to the snow.

"Hold her!" he barked at his friends.

Two sets of hands grabbed her wrists and forced them down and the man on her resumed his grunting and thrusting. His hands now free, they began to roam, tearing the shredded remains of her clothes from her.

His hard hand found her right breast and there it stayed, pushing and squeezing and pulling until he cried out and spasmed against her. He licked her cheek once more before he rolled off her.

Seraphimé forced herself upright before a new set of hands pushed her back down into the snow.

"No you don't," the new assailant said. "It's my turn now."

The men all laughed as he forced himself between her thighs. She struggled and bit and kicked, tears and fear choking her throat and blurring her vision. The shooting pain of the knife wound tore at her side as she fought the rapists. The pain drove the air from her lungs, crushing the breath from her.

Bran's lips were everywhere. He kissed her beautiful skin as his hands groped savagely at her breast and between her perfect thighs. He tore at her clothes, trying to remove them quickly as she struggled weakly, biting and kicking.

It was the most active she had ever been beneath him. It aroused him.

He caught her wrist as it broke free and swung towards his head and forced it down to the ground. Her struggles were weakening.

What am I doing? Bran's mind demanded of his unheeding body. *Stop! Stop! STOP!*

Bran stopped suddenly and let his weight fall on top of her.

Seraphimé ceased her struggling and concentrated instead on trying to draw breath. Bran trembled with the effort of restraint. *It is done now. She will never love me after this. I have destroyed it all.*

"Damn you," he whispered hoarsely in her ear. Then he was gone, off Seraphimé's trembling frame and out the door into the night.

Seraphimé's senses returned slowly. Her vision cleared as the tears slowly died away. She realised that she was not in the tundra, though she felt as cold as if she was. She was on the floor in her house in the royal compound in the capital city of Baveii territory. She was far from home, and she was hurt, angry and afraid. Fighting rising bile, Seraphimé curled herself into a tight ball and hid her head in the crook of her arms.

Thirty

𝒜mwyl was on her way to visit the Queen when she noted that Bran's door stood open. It was dark and silent inside, as it ought to be at this hour, yet something felt wrong. Almost timidly, Amwyl approached the house and entered. She did not expect to find what she did.

Seraphimé lay curled on the floor, trembling like a leaf in the autumn wind. Her face was bloodied from a cut lip, and her cheek was swollen and starting to turn purple. Her beautiful red gown was torn. Amwyl gasped in horror and ran to the girl's side.

"Otsana," she breathed, laying her hand on Seraphimé's shoulder. "Otsana, can you hear me? Are you all right?"

Seraphimé lifted her head and looked at Amwyl with desolate eyes.

"Goodness child! What happened?"

Seraphimé shook her head and struggled to push herself up. She cried out in pain as her bruised body protested. The adrenaline of the fight had concealed the extent of her injuries. Amwyl managed to catch her as Seraphimé's strength gave out and she collapsed. The third queen of the Baveii pulled her close as Seraphimé burst into tears. The tears were short-lived though. She simply did not have the energy for them.

"Let's get you upstairs and into a bath," Amwyl said gently.

Seraphimé nodded and, with considerable help from Amwyl, stood. It was a slow, painful walk up the stairs, but Seraphimé did not complain. Amwyl drew Seraphimé's bath personally, helped her undress and settled her into the water. Amwyl washed Seraphimé's face first. Though she was tender, Seraphimé could not help but wince as the kindly woman tended to her cut lip.

"Did Bran do this?" Amwyl demanded.

Seraphimé turned her eyes down at the bathwater and did not answer. Silence was all the confirmation Amwyl needed. She paused in her work, horrified. She had not raised such a man, or so she had thought. She sighed and put down her cloth.

"I'll get some Sooth Flower and make you a tea. Soak awhile. It'll help the ache."

Seraphimé watched Amwyl go and then tried to do just that. Seraphimé could not relax in the water. Her skin crawled and her stomach rolled. She felt unclean.

Taking up Amwyl's cloth, Seraphimé set to work, scrubbing herself hard. The efforts turned frantic as memories of violence raced through her mind. The more she scrubbed, the filthier she felt. She scrubbed until her soft skin was rubbed raw.

Amwyl returned in time to stop Seraphimé from drawing blood. She immediately put aside the tea and ran to Seraphimé, catching her frenetic hands and pulling her close to stop her struggles. Amwyl was surprisingly strong.

"There, there," she soothed when Seraphimé cried out in anger and grief. "It's all right now. It's all right. I'm here. Come on. Time to get out of the tub."

Seraphimé slumped in defeat. Calm once more, she nodded and stood. Amwyl lovingly wrapped a soft towel around her and dried her off. She applied a salve to calm the scratches Seraphimé had given herself and helped the girl dress. She supported Seraphimé the short walk to the bed and piled pillows behind Seraphimé's back before pouring a cup of steaming Sooth Flower tea.

"This will help calm you and aid your sleep," Amwyl said.

Seraphimé nodded, but still did not speak. Amwyl sat with her for a time as Seraphimé sipped the brew. She had not finished the cup before her eyes started closing of their own accord.

Amwyl smiled sadly and gently took the cup away. She rearranged the pillows and gently stroked Seraphimé's face.

"Sleep now, Otsana." She said gently. "Sleep. It will all be better in the morning, you will see."

Seraphimé soon fell in a deep, drugged sleep. Nothing would wake her this night.

* * * *

Bran did not know where he was going. Hurt and anger drove his feet forward, plunging into the darkness unheeding. Were he to come across a bluff, he might well have walked over its edge unawares in his current state. He wished he might. Better the peaceful sleep of oblivion than the turmoil that now burned deep in his living chest.

When he was calm enough to take stock of his surrounds, he realised that he was beyond the walls of his oppidum, amidst the tall mounds of the burial grounds. He recalled that Seraphimé came here often when she wished to be alone, and it was here that she had consented to marry him.

And what did she get for her sacrifice? Bran thought bitterly. *What have I done?*

As soon as he asked that question of himself, the tears came, hitting him like blows from a war hammer. They felled him, and the bear sank to his knees and hung his head.

"I'm sorry," he whispered. "I'm so, so sorry."

He did not sob, or keen. He simply knelt and let the tears stream down his face as he stared listlessly at the mound before him. This place felt suddenly sad, its mood changing to match his own.

Normally he did not take heed of these graves, but Otsana often spoke of this place. She said that it was restful. There were no angry spirits. Sometimes, she said, she could hear the sounds of feasting, laughter and the clink of drinking horns.

Bran could hear none of that. Yet he felt something, something outside of himself. He felt a deep, external sadness that pressed on his shoulders even as his own misery squeezed at his heart. Had his own ancestors heard his pain and were now grieving for him?

He had never believed in the spirits of the ancestors lingering to help or hinder him as Otsana did. Yet tonight, he needed someone near. He tried something he had never tried before. He spoke to the dead.

"I've done a terrible thing," he said quietly. "Such a terrible thing to the woman I love. Gods help me. I love her so much. But she doesn't love me." Bran broke down again, and this time he did sob, though he tried to be strong and fight the tears. "And now she never will," he whispered when at last he was in control of himself again.

"Gods, what I've done…"

Bran felt ill. Bile churned in his stomach and a sour taste filled his mouth. He buried his head in his hands and fought the urge to be sick everywhere. If the ancestors did hear and were watching, he doubted very much they'd appreciate such a gift. When he had recovered enough he lifted his head again.

"Help me. Help me make it right."

Stony silence answered his plea and Bran became strangely aware of the cold blade tucked into his boot. He looked down torpidly before drawing the blade out. It seemed to glow in the light of the half moon. Blankly, as if he were not quite in his own body, he rolled up his left sleeve. He placed the tip of the knife on the inside of his forearm near his elbow.

"I vowed to be faithful," he said as he pressed the blade into his arm. The pain, though sharp and severe, carried with it a strange catharsis. "And to that I hold."

He began to pull the blade up towards his wrist. Three vows he swore as he slowly pulled the blade through his own flesh. "I vow to love her. I vow to honour her…." The last vow was the most difficult to make.

"I vow to free her."

Bran withdrew his blade and watched distantly as the blood flowed freely from his wound. He followed the line of blood as it ran down his forearm, pooled a moment in his palm before sliding through his fingers and onto the sacred earth of the burial ground.

A gentle breeze blew then, lifting the oppression that hung on Bran's heart like a yoke. He closed his eyes and smiled. When he opened them again, a small grey line in the sky told him that dawn was coming. With a sigh, he put away his knife and turned to go home. The blood loss spun his head like a top, but still he managed to find his way.

* * * *

Amwyl walked wearily down the stairs, carrying the tea. No sooner had she set the tray down on the small table that stood at the foot of the stairs than Bran appeared in the doorway, looking exhausted.

"Bran!" Amwyl exclaimed, running to him. "Bran, what happened?" She moved to take his arm, but Bran pulled it out of the way. It was then she noticed his gash.

"What happened?" she demanded more insistently.

"Where is she?" Bran asked his mother. His tone was calm and kind, and his eyes gentle and sad.

Amwyl could not imagine that he could ever have done Seraphimé any harm.

"She's sleeping upstairs."

Bran moved before his mother finished speaking. He moved quietly and purposefully, with Amwyl close behind. She did not follow him into the bedroom, but watched carefully from the open door.

Bran went immediately to Seraphimé's side and sat down. The girl barely stirred. Amwyl watched as Bran brushed loose strands of Seraphimé's beautiful auburn hair away from her face. He simply watched her for a time, his expression melancholy. With a small sigh, he bent over and kissed Seraphimé on her forehead and quietly made his exit, closing the door behind him. He turned to his mother.

"I hurt her," he said quietly, casting his gaze to the floor.

Amwyl was stunned into silence. Bran sniffed and looked up. He looked so lost that Amwyl could not help but fold her arms around him. Bran accepted the embrace gladly, wrapping his unbloodied arm around his mother.

"Did she cut you?"

Bran shook his head. "I did," he said quietly. "As recompense."

"Bran!"

"I'd do it a thousand times over if it meant I could undo what I have done. Mother..." he choked.

Amwyl sighed. "Come," she said gently. "Let me tend to your arm."

Bran allowed his mother to lead him back downstairs. He sat quietly as she cleaned, stitched and bandaged his arm. Bran's eyes were hazed and distant as he sat deep in thought. Amwyl observed him carefully. In just one night he seemed to have aged a decade.

"Tell me what happened," she said when she was finished.

Bran did, leaving nothing out, except his strange ritual in the burial grounds. He felt foolish speaking about it, though it had moved him deeply. When he was done, Amwyl shook her head in disbelief and dismay.

"Oh, Bran!" she murmured.

"I know," Bran replied softly.

"She may divorce you for what you have done. I do not think I blame her."

"Nor would I," Bran replied. "If that is what she wants, then I can naught but let her. I do not know what madness possessed me. It is right that I should suffer for it."

"Bran," Amwyl said, taking his hand. "I will speak to her for you."

"Don't," Bran said. "This was all my doing, and I am a man grown. Whatever happens now, I will accept it."

Amwyl wondered briefly how it was possible for her to be both appalled and proud.

"Mother?"

"Yes, Bran?"

"Will you stay a while? Otsana will probably not want to even see me for some time. I fear that she will get lonely. You and her are friends. She may appreciate your company."

Amwyl smiled and nodded.

"Good," Bran said. "I will prepare your room." He stood, or tried to. The blood he lost affected him more than he thought it would. His head swam and he swayed dangerously. In an instant Amwyl went to his side.

"You're in no fit state to do anything. You need to eat some and then sleep a lot. I can prepare my own room. Come, let me take you upstairs."

Bran grunted. "I'll sleep on the cushions down here."

Amwyl nodded. Her son's pale face and gently swaying body indicated that he might not make it up the stairs. She helped him over to the cushions and lay him tenderly down, then left to fetch a blanket.

When she returned, Bran was sound asleep. She laid the blanket over him, kissed him gently on his cheek, then retired upstairs. She found that she was exhausted herself and fell rapidly to sleep.

* * * *

Amwyl awoke the next morning to bright sun and singing birds. When she crept downstairs to check on her son, she found him awake, staring blankly up at the ceiling.

"Bran," she said softly.

Bran sat up quickly and immediately regretted it. He pressed his palm into his forehead. He grunted in pain as Amwyl sat by her son's side.

"Otsana?" he asked.

"Still asleep. Sleep brought on by tears is a deep and long one. She will not wake for a while."

Bran nodded and pulled his long legs up to his chest. "My head," he mumbled.

"Well, you need to eat and then it's back to bed."

Bran glared at her, though his lips twisted into a half-smile. "A man grown?" he asked wryly.

Amwyl laughed. "Yes, but first and foremost my child. Now lie back. I'll fetch the servants."

His morning meal prepared, Bran rose and stumbled to the table. He had not yet finished eating when the bath was ready. He sunk gratefully into the warm water and allowed the servants to scrub him down. Half the morning had passed in the blink of an eye.

Bathed and dressed, Bran ate a small meal, then returned to his make-shift bed. Before long, he was soundly asleep again on the cushions on the floor.

"Why is he sleeping there?" one bold servant asked Amwyl.

"Lady Otsana is ill," Amwyl answered simply. She knew that the servant did not believe her and that soon there would be talk of a rift in Bran's marital bliss, but that did not concern her. Chances were, Seraphimé would divorce Bran soon in any case and then everyone would know. With a sigh, Amwyl went upstairs to check on her.

Even grief-induced sleep could not survive the commotion of the royal compound in the morning. Seraphimé was awake, though she had not risen from bed. She looked tired and drawn when Amwyl greeted her. Her left cheek was still swollen and had turned a terrible, mottled purple.

Amwyl sighed. Her son had done that, her seemingly gentle child. She smiled encouragingly at Seraphimé and sat by her in her bed, stroking her hair.

"Bran is downstairs," she said quietly. "Sleeping on cushions in the lounge."

Seraphimé's eyes closed and her forehead creased a little.

"According to our laws, Otsana, you have grounds for a divorce, if you want it."

Seraphimé's eyes fluttered open and she turned her head to look at Amwyl. Her expression was puzzled. "You want me to divorce your son?"

Amwyl smiled a little. "I want you to do what's best for you. I think of you as a daughter, Otsana, and I would never tell my daughter to stay with a man who has struck her."

Seraphimé smiled. She reached out and took Amwyl's hand. The gesture touched Amwyl deeply.

"I am hungry," Seraphimé said.

Amwyl nodded. "I'll tend to you myself. Would you like another bath?"

Seraphimé nodded. "Please."

Amwyl left and soon returned with a warm breakfast of cumin-spiced fish wrapped in thin strips of pork, heavy dark bread and a large cup of honeyed milk. Seraphimé surprised herself with her hunger and ate it quickly while Amwyl prepared a rose-petal strewn bath. Soon the room was filled with the scent of roses.

Her hunger satisfied, Seraphimé allowed Amwyl to help her bathe. Amwyl tutted and tsked as she removed Seraphimé's nightclothes, revealing large, deep bruises.

Seraphimé ached sufficiently that she needed to lean heavily on Amwyl in order to step into the warm water. She sunk down gratefully. Amwyl set to work, combing through Seraphimé's shining waves of hair and then washing them.

"It must have been quite a fight," Amwyl noted sourly when she spied another bruise on Seraphimé's neck.

Seraphimé smiled a little. "We are matched in skill, but Bran's strength is greater than mine."

"Then you must learn a way to overcome that, for most men are indeed stronger than most women."

Seraphimé nodded. After a time, she spoke again. "I will not have the warriors I require if I divorce him, will I?"

Amwyl paused. "A divorce renders the contract null and void. You each will receive what of yours you brought into the marriage and exactly one half of the property accumulated afterwards."

Seraphimé nodded. "Then I will remain his wife," she said quietly.

"Are you certain, Otsana?"

Seraphimé nodded. "I came here in the hopes that I might return home with something to help my people fight the Ottal raiders. The Baveii have offered me their warriors. I cannot turn that down. Not for any price. Bran was gentle to me before. Perhaps he will be again."

"Bran is not a bad man," Amwyl said quietly. "I do not understand what possessed him to strike you."

"He had a lot to drink at the feast," Seraphimé replied. "And I had angered him."

"That is not an excuse."

"No, it is not."

Amwyl sighed as she began to anoint Seraphimé's hair with rose oil. "I have a salve to massage into those bruises. They will fade faster."

Seraphimé smiled. "Thank-you. It will not do to present myself to Bran's warriors bruised before battle."

Amwyl wanted to hiss in anger. Instead she said darkly, "Perhaps you should, and shame him for what he has done."

"What would that achieve but to sew more discord?"

Amwyl nodded. Seraphimé was right. It would do nothing but create yet more tension between the couple and give ammunition to those who were sceptical about the union.

"Out of the water," she commanded.

The girl did as she was told without complaint and struggled out of the tub with Amwyl's help. "Go lie on the bed, dear, and I'll fetch the salve."

Seraphimé nodded and retired to bed, finding herself exhausted once again. She was almost asleep by the time Amwyl returned. In tender silence, Amwyl dipped her hands in the wooden jar of thick black muck that smelled a little like mint and a little like rot. She rubbed it firmly into all of Seraphimé's bruises. A few times Seraphimé sucked in her breath and recoiled, but she never once complained.

Not long after Amwyl was finished, Seraphimé fell to sleep. Amwyl washed her hands and went downstairs to break her fast. She found Bran awake.

She laughed. "You wake, she sleeps. She wakes, you sleep."

Bran smiled. "It might be better that way."

Amwyl grunted and went to the table where, she noted happily, a hot breakfast awaited. Bran joined his mother at the table, sipping Sooth Flower tea.

"How is she?" he asked.

"Bruised," Amwyl replied. Bran winced and dropped his gaze down to the table.

"You split her lip, Bran."

Bran nodded and did not look up.

Amwyl sighed. "She will not divorce you."

That brought Bran's head up sharply. He looked astounded.

"She needs your men to save her people. She will do anything for them, it seems. But the gods help me, Bran, you take advantage of that and I'll beat you myself!"

Thirty - One

$\mathscr{I}$t only took a few days of Amwyl's careful attention for Seraphimé's bruises to heal and vanish. It took a great deal longer for Bran to face Seraphimé. In that time, Bran had informed the warriors who would accompany him to the Great Gathering. They prepared for their northern adventure together. Bran found he rather enjoyed their company. They all were intelligent men.

From them, Bran chose three who would be his counsellors. He would rely on their advice him once they learned of the situation the Sierran nomads faced. He did not tell them as much. He simply made sure that they knew he respected their counsel.

Seraphimé instructed the chosen men on the language and customs of her people daily. Not many were able to learn quickly. Seraphimé found herself laughing often at their nonsensical babbling. Her daily lessons with them lifted her mood somewhat. Away from the warriors, however, the tension between herself and her husband remained.

Bran slept downstairs on the lounges and Seraphimé upstairs in the bedroom. Entrusting her own household to her sister Catrin, Amwyl moved in with her son. She was Seraphimé's only company for months.

The rest of autumn passed without event. Early in the winter, Bran and Seraphimé accidentally met in the upstairs hall. Bran immediately froze, his mouth agape.

"My Lord," Seraphimé said softly, bowing a little.

Bran shut his mouth. "Please Otsana, my name is Bran." He spoke gently.

Seraphimé did not look directly at him.

"I'm sorry," Bran blurted. His heart pounded as it had done when he first saw her. She was so beautiful to him that he forgot to breathe.

Seraphimé nodded but still did not look him in the eye. "Please excuse me," she said quietly. She bowed again and then brushed past him.

Bran wanted to groan. She smelled faintly of roses and honey. It woke in him a desire he long thought dead. Turning on his heel, he searched frantically for a place where he would not be disturbed.

The Festival of the Dead, a now hollow ceremony for the Greyls, its meaning and use long forgotten, came and went. Whenever the occasion required both of them to be present, Bran and Seraphimé appeared together, smiling. Servant gossip notwithstanding, they looked to the outside eye as any happily married couple.

It saddened Amwyl to know that all the warmth they displayed in public was lost to frost once they were shielded from the masses. Bran had not slept with his wife for months. Yet he still stoically refused to take anyone else to his bed. Amwyl had surprised herself by suggesting he take a mistress.

Bran had simply touched the scar on his arm absently and shook his head. "I swore a vow," he said.

Amwyl gave up. It seemed to her that Bran did as well.

In public, he stood tall and smiled and laughed. He appeared his wild, carefree self. In private, however, he was sad and defeated.

Amwyl often spied him standing at the bedroom door at night, one palm and his forehead pressed against it, as if he might be able to feel Seraphimé through the thick wood. He did not sleep well without her, waking often. Sometimes he wept in his sleep.

Amwyl worried constantly for him. Seraphimé, however, did not seem to be much affected.

Why would she be? Amwyl reasoned. *The marriage was all but forced on her in the first place.*

"Bran, go speak with her," Amwyl said firmly one late winter evening as Bran poured over the maps of the northern territory. They were long out of date and next to useless. Still, Bran stared at them, trying to figure out the best way to defend the Sierrans against the Ottals.

"And go to bed. You look exhausted."

"Hm?" Bran replied, not listening.

"Go. Talk. To. Her."

Bran looked up. "No. She's happier without me around. Let's leave it that way. We'll have plenty of time to play-act a happy couple when we're on the way to the Great Gathering." His tone was bitter.

"Bran, you are destroying yourself from within."

"Mother, please. I have work to do."

"Do you still love her?"

Silence.

"Bran?"

Bran sighed and put down his quill. He rubbed his face. He sighed again and looked at his mother.

"Yes, Mother. Yes, I still love her. I married her because I love her. She married me because she loves her people."

"And when her people are rescued? Then what?"

"Then I will dissolve the marriage."

That Amwyl did not expect. "*What*?"

"You were right when you said Otsana was a bird who needed to fly free. When all this is over and the men return, Otsana will remain with her people, as she should; as she needs. What right have I to keep her bound to me?"

"You are her husband!"

"And I love her. She is happier free and I am happier when she is happier." Bran's tone softened. "I don't deserve her," he muttered finally.

"Oh, Bran!" Amwyl embraced her son. "You deserve ten thousand of her!"

Bran laughed a little. "Just one of her is enough. If only...." Bran didn't finish the thought. The words choked in his throat and there they died. Amwyl knew, however. Amwyl knew the words he could not say. *If only I hadn't beaten her. If only I hadn't tried to force myself on her. If only she did not love another. If only...*

Amwyl released her son and kissed him gently on the cheek. "Go to bed," she said simply.

Bran smiled sadly. "In a moment."

Amwyl sighed and left, leaving Bran behind to brood by the dying fire.

The following evening, Bran summoned Seraphimé. He did not pull his gaze from the window, beyond which the snow fell in large flakes, when Seraphimé arrived. The servant excused himself quietly, his eyes lit with curiosity.

"Tell me about him," Bran said softly. "Tell me about the man you love."

Seraphimé stood in silence for a long time. She observed Bran in her silence. He looked as if he hadn't slept in days. Dark circles sat under his blue eyes and his hair was dishevelled. She found herself feeling sorry for him, though the anger of his abuse had not yet faded.

"You already know him, my Lord," Seraphimé replied at last.

"Do I?" Still Bran would not look at her.

"Yes."

"How so?"

Seraphimé sighed. She went to one of Bran's books. Though she did not find any use in reading, there were often illustrations that she could relate to. She pulled down a thick volume and riffled through the pages until she came across the illustration she was looking for. Leaving the book open at the appropriate page, she laid it on Bran's desk.

He pulled himself away from the wintry window and looked long at the image Seraphimé had found. It was a drawing of a creature that was neither man nor stag, but both. In one hand he held a torque and in the other a ram-headed serpent. At his feet milled three hounds.

He wasn't quite sure what to make of it. He looked up at Seraphimé in confusion.

Seraphimé smiled sadly. "I told you that it was Inna of the Ice Bear Clan who came to my rescue. That was not entirely true. Inna found me, wrapped in a thick deer-hide cloak, my attackers dead, torn to pieces all around me."

Bran frowned.

"When I lost consciousness, I had a dream. I stood in a clearing. It was lush and green and full of trees. There was a man there. He was tall and had skin the colour of honey. On his head he wore the skull of a great stag, still crowned with its antlers. He had a number of weapons about him, knives made of black glass and a quiver of arrows. We talked a time and he told me his history."

Bran watched Seraphimé in silence. She spoke distantly, as if pulling from her deepest reservoir of memory. It seemed to Bran, by the expression she wore, a sad place.

"While my body lay wrapped in a cloak in the snow, my dreams took me away to him, and while I was with him, I was never wanting of warmth. Inna told me later that he had been hunting a stag and that one night the stag approached him and spoke to him."

"Spoke to him?" Bran's incredulous tone expressed his disbelief.

"He, the deer, and a Black Hound, led Inna to me and Inna took me back to his clan where I remained until I was well enough to journey south."

"To find allies," Bran finished. "A dream, Otsana?"

"I do not expect you to believe me, my Lord."

"My name is Bran, Otsana. Please use it."

Seraphimé looked at the floor.

"Where is he now?"

"Gone," Seraphimé replied. "I do not know where."

Bran could tell from her tone that it was a painful truth she spoke.

A dream? Bran wanted to groan. How was he supposed to compete with a dream?

"I have heard tales of men and women who fell in love with dreams," Bran said gently. "And they wasted away into nothingness, forever unfulfilled."

Seraphimé nodded. "Even so, I love him." There was a short, uncomfortable silence before Seraphimé cleared her throat. "May I be excused, my Lord?"

"Yes," he replied. "You may."

Seraphimé bowed a little. Never once having met Bran's eye, she exited his study. Bran sat sullenly at his desk and pulled the book towards him, studying the image therein.

* * * *

"A god?" Amwyl asked incredulously the following morning.

Bran's mouth twitched. He had never put much store in gods and ancestors. His mother, however, was wildly superstitious. She snatched the book from Bran and stared down at the image. Bran relayed to her all that Seraphimé had said. She stared at him incredulously whenever she wasn't looking down at the image.

"Bran," she said at last. "I know that you do not much believe in tales such as these, but if she's telling the truth…"

"Mother, please. A god?"

"It has happened before."

"Mother…"

"Bran, it could be."

"Then where is he now?"

"The politics of men are not a god's problem, and certainly out of the realm of the First Hunter."

"Then why is he involved with Seraphimé, if indeed this outlandish tale is true?"

Amwyl frowned. "Perhaps he is bound by some ancient promise. You might do well to ask the Wise One. The trees will know, for their memories are long, and the Wise Ones know the language of the trees."

"You sound like a madwoman."

"Stop it Bran! Go ask him!"

Bran sighed. "If you say so."

"I do. I shall go with you."

Bran grunted. His mother's stern gaze might help him keep from bursting into peals of laughter during the conversation, he supposed.

Amwyl and Bran sought the counsel of the court Wise One that same evening. He, like most of his kind, remained removed from society, though he kept a simple house in the royal compound.

Amwyl nervously pulled at her gown and played with her fingers as they approached the small, round house where the Wise One dwelt. They barely reached the doorstep when it swung open, seemingly of its own volition.

"Come in my Lord, my Lady," the Wise One called from inside.

Bran blinked as a light flared and then settled. The bent old man had lit a candle. Bran stepped inside, suddenly cowed. The atmosphere of the place sent chills along his spine.

The Wise One was dressed in his night robe, and looked as though he had just woken. He rubbed the sleep from his eyes and blinked at Bran and his mother.

"You are come seeking truth about the Tundra Wolf, yes?"

"Otsana," Bran replied.

"Yes. Otsana is an old word. It means 'wolf,' Little Crow."

Bran frowned. Only family were allowed to call him by his pet name.

"Well then. What have you come to ask?"

"You tell us, Wise One," Bran grumbled.

Amwyl slapped her son's arm hard and the old man chuckled. He shuffled to the back of his home and took out more candles. Using the one already lit, he started to light more.

"You are troubled because she does not love you," the Wise One said.

"That is common knowledge," Bran replied dismissively.

"Not as common as you might think. The tundra wolf is a consummate actress," the Wise One said with a smile. "And any fool can see that you are still desperately in love with her."

"Well," Bran replied sourly. "She is in love with a dream."

The old man raised one eyebrow and waited in silence.

Bran could not contain himself. "The First Hunter," he blurted.

The old man raised both his eyebrows and looked at Bran in surprise. "Do you know much of the First Hunter?" he asked Bran.

"That he is Lord of the Wilds, and Death and that he helps hunters should the whim take him."

"He is the oldest," the old man interjected. "The oldest of them all. He came before the Bride of Fire, even. He will outlive the last of us, I am certain. It takes a particular cause to rouse him from his slumber. This is an ill omen indeed."

"What do you mean?"

The Wise One shrugged his shoulders and Bran stamped his foot.

"Patience," Amwyl said to him. She turned to the Wise One. "Why would he wake for the people of the tundra?"

The old man shrugged again. "I could ask, but the trees give cryptic answers. Perhaps the reason is not so important. All you need know is that he is aiding the Sierran nomads."

"So are we," Bran muttered. "Or will be shortly."

"Indeed?"

"When the passage north is clear, Otsana and I and some warriors will be joining the nomads at their Great Gathering. We can assess the situation better from there and decide what to do."

"It was in your marriage contract, then?" The Wise One nodded. "I thought as much."

"I'd do it regardless!" Bran snapped hotly.

The old man regarded Bran with eyes that seemed to know too much. "I do not doubt you, boy," he replied coolly. "The Ottals, I fear, will press an attack as soon as they can."

"How did you know it was the Ottals?"

"My ears may be old, Little Crow, but they still hear. I am still welcome on the council that hears of matters that concern the Greyls in general and the Baveii specifically. The movements of the desert men have escaped no one's notice."

Bran grunted.

"Stop pacing, boy, and sit."

Bran ignored him. "There's no use asking you whether you believe her."

"I do not doubt that she dreamt of the First Hunter."

Bran rubbed his temples. "But it was only a dream, right?"

"And what is a dream, Little Crow?"

"Just a dream. It is not real."

"Yet the feelings she has towards the First Hunter, they are real, are they not?"

Bran grunted. "But he's just a dream!"

"A dream that ensured the wolf's survival."

Bran stopped pacing and stared hard at the old man, who kept his expression impassive.

"You do not put enough stock in dreams, Little Crow. I dreamt that a crow landed on my doorstep and when I woke, there you were."

"Coincidence."

"I have had enough dreams to believe otherwise."

"Lucky you," Bran grumbled.

"I dreamt a few nights ago of an old man," the Wise One said. "He carried a spear of stone, but it was clear who he was. Those dark blue eyes of yours run deep in your family."

Bran looked up at the Wise One, startled.

"He said his name was Bran, can you imagine? It seems the Baveii kings felt a kinship with the crow. If we were still living as the Sierran nomads do, no doubt we would learn that we were once the Crow Clan."

"What did he have to say?" Bran asked cautiously.

"He said that you were heard."

"That's all?"

"That's all. He seemed pleased that you remembered him, though."

"I don't."

"You called to him as a kindred spirit. That is remembering."

Amwyl was looking strangely at her son and her gaze fell to the purple scar on his forearm. Bran felt it burn.

"He also said you needn't go to such drastic measures, next time."

Bran scowled.

The old man chuckled. "There are some gods that might require cruel sacrifices, but your own ancestors do not."

"Oh, Bran!" Amwyl whispered.

Bran ignored her, setting his jaw in a typical indication that he was less than impressed. He resolutely said nothing.

"I suspect that the Bran who came to me in my dreams was the first king. The spear seemed ornamental rather than functional." The old man chuckled. "The first sceptre. A stone spear, given by and accepted from the last of the Old Ones in our clan as a token."

"A token of what?"

"That we are now custodians of the earth - she who walks in her dreams in the pelt of a wolf."

Bran started.

"Hmph," the old man grunted. "You aren't as daft as you seem. Yes, there seems to be a connection. The earth may be dreaming now and has chosen her skin."

"Otsana?"

"Perhaps."

"But how? When? *Why*?"

"I cannot be expected to know the will of the tundra, child. All I know is that Otsana is likely her dream and in this dream she chooses to defend the people of the tundra. She has a plan, the Great Mother, but I do not possess the arrogance to presume I know what it is. We must go with her when we can."

"What happens if we choose not to?" Bran asked quietly.

"There have been civilisations in this place long before us; great dynasties that have risen and then fallen, all at her whim. If we displease her enough, we face total obliteration, just as the others that have come before us. Men and gods alike are powerless before the will of our Great Mother."

"Does she… does Otsana know?"

"Know that she is the incarnation of the Great Mother in the mortal realm? I very much doubt it."

"A strange dream," Bran muttered.

"Do you know that you are dreaming when *you* dream?" the Wise One replied.

"Otsana has parents! She was *born!* She has lived almost eighteen *years!*"

"And to one that has lived through eternity, what is eighteen years but a blink of the eye, a short sigh?"

Bran had no answer. He sat down abruptly. "If this is so, Wise One, why does the Great Mother not simply destroy the Ottals with her power?"

The Wise One shrugged. "I do not know. Perhaps she is giving us a chance to prove ourselves. Perhaps she cannot, in her dream state."

Bran snorted.

"Ever dreamt you were falling, Little Crow?"

Bran stared maliciously.

"Can you always command your dream-self to fly?"

Bran turned his head away, quite done with this conversation.

"I thought as much." The old man sniffed sourly. "I think I have answered all your questions as best I can. I am an old man and I beg to return to my bed."

Amwyl stood. "Of course, Wise One. Thank-you for your time." She glowered at Bran.

"Thank-you," he said stiffly, rising from his seat.

The Wise One tilted his head. "You are welcome, Little Crow."

Once Bran was sure he was out of earshot of the old man in his tiny hovel he turned to his mother.

"What rot!" he spat. Behind him, a thin old voice cackled raucous laughter.

"Bran!" Amwyl hissed at her son. "You have no idea what that man knows!"

"He is an old, superstitious fool," Bran replied. "We can't trust his word."

"I would trust his words more than I would my own desires, if I were you Bran. He has been to the Aqyl and back. He has met the First Hunter and the Bride of Fire. He has *seen* things, Bran."

"You don't really believe that do you?"

"If you did not, why did you spill your blood for the ancestors?"

Bran gritted his teeth. "I didn't," he lied.

Amwyl stopped walking and looked at her son.

Bran sighed. "I was upset. It helped. That is all I know."

"You made a blood vow, didn't you?"

Bran grunted.

"Now you're trapped, Bran. Terrible things happen to people who break a blood vow."

"I don't intend to break it."

"I hope not."

"Can we not, Mother?"

Amwyl resumed walking and she and Bran returned to Bran's home without another word uttered.

Thirty-Two

*T*he Tigil Mtsusa had been drunk for close to three months. He sat sourly at one of the long tables in the guildhall, reeking of stale ale and roib. The Guild Master sat across from him in expectant silence.

"They killed Uma," the Tigil slurred. "Bastards."

"You expected to take them without a fight, did you?"

"Those stupid bitches!" the Tigil fumed as if he hadn't heard. "I'll make them pay, I swear it!"

The Guild Master sighed. He was tired of having to deal with this. "Losses are to be expected in this trade. We've had a good crop for two seasons now, it was about time they pulled together a defence."

"And the stag-man?"

"You're not still on about that are you? There is no such thing."

"I've been talking to one, one of those tundra bitches. She says he's a god too. They all say he's a god."

"Gods and ghosts," the Guild Master sighed. "When will you give up that story? I saved you from the Suma, I doubt I'll be able to do the same from the asylum."

"I saw it with my own eyes!" Mtsusa roared. The other members of the guild, now well used to the drunken Tigil, paid his outbursts no heed.

The Guild Master sighed again. "Perhaps you should return to your heartland for a time and rest."

"Don't you try and send me away!" the Tigil growled. "I'm going after those sons-of-bitches as soon as the wet season comes!"

The Guild Master rubbed his face in frustration. "I'll write to your father if I have to."

At this the Tigil narrowed his eyes, looking truly vicious. "Don't. You. Dare."

"You don't leave me much choice, you know."

The Tigil burst into tears unexpectedly, his shoulders shaking with grief. "Don't," he begged. "Please don't."

The Guild Master's brows rose in shock. For all the months of hard drinking and roib-induced rages, he had never before seen the large son of a warlord break like this.

"Ghosts," the Tigil moaned. "Hounds and ghosts. Great Susa, but that place is cursed."

"Then you had best put aside any ideas of riding in alone. We will begin raiding together when the wet comes. We'll be safer from the hounds and ghosts if we stick together."

The Tigil, still in tears, nodded before suddenly dropping his head on the table and snoring fitfully. Feeling uneasy, the Guild Master stood and went to his room.

He knelt before a low table set at the edge of the bed. There, unbeknownst to anyone save himself, stood a small clay idol of a headless woman with swollen breasts and thighs.

"Save us from the Tigil's ghosts," he prayed.

The wolf is there, came the soft response, no more than the whispering of gossamer curtains in the breeze. *Stay away, the wolf is there.*

* * * *

Bran watched Seraphimé the entire first day of the trip. She dressed in the fashion of her people, though in the lighter fabrics of the Baveii to match the warmer climate. She brought with her heavier clothing for the northerly climes as well as a sword Bran had given her as a gift.

Nothing about her appearance suggested that she was a dream of the earth. Bran dismissed the idea often, for it came crawling back into his thoughts repeatedly, like a beaten cur with nowhere else to go. It simply was not possible.

For three days, after each evening camp was set up, there were snow fights. Bran and his men would chase each other like children, laughing and dancing in the still warm air.

The spring snows were light and fluffy, the sort of snow that wouldn't pack well. Snow fights usually consisted of people flinging handfuls of loose snow at each other. The wind, more often than not, would blow the snow into the eyes of the attacker.

For Bran, this frivolity was feigned and empty. Every night he lay in his pavilion, in his bed with his wife. Every night he reached out to touch her, only to lose heart and withdraw. He yearned desperately for her warmth and received only her back. It was no less than he deserved, he reasoned.

Thinking so did not assuage his profound loneliness.

In the daylight hours, he kept up the pretence. If the lords of the Baveii tribe knew that his marriage was less than happy, they would guess the sole reason for the union and frown upon it. They would never offer their warriors to protect his wife's people.

Seraphimé and Bran rarely spoke in the evenings, though in front of the men they talked and smiled as though all was well. It came as a shock to Bran, then, when Seraphimé spoke to him in the evening of the fifth day.

"I feel dishonest," she said at length. "All this lying; it's wrong."

Bran shrugged as he unlaced his boots and watched Seraphimé comb her hair. "It's not exactly lying."

"We're pretending."

Bran smiled tautly. "You are pretending."

Seraphimé turned to him, her green eyes narrowed.

"I don't have to pretend to love you, Otsana. I do love you."

Seraphimé immediately turned away, trying to hide the sudden guilty tears that struck her eyes.

"Don't worry," Bran said gently. "I knew you loved another when I married you. I cannot rebuke you on that score."

Seraphimé stopped brushing and looked down at her hands. "I'm tired," she announced in a whisper. She rose and put away her comb. Without another word, she slid between the sheets, rolling on her side and presenting her back to her husband.

Bran sighed. "Goodnight," he said gently. In silence, he pulled off his boots and slid into the bed.

Once more he reached out to touch his wife, only to draw his hand back at the last moment. In misery, he closed his eyes and fell into a fitful sleep.

It continued this way for the many months it took to travel north into the Sierran Tundra. The miles and physical proximity did nothing to unite Seraphimé and her husband. She remained as the tundra remained, frozen, despite outward appearances. When they reached the edge of the tundra, Seraphimé smiled genuinely for the first time. Bran could understand why.

He had never been this far north. He found the scenery simply spectacular. Wildflowers of every sort bloomed lush and bright over the grey-green rocks. The winds kept the snow from covering the rocks. Even so, it sparkled clean and white in crevices and cracks.

The sun shone brightly, though it did nothing to lift the chill in the air. The temperature had Bran and his men wrapped in as many layers of wool as they could manage without suffocating themselves. The terrain was largely flat, despite the rocks, with the occasional small hill scattered here and there.

"Do you know where in the tundra we are?" Bran asked Seraphimé. He had spoken to her the entire journey in the Sierran tongue and had insisted his men do the same so they kept practiced.

"I think this is the Ouruq Clan's territory," Seraphimé replied.

"Will we be allowed to cross?"

Seraphimé nodded. "All the clans are now on their way to the centre of the tundra," she replied. "During this time, all lands are open to all clans. We will not be hindered."

Bran grunted and squinted up at the sky. "The Gathering happens at summer solstice?"

"Yes."

"We only have a few weeks then."

"That is not a concern. The Ouruq Clan territory borders on that of the Osprey Clan, and both are close to the centre. We should reach the gathering in a fortnight."

"Which way?"

"This way," Seraphimé said with a smile. She nudged her horse forward.

Bran followed. "How do you know?"

"We never forget the tundra," Seraphimé replied. "It's in our blood."

Bran shrugged and let it be. He certainly did not know the tundra, so he was content to accept the word of a person who did.

They found the way slow-going. The delicate hooves of the southern-bred horses had difficulty over the treacherous rock of the tundra. Not two hours into the ride, a packhorse trapped his hoof and his ankle broke. The beast squealed in pain. It was terrible to bear. Bran quickly put the animal out of its misery.

They lost time rearranging the baggage and night fell quickly. They had not gotten far.

"Perhaps we will take three weeks," Seraphimé noted wryly. Bran laughed.

* * * *

The journey did take three weeks. As they approached the site of the Great Gathering, Bran noted with interest the array of onion-shaped pavilions. They sprawled all over the wide, shallow valley in a vaguely circular pattern.

In the centre of the valley stood a crumbling ruin, now reduced to a few standing stones, most of which had lost their lintels.

The paved ground at the centre of the ruin, overrun with wildflowers and stunted shrubs though it was, was still clearly visible. Bran marvelled at the intricate mosaic of expertly cut coloured stone that formed the paving of this ancient plaza. It did not depict anything in particular, though Bran could recognise several symbols that were considered sacred amongst the Wise Ones of the Greyls. Bran thought back to his tutor. He smiled slightly at the thought of the old man's life-long desire to attend a Great Gathering.

Bran watched as a large train of people streamed in from the north, dismounted and immediately began setting themselves up. He turned to look at Seraphimé, who seemed, for the first time Bran could remember, at ease and happy.

"Otsana?" a young voice called when Seraphimé and her entourage crested the hill nearest to the centre of the valley.

Despite the time apart, Seraphimé would have recognised that voice anywhere. She scanned the horizon until she found the voice's sightless owner.

"Ur!" she replied.

The boy came running. He ran directly to Seraphimé over the rocky terrain without a single misstep.

Bran marvelled at how he managed to do so completely blind. Still he succeeded and, without seeing, flung himself into Seraphimé's open arms. Bran had not noticed her dismount.

"Oh, Ur!" Seraphimé said, clutching the boy tightly. Many heads turned and almost the entire settlement watched the reunion. Bran felt uncomfortable.

"I knew you were coming!" Ur said. He would have been crying if he still had eyes. "I had a dream. The wolf ran north with a flock of crows at her heals. I knew it was you! But the crows?"

"I have indeed brought crows," Seraphimé said. She was denied the chance to fully explain. A man emerged from one of the closer pavilions. The moment he spied Seraphimé he stopped dead.

"Otsana!" he called.

Seraphimé looked up and smiled. A surge of jealousy ripped through Bran. She had never smiled like that for him.

"Otsana," the man said again, scrambling over the rocks just as nimbly as the blind boy had.

"Inna," Seraphimé greeted with a laugh. She laughed harder when the short, but strongly built man lifted her off the ground and swung her around in a tight embrace.

Though Bran desperately wanted to take the man's head off, he had no choice but to smile and pretend he was happy his wife had found her friends again.

"Inna, where is Old Mother?" Seraphimé asked.

The man named Inna immediately fell silent.

Ur answered. "She did not survive the journey south."

Seraphimé's heart broke. She loved the old Shamanka. She pulled Inna and Ur, now the last remaining survivors of the Ice Bear Clan, into a tight embrace.

"I am so sorry," she whispered.

Inna shrugged. "It was her time," he said easily, though his voice choked a little.

"Seraphimé?" another voice, a woman's voice, enquired. Though spoken quietly, the voice could be heard over the gathered crowd.

Seraphimé turned and faced its owner. Her sister, Gabija, stood only a few paces away, her lieutenant at her right shoulder. The Chieftain of the Osprey Clan could do naught for a full five minutes but stand and stare.

"Gabija," Seraphimé replied. Relief and joy cast tears into her eyes and tightened her throat.

Gabija burst into tears. She ran to her sister and embraced her tightly.

"I thought you were dead?" she murmured. "How?"

Seraphimé did not let go of her sister to reply. The tears that stung her eyes now streamed freely down her cheeks. "It's a long story, Gab."

"But you were dead. Oh gods, we *left you*! How could we?"

"Hush Gab," Seraphimé replied. "You did what was right."

Bran was confused. "Seraphimé?" he asked to no one in particular.

Ur's sharp ears heard. "Otsana was *his* name for her. Are you a crow?"

Bran had to wrestle with himself for a brief moment before he could answer. He knew exactly who *he* was – Seraphimé's dream lover. She had presented herself as his creature right from the off. Bran never had a chance.

"Yes, Ur," Seraphimé said, noting Bran's inability to talk for the moment. She detangled herself from her sister's arms. "He is a crow. His name is Bran."

All eyes turned curiously towards Bran and his men.

Seraphimé hesitated a moment. "He is my husband."

Gabija was astounded and did not care to conceal it. She stared at her younger sister with wide eyes and an open mouth. "You got *married*?"

Seraphimé shrugged. "It was duty," she mumbled quietly.

Bran heard it nonetheless, and though it was true, it hurt. The wound flashed across his eyes and vanished the instant it came. Gabija, however, did not miss it. Looking at her sister with an expression that asked a mountain of questions, Gabija turned to Bran. She embraced him with genuine warmth.

"Welcome, Bran Crow," she said in Touan.

Bran rather hesitantly returned the embrace. It had been a very long time since a woman had touched him, let alone held him. He was nervous about what that might do to him, especially since Gabija was almost as beautiful as her sister.

"Thank-you," he murmured.

If Seraphimé was frozen stone, Gabija was warm honey.

Gabija seemed surprised that Bran could speak the Sierran language. She smiled slowly. "Welcome to the Osprey Clan. You and your men will camp with us. Have you pavilions?"

Bran nodded. "Yes, we have brought all our own provisions."

"Wonderful! My men will show you where to set up."

Gabija's lieutenant, hitherto silent, grunted and motioned for Bran to follow. Bran looked at Seraphimé.

Gabija noted the unspoken longing in his dark blue eyes. She frowned slightly at her sister as Bran led his men past. She took her younger sister's hands.

"Come with me," she said. "We were about to eat."

"Otsana?" Ur asked from Inna's arms. "Can we come?"

Gabija looked enquiringly at her sister.

"Ur and Inna of the Ice Bear Clan. They saved my life."

Gabija turned to Inna and the young boy with no eyes. "The Ice Bear Clan? We thought you long dead. No matter, I owe you the world for saving my sister. You and your clan are welcome to camp with us."

Inna smiled a little. "We are the clan."

Gabija blinked in surprise.

"It will all be told on the first night."

Gabija nodded. "I'll send someone to help relocate your pavilion."

"Not necessary, Chieftain. There isn't much that one man and one boy can bring," laughed Inna.

Gabija smiled and nodded. They parted ways and Gabija walked with Seraphimé to her pavilion, where steaming cups of honeyed sage tea sat waiting. They talked and laughed together well into the evening, joining Bran and the rest of the Osprey Clan once the sun set.

Not surprisingly, in Bran's esteem, Seraphimé chose to sit with her sister and the Lieutenant rather than her husband. Gabija silently noted it, but did not comment. Bran behaved as if nothing was wrong, as if he had every confidence that he was not losing his wife. He did well to hide the fact that his heart felt like it was trying to tear its way out of his chest with many-barbed claws.

Thirty-Three

For the two days that followed things remained much the same. Seraphimé remained close to her sister and Inna and Ur. Bran chose to remain with his men. He did well in his efforts to hide his jealousy. So far removed from home and his mother's guidance, he found it difficult to cope.

He mused on that very thought as the clan leaders gathered in the ancient stone-strewn plaza and sat in a circle. Their kinsmen milled behind them as they tried to find a good vantage point to view the proceedings.

Bran watched with interest as eight young women dressed in grey smocks stoked a fire in a hearth that sat in the middle of the circular plaza. Three tall torches were lit from the fire and driven into the rocks that surrounded the plaza.

Then the Shamans and Shamankas from each clan gathered around the fire to set alight long thick herb ropes. The ropes smouldered and smoked, giving a spicy, sweet fragrance, but never caught ablaze.

Drums and small pipes began to play. The Shamans and Shamankas danced around the fire, chanting and singing.

Bran, invited into the circle, forced his way to Seraphimé's side. He sat between her and Gabija. Seraphimé and Gabija both chanted back the appropriate responses. They sang all the songs. Bran, lost and bewildered, found himself flowing in and out of a trance-like state as the rites progressed.

Before long, Bran did not see Shamans dancing, but animals circling around the fire. There was the many-tusked mammot, the shaggy tundra boar, ouruq, elk, and strangely enough, a whale, amongst other animals that writhed and danced around the flames.

Bran looked down at himself, and noted with dim shock that he was no longer himself, but a large crow with yellow eyes. He sat beside a large, whitish-grey wolf, who stared intently at the parade of animals with keen eyes. Bran thought the wolf might attack at any moment. Then a voice spoke. It was deep, but distant. A shadowy man holding a smoking stick that glowed at the tip spoke his name.

"I am Inna," he intoned. "Of the Ice Bear Clan, which is no more."

The words vanished, replaced by images of strange yellow-faced, orange-toothed men attacking the pavilions of the Ice Bear Clan. People screamed and ran in every direction, scattered by the unexpected onslaught. Men were hacked down where they stood and women bound and dragged away. Those who fought were raped and killed.

A little boy screamed for his mother as his eyes were removed with burning metal bars. Then the attackers left, and the only thing that stirred was an old woman, stripped of her thick white cloak.

She scrambled over the snow and rocks, searching for bodies that still breathed.

The boy with no eyes she found first. With surprising strength, she lifted him in her arms and disappeared into one of the few pavilions that remained standing. Moments later she returned. Drifts of snow began to swirl down. She found a young man still breathing. Of the forty members of the clan, only three remained. The rest of her clan had been either taken or killed.

The images faded and a different voice spoke. "My name is Bahana, and I am Chief of the Arrluk Clan. Long have we been strong...."

The voice faded and new images began.

Seven times names were announced, and seven times images of each clan's experiences flashed before the crow's eyes. In almost all, the vile men with painted faces featured again and again. Then the eighth voice spoke, and the crow recognised it immediately. It belonged to the wolf sitting beside him.

"My name is Seraphimé..."

The whole horrid truth of Seraphimé's trials flashed before the crow; even the dreams. He watched everything, unable to speak or cry out as Seraphimé was stabbed, dragged away, then raped. He saw everything as Seraphimé had seen it. His heart pounded fitfully against his chest. He felt it might explode for the grief.

Then all the images faded. The dancing stopped. The drums ceased and all fell into a deep silence. Bran felt movement at his side. He turned his head and watched Seraphimé toss the stub of smoking herbs into the flames and sit down. He instinctively took her hand, and to his surprise, she did not pull away.

"These desert devils will come again," someone shouted from the gathered crowd.

"We cannot hope to hold them off!" another one wailed. "We will all be killed."

"You will not," Bran said softly. All eyes fell on him. "I have come from the south, from the land of the Baveii, and I promise that my people will do all it can to help the people of my wife's land."

A murmur spread through the crowd. At that moment, Gabija understood Seraphimé's comment about duty.

Poor man. You love her so, and she loves you not.

"You have brought barely twenty fighters," one of the chieftains noted.

Bran smiled. "For now."

Talk went on around the fire until the diminished light of a twilight that never quite ended began to lighten. The clans broke up. Each family disappeared into their respective pavilions, resolved to meet again the following evening.

Bran, exhausted, fell asleep on the bed before Seraphimé had finished brushing her hair. He missed her brief display of tenderness as she covered him with a blanket to guard against the chill of the tundra, present even in the middle of summer.

* * * *

For three more nights, the clans gathered in the plaza to talk around the fire. Thankfully Bran had no more strange visions, though he often found himself at the centre of conversation. There were many things the Sierran nomads were curious about.

Where was the land of the Baveii? How many men could he bring? What could they do? How did he intend to fight the Ottals? What was the price for such a favour?

To that last question Bran could only smile sadly. "I have all I could desire from the tundra," he said, taking Seraphimé's hand and squeezing it briefly before letting it go. He knew she did not much like to be touched. Seraphimé looked down at her lap. To the outside eye it might have looked like demure embarrassment, but all Seraphimé felt was a burning barb of guilt.

The questions and answers flew back and forth for three evenings before the Shamans and Shamankas collectively came forward and conferred around the fire in a language that, as Bran learnt later, no one else knew. At length they turned to Bran and regarded him in silence with their deep, knowing eyes. Bran wanted to squirm and run away, but he held their gaze firmly. At length one nodded.

"The crow is welcome," he said solemnly.

Bran looked enquiringly at Seraphimé.

"They believe you to be honest and trustworthy," Seraphimé whispered to him. "You are now considered a Chief and you can confer with the other Chieftains as an equal and negotiate terms for crossing their borders in order to do whatever it is you need to do to fight the Ottals."

Bran nodded and smiled at the Shaman who had spoken. "Thank-you," he said.

A Shaman grunted. Turning to the masses, he raised his meaty hands and said, "The circle is complete! The games begin!"

There was a general cheer and the crowd dispersed to get some sleep before the feast that was to come the following night. The competitions, games, marriage negotiations and trading would all be held after the opening feast.

Bran turned back to where his men sat and shrugged at them. They grinned back in return, before taking the cue from their hosts and retiring to bed.

The entire day following, the camp remained silent as people slept. The nervousness of the Sierran nomads, however, was plainly evident. For the first time in their history, armed sentries guarded the sprawling encampment, each keeping watch in four-hour shifts.

Life began again at dusk. The Shamans, Shamankas and their apprentices became the servants for this festival. They lit the fire, chanting over it in a blessing for the meat that would soon be roasting over the flames. They covered the stones for sitting with cloths, and wiped down and set platters down in tall piles.

There were two piles of platters. Ornately carved and enamelled wooden platters sat in a short pile of their own. Other platters, in various materials and states of care, including cold beaten copper and bone, were piled haphazardly in several other tall stacks. The wooden platters were reserved for the Chieftains and their families, wood being harder to find in the tundra and thus more valuable than copper.

Lit torches encircled the fires. The meat was spitted, seasoned and set over the brightly dancing flames of the enormous cooking fires. Into the flames themselves, a Shamanka threw large helpings of fresh and dried sage and rosemary, flavouring the smoke, which in turn would flavour the five tundra boars that rotated slowly on their spits.

The smell of cooking meat woke Bran. Seraphimé still sleeping soundly, Bran took care as he slipped out of the bed and dressed himself. He did not want to wake her. He wandered out of the onion-shaped pavilion and followed his nose to the fires.

The amount of food astounded Bran. Not only were there five tundra boars, but also one enormous ouruq slowly rotating over the flames. Along the sides of the fire pit, large cauldrons bubbled away filled with garlic, mushrooms and vegetables. Bran's stomach grumbled hungrily. The aroma sent his mouth watering.

Bran watched as the Shamans worked, talking in their secret language and laughing. He even noticed two pretending to sword-fight with root vegetables. It was hardly a sight to inspire awe, and yet always there seemed to be a power about these men and women.

The ages of Shamans and Shamankas varied. Young, old and various stages in between interacted as equals. There were even a few solemn children dressed in the grey of an apprentice.

Other people had begun to wake. There were hushed conversations and peals of loud laughter. Someone had started to play a drum, and before long someone else joined in with a bone pipe.

Bran listened to the sounds that slowly filled the camp. It seemed to him the most natural of things; relaxed and happy. He breathed deeply and looked up at the sky. It fanned out to eternity with plumage of brilliant colours.

Yellow and orange, fuchsia and purple all in various shades streaked across it, blending into one another and constantly changing as the sun continued its descent behind the horizon. Stars began to show.

The day of the feast always occurred on the day of the summer solstice, the longest day of the year. Bran surmised that it must be close to midnight.

The sun would not fully set here. It would simply allow half of itself to disappear behind the horizon before pulling itself back up into the sky. As it did so, it displayed the most stunning sunset Bran had ever seen. Now he understood why the Sierrans lived here.

Life could be hard, yes. However, the tundra provided well, hosting a plethora of game, offering warm skins as well as food. More striking though, was the freedom. There were no buildings to cage people in, no limits to the horizon and an endless display of beauty.

Bran felt that he never wanted to leave the tundra. He turned his attention back to the feast preparations and his eyes met the Shaman of the Arrluk Clan.

The Shaman smiled at him, for a moment looking exactly like the hunting whale from which his clan gleaned their name. Bran smiled easily in return. It suddenly struck him as odd that seeing the image of the black and white whale in a man seemed completely natural. Bran shook his head in an attempt to dislodge the image. Perhaps he was losing his mind.

A young girl in a grey robe and carrying a bucket of warmed honey water, suddenly appeared at Bran's side. In silence, she handed him an ouruq horn filled with the liquid. Bran smiled and accepted it. The girl smiled shyly in return and continued her rounds of the encampment, offering a horn to anyone awake. She returned often to the fire to collect more horns or heat up her cauldron.

Bran noticed that many of the grey robed children were doing the same. He sighed contentedly and decided to walk around the encampment to explore. Many families were now awake. Some stood outside their own pavilions, gathered around their small personal fires singing or exchanging stories.

The women wove baskets out of the tall lavender-coloured grass that grew in profusion in the tundra during the summer months. Others tended to each other's hair, weaving in flowers and feathers and bright stones in preparation for the feast. Children played with smooth pebbles at some game Bran did not know and could not understand. A relatively large group of men gathered at another pavilion, talking in low voices. They smiled or nodded at Bran in greeting as he wandered past.

Since the Shaman had welcomed him into the tundra as a chief, Bran had been affectionately accepted. He found their warmth and acceptance refreshing. For all the vaunted hospitality of the Greyls, the warmth was buried and forgotten, replaced by ritual and social expectation. Here in the tundra, everything felt much more genuine.

His passing held some curiosity for many children, and they trailed him, whispering and giggling to each other. When Bran turned, one little girl screamed and ran away, prompting the others to do the same. Bran burst out laughing. It became a game. Every time Bran was certain the children had regrouped behind him, he would turn suddenly, scattering the squealing children in all directions. Their laughter could be heard from behind the round pavilions where they hid until they felt it safe to gather behind him again.

Mothers, fathers and older siblings looked on, grinning broadly as Bran and the children played. The game left Bran grinning like a fool from ear to ear.

Arriving back at his pavilion, he slid inside and found Seraphimé awake and speaking with her sister over horns of steaming honey water.

The conversation ended abruptly. Gabija threw Bran a stunning smile. He smiled in return, his sombre mood returning once inside and away from the laughing children. Seraphimé smiled at Bran also, but it was a hollow, empty sort of smile. She seemed sad.

"I'll be back in a few moments," Gabija said. "I have to get the beads and feathers for your hair."

"That isn't necessary," Seraphimé said. "I'm married, and not trying to attract another husband."

Bran smiled a little. She intended to remain faithful, at least.

"Even still, you are far too beautiful to hide behind leather armour and riding breeches."

"I'm not wearing a dress," Seraphimé said flatly.

"Don't be tiresome, of course you are."

"No. I'm not."

Gabija threw her hands in the air. "Fine, but I'm putting beads and feathers in your hair!"

Seraphimé narrowed her eyes and opened her mouth to protest, but Bran's chuckle reached air before her words did. She shut her mouth and looked sour.

"Fine."

Gabija clapped her hands together and squealed in delight. She exited the pavilion in a flash, kissing Bran lightly on the cheek as she did so.

Bran smiled cheekily at Seraphimé. "You'd look wonderful with a head full of feathers."

Seraphimé could not help herself. She laughed. "Perhaps we should put some in your curls also?"

"Not on your life!"

The laughter died down into an awkward silence. Bran went to his wife and cupped her face in his hands. He studied her for a moment, noting how wonderful she looked when her face flushed in embarrassment.

"You really are beautiful," he murmured to her before releasing her.

"Thank-you," Seraphimé managed to mumble, casting her eyes once more to the ground to avoid his gaze. Bran kissed the top of her head and left the pavilion to amuse the children once more.

Thirty-Four

"Where is your husband?" Gabija asked as she walked into the pavilion carrying a woven basket filled with beads and feathers on thin leather thongs.

"Outside," Seraphimé replied.

Gabija nodded and laid her basket on the table. "Well, you'd better dress in what you'll be wearing tonight," she said. "It won't do to mess up your hair after I've worked it."

Seraphimé rolled her eyes but did as she was told.

Gabija sighed as Seraphimé struggled into her armour. "You don't have to be the marshal at a feast," she said with distaste.

"So you are giving me my old title back?" Seraphimé said with a smile.

"Of course. Though I've selected a lieutenant, I couldn't bring myself to appoint a new marshal. Besides, how could I not? You saved all our lives."

"Not enough," Seraphimé replied quietly.

It occurred to Gabija from her sister's tone, that Seraphimé had yet to mourn for the loss of her beloved father and the good men who died defending the clan.

Gabija kissed the top of her sister's head. "You were his favourite, you know," she said as she began to comb Seraphimé's hair. "You were always getting into some mischief, beating up the sons of other chiefs if they annoyed you, stealing things from mother and hiding them. You drove us all wild, but father just laughed and laughed."

Seraphimé remained silent.

"You could have turned into a little bully, but you only raised your stick to defend someone. You remember that stick don't you? You used to wear it in your belt like it was a sword."

"Long Tooth," Seraphimé said with a gentle smile. "I named it Long Tooth."

Gabija chuckled. "Father used to call you his little marshal. And when you grew up, you became his marshal in fact."

"He still called me 'Little Marshal'," Seraphimé said.

"Yes, even when you came into womanhood. You hated it."

"I'd give anything to hear him call me that again," Seraphimé whispered. Unexpected tears struck her eyes. She bit her lip in an effort to prevent them spilling over her cheeks.

"I know. So would I."

Bran returned an hour later. "The food is ready," he said, never taking his eyes of his wife.

Gabija had let Seraphimé's hair fall loose, for the most part, though half of it was braided back away from her face.

One strand of the braid was covered in amber beads strung on thin thongs of leather. At the end of the braid hung three brilliant blue tundra goose tail feathers.

"You look wonderful," he breathed.

Gabija smiled as Seraphimé flushed. "She would look better if she wore a dress," she said wryly.

"I don't see how," Bran replied.

Seraphimé looked up at him and smiled in gratitude. She turned to her sister and stuck out her tongue.

Gabija laughed. "Come then, Little Marshal," she teased. "Let's go eat!"

Gabija led the way, escorted by her lieutenant. Seraphimé walked with Bran. The chieftains took their seats on the cloth and fur covered stones and their clansmen settled themselves where they could behind them.

Bran was parted from Seraphimé, who chose to sit with the Osprey Clan Lieutenant and his men. He himself was beckoned to sit with Gabija.

As soon as the crowd fell silent, the Shamankas led the gathering in a blessing over the souls of the animals that they were about to ingest. Then one turned to Bran, holding out a wooden platter and the gathering seemed to hold one collective breath. He looked enquiringly at Gabija.

"You are the honoured guest," she explained. "And you get to select the first cut of meat."

Bran hesitatingly took the platter and rose. The Shaman handed him a knife and Bran went to the first tundra boar. It was almost twice as long as he was tall.

Carving carefully, he sliced a large piece off the beast's belly, letting it fall onto the plate in a sizzling lump. He then went to the ouruq and cut a similar piece.

From the cauldrons he spooned out whole cloves of garlic and a large helping of mushrooms. Bran turned back, but instead of walking to where he sat, he walked to Seraphimé and bowed, offering her the platter.

The gesture of honour sent swooning gasps from the women in the crowd, with whom Bran was unknowingly popular. One woman turned to her husband and, looking highly unimpressed, slapped him hard on the arm.

"Ow!" the man protested. "What was that for?"

His wife faced forward again in angry silence. The man rubbed his arm sourly.

All attention was now on Seraphimé as she slowly accepted the platter from her husband. He smiled warmly at her and kissed her gently on the cheek. The young girls swooned again.

Seraphimé offered him a shaky smile and Bran turned back to find the Shaman offering a second plate. Bran took it and repeated the act, this time walking to Gabija.

"Unless you intend to tell them all that you want me as a second wife, you'd best keep that platter to yourself," Gabija said gently, her eyes sparkling.

Bran nodded and sat down. He tried to eat slowly, but his nagging hunger made even trying almost impossible. He ate and watched as the Shamans and Shamankas of the various clans passed out the wooden plates to the chieftains and their families and each took their fill. Then the apprentices carried platters of metal and bone to the waiting clansmen.

Soon, people vying for a good cut of meat surrounded the fire. When the crowd parted, there was nothing but bones left on the five tundra boars, and the ouruq carcass had fared little better.

Bran spoke to Gabija and the nearby chieftains for the majority of the night. His attention was drawn often to Seraphimé, who remained surrounded by the fighting men of the Osprey Clan. They were largely sombre and the discussion looked intense. They were talking strategy, Bran was certain. He could see Seraphimé's brow furrowed in thought as she nodded or shook her head every so often.

The sun did not stay in sunset very long. Bran noticed the deepening colours begin to lighten as the sun that never finished setting reverted back to sunrise.

The youngest of the apprentices walked around, serving mead and warm water to any who wanted it. Gabija was a very attentive hostess, eager to keep Bran occupied and not brooding over the situation between himself and her sister.

"Tell me about the lands of the Baveii," she said, raising a small piece of pork to her lips.

Bran smiled. "It is beautiful. The kingdom holds three rivers that run from the same source and snake into one another. At the southernmost edge, the three finally join into one before flowing out through the kingdom of the Doitchu to the sea. We have every kind of terrain one could want. Our city is built on an artificial hill in the middle of the chalk downs and from our hall, you can see for miles and miles, as far as the mountains in the west, and the old forests in the north and east. You can even see a Doitchu fort near the joining of the rivers. Until I came to the tundra, it was the most beautiful place I had ever known."

"And now?"

Bran shrugged. He thought a moment before replying. "This place," he said quietly. "It truly is *free*. There are no walls, there are no trees to conceal the horizon, and the horizon stretches on into eternity, it seems. You could ride for days on end with no fear. And the air, it's so crisp, so clear." Bran grinned self-consciously. "I find this place peaceful and welcoming. I can't really explain why."

Gabija smiled at Bran. "People were made from the land, just as the animals were," she said. "I do not think we were made to be walled in."

Bran laughed. "Sometimes those walls are necessary."

"For protection. Yes, I know. Even still, I would rather face an enemy in the open, where I can move and see in any direction I wish, than be penned in like a frightened lamb."

Bran nodded. "I can appreciate that. That might need to change if you hope to defeat the Ottals."

Gabija smiled sadly. "You will not find any place to build your walls, Bran, husband of my sister. Most of the tundra is solid rock. Where it isn't, not three inches beneath the earth the ice starts, and it continues on and on. You will have no foundation on which to build."

Bran grunted. "It can be cut."

Deciding that a change in subject was in order, Bran nodded his head at one of the many massive black horses that grazed near a pavilion. "How did it come to be that the nomads of the Sierran Tundra became horse-breeders?"

"That is a very long tale."

"Good! I like long stories."

Gabija smiled. "It starts at the very beginning, at the dawn of our life. The Old Ones lived on the tundra for a long time before we came, and a long time after. Further south, our people had hunted and killed almost all of them.

"Here in the far north, near the great rivers of ice, we understood that we could not live without them. They knew things we did not. They were gentle and wise. They taught us how the birds knew the snows were coming before anyone else.

"They taught us how to hunt without killing the herd. They taught us how to find water, where to seek shelter and all the routes the game took in their journey south. They taught us the herbs and what they were for and how to heal, and they taught us about the spirits and the gods.

"They had only two gods, the Lord of the Hunt, who was also the God of Death and the Master of the Wilderness, and the Bride of Fire, who was also the Goddess of Childbirth and Mistress of Song. They showed us the dances and the songs that woke the spirits and roused the gods. But when the last of them died, we forgot what they had taught us. Some of our ancestors built great buildings out of stones carved from the earth, paved roads and dug deep and greedily into the ground for things that sparkled and shone.

"One girl was born then, before the gods tore down the false caves we had made. She was a small thing, not very strong, but she had a gift. The animals of the wild seemed to know her and she was as wild as they were. She did not enter buildings and grew frightened and dangerous if ever forced in one. When her clan tried to force her to marry, she ran away.

"Where she went, no one knew. Autumn followed summer, and winter followed autumn. For five winters the girl was neither seen nor heard from again, until, one summer, hunters stumbled across a large herd of wild horses. And there, running with them, was the girl, now a young woman and fully-grown. Naked as her birthing day, she ran with the horses as one of them. The horses allowed her onto their backs, and the hunters were filled with wonder.

"They returned then to the great stone buildings of the ancestors and told their lords what they had seen. The lords went out to see it for themselves. The girl saw them approach. She stood and watched them with suspicious eyes.

"'Girl!' one lord called. 'Come home to us, and submit to your lord.'"

"And she replied, 'I choose my own lord!'

"The men jeered and laughed and told her she was a fool, and that the stallion could not be her lord for she was no filly. The girl just laughed at them and claimed that she would sooner lie with the stallion than false lords of false caves, for she would lie with no one unless he was truly a lord.

"The men grew angry and plotted to capture the girl and take her away by force. But the girl was as wild as the horses she ran with. She was one of the herd. The stallion protected her fiercely. When one lord saw how well the stallion fought, he realised what power he would have if only he could ride it as the girl rode it. He plotted to take the stallion for himself, for any man with such power beneath him would truly be king.

"It took many weeks, but at last they caught the stallion and dragged him back. But the stallion would not submit. He would not let them ride his back as he had allowed the girl, no matter what cruelty the lord threw at him. The lord fumed and raged until one of his men suggested to him that he could be made a lord if he had the girl lie with him. Then perhaps the stallion would submit.

"And so they captured the girl who, without her lord and protector, was lost and vulnerable. Yet try as he might, he could not get her to submit either and though he tried to force her, she was now as strong as a horse, and she kicked and screamed and bit until at last he threw her from his bed and declared, 'If you think yourself a horse, then you will act as the horse I want to own! You shall carry every traveller who wishes to enter my home from the outer gate to the inner gate and when you are tired and spent, perhaps then you will lie with me.'

"'I will not lie with a man unless he is a true lord!' she replied and the false lord was enraged. He had her lashed and bound to the inner gate with a chain that was as long as the road to the outer gate, and so she had no choice but to do as he told her, or else lie with him. For almost a month she carried men back and forth like a beast of burden. Her feet cracked and split and bled and her back ached until she could not stand upright.

"Then one day, a man came dressed in simple leathers and furs and he stopped at the outer gate. He greeted the girl as if she were more than a beast. 'Why are you chained?' asked he. She told him everything, and how the brave stallion, the Lord of Horses, was still tied in the stable, wasting away for want of freedom. The man was appalled.

"'And who are you?' the girl asked.

"'I am Running Elk,' the man replied. 'Chief of my clan on the plains beyond the mounds of the Old Ones where we live as the Old Ones did. I have come to trade furs and axes. Let me free you and come back with me, and I will protect you.'

"'I will go nowhere without my lord,' the girl proclaimed.

"'Then I will free your lord,' said the man. He entered the gate alone and on foot so that the lord of the false cave grew angry with the girl. While he ranted and raved, the Chieftain stole the key to the girl's chains and then traded his wares as if nothing had happened. After, he stole into the false cave for horses and freed the stallion. The horse bolted, running through both gates before an alarm could be raised.

"In the confusion that followed, the Chieftain managed to free the girl and they ran together towards the land of his clan. But they were followed and the lord, who could not bear the thought of her declaring anyone a true lord but him, loosed an arrow that struck her in the chest. The stallion, who had waited for them at a safe distance, screamed and the jealous lord, who could not bear the thought of the stallion being lord in his lands, loosed his arrows on him as well.

"Running Elk went first to the girl, who was alive but barely. 'I will lie with no one who is not lord,' she whispered. Then she said, 'Please care for my family.' And she died in the Chieftain's arms. The stallion was still standing, and saw it all.

"At length, the Chieftain rose and turned to the stallion. 'My Lord,' he said. 'Allow me to treat with you. If you become a part of my clan, I swear to keep you safe from harm if you promise to help my clan and I as you can.'

"'That is well,' said the stallion. 'For my life bleeds from me swiftly and I will not be able to care for them myself.' So the Lord of Horses called his herd to him and he told them of the pact he had forged with the Chieftain.

"'He is your lord now, and he will protect you as I have, and in return you must serve him as you have served me.' And then the stallion went to where the girl lay. He lay down beside her and died, bled of his life.

"The girl and the horse were buried together in the mounds of the Old Ones, and their spirits combined. The Chieftain returned to his clan on the back of a horse, with the herd following, and his clan marvelled at the sight. From then on, herd and clan were one and the same, and to this day, the clans of the tundra have walked with their horses as one of them.

"The following summer, the Chieftain met a lovely girl whom he could not deny. He wed her that very season. It seemed to him that he knew this beautiful girl. After their hand-fasting and the vows, the maiden leant towards the Chieftain and said, 'I will not lie with a man unless he is a true lord.'

"The Chieftain knew it was the returning spirit of the girl he had released the year before, and she had come to honour her words. To this day it holds that the first wife of any Chieftain is the spirit of the girl returned to proclaim him chief – a true lord."

Bran was silent for a while after Gabija finished the story. "We have the same tradition," he said. "Though I never knew how we acquired it."

"Of course you have the same tradition!" Gabija said with a smile. "The Greyls and the Touans and the Sierrans are descendent from the same tribe that made the pact with the tundra horses. You Greyls are simply descendents of those families that travelled south and liked it, so they stayed."

"Did we ever attend the Great Gatherings?"

"I do not know. Perhaps, or perhaps not. It may have begun too late for that. Who knows?"

Bran jumped as a young girl in grey robes tugged at his empty plate, startling him. He relinquished it with an apologetic smile.

"That was a wonderful meal," he said.

Gabija nodded in agreement, accepting another horn of mead. Bran followed suit and until roughly midday, the feasters continued to eat and drink.

The laughter stopped abruptly as four ayals suddenly appeared near the sizzling carcasses of the devoured boars. It was rare for them to join the feasts at the Great Gathering. Something particular must have brought them here this evening. A respectful, even fearful hush fell over the crowd as, one by one, the ayals brought forward bundles wrapped in furs and laid them before Seraphimé.

Seraphimé immediately recognised the furs – red fox and snow hare, the traditional wrappings for wedding gifts. The meaning was lost on no one save Bran and his men. That it was the ayals, messengers of the Master of the Wild, who presented them left no doubt as to whom they were from.

It stung like a slap in the face and felt, to Seraphimé, slightly mocking. Even still, the ayals were very respectful and bowed low with each presentation.

She was under obligation, having been presented these gifts publicly, to open them publicly. Seraphimé's hands shook as she reached for the furthermost one on the right. Placing it upon her lap, she opened it carefully and froze.

Everyone strained to see what it was that had been wrapped in the fox fur. Bran saw it clearly and frowned in confusion. A gasp escaped the lips of those who saw it.

Seraphimé extended a pale hand and stroked the pair of jagged looking daggers made from what looked like chipped black glass. They were small and came with neither a sheath nor a thong with which to tie them on. Bran correctly guessed that these daggers were intended to slide into the cuff of a boot. Seraphimé looked pale as she placed them aside and picked up the next parcel.

Every gift was a weapon or a pair thereof, and they were all made of the same strange black glass. There were two thick-bladed daggers in sheaths with thongs to be tied to the thigh and a long sword. How, Bran wondered, could a blade of long, narrow black glass not shatter on the first strike? Bran thought the weapon entirely useless.

Other gifts included were two shorter swords to be strapped onto the back, one blade to be strapped to the upper arm, and one to be strapped on the forearm, a variety of very small throwing daggers, and a long recurve bow of oiled bone replete with two quivers full of glass-tipped arrows. One quiver was designed to be strapped on the back over the swords and the other hung at the hip.

It took Seraphimé time and a great deal of help from the Lieutenant to figure how the pieces of this morbid jigsaw fitted together. Once fully armed, Seraphimé, already in full armour, appeared formidable indeed; a frosted beauty wrapped in a nightmare. Her eyes met Bran's. They were distant and closed off, giving no indication of what was happening behind them.

One Shamanka came forward and grasped Seraphimé's hand. "Marshal of the Tundra," she said.

A whisper rippled through the crowd before the Lieutenant of the Osprey Clan took up the call.

"Marshal of the Tundra! Marshal of the Tundra!"

The entire gathering joined the chanting. In that instant Seraphimé became universally accepted as the leader of all men in the tundra, and with her, Bran, now the husband of a queen.

Thirty-Five

The old woman leant back. She sat on the rock near the mounds, weaving a basket from the tough, lavender-coloured grass of the tundra.

"Well, now you've done it," she noted casually, barely looking up as the Lord of the Hunt walked into his clearing.

"This is my clearing, old woman," he growled.

The woman did not respond, concentrating on her weaving. Cabal did not mind her presence and happily bounded to the woman to settle down beside her.

"Traitor," the Lord of the Hunt muttered.

"I'm here to keep you humble," the woman said with a smile.

The Lord of the Hunt grunted and sat down next to Cabal.

"She's mad at you," the woman said.

"Because of the gifts?"

The woman nodded.

"She will need them."

"But as *wedding* gifts?"

"She got married."

"At your insistence."

The Lord of the Hunt grunted and stared off into the distance.

"How are you going to feel when she finally accepts him and lies with him for more than duty?"

The Lord of the Hunt turned to the woman, a thousand questions glittering in his dark eyes. The old woman smiled a secretive smile and continued to weave. He did not want to admit it, but the thought drove a cold blade of jealousy straight through his chest.

"Admit it, you proud fool," the woman said. "You love her."

"Go away," he replied irritably, tired of these exchanges.

The old woman shrugged then vanished.

Alone in the clearing, the Lord of the Hunt and Master of the Wild sank slowly to the ground and drew his knees to his chest.

* * * *

"Well now," the Tigil Mtsusa said. He appeared at the threshold of the Guild Master's private chambers, sober at last; sober and exceptionally dangerous. "What's this?"

The Guild Master stood. "What are you doing in here, Tigil?" he asked in return.

The Tigil ignored him. "An altar, Guild Master? Truly? Idolatry has been outlawed for several thousand years. There are no gods but one. Didn't you know that?"

The Guild Master squared his shoulders. Inwardly his heart beat a furious rhythm. Outwardly, he remained the Guild Master. "You have no right to be in my personal quarters, Tigil."

"The courts would surely be interested in this," the Tigil continued quietly, appearing slightly bored as he examined his fingernails. "There hasn't been an idolatry trial in a lifetime."

The Guild Master narrowed his eyes. "What do you want, Tigil?"

"I want to go back there and tear out the throats of those murdering bastards."

The Guild Master rolled his eyes. He thought he had dealt with this already. There was something to be said for the complaints of women regarding the promises of drunken men. They were hastily made and quickly forgotten.

"We've been over this already, Tigil," the Guild Master said, sounding level and casual. "We both decided against it."

The Tigil shrugged. "I've changed my mind." He walked around the room, noting that it was sparsely furnished. The Guild Master obviously didn't believe in decorating. The Tigil brushed passed the Guild Master and snatched up the headless statuette.

"What is this grotesque thing?"

"A Bulgan girl gave it to me," the Guild Master replied. It had been many years ago, but he still remembered her clear as day; her stunning deep red hair and freckled, pale skin. She had a sweet smile and saved it only for the Guild Master. He had been young then, and a newly made Tigil.

She was raped when Tigil Gafa's men had raided her village. The Guild Master spied her when the caravans joined to journey back. He could not take his eyes off her. In one hand she clutched the idol tightly.

The Guild Master had gone out of his way to ensure she was fed enough. They had become friends, of a sort. She told him her name was Iris. When they arrived at the market, he bid heavily in an effort to buy her, but was outbid at the last by a very wealthy Suma. At their parting, she had given him the idol.

'You are a good man,' she had said. 'Take this, and the Great Mother will watch over you.'

Then she was gone. He saw her, not one month later on the top of a death cart en route to the mass graves reserved for slaves.

The Guild Master grieved for her as he had never grieved before or since.

The Tigil scoffed derisively. "Did she? Well, it's mine now. Evidence you understand."

"Put it back," the Guild Master growled.

"I'll think about it if...."

"If?"

"If you stand aside and declare me Guild Master."

"*What?*"

"Come now, I can't invade the tundra all by myself, can I? I need an army, and the Guild of Fortu is an army unto itself, every man within it a trained fighter."

"Invading the tundra will serve no purpose but to get yourself and any fool willing to follow you killed."

"Don't tell me you believe in the ghost stories now?"

"Your entire band was obliterated, Tigil."

"We didn't know what we were dealing with then."

"And you do now?"

The Tigil grinned viciously. "Don't you worry, Guild Master. We will have the entire desert behind us by the time I'm done."

The Guild Master shook his head. "It's utter foolishness," he said. "I can't just stand aside and let it happen."

"You have a choice, Guild Master. You stand aside and I let you live. You deny me, and I'll take this little clay grotesque to the magistrate and you'll be put to death; painfully and slowly, I'll make sure of it. My grin will be the last thing you see."

The Guild Master left in the night, leaving naught but a short note stating his unplanned retirement and announcing Tigil Mtsusa as his replacement.

* * * *

Seraphimé silently slipped into the tent to remove her new weapons. Bran was quieter still and Seraphimé did not notice his presence until he touched her to help. She jumped in surprise when he did.

Bran smiled a little. "Sorry. I didn't mean to startle you."

Seraphimé did not reply and returned to her task. Bran's heart sank a little. Whatever warmth he had managed to glean from her had faded and she was once again a pillar of ice. Bran continued to help her in silence.

Once disarmed, she moved away and sat on the bed. Bran sighed and turned to speak to her, but was interrupted when Inna and Ur entered the tent.

"Otsana?" Inna asked quietly.

Seraphimé was distant even with him. It helped take the edge off Bran's hurt.

"Yes, Inna?" she replied, looking dimly at the pavilion wall.

"I... I too wish to give you a gift to celebrate your marriage."

Some celebration, Bran thought bitterly.

Seraphimé turned and frowned slightly at Inna.

"The Ice Bear Clan had warriors and when each warrior came into manhood, he was given tattoos to mark his status."

Seraphimé waited in silence and Ur spoke.

"You are Marshal of all the tundra, including the Ice Bear Clan. That makes you one of us, one of our warriors. To honour you Inna and I wish to give you tattoos as we used to give to our own warriors."

"Tattoos?" Bran exclaimed.

Seraphimé ignored him, as did Inna and Ur. Bran gritted his teeth and balled his hands into fists as his blood boiled. He tensed every muscle in his body in an effort to contain the hot flash of anger that raced through his entire being.

After taking a moment to observe Inna and Ur, Seraphimé nodded. "Thank-you. I would be honoured."

"Don't you think we should discuss this?" Bran protested.

Still Seraphimé refused to acknowledge him. Bran pressed his lips into a thin line.

"Thank-you, Inna," Seraphimé said, turning away from all three.

Inna nodded and left, throwing Bran an apologetic look as he did so. Honoured guest and married to a Sierran though he was, he was now, and forever would be, an outsider.

Bran turned to Seraphimé. "You are not getting your skin stained."

"You won't stop me," Seraphimé said softly, distantly.

"Otsana…"

"It is *my* flesh and I shall do with it as I please!" She spat the words in sudden fury. Seraphimé had been powerless against men before. She would never be again. Though Bran knew and understood this about his wife, her tone and refusal to listen to him threatened to tear away the bonds of his tightly tethered temper.

With a snarl, Bran stormed from the tent and marched passed the pavilions and out into the tundra. He walked and walked until the ocean of tents was nothing more than a grey smudge. He sat down on a rock and fumed.

Shortly after his departure, Seraphimé's sister arrived with tea. "Hello Seraphimé," she said with a smile. "Where is Bran?"

"Sulking."

Gabija looked at her sister in silence. "You look like you're not far from it."

"Arrogant bastard!" Seraphimé spat. "How *dare* he presume to dictate what I would do with my own skin!"

The anger surprised Gabija. She went to her sister's side. Seraphimé first resisted her sister's touch before permitting Gabija to wrap her arms around her shoulders. Seraphimé was so angry she trembled.

"Tell me what happened."

Seraphimé shook her head and tried to pull away, but Gabija would not let her. "Talk to me, Seraphimé."

Seraphimé remained silent for a brief moment before saying simply, "The Ice Bear Clan is tattooing me in the fashion of their warriors."

"Bran does not approve?"

Seraphimé shook her head and Gabija sighed.

"He is not used to the tundra and the customs of our people. Perhaps you could have been gentler in telling him you intended to have the tattoos."

Seraphimé scoffed. "He is a man grown. He can deal with it."

"He is a man in love," Gabija said. "And that makes him no better off then the most defenceless of children. Be kind to him Seraphimé. He has been kind to you."

At that Seraphimé pulled away and once again grew distant. "Please go. I am tired."

Gabija sighed and nodded. She gathered up her tea tray and left, casting one last look back at her sister. Seraphimé remained seated on the bed, staring blankly at the wall.

Once she was quite certain she was alone, Seraphimé curled on the bed and fought a losing battle with tears until, exhausted, she slept.

Out in the tundra, Bran curled against a rock. It was still freezing to the touch despite baking in the sun for days on end. He rested his head on his arm and closed his eyes, letting the warmth of the sun calm him. He did not remember falling asleep.

Thirty-Six

Seraphimé was surprised to find herself in a familiar clearing. She stopped apprehensively at its edge.

"Hello, Otsana," a familiar, deeply seductive voice greeted.

Seraphimé turned to find the Lord of the Hunt standing beside her, naked from the waist up. She scowled at him, then delivered a hard slap across his cheek. She turned to leave and he grabbed her wrist. She tried to pull away.

"Let me go!"

He would not. The Lord of the Hunt gripped her wrist tightly, watching her with his dark eyes.

"Let me go!" Seraphimé demanded again.

"No." It was spoken softly and gently, with no malice.

Seraphimé felt her heart beat hard against her chest. She struggled in earnest, panic overcoming her. No matter how she raged against him, his constant strength never yielded an inch. When at last she began to weaken, he pulled her in close.

"Are you done?" he asked in a calm voice, an undercurrent of tension indicating his arousal.

Seraphimé felt her body turn traitor. She trembled for want of him, a sensation she thought had died once she married, a sensation she could not feel for her own husband. Rage thrilled through her and she unexpectedly slammed her fist into his chest.

In surprise and pain, the Lord of the Hunt released her. Seraphimé turned and ran. She did not get far before she felt his strong arms wrap firmly around her waist. Seraphimé twisted and tried to strike his head with her elbow, but the Lord of the Hunt was prepared for it.

Taking her elbow, he managed to twist her, one arm still wrapped around her waist, and push her hard against a nearby tree trunk. Seraphimé could do precious little. Her feet did not touch the ground. The Lord of the Hunt held her firm against the tree by the pressure of his body against hers and little else. Both of them breathed hard from their exertions.

The Lord of the Hunt leant forward and kissed Seraphimé hard on the lips.

"I hate you!" Seraphimé breathed in the short intermission between his lips leaving hers and hers finding his again.

They were frantic as their greedy hands clamoured for each other. In the rush they collapsed onto the ground. Seraphimé could not remember being undressed, yet she was acutely aware of being naked beneath the smooth, honey-coloured skin of the Lord of the Hunt. It seemed no time at all before he slipped inside her, thrusting as she arched and dug her nails into his back.

It was not over quickly. The Lord of the Hunt had been away from her too long. He needed to assuage the profound frustration that developed since the last time he had Seraphimé beneath him. Seraphimé lost count of the dizzying number of times he quaked against her. Neither returned to their senses until, their lust slaked, they were too exhausted to continue.

She rested her head on his chest and stroked it gently as he fell to sleep. His arms were wrapped firmly around her, as if he would never let go. She desperately wrestled against sleep, knowing that when she next opened her eyes he would be gone and may never return.

She fought valiantly, and lost.

* * * *

Bran dreamt a different dream. In his dream, he walked through a cool glade. He heard yelps and whimpers of pain somewhere nearby. He walked as fast as he could toward the sound and stumbled across a large, pale wolf in distress.

Her two front paws were chained thickly in metal and tied to a great oak. Her back legs were similarly bound, tied to another tree covered in pink, sweet-smelling blossoms.

The wolf herself struggled hard against both bonds. The metal had worn away her fur and where the chains touched flesh, blood flowed from rips and tears. The wolf attacked itself, attempting to devour itself in a desperate effort to break free.

With tears in his eyes, Bran ran to one of the chains and tried desperately to break it, only to discover that he had only clawed feet and a beak for weapons. Against such a thick chain he had no hope.

The wolf either did not see him or could not. In any case, she continued her relentless struggle, snarling in frustration and howling in agony. Frantic, Bran kept trying to calm her, but could not find voice other than a raucous croak. Something cold touched his shoulder.

In an instant Bran jerked from his restless sleep. He sat upright with a strangled cry to find one of his men kneeling at his side, looking pale.

"My Lord, are you all right?"

Bran fought to steady his breath and nodded. "A bad dream," Bran managed at length, even as the dream faded from memory. "Strange dream."

"What are you doing out here, my Lord? It's not safe."

"I was feeling claustrophobic. I needed air."

The man gave him a strange look and Bran immediately noted how odd an excuse it was.

The onion-shaped pavilions of the Sierran nomads were spacious and airy, and were not erected nearly as close together as the Greyls preferred to camp. Moreover, there was enough sky to satisfy anyone's desire for open air.

Bran grunted and struggled to his feet. He looked around him. The shadows were a little longer. He must have slept several hours. Soon the sky would change into a sunset that never quite sets.

"I think I'd be more comfortable in my own bed," he muttered to the man. The man nodded and watched with a worried frown as Bran made his shaky way to his pavilion.

Once inside, he noted Seraphimé asleep on her side in the bed, clutching a cushion to her like it was a child. Sighing, Bran removed his shirt and his boots and crawled into the bed beside her. He gently removed the cushion and pulled her close.

In her sleep she shifted so that her head rested atop his chest. Bran knew that she must have been dreaming about *him*. It did not matter. She was sleeping beside him now.

Bran wrapped his arms firmly around her and held her as if he would never let go.

* * * *

Bran woke first. At home it would be barely first light. Here it was as bright as midday. With a sigh, he carefully slid out from beneath his wife's sleeping form. He would have gladly stayed, but he did not want to see the look on her face when she awoke to discover that the man who had been holding her all night was not the god she loved. Bran could spare her that much.

Still bitterly cold despite the morning sun, Bran shivered as he pulled on his woollen tunic, ignoring the flurry of itches it sparked. He placed a cauldron filled with water on the coals of the hearth that sat at the centre of the pavilion. After he had put life back into the fire, he stood and looked around him.

The round shape of the pavilion, while odd to his eyes, was in truth very soothing. It was almost impossible to be tense when enclosed by a sphere. He had been outside of the pavilion often at night enough to marvel at its structure. Sliced Mammot ribs provided the frame. Wetted, bent and then fired into a shape that resembled half of a strung recurve bow, the treated bones were far more solid than wood, and lighter than stone.

Ouruq hides were then sewn around the entrance, one rib at either side, and stretched and tied around the remaining ribs. The entrance flap was sewn on at the top, then left to hang, tying up at either side if privacy was required. The whole thing collapsed and unfolded like an enormous circular accordion, making emptying the pavilions the greatest part of striking camp.

At night, the hides of the pavilions glowed with the light of the internal hearths, while the animals painted upon it in white ochre became shadows that came alive and danced to the movement of the flames.

"They protect us," one of Seraphimé's men explained when he spied Bran staring dumbly at the scene. From afar, the softly glowing pavilions looked like orbs of flickering light, as if faeries had built lanterns to light the tundra.

Bran marvelled at the ingenuity of the people of the Sierran Tundra.

A loud snap of cracking fire-bone made Bran jump and pulled Seraphimé from her sleep. She stretched and sat up, looking quietly at Bran.

"Good morning," Bran said. "If it is indeed morning. With so much sun all the time, I lose track of days."

Seraphimé smiled a little and Bran sighed. "Would you like a cup of tea?" he asked.

Seraphimé nodded. "Yes, please."

Bran went to the teapot to prepare. Seraphimé watched him closely and it made Bran uncomfortable.

"The tattoos," Bran said quietly. "If they truly mean a great deal to you, then I won't begrudge them."

Seraphimé looked down at the flames. "Why do they bother you so?"

Bran shrugged. "The practice of tattooing was abandoned generations ago, and even then, it was only the men who were tattooed. Now it is considered a barbaric practice. I am a product of my upbringing, I'm afraid. You're not getting any on your face, are you?"

Seraphimé shook her head and Bran nodded, relieved. The camp outside was also beginning to rouse, and the sounds of the first day of the games began. Bran did not leave the tent until he had made the tea and washed with the remaining warm water. Even then, it was only when Inna and Ur arrived with the tattooing implements that Bran left the tent.

Outside was bedlam. All manner of activities were being conducted. There were trade exchanges, gifts being delivered, meetings between families with children to marry, and marriage contracts negotiated. All this occurred between various martial contests.

Bran watched in awe as mounted archers raced past targets, managing to fire multiple arrows before the short gallop was over. The winner of that contest hit the target square on five times, once splitting his own arrow. More horse-skills were contested, jumps and war manoeuvres, races, mounted javelin throwing and even acrobatics on horseback. The Sierrans were, Bran noted, extremely proud of their horses, and they had every right to be.

The tall, broad-hoofed mounts of the tundra were extraordinary. Their steady strides and remarkable recoveries if a slip did occur made Bran quite envious. It also gave Bran an idea. If ever they could be trained, the Sierran nomads would make a formidable cavalry indeed.

There were also contests on foot – archery, javelin throwing, stone tossing, slinging, races, armed combat, unarmed combat, and there were even dancing contests.

In the meantime, the Shamans and Shamankas continued their role as servants. They were exempt from the trading and the competitions just as they were exempt from the normal rules of society itself. They continued to prepare the evening meals, which were taken communally in the plaza. The other meals the clans and families had to provide for themselves.

On the first day, Bran watched archery contests, mounted and on foot. The rest of his time was spent wandering around, observing the frantic trading and marriage negotiations. Occasionally he would bump into one of his own men, who were equally fascinated with the spectacle of the Great Gathering. Bran had been fortunate in that these men did not need to hang on to him in these strange surrounds.

"Oisín," Bran greeted, drawing one man's attention away from the dancing contests. "Enjoying the scenery?"

Oisín almost blushed. "They are fine dancers, my Lord," me managed to mumble.

"Indeed. Fine women also, no?"

Oisín grinned. "I won't argue."

"Well," Bran said with a shrug. "I married one, so don't."

The man laughed and turned back to the dancers. Feeling restless, Bran moved on. He knew his men did not require his presence.

They were confident enough and felt safe enough to spend time wandering on their own or with one or two friends. Knowing the language as they did, it did not take long before they had made friends among the Sierrans.

Bran smiled at them as he passed. He stopped to talk if they had something particularly pressing to relate to him. Through their connections, many had learnt much about the tundra and had many ideas on how to best defend it. The horror of the tales the Sierran's related during the three day ceremony at the commencement of the Gathering had them riled and ready for war.

Bran almost felt guilty for having deceived them. Near as they knew, this visit had purely been to establish a relationship with the people of Bran's wife.

At roughly midday, Bran returned to his pavilion to check on Seraphimé and Inna. Ur sat on the bed beside Seraphimé, holding her hand as Inna worked quickly and diligently with a hollowed, sharpened bone.

Seraphimé herself looked pale. She focussed hard on the pavilion wall where, directly in her line of sight, was the painted form of a wolf.

Bran remained at the entrance, unsure if he ought to enter. He did so, noticed only by Ur, who turned his sightless head towards him and smiled in greeting. It unnerved Bran. How could a boy with no eyes see what everyone else did not?

Bran smiled shakily in return and Ur laughed, drawing Seraphimé's attention. When Seraphimé turned towards the boy, he whispered something in her ear and Seraphimé turned her head to greet her husband.

"May I come in?" Bran asked uneasily.

Seraphimé's melancholy face split into a smile. "This is your home also," she said quietly. "You may come and go as you please."

Bran smiled and walked forward. He spied a rag covered in blood and ink on Inna's knee and he watched as Inna carved into Seraphimé's skin, stopping every so often to wipe the blood and ink away. Bran shuddered.

Seraphimé's right forearm was finished, or so Bran gathered from the thick bandages that wrapped around it. The bandage covered Seraphimé's hand and middle finger, leaving her thumb and three other fingers free to use. Bran looked at Seraphimé, who had returned to concentrating on the images painted on the pavilion walls. He imagined she was working on controlling her pain, something she was yet to master, judging from the winces and grimaces she occasionally made.

Inna stopped carving suddenly and rubbed Seraphimé's forearm down with a thick, opaque paste. Seraphimé drew in a sharp breath and twitched.

"That is all for today," Inna said, bandaging the arm. "You eat and sleep. Tomorrow I come back and do your upper arm and shoulders."

Seraphimé nodded and Inna stood. Ur slid off the bed and trailed silently behind Inna who went to his own pavilion to clean the instruments and prepare for tomorrow's session. Seraphimé flexed and rubbed her bandaged forearms thoughtfully.

"Painful?" Bran asked. Seraphimé nodded silently, distantly.

"They'll be serving dinner soon. Would you like me to bring it in here?"

Seraphimé turned to Bran and smiled. He had been talking to people, she knew, and had learnt that the tattooing was a rite of passage of sorts. The magical enchantments that Inna had whispered over the tattoos as he carved them into her flesh could not be disturbed. She should not be seen by anyone except family and a Shaman or Shamanka until it was complete, or it would all be for nothing.

"You look tired," Bran said. He went to the bed and pulled back the blankets. "Rest until I bring you something to eat."

Seraphimé did not struggle or even complain. She quietly leant back and allowed Bran to adjust her pillows. She looked at him with hazy eyes for a moment before falling unceremoniously to sleep.

Bran kissed her gently on her brow and went to the fire to build it up again. He slipped out quietly and went to the dinner.

Thirty-Seven

*B*ran ate with his men that evening, talking and laughing with them as they exchanged tales of their experiences with the Gathering thus far. One unfortunate soul had been approached five times with marriage offers. Some of the father's were very insistent. When questioned about Seraphimé, Bran saw no reason to lie.

"She's being tattooed in the fashion of the warriors of the Ice Bear Clan," he explained. "I gather it's a rite of passage of sorts. She is allowed to see no one but her family or a Shaman until the tattooing is complete otherwise it's all for naught. I don't know why. There is some invocation involved. I didn't pry too much."

One man scoffed. "You know Queen Hafwen is not likely to approve of this."

Bran shockingly replied, "The Queen can go stuff herself."

The men enjoyed that immensely.

Before the meal was officially called, Bran went to the Shamans and Shamankas to request that food be set aside for his wife. He did not need to explain why. One Shamanka was so overjoyed that she clapped her hands together before embracing Bran.

"It has been a long time since women were tattooed," she enthused. "That was before the last of the Old Ones had died. I am happy to see it has not all been forgotten! I will save her good food, you'll see!"

When Bran left his men to collect the food, he found mushrooms that had been skewered and roasted along with a large helping of fried dried fish in a bright yellow sauce. A bizarrely twisted root vegetable that Bran could not identify accompanied it. Last of all, he noted a small basket filled with sweet cakes made from pounded grass seeds, flowers and honey.

The Shamanka smiled as he handed Bran the meal and said, "There is an extra sweet cake for her husband, who is taking good care of our marshal."

Bran smiled and thanked her. He walked to his pavilion, careful not to overturn any of the platters. Seraphimé was still asleep when Bran arrived, but the smell of food dragged her from slumber. She sat up groggily, looking, if possible, more tired than she had before.

"That smells good," she said.

Bran nodded. "It is good. Come to the table."

Seraphimé did so. Bran placed the food in front of her, then went to the fire to stoke it and start boiling water for tea. Seraphimé started by nibbling at the fish, but hunger overcame her and she devoured it far too quickly, giving herself the hiccups.

Bran could not help but laugh as each little spasm created a soft, mousy sound. Seraphimé stared at him flatly as she tried to eat her mushrooms while hiccupping. That too was entertaining and, though Bran managed to control the laughter, his grin was unavoidable.

Despite the hiccups, Seraphimé managed to eat everything on her plate, as well as half a sweet cake and a cup of grass blossom tea, before she could no longer keep her eyes open. She crawled back into bed.

Bran covered her in blankets once more and returned to the table, enjoying the rest of the cakes and tea before joining her. He wrapped one arm solidly around Seraphimé's waist before falling soundly asleep.

Morning came and went. Only when Inna returned did Bran bother to get out of bed and rouse his sleeping wife. He stoked the fire and dressed as he watched Inna unwrap Seraphimé's forearms. The design was clear.

On each arm two ram-headed serpents wound their way around the arms with their tails entwined around Seraphimé's middle fingers and their heads resting at her elbows. Bran recognised them, *his* serpents; the messengers of the Land of the Dead.

Jealousy ripped through Bran like a cold knife. Gritting his teeth, Bran excused himself and stormed from the tent. He tried hard to conceal his ire, but no one in the pavilion missed it. Seraphimé looked down at her hands sadly.

"It is good he is jealous," Inna told her. "It means he loves you."

Seraphimé shook her head. "Everyday he will look at these and be reminded that my heart is not his. Everyday brings a new hurt to him. I wish I could love him."

Inna said nothing and Ur placed a gentle hand on Seraphimé's shoulder. In silence, Inna resumed the tattooing.

* * * *

Bran marched out past the valley where the Sierrans had set up camp. He walked until the pavilions were barely visible and then he sat abruptly down on the ground, feeling much like a lost, angry child. With no one around to see, he even let himself pout. Closing his eyes he forced his boiling blood to calm with slow, deep breaths.

He tried to reason away his jealousy. He already knew what it would be like. He had made his vows, and that was that. There was no point in getting jealous. He would free her as soon as the battle was won. Caught in the effort of constraining his rage, Bran failed to notice a figure approaching until it stopped directly in his line of sight.

Bran tensed and scrambled to his feet. Before him, some distance away, stood a stag, the likes of which he had never before seen. It was tall and broad with a pelt of red and tan that was spotted on the hinds and striped on the legs. Milling around it were three very large, very black hounds, each with a ruff that suggested a kinship with wolves.

The dogs observed Bran with nothing more than idle curiosity. The stag was another matter entirely. Bran could feel its hostile gaze burn in his mind. Standing his ground, he stared back. Behind his glare, he put the force of every jealousy, every disappointment he had ever felt because of the Lord of the Hunt. It became a silent contest of wills until, at length, the stag turned and walked proudly away, followed by the three hounds.

One of the dogs stopped to look behind, surprising Bran with its gentle expression. Bran turned on his heel and marched back to the camp. He grumbled irritably about how, in spite of the vast emptiness of the tundra, he could find no peace.

He entered the tent with none of his previous caution and pulled himself short when he noted Gabija there, combing through Seraphimé's hair. The Chieftain of the Osprey Clan looked up briefly and smiled.

"Hello, husband of my sister," she greeted.

Seraphimé turned her head to look at him. Her forearms had not been re-bandaged. Her left upper arm and torso were now wrapped in fresh dressings. Bran wondered what designs lay beneath the bandages. His mind immediately turned to running his fingers along the designs.

He forcefully pulled his mind away from such thoughts. There was no point in even wishing it. It would not happen. The thought sent another rush of searing jealousy through his tall frame. Bran turned away.

After pausing a moment to collect himself, Bran turned back to Seraphimé. He smiled forlornly.

"I saw a stag on the plains today," he said quietly. "And with him were three hounds." Bran's tone was not angry, it was sad. "I think he had come to see you. He hasn't abandoned you."

It hurt to say it, and Bran did not care to conceal it. Tears struck his eyes as he gazed at his wife's face. She looked surprised and confused.

"Why are you telling me this?"

Bran came forward and took Seraphimé's hands in his own. "Because I love you, Otsana," he said. "And I want to see you smile."

He bent over and kissed Seraphimé on her brow and then left, not looking back, leaving Seraphimé stunned and in turmoil on the bed.

A gaggle of grinning children, who had grown tired of playing whatever game they had been playing and had come seeking new fun, greeted Bran outside. Immediately Bran put aside his misery. A cheeky grin answered the smiling faces he saw before him and he let loose a roar. He chased the children, who scattered, squealing with delight. He played away the ache in his chest.

Gabija went to the pavilion entrance and watched, soon joined by her sister. Gabija smiled. "Handsome and good with children. He will make a fine father. You are very lucky, Sera."

At that, Seraphimé burst into tears and returned to her bed, sobbing hysterically. Gabija joined her, wrapping her slender arms around her sister's heaving shoulders. She said nothing as Seraphimé wept and wept, until the latter was calm enough to speak.

"I don't love him," Seraphimé sobbed. "He has been so kind and patient and still I don't love him."

Gabija understood as only women could why this caused Seraphimé grief. Good men deserved to be loved, and causing any one any pain was a difficult thing to do.

"You haven't tried, Sera," Gabija said gently, pulling her sister in closer. Seraphimé's sobs stopped abruptly and she frowned.

"You're tired," Gabija noted. "Go to sleep. It will be better in the morning."

Seraphimé did as she was bid in silence still frowning, deep in thought over her sister's words. She fell asleep and Gabija silently left, sad for her sister.

* * * *

Bran played with the children until too much running winded him. He was grinning and in good humour when he sat with his men, and for them, at least, it seemed that their prince was supremely happy.

The Shamanka who had given Bran a meal for Seraphimé promised to do so again before Bran even asked. Bran found himself standing once more before Seraphimé sleeping on the bed. He didn't want to wake her. She seemed so peaceful. He turned and placed the food on the table.

With a reluctant sigh, Bran placed his hand on Seraphimé's shoulder, noting that, for the first time since he had known her, she was naked beneath the blankets. He grew hard at the realisation. He leant in close to her ear, taking in her scent. For a moment, Bran forgot himself and kissed her on her temple.

"Otsana," he said softly.

Seraphimé stirred and turned to face him, her green eyes dark in the dim light of the pavilion.

"Dinner is here." Bran didn't know why he was whispering. It just seemed appropriate. He turned to go to the table, but Seraphimé grabbed his hand and pulled him back. Bran frowned. His frown turned into an expression of surprise when Seraphimé pulled herself up to kneel on the bed, letting the blankets fall around her.

Seraphimé's torso was still bandaged, as was her right upper-thigh, but that did nothing to make her form any less appealing. Bran's breath caught as he drank her in. Seraphimé inched her way forward on her knees and placed Bran's hand around her on the small of her back. She wrapped her arms around his neck.

Bran was rooted to the spot, frozen still in surprise. He was roused from his state of shock when Seraphimé's lips touched his; twice. The third time Bran responded, releasing his endless longing and hunger in a single kiss. He pulled Seraphimé so close she could barely breathe and kissed her so deeply that what little breath remained was stolen away.

Bran's skin trembled beneath his clothes as his muscles tensed with the effort of self-control. It made Seraphimé smile. She looked him in the eyes as her hand travelled down the length of his torso. Bran's eyes closed as her fingers touched the top of his belt.

Seraphimé moved painfully slowly in undressing him, using the time to touch and stroke and explore. It drove Bran closer and closer to the brink of insanity. He rained kisses down on her like a thunderstorm, his calloused hands running lightly over her skin. He lifted his hands to cup her bandaged breast, and finding that unsatisfactory, wiggled his thumb between the bandages until he felt flesh. There he parted the bandages, exposing her nipple to the cool air.

Bran wrapped his arm just below Seraphimé's buttocks and lifted her up until his lips found and closed over her exposed nipple. Under the loving caresses of his tongue, Seraphimé's nipple grew hard and pert.

Shirtless, but still wearing his trousers and boots, Bran crawled onto the bed and gently lowered Seraphimé down onto her back. She willingly parted her legs to allow for Bran's hips, but it was his fingers that found their way there first. Seraphimé gasped.

Stopping Bran, Seraphimé pulled herself up again. She forced him to sit while she rested atop his thighs. Very slowly she undid the laces of his trousers as Bran reached behind her and frantically unlaced his boots. He managed to kick them off just as Seraphimé had finished with the laces and once more Bran lowered her onto her back.

Bran could not stop himself now if she had screamed and fought. His mind was gone. He could smell her creamy skin, hear her gasping breath, feel her legs wrap around him, but that was all. He was entirely lost to the more primitive part of himself.

Sensation soared as he entered her. Every moan that escaped her lips sent a chill of pleasure running down his spine. Every time her body brushed against his as she arched her back in time to his thrusts, he grew harder, more desperate until at last he was nothing but sensation.

His first ejaculation did nothing to quell his desire. Neither did his second, nor his third. Countless times he spilled inside of her, each time no less frantic or desperate than the last.

Tonight, she was his; wholly and completely his. Tomorrow she may change her mind. So tonight he took and gave all he could.

At last Bran could hold himself up no longer. Panting hard and drenched in sweat, he collapsed on top of her. He pulled her close and kissed her briefly before requiring more air.

Seraphimé responded in kind, feeling at once drained and light. Her arms remained around Bran as he lay on top of her, fighting the sleep of heady exhaustion.

"Sleep," she said, running her fingers through his dark curls and kissing his head.

Bran mumbled something incomprehensible before falling asleep. Seraphimé smiled and, enjoying Bran's weight on top of her, she too fell to sleep.

* * * *

Guild Master no more, the lonely man walked among the rows of caged slaves, unaware of where he was and not caring where he was going. It must have been close to midnight and the sun was nowhere to be seen. It was cold in the desert without the sun blasting down. A strong, northerly breeze made it colder yet.

The man crossed his unclad muscular arms over his broad chest. He had nowhere to go. He was friendless, jobless and, now, homeless in the brutal world that was the desert. He had held onto that idol for most of his wasted life. It was the only thing of Iris he had left. Where had it gotten him?

Nowhere, that's where.

A grimy hand shot out from a cage and caught the arm of the former Fortu Guild Master. The touch was light and gentle, but enough to stop the big man in his tracks. He stared incredulously at the owner of the hand – an old woman who had the flat features of the ice-dwellers in the far north. In her hand, which she now stretched out and opened, sat a small, beautifully rendered clay wolf.

"It has given you a new direction," the woman croaked in broken Ottalan.

Gingerly the man reached out and took this new idol. The woman withdrew her hand and curled up with the rest of the slaves, turning her back to him and speaking no more.

The man stared dumbly down at the wolf statuette, turning it carefully in his hands. For eyes the artist had pressed tiny green stones into the clay. Otherwise it remained undecorated. For all its simplicity, he felt some strange sense of power emanating from this little statue, and with it, a sense of purpose.

Northwest. He would go northwest. The Tigil would rue the day he made an enemy out of this man.

"The enemy of my enemy is my friend," he whispered, a small smile touching his face.

With other option, the former Guild Master slid the wolf, his only possession, into his pocket and made his way from the shadows of the Fortu Guildhall.

Glossary of Terms

Aqyn: Home to the spirits of the deceased, Aqyn is a series of islands, rather than a single landmass. Ruled over by the King of the Dead and guarded by his three Black Hounds, each island is said to have peculiar properties specific to that island. The spirits of the dead inhabit only one of these islands. This island appears no different from the Sierran Tundra. *See also: Black Hounds, Lord of the Hunt.*

Ayal: Servants of the Lord of the Hunt, ayals are stag-helmed warriors returned from the dead and assigned to a clan. There may be only one ayal per clan at any given time, though it does not follow that all clans will have an ayal. They are said to appear when times of strife approach. *See also: Lord of the Hunt; Sierrans.*

Black Hounds: The famous hunting dogs of the Lord of the Hunt, there are three Black Hounds – Cabal, Guira and Valla. They are said to guard the gates of the Otherworld when not accompanying their master on a hunt. *See also: Lord of the Hunt.*

Braddard: In the hierarchy of the Fortu Guild, the Braddard stands second only to the Guild Master. There are only five Braddards in the Guild. They are given the same status as Lords in Ottalan society. *See also: Fortu Guild, The; Ottalan Empire; Ottals.*

Bride of Fire: Goddess of fire, healing, and artistic inspiration for the Sierrans and the Greyls. Her shrine is located at the same site as the summer solstice festival called The Great Gathering, where a perpetual fire dedicated to her is tended by virgins – one from each clan of the Sierran Tundra. Unlike her masculine counterpart, the Lord of the Hunt, she is referred to by only one name. *See also: Great Gathering, The; Greyls; Sierrans.*

Cabal: The Lord of the Hunt's favourite hound. *See also: Black Hounds.*

First Hunter, The: *See Lord of the Hunt.*

Fortu Guild, The: A guild of Ottalan hired swords. They are hired as assassins and soldiers, though more often are used as guardsmen for trade goods en route. The structure of the guild is feudal, with the Guild Master presiding over the entire Guild. Next in command is the Braddard. There are only five Braddards in the Guild at any one time. They command the Tigils, who in turn recruit and command their own regiment of hired swords. *See also: Braddard; Tigil.*

God of Death: *See: Lord of the Hunt.*

Great Gathering, The: Occurring once every three years during the summer solstice, this is the largest festival of the Sierran Clans. It is so famous that it is known to the Greyl kingdoms and the Touan Federation. The festival begins with the ceremonial relaying of important events to the clans. A spokesman from each clan, usually a chieftain, joins in a circle and speaks only when a lit sweet-grass stick is handed to him or her. This is followed by three weeks of feasts, trade, contests of skill and matrimonial negotiations. *See also: Greyls; Sierrans; Touan Federation.*

Great Stag, The: Taking the form of a breed of deer made extinct by excessive hunting (giant deer), the great stag is said to be the Lord of the Hunt's preferred corporeal form when walking in the land of the living. *See also: Lord of the Hunt.*

Greyls: The general cultural name given to the peoples of the kingdoms of the southwest. Descended from a singular tribe, the Greyls live in autonomous kingdoms and are as prone to raiding one another as much as anyone outside of Greyl territory. The Greyls hold to the archaic gods of their past, sharing two of them with the Sierrans. *See also: Bride of Fire; Lord of the Hunt; Sierrans.*

Guira: A Black Hound; one of the three hunting dogs of the Lord of the Hunt. *See also: Black Hounds.*

High One: The name the Sierrans use when speaking to their Shaman or Shamanka. *See also: Sierrans; Wise One.*

Holy City, The: *See Yellow City, The.*

Ice-Dweller: Though strictly the name of the people who lived in the tundra before the Sierrans, it is used most often as a derogatory term to describe the Sierran nomads. *See also: Old Ones.*

Keeper of the Otherworld: *See Lord of the Hunt.*

King of the Dead: *See Lord of the Hunt.*

Lord of the Hunt: The masculine counterpart of the Bride of Fire, the Lord of the Hunt has many functions. He is responsible for the care of the wilds, and the wild animals, on which the Sierrans and Greyls both rely for food. He is also the spirit that aids or hinders a hunter, and sometimes punishes a hunter should they hunt needlessly or carelessly. He is also considered King of Aqyn, the Otherworld, and rules over the spirits of the dead who dwell there.

—He keeps for company three Black Hounds, Cabal, his favourite, Guira and Valla. It is believed that he takes the form of the now-extinct giant deer most often, though some sightings of him in his more human form have been reported. It is considered rare that he would walk the land of the living, and any sighting of him is considered an ill omen.

Unlike his female counterpart, Bride of Fire, the Lord of the Hunt goes by various names including, but not limited to, God of Death, Master of the Wild, The First Hunter and Keeper (and sometimes King) of the Otherworld. Use of any one of his alternate names seems to be indiscriminate. *See also: Black Hounds; Bride of Fire.*

Master of the Wild: *See Lord of the Hunt.*

Old Ones: The term by which the Sierrans most often refer to the people who came before them. According to Sierran tradition, it was the Old Ones who first taught the Sierran ancestors to live on the tundra. *See also: Ice-Dweller.*

Ottalan Empire: Named for the first man to unify the slaves of the eastern desert, Susa Ottal. The Empire now spans the entire desert, unifying all the peoples therein under one religious rule. *See also: Yellow City, The.*

Ottals: The name of the people of the Ottalan Empire. They live exclusively in the desert of the east. *See also: Ottalan Empire.*

Roib: A medicinal desert shrub the flowers of which are chewed before battle. It is said to numb the fear response and increase aggression. It can be addictive and prolonged use can result in severe mental disorders (psychosis, paranoid delusions, etc.).

Sierrans: Also Sierran nomads. The general cultural name used to describe all peoples who live in the Sierran Tundra. Unlike the people of the other regions, it was the name of the land that was bestowed upon the people, and not the other way around. The society itself is divided into large family groups, or clans, each ranging within a defined territory. Each clan lives independently of the others save for once every three years, when all clans attend the summer solstice celebration known as The Great Gathering. *See also: Great Gathering, The.*

Suma: The title afforded to merchants of the Ottalan Empire, specifically those who deal in the slave trade. *See also: Ottalan Empire.*

Tigil: The Tigil is an officer of the Fortu Guild. Answering directly to a Braddard, the Tigil is responsible for recruiting, training and commanding their own regiment of hired swords. The number of Tigils in the Guild varies in accordance with a man's ability to recruit. There are generally around thirty Tigils at any given time. Tigils do not get to choose which Braddard commands them. *See also: Fortu Guild, The, Braddard, Ottalan Empire, Ottals.*

Touan: The name given to any citizen of, or anything to do with any kingdom within the Touan Federation. *See also: Touan Federation.*

Touan Federation: Though strictly sharing ancestry with the Greyls, the Touan Federation is a conglomerate of formerly independent kingdoms that were converted to the religion of the Ottalan Empire. Though given some independence from Ottalan rule, all kingdoms of the Federation answer to the Yellow City, share currency with the Ottalan Empire and are expressly forbidden to make war upon one another. *See also: Greyls, Ottalan Empire, Ottals, Yellow City, The.*

Valla: One of the three Black Hounds of the Lord of the Hunt. *See also: Black Hounds, Lord of the Hunt.*

Wetouan Council: A branch of religious officials assigned by the Yellow City to rule over the Touan Federation. They hear matters concerning the Federation that are not deemed important enough for direct intervention from the Yellow City. *See also: Yellow City, The.*

Wise One: The Greyl equivalent of the Sierran "High One." *See also: Bride of Fire, High One, Lord of the Hunt.*

Yellow City, The: The name of the Holy City of the Ottalan Empire, and the heart of the Empire itself. From the Yellow City come all laws and edicts, as well as commands to battle. History states that the Yellow City was destroyed by Susa Ottal in his bid to escape slavery and avenge his family. It later became the seat of his rule. *See also: Ottalan Empire.*

The Winter Wolf
The Seraphimé Saga, Volume Two
Chapter One

Walking the breadth of the desert was not easy.

I should have taken a horse, Guild thought bitterly to himself.

Guild was not his name but, in fear of his life, he had forsaken his given name when he abandoned his position as master of the Fortu Guild to the Tigil Mtsusa. There was safety in namelessness. He now called himself Guild. He would not go back to the name of his former self. A new life awaited.

I should have taken a horse.

On horseback, it was no more than three days between villages, between water and beds and food. On foot, it was over a week between them. A week without water did strange things to a man. Shapes appeared in the shimmering desert heat. Translucent women rose from the shimmering sands and danced strange dances, skinless dogs loped at his side and, once, Guild swore he saw a serpent take flight. After months of walking, he almost believed in ghosts.

"Iris," he whispered, tears of regret staining his dusty cheeks as he stumbled across a dune. Iris. Her memory haunted him now more than ever. She had been no more than a slave, and yet remained the only woman to have ever captured his heart.

"I'm sorry. I'm so sorry. I should have done more."

Yet what more could he have done? He did not have the money to buy her, and even if he did, there could not have been any guarantee that she would not have died in a month regardless.

Guild reached into his pocket and his hand closed around the clay wolf idol that remained there, hidden from the unfriendly eyes of the desert. The clay was, despite being alternatively pressed against his body and beaten by the sun, ice cold to the touch.

Guild smiled grimly. It was winter in the tundra. He pulled the wolf out and pressed it to his chest. The cold hurt a little, but it was welcome relief from the unrelenting heat of the desert.

"Can you hear me, winter wolf?" he whispered, directing his thoughts to the idol at his chest. "I'm coming. I'm coming."

****

Seraphimé shifted uncomfortably in her sleep. She was sweating profusely, though it was the middle of winter.

"Otsana?" Bran whispered softly. He shook her gently. "Otsana? Are you alright?"

Seraphimé slept on, groaning a little as she shifted yet again. Bran chewed on his lower lip. He looked at the walls of the onion-shaped pavilion that had become his home. They were starting to lighten, the painted forms of the animals and symbols that decorated them slowly becoming shadows cast by the wan sun.

Bran had chosen to stay with his wife's people after the Great Gathering. The majority of his entourage were sent back home to the territory of the Baveii. There, they would inform the Baveii council of the threat the people of the tundra faced. It was a cheap trick, but necessary if Bran had any hope of moving his people to war in defence of his wife's kin.

The tribesmen of the Sierran Tundra were now, after all, his own kin.

Bran placed his cool hand on Seraphimé's burning skin once more. "Wake, Otsana," he whispered. "The sun has come. It is day now."

This time, Seraphimé's eyes fluttered open and she looked around. Her green eyes met Bran's and she smiled.

"Hello, little crow," she said. Bran smiled in return. His heart still skipped a beat when she looked at him.

"Are you alright? You are burning to the touch."

"I had a dream."

"Oh?"

"I saw a small desert wolf. He was orange, like the sand, and the sun. He was coming, coming to me, in answer to my call."

"The desert is Ottalan territory. They are all snakes there."

"Perhaps one is a wolf."

Bran smiled. "I think you place too great an import on dreams, Otsana."

Seraphimé smiled. "I think you place too little import on dreams, my crow. When we are sleeping, we travel to the spirit world. We are shown things."

Bran chuckled. "In this, I think we can agree to disagree."

Seraphimé nodded. "When are your messengers expected to return?"

"Not until the war council has decided."

"Will they decide in our favour, do you think?"

"I certainly hope so."

Seraphimé stretched, exposing part of her naked body to Bran. Bran leant forward and kissed Seraphimé on the now exposed crest of her hip. Seraphimé laughed and turned to face Bran.

"We can be late to breakfast, can't we?" he asked.

Seraphimé laughed again and traced Bran's face with her fingers. "I don't think anyone will mind."

****

"Your fault."

"Go away."

"Don't you growl at me. You might be a god, but I'm her kin. She'll listen to me before she listens to you."

"You're an annoying hag."

"Perhaps."

The Lord of the Hunt, Master of the Wild, and God of Death turned his gaze to the old woman on the rock in his clearing. His expression was hostile, twisted by unexpected jealousy. Hers remained perfectly amiable, except the twinkle of mischief that sparkled in her green eyes.

"Why are you here?"

"Because, when you so callously drove her away, she asked me to intervene on her behalf. And so I came here to tell you precisely what I was thinking. God or no, you are an idiot."

The Lord of the Hunt turned away again. The constant howling that had sounded in his private world since he had banished Seraphimé to marry had stopped some months ago. Some part of him yearned to hear it once again, to know that she had not forgotten him.

"You should be glad she's made peace with it. There is no more pain."

"I should be," he agreed. Here in the clearing, it was winter, and the Lord of the Hunt wore his armour and helm of the skull of a great deer.

"But you are not."

The Lord of the Hunt rolled his broad shoulders in a bid to try and relieve the tension that had settled there.

"I knew it! You love her."

"Go. Away."

"No. I. Won't."

"Do not mock me, woman!"

The old woman sighed. "You are just going to have to compromise."

The Lord of the Hunt turned back and looked at the old woman with an expressionless gaze. She had been around him long enough to know that meant he was curious, though he did not want to be.

"You've fashioned her into the winter wolf; the mortal dream of the sleeping tundra. She is on her way to ascendancy. If all goes according to plan, she shall become the tundra, yes? She shall choose her kings, yes?"

The Lord of the Hunt cocked his head in acquiescence.

"Then you have no choice but to let her be free to make that choice."

The Lord of the Hunt turned away again. "I want her."

"Yes, well a god cannot be a mortal king as well. She cannot lie with you anymore. Not again. Not yet."

"Not yet?"

"The kings of the tundra will need her blessings with the return of the sun and the herds. The spring and summer months belong to the mortal kings. But the winters, my Lord; the tundra bears no fruit then."

"So I must share her."

"If she will have you," the old woman said with a smile.

The thought was enough to drive the Lord of the Hunt wild. "I will not!"

"Fine. Then you must learn to live without her at all. She will not abandon her husband now."

The Lord of the Hunt growled.

"Besides," the ancient woman said as she closed her eyes and leant back. "I like him."

****

Ur woke first, carefully dressing and exiting the pavilion so as not to wake Inna, who was still fast asleep. Precious few others were awake. None had started a fire yet. Ur stretched and yawned, turning sightless eyes towards the birthing sun. He paused for a moment at a lone figure on the horizon. A man, dressed in the skins of a deer and wearing a helm made of a great stag. He was not an ayal.

Ur smiled a little and walked towards him, knowing who and where he was by some power other than sight. Once at his side, Ur turned back and looked at the village of the Osprey Clan. It was not as big as it ought to have been.

"You are sad," Ur said after a deep silence.

"Yes," the figure replied in his deep, silken voice.

Ur smiled a little. "About Otsana."

The figure did not speak for a long while. "Yes," he said at last.

Ur remained silent. "Two men who love the same woman," he said, shaking his head. This time the figure drew his attention away from the portable village and looked down at the boy at his side.

"You see much, for one who has no eyes."

Ur smiled. "I have been gifted," he said. "When my eyes were taken, I received sight in return."

"What else do you see?"

"I see Otsana as Chooser of Kings. I see her as the Wolf of War. I see her as High Queen. Not just now, but always."

"What is she queen of?"

"That depends on you, King of the Dead."

With those words, Ur smiled serenely and walked back to the village. The Lord of the Hunt watched him go with a frown.

"Clever boy that," the old crone said from behind the Lord of the Hunt.

He groaned.

****

"I don't believe it," Algar said bluntly as he paced in front of his brother at dinner. He had been in a meeting all day with his father and a member of the Wetouan Council. "The yellow robes have declared Holy War on the tundra."

Alam almost dropped his cutlery. "*What?*"

Algar threw his hands in the air. "Convert or kill. They aren't pleased with the ascension of a heathen war-leader over all the tundra. They consider it an act of treason and have declared war."

"There wouldn't be a heathen war-leader if the damned yellow robes told the desert idiots to stay the hell away."

"It's a culture of slavers, and they aren't allowed to acquire goods from the desert. Where else were they to range?"

"Acquire goods. They're people, not cattle! And that is no justification! What has father said?"

"What can father say? What the council decrees we must ratify."

"We were going to trade with them. Now we must fight them?"

"So it seems."

"That's just stupid." Alam lost his appetite, infuriated beyond words. They once had dispatched a messenger to the Osprey Clan informing them of their desire to trade, and now the next message was likely to be in blood. Prince Alam's mind turned to Gabija, the Chieftain of the Osprey Clan. He had promised her friendship, and had hoped for more.

Algar grunted. "The word is, the tundra has enlisted the help of our Greyl neighbours."

"Which ones?"

"Our closest ones."

"The Baveii?"

"Yes."

"Oh dear."

"Hardly surprising, though, is it? They share gods still. The Greyls are primitive and yet to convert. And then there was that Otsana girl who married one of the Baveii princes."

"How so very convenient."

"Political marriages happen all the time."

Alam grunted. "If the Baveii have joined the fight in the tundra, we'll have an enemy on our left flank. That's a terrifying thought. Pulling the Baveii into a holy war will draw in the rest of the Greyl tribes. They're trouble enough without a holy war. Do you know the size of the Greyl fighting force?"

"Expansive, I'd imagine."

"That's putting it lightly."

"They lack discipline, Alam."

"And more than make up for it in courage and zeal."

Algar grunted. "This is going to get messy."

"Very."

"Damn it."

****

Once Tigil, now Guild Master, the head of the Fortu Guild had been busy indeed. He had been twice to the Yellow City to speak with the Ottal High Council. The council members had, at first, been dismissive of the Guild Master, but were moved by the threat of members of the guild converting to the religion of the tundra.

It was not true, at least as far as the Guild Master knew, but a perceived threat was the same as a true one. He intended to leverage that to its fullest potential.

The stories of ghosts and gods in the tundra had made the circuit more than once, and the Guild Master had noticed a growing reluctance on the part of the Guild members to venture to the land of frost again. It irked him. The hired swords of the Fortu were famous throughout the desert as men of courage. He would rather be fed to a nest of snakes than permit a handful of these damnable cowards tarnish the Guild's reputation.

The second visit to the Yellow City proved much more promising. The council had voted in favour of the Guild Master's proposition of war. Mtsusa knew enough about the Holy Council to know that it was new slaves they desired, though they had used the excuse of ghosts and gods just as he had.

The Ottals all shared a penchant for power and wealth. It was a good thing, for more righteous men were less easy to manipulate. The Guild Master smiled with smug satisfaction as he rode away from the Yellow City.

Those frozen tundra bastards would pay for all they had done.

The council need only send out word to all the converted peoples under its control, and they would have an army like no other. The tundra would be crushed, and their cursed gods and ghosts with them. The thrill of the thought reminded Mtsusa of the benefits of his current employment. He had, upon his ascension to the position of Guild Master, taken a Sierran girl as a personal slave. He allowed himself the luxury of anticipation wash over him as he rode back to the Guild. No beast of the ice would ever match the ferocity of his ravishing, he promised himself that.

His self-satisfied smile became vicious.

About the Author

Born in 1983 in Quito, Ecuador, S.M. Carrière has lived in five countries around the world including Ecuador, Gabon and The Philippines. The family moved to Australia from The Philippines shortly after the commencement of hostilities there in 1989.

After graduating High School, S.M. Carrière worked full time as an Office Junior at a law firm in Brisbane, Queensland before moving to Canada in 2001. In 2002 she began her academic career in Criminology, but switched to Directed Interdisciplinary Studies (focusing on Celtic Studies) after her first year. She graduated with honours, earning a B.A. Hon from Carleton University in 2007.

It wasn't until well after graduation that writing found her. She hasn't looked back since.

S.M. Carrière now resides in Canada with her two cats and a growing collection of books.

www.smcarriere.com